Outside Context Problem

Outside Context Problem

Christopher G. Nuttall

ISBN-13: 9781537411705
ISBN-10: 1537411705

Book One: *Outside Context Problem*
Book Two: *Under Foot*
Book Three: *The Slightest Hope of Victory*

http://www.chrishanger.net
http://chrishanger.wordpress.com/
http://www.facebook.com/ChristopherGNuttall

All Comments Welcome!

Dear Reader

A slightly embarrassing problem is that I wrote this book before NASA terminated the space shuttle program. The handful of sections that feature a space shuttle are outdated. I apologise for any confusion this may cause.

In addition, the team Outside Context Problem was devised by Iain M. Banks, one of the most inventive SF writers in the world today. This book is dedicated to him and those who believed in my writing enough to help.

Thank you. If you enjoyed this book, please leave a review.

Christopher G. Nuttall
Edinburgh, 2016

"*An Outside Context Problem was the sort of thing most civilisations encountered just once, and which they tended to encounter rather in the same way a sentence encountered a full stop. The usual example given to illustrate an Outside Context Problem was imagining you were a tribe on a largish, fertile island; you'd tamed the land, invented the wheel or writing or whatever, the neighbours were cooperative or enslaved but at any rate peaceful and you were busy raising temples to yourself with all the excess productive capacity you had, you were in a position of near-absolute power and control which your hallowed ancestors could hardly have dreamed of and the whole situation was just running along nicely like a canoe on wet grass...when suddenly this bristling lump of iron appears sail-less and trailing steam in the bay and these guys carrying long funny-looking sticks come ashore and announce you've just been discovered, you're all subjects of the Emperor now, he's keen on presents called* tax *and these bright-eyed holy men would like a word with your priests.*"

-Iain M. Banks

Chapter One

"All ready for another fun-filled evening in front of the box?"

Airman First Class Robin Lance rolled her eyes as she took her place in front of the radar screen. Night duty, even at one of the most vital facilities in the Continental United States, was almost always boring, without even the prospect of a stealth aircraft trying to fly through their area of responsibility to look forward to. She had learned to enjoy the times when a new and exotic aircraft would be put through its paces, when she would be charged with detecting it before it got into position to do harm to the base, but there wouldn't be one tonight. It would be just another boring evening, enlivened only by her ongoing project.

"Yes, dad," she said, simply. "I brought my homework to do when nothing was on TV."

Technical Sergeant Dave Heidecker laughed. Robin had worked under him for the last six months and he'd taught her a great deal, including some of the mysteries of USAF protocol, which she had regarded as a closed book. Her interests lay in radar and some of the more exotic applications of passive sensors, not in standing up and saluting when someone with a higher rank talked down to her. Heidecker understood her and that was all she needed to blossom into someone the USAF needed desperately.

"There's nothing in the log book," Heidecker confirmed, as she skimmed through the brief list. A handful of civil aircraft had been tracked, along with a couple of fast jets from the nearby AFB, but nothing particularly special or important. There were no warning notes about the equipment, nor any signs that the radar system might need urgent repairs, but she checked it anyway, just in case. The systems were far more fragile than civilians tended to believe and Robin had no intention of allowing a faulty system to remain online any longer than absolutely necessary. The Bill of 2017 authorised the rapid replacement of any faulty system charged with defending America's heartland.

Schriever Air Force Base handled most of the space-based military systems that had been launched into orbit by the United States. As such, the 50th Space Wing – which was charged with overseeing the complex network of satellites, ground-based radar stations and other, highly-classified systems – was one of the most important units in the USAF, although most of the fast-jet pilots would have hotly disputed that claim. Robin had no arguments with it. The rapid detection and identification of anything that might be remotely hostile to the United States was critically important in a world where more and more rogue states were developing the technology required to launch ballistic missiles towards her country. It didn't help that most of the space-faring powers had encircled Earth with thousands of pieces of junk, from old rocket components to dead satellites, that presented the space-monitoring teams with a challenge. A new contact could be anything from a glove lost by the ISS to an incoming enemy missile.

She looked down at the radar screen and sighed. There was nothing exotic or even remotely interesting in her work at night, so she checked with Heidecker and brought up the radar data from the recent clash between Israel and Syria. Her supervisors had been very keen that she – along with hundreds of other analysts – should study the data carefully, perhaps in the hope that a younger mind would see a way to determine new programs that would allow rapid target identification. The Syrians had launched over thirty Scud missiles at Israel, but they'd loaded half of them with decoys and successfully tricked the Israelis into wasting some of their Patriot missiles on harmless duds. A Scud could be had for less than a hundred thousand dollars; a Patriot cost well over a *million* dollars. The balance of expenditure had fallen squarely against Israel and the USAF had no intention of allowing Iran, or any other possible foes who possessed Scud missiles, to do the same to them. If the radar data could be used to separate the decoys from the real missiles, they could avoid wasting millions of dollars worth of irreplaceable missiles. Congress would definitely approve.

There was no point in keeping her eyes on the main radar screen. Even without Heidecker watching over her shoulder, and keeping one eye on his own console, the computers would alert her at once if anything entered the base's air defence zone. It was hard to keep radar operators at night from goofing off – their job was boring and often unrewarded – but as long as she could split her attention between her homework and the console, she was fine. Others didn't manage this nearly as well and were eventually streamlined into different units, or more rewarding positions. Robin couldn't understand why some people didn't want to study radar with more interest. She'd been fascinated ever since her father had introduced her to the concept.

She caught a glimpse of her reflection in the glowing screen and smiled. At nineteen years old, with long blonde hair, she looked more like a cheerleader than a radar specialist – indeed, she was ridiculously young for her rank. It bothered her from time to time that she had to progress slowly, rather than rising to a level where she could set her own priorities and make the breakthroughs she knew were waiting to be made, but the USAF didn't have that much flexibility in it. It had already paid for an education well above the norm and…well, now she had to repay it with her service. She didn't mind most of the duties, but there were times when she just got exasperated.

Or perhaps I'm being punished, she thought, wryly.

Seven months ago, just after her promotion, she'd been assigned to a mobile radar station during an exercise involving F-22 Raptors and a couple of highly-classified next generation stealth platforms. Robin had seen the deployment of the stealth aircraft as a challenge and, rather than wait for them to start dropping bombs, had managed to link the various radar stations together and track the disparate aircraft, shooting several of them down. The losses might have only been simulated – the USAF had never lost a Raptor in combat – but the embarrassment was real. Robin had ignored most of the angry disputes at higher ranks, or the amused response from the Army or the Marines, yet she did wonder at some of the senior officers. America might have the best equipment in the world – and the only known deployment of combat-capable stealth aircraft – but any opponent could adapt their own tactics to confront the stealth jets. Surely it was better to have their flaws and disadvantages pointed out in an exercise, where no one died, than in a shooting war?

She bent her head over the radar traces from Israel and frowned. There seemed to be little that could be used as a basis for determining which missiles were real and which were decoys, even in hindsight. The decoy missiles might be impossible to separate from the real missiles - at least quickly enough to matter - even though Robin enjoyed the challenge. If it were possible...she was deeply immersed in her work when the console chimed an alert.

Robin sat up instantly, switching the display back to the live feed from the radars and other sensor systems surrounding the base. A contact had flickered into existence on the display, approaching the base a little faster than an Apache helicopter, although it was quite high in the sky. A moment later, it flickered out of existence and vanished. Robin scowled and triggered a handful of analysis programs – including a pair she'd designed herself – in the hopes that they would reveal more than she'd seen, but she wasn't hopeful. The contact had just vanished.

Radar was a notoriously imprecise science; indeed, the reason the USAF put up with some degree of eccentric behaviour from Robin and her peers was that they had an instinctive understanding of radar. Anything from another radar station to a flock of birds could trigger an alert, convincing operators that an attack was underway and combat jets should be launched to deal with the threat. Robin had studied events back in the days after 9/11, when USAF jets had been launched to do battle with flocks of birds and transient atmospheric conditions, yet *this* contact had been amazingly solid. Robin felt a tingle running down her spine. Her instincts told her that something wasn't right. A moment later, the contact flickered into existence again.

It was lower now, heading towards the ground. The radar beam washed over it again and allowed her to track its course and speed. She knew what was happening before the computers confirmed it. The mystery target – and it had to be real; a real solid contact – was going to crash. The results were odd, but there was no doubt that *something* was out there. What was it?

"Sir," she said slowly. "We have a contact."

Heidecker stepped forward and leaned over her shoulder, his face illuminated by the glowing light from the radar screen. "What the hell is it?"

"Unknown," Robin said, flatly. There were ways to identify the type of aircraft from the exact radar returns, using them to map the hull, but the unknown aircraft didn't seem to fit any known pattern. "It's crashing."

The screen flickered again. "It's crashed."

Heidecker grabbed for the secure telephone. "Get me the Security Commander," he snapped, as he picked it up. "Whatever that thing is, it shouldn't be here."

———

Master Sergeant George Grosskopf hefted his M16 as the Humvee drove towards the crash site. He could see a flickering white light in the distance, like burning magnesium, suggesting that the unknown aircraft had come down hard. It hardly mattered. His duty was to secure the crash site before fire and other emergency services arrived to complicate matters. George's five-man security team checked their weapons quickly. If inquisitive reporters – or anyone else – tried to approach the site, they'd have to warn them off or take them into custody.

It wasn't something that sat well with him – there might be survivors in the mystery aircraft – but he understood the logic behind it. No one should have been flying anywhere near the base without clearance and that meant that the mystery aircraft was being flown by reporters, terrorists…or, perhaps, it was a stealth USAF aircraft that no one had bothered to warn him was in the area. If there were injured in the craft, they'd have to take their chances until the crash site was secured, particularly if they were reporters. George had been briefed on some of the more idiotic stunts reporters had pulled to try and gain information they had no need to know and if a few of them had been killed, it could only improve the gene pool. Personally, he doubted that any reporter would actually understand what they were seeing when they flew over the base, but that wasn't his concern. He was charged with keeping the base secure…and, after several shooting incidents at American bases, he wouldn't take any chances.

The cool night air was growing warmer as the vehicle stopped, a safe distance from the crash site. He felt an odd prickling on his skin as he jumped out of the Humvee and barked orders, motioning for three of his men to form up and advance behind him. The fourth would remain behind and report if anything happened to them, although George doubted that anything would. Neither terrorists nor reporters would offer any resistance after such a crash.

It occurred to him that it might be a Russian or Chinese aircraft – there had been rumours that both powers were deploying stealth aircraft capable of reaching the Continental United States – yet it seemed unlikely. No one would fly a spy aircraft right into the heart of America's radar defences – and the firepower that backed them up – unless they intended to start a war, but the world had been remarkably peaceful lately. There were still brief bloody skirmishes against a hornet's nest of terrorists and other scrum bags in the Middle East, and there were dozens of minor disputes all over the world, yet there was nothing worth risking an all-out war over, was there? It was far more likely that the aircraft had been hijacked by terrorists intent on using it as a weapon when they lost control and crashed it into the ground.

The M16 felt reassuringly solid in his hands as his team advanced. The flickering light seemed to be fading, along with the temperature. The mystery aircraft had come down hard enough to be half-buried in the ground, yet he could see a trail of debris surrounding the wreckage. There was something about the wreckage that sent a shiver down his spine. He'd seen aircraft crash sites before and this was no different, yet there was something... not quite right. He reached for his radio to call for reinforcements, and then halted his hand by sheer strength of will, cursing himself for allowing the crash site to spook him.

He looked down at one of the pieces of debris as he almost stumbled over it in the fading light. It was a piece of silvery metal, completely beyond easy identification. He reached out to touch it and was repelled by the heat; the ground was scorched all around where the mystery craft had crashed. The feeling of danger kept rising within him and he waved his men back as he stepped forward. For the first time, he looked down at the main body of the unknown aircraft...and stared.

Civilians always believed that aircraft that hit the ground exploded, or were destroyed completely, but George had seen enough crash sites to know that the main body of the aircraft often remained intact. It depended on the size of the structure, and what had actually happened to make it crash, but it wasn't unknown for most of the body to survive. The aircraft he was looking at was surprisingly intact – he could see crumpled hull metal and other, less visible, signs of damage – and it *glowed*, wrapped in a fading white light. The feeling of danger only grew stronger. Whatever the exact nature of the craft – he was starting to believe that it was something truly exotic, perhaps out of Area 51 or one of the more classified testing locations – it wasn't anything remotely mundane.

"Contact the base," he said. His voice came out in a throaty whisper and he coughed to clear his throat. There was something about the scene that forced him to be quiet, as if something was watching them in the distance. "Tell them we need the emergency trucks out here now."

The light vanished, as if someone had turned off a switch. George could see the lights of the base, and the stars high overhead, but the mystery craft had gone completely dark. His eyes hurt – from the curses he could hear behind him, he wasn't the only one – and he squeezed them closed, remaining still to avoid stumbling over a piece of debris. The temperature fell rapidly back to normal, leaving them shivering in the darkness. He reached for the flashlight he carried and shone it onto the craft. It looked, somehow, even more exotic in the sudden illumination, yet it was still dark. The craft almost seemed to be absorbing the light.

"Sergeant," one of his men said, from behind him, "what the hell is it?"

"I don't know," George admitted. It hurt to admit ignorance, yet there was no choice. He was tempted to fall back and wait for reinforcements, but there could be an injured or dying pilot somewhere within the craft. If it was a USAF craft, the pilot had to be kept alive, if only so that he could report on his experience. "Follow me."

He stepped forward towards the craft, suddenly aware of a spicy scent that seemed to hang in the air. Up close, he could feel a tingle in the air, like an approaching thunderstorm. The largest gash in the hull was big enough to allow him to stick his head into the craft, so he unhooked his flashlight and leaned forward. The scent grew stronger as he shone the light into the interior of the craft.

"Be careful, Sergeant," someone said, from behind him. The man who had secured air bases in Iraq and Afghanistan sounded spooked. George would have chewed him out for it, were it not for the fact he felt the same way. There was something about the mystery craft that left an air of unreality hanging over their heads. "Sergeant…"

George said nothing, shining his light around inside the craft. The interior looked…odd, almost as if it hadn't been designed with any concerns for comfort or even for functionality. Great piles of equipment of unknown design lay where they'd fallen, or smashed against the hull. The scent was almost overpoweringly strong and he found himself wishing for a gas mask, or even a MOPP suit. In the darkness, he only caught vague glimpses of things, lurking just beyond reach of his light. His imagination filled in the blanks…

And then he saw the bodies.

He had shied away from one possible origin for the craft, because it had been unbelievable. The bodies showed that it wasn't unbelievable. He wanted – desperately – to deny what he was seeing, but how could he? The bodies weren't people wearing bad outfits, or the results of CGI created by technicians stoned out of their minds…they were *real*.

"Sergeant?" A voice asked. He hadn't even realised that he'd almost fallen out of the craft in his shock. His heartbeat was terrifyingly loud in his ears. "*Sergeant?*"

"Contact the base," he said. There was no SOP for *this*! He hadn't spent most of his life watching science-fiction, or anything that might tell him how to proceed. "Tell them…tell them that we need an NBC team here now. We've got visitors."

Chapter Two

Near Washington DC, USA
Day 2

Alex Midgard looked up blearily as the car turned into a wooded driveway and drove up towards a manor house in the distance. He felt like he hadn't slept for a week. He'd been scheduled to take a few days off to attend to visit his parents, but his superiors had been explicit. The Air Force's Foreign Technology Division had been ordered to send a representative to a new team being formed by Executive Order and Alex – being the one who could be spared for anything unexpected – had been ordered to report to Washington, where he'd been picked up by a car. He'd expected to be driven to the Pentagon, but as the driver had taken him further from Washington, it had become apparent that they were going to a more secret location.

The car stopped at a small guardhouse, carefully concealed within the trees, and the driver handed over a small sheet of paper. The guard – he wasn't wearing a uniform, but Alex had no difficulty recognising him as a trained and experienced soldier – checked the paper quickly, glanced inside the car to ensure that Alex was the only passenger, and then waved them through. Alex hadn't realised he'd been sweating until the car passed onwards towards the house. He'd been in too many places where a single error in the paperwork could lead to disaster.

He watched as the car swept by the front entrance – the house had probably been built by an internet millionaire; it had the standard complete lack of taste – and into the garage. Someone had invested a great deal of money in upgrading the house afterwards, he realised, as the garage was quite obviously a secure environment. The two guards standing at one end held M16s and watched carefully as the driver climbed out and opened Alex's door, inviting him to exit. He stood up, stretched, and nodded to the guards. They didn't smile back.

"This way, sir," one said, and led Alex into a second room. It was barely large enough to swing a cat. His tone was bored, but Alex wasn't fooled. The guard was on the alert. "Place your fingers against the sensors."

Alex nodded, recognising the scanner on the table. He pressed his fingers down on it and saw the red flash of laser light as the scanner checked his fingerprints against the ones in the main directory. The military and intelligence services tended to have tech two or three generations ahead of anything in the civilian world – at least in theory - but Alex knew that it wouldn't be long until it was released to the public. The banking sector, in particular, wanted to use it to combat identity theft, although Alex could see at least two ways to fool the scanner. As technology advanced, the technology required to fool it advanced as well. The Foreign Technology Division had a hand in developing most of it.

The guard waved him through when the scanner cleared him and Alex found himself in another room. "Place your cell phone, PDA and anything else electronic in this box," a second guard ordered. His voice was none the less alert. "Attempting to carry electronic devices into the secure compartments is punishable by a long spell in jail."

Alex nodded as he unloaded his pockets. He'd been in places where the security requirements were truly paranoid, although not without reason. His time on Wright-Patterson Air Force Base had included time spent in compartments where no one left if they could avoid it, just to avoid going through the entry procedure again. It wasn't pleasant.

"Done," he said. He felt naked without his cell phone, or bleeper. It was unlikely that something would happen requiring his presence, but even so being without communications still bothered him. "Now what?"

The guard stood up and waved a magnetic wand over his clothing, before waving him through another door. Alex stepped through and was confronted by an older man wearing a grey suit. His hair was shading to grey and he walked as if he was bent over, carrying some horrible weight. Alex had seen similar looks from men who'd been behind enemy lines in the war on terror, or scientists who'd researched chemical or biological weapons; he wondered, vaguely, what his new friend's story was. It could be anything.

"Alex Midgard, I presume," the man said. It wasn't a question. "If you would like to follow me…?"

There were no signs inside the building, nothing that a spy could use to find his way around. That wasn't uncommon in secret bases, although Alex did tend to think that they overdid it. A spy who penetrated the heart of such a base would find it easier to get around than an outsider might think, unless the base was very small and everyone knew who was permitted within its confines. People tended to assume that anyone inside had already been cleared by the guards. Alex looked from side to side as he was led through a set of interlocking corridors, but saw nothing of great interest. The interior designer had gone for *boring*, rather than anything more spectacular. That, too, was fairly typical of secret bases.

They stepped into a small conference room and Alex was waved to a seat. The conference room was nothing more than a table, with a jug of water and a handful of glasses, surrounded by five other people. They looked up as he entered and some of them smiled, but most of them looked tired and nervous. Alex guessed that they'd been summoned on very short notice as well and started to realise that something was definitely up. No one would have summoned them at such short notice for anything other than a real emergency. Their emergency drills were always pre-planned to avoid causing disruption to schedules.

"Please be seated," the grey man said. "My name is Tony Jones, special advisor to the President." He paused to allow that to sink in. "You have all been summoned here to serve on…ah, a task force investigating a new situation. You will be expected to spend at least a month in lockdown at a classified location, perhaps longer, and full security requirements will be observed. Anyone who discloses information relating to this…ah, *project* will be charged with breach of official security and spend the rest of their lives in Leavenworth. If you'll read the documents and release forms in front of you…"

Alex looked down at the small folder. He'd seen release documents before. "If you want to leave now, you may do so," Jones concluded. "If not, sign the documents and pass them over here."

There was no point, Alex knew, in asking questions. They wouldn't be told anything else until they signed their lives – at least for a month – away. He skimmed the document quickly, just in case, but there were no real surprises. The signer agreed to complete nondisclosure without prior permission, which could be obtained from the White House. That meant Cabinet-level, if not the President himself. A month on a secure base didn't have to be boring. Besides, it was now clear that his superiors had hand-picked him for the task.

He signed with a flourish and passed the paper over to Jones.

"Thank you all," Jones said, when they had all signed. There had been no questions. "I will make introductions first. Ben Santini, military adviser; Alex Midgard, USAF Foreign Technology Division; Jane Hatchery, medical researcher; Neil Frandsen, advanced propulsion specialist; Gayle Madison, communications and cultural specialist – and, finally, Steve Taylor, Intelligence Analyst. Welcome to this safe house."

He sighed. "There's no easy way to say this, so I'll be blunt," he continued. He sounded, Alex realised, like a man who didn't believe what he was saying. "Last night, a…structured craft of unknown origin crashed outside Schriever Air Force Base."

It was Gayle who spoke first. "This is a joke, right?"

Oddly, her words seemed to give Jones courage. "No," he said, grimly. "The crash site was secured by the base security team, who made the preliminary assessment of the craft. They found bodies that were…ah, not human. They found bodies from at least two alien races present within the craft."

Alex went numb with shock. He'd believed in UFOs ever since he was a kid, believed in them to the point that he'd joined the USAF and found himself streamlined into the Foreign Technology Division, yet somewhere along the way he'd lost the sense of wonder. The USAF collected UFO reports without quite knowing what to do with them, because most UFOs were actually misidentifications or secret military aircraft. Alex – granted a security clearance that civilian UFO researchers didn't know existed – had succeeded in identifying most 'unknown' UFOs as civilian sightings of classified military aircraft. The wonder had faded away…but there were still some reports that he hadn't been able to identify.

The Foreign Technology Division had taken an interest, of course. If the UFOs were real, someone was flying them over American territory – and *that* was a hostile act. If they were Chinese or Russian spy planes, or even something from a more…exotic origin, they had to be identified. They had been delighted to pass the job to Alex, who had actually wanted to do it; most Foreign Technology Division researchers regarded UFO research as the kiss of death to their careers. Alex hadn't cared. All *he* cared about was solving the mystery.

Jones stood up and tapped a remote control, activating an overhead projector. "The…ah, alien craft was detected on radar as it fell out of the sky," he said. "It did *not* show up before it ran into trouble – as yet, we don't know why – and the radar operator scrambled a recovery team. An NBC team cleaned the crash site after the craft was moved to a nearby location, where it was transported to a classified location. The news was passed rapidly to the Chairman of the Joint Chiefs of Staff and from him to the President, who was woken in the middle of the night. He wrote out an executive order authorising the creation of a Tiger Team to examine the wreckage of the craft and what it means for us."

"It means that aliens have been watching us," Alex said. He was familiar with some of the installations at Schriever Air Force Base. There weren't many places that were more secret – or important. "Sir…what does the public know?"

"Nothing, as yet," Jones said, shortly. "We believe that the crash was reported as a light aircraft crash – we've registered it as such – and…well, that's not important enough to attract attention. We suspect that some news will start leaking out sooner rather than later – we can't put the entire base into lockdown – but the President has ordered a complete news blackout until we can get to grips with the situation."

"They're not friendly," Santini said. He was a tall man, with dark hair and powerful muscles, who would have been handsome, were it not for the scar covering his right cheek. His voice was gruff and no-nonsense. "If they're sneaking around near one of our most vital facilities, they're not being friendly at all. We need to start making preparations for an invasion."

Jones looked, if possible, even paler. "We don't know that they're coming to invade," he pointed out. "They might be friendly."

"If they were friendly," Santini argued, "then why don't they land in front of the White House, or the Kremlin, or in London, or somewhere that isn't of vital military importance?"

"The White House is closed airspace," Alex said. He'd wondered about that himself. "If they flew into Washington, they'd have fighter jets on their tail before they could land and meet the President. The last thing they might want is to be shot down by paranoid defenders."

"Then they could contact us and arrange a meeting directly," Santini countered. "I really don't like the implications of them sneaking around one of our bases – and particularly not that one." He looked over at Jones. "What sort of precautions are we taking, sir?"

"The President has ordered a low-level alert over most of our airbases and other defence installations," Jones said. "We were preparing for the annual exercise in any case, so we have an excuse to make all kinds of military manoeuvres without attracting much attention from the press. We'll intermix it with reports that the CIA has picked up warnings about another terrorist plot and use that to justify putting various bases on a combat footing. In the long term…"

He shook his head. "That's for you people to advise," he concluded. "We don't know what we're facing."

Alex looked down at his hands. "We need to tell everyone," he said, slowly. "We need to warn them about the aliens."

"That would cause a panic," Jones said. "The President is very keen to avoid a panic."

"Speaking for myself," Neil Frandsen added, "keeping the crashed ship a secret could only be beneficial to us. A craft capable of interstellar travel… if we could reverse-engineer it and put them into production ourselves, what couldn't we do?"

"He has a point," Santini said. "If the aliens don't know we have the craft…"

Alex shook his head. "If we lost a JSF from one of our carriers over Iran, would we conclude that the craft was smashed to pieces and the pilot was dead, or would we attempt to rescue the pilot – or at least confirm his death?"

He leaned forward. "The aliens already know that they've lost a craft," he said. "The presence of one craft implies others – others still out there in alien hands. As I see it, assuming the aliens are hostile, they've just lost their cloak of secrecy. That gives them only a handful of choices. They can back off, they can make contact with us, they can continue with their original plan – whatever it was – or they can attack at once. The first attack wave might be on its way to Earth now.

"And there are political implications," he added. "What will happen if the news gets out that the President ordered this clear and present danger *concealed* from the public – and the rest of the world?"

"Let the President worry about that," Jones advised, dryly. "If you wish to argue for full disclosure, I will take a note to the President about it. For the moment, however, the President's decision stands."

"There is another issue," Jane Hatchery said. "I've seen movies suggesting that we could catch alien diseases from the release of alien biological matter into our atmosphere. I know that scientifically it's unlikely, but what precautions have been taken to prevent mass infection?"

Jones looked oddly relieved to get that question. "The NBC team used flamethrowers and…sanitised the remains of the crash site," he said. "It's true that some alien biological material might have escaped, but we don't think that it will pose a threat. Once the alien bodies have been examined, we should be able to make a more informed judgement."

He scowled. "For the moment, everyone who had contact with the alien craft has gone into a biological warfare quarantine ward as a precaution," he added. "I hope that you can clear them soon, Doctor. We need to know if the aliens are capable of tolerating our atmosphere…"

"To see if Earth is any use to them," Alex said.

"Exactly," Jones agreed. He clicked the remote control and displayed an image of the alien craft. The scale on the display suggested that it wasn't much bigger than a small luxury jet. It was definitely larger than a fighter jet, yet smaller than a massive C-5 Galaxy or another heavy transport. "Now, this craft…"

———

The remainder of the day had passed slowly. Alex had expected that they would be transported to the research site at once, but the military had a hundred and one briefings to give them first. There was no plan to deal with alien contact – or, at least, no overall plan; Alex had suggested developing one, but his superiors had nixed the idea – and it was starting to look as if someone was making it up as he went along. There was little for Alex to argue with – whoever was doing it had clearly thought about the implications – yet he couldn't shake the feeling that they were in a race against time. After the briefings had concluded, he wandered the house until he found himself in an observatory, looking up at the stars.

They had been a disappointment to the small boy who had dreamed of alien life. Mars and Venus were barren of life, the space program had stalled after Neil Armstrong had walked on the moon and most of the people who claimed to have seen aliens were lying or deluded or drunk. There were no alien spacecraft concealed in hidden bases, no massive City Destroyers hanging over Earth's cities, no tiny grey aliens abducting humans from their beds and performing medical experiments on them. Alex had investigated a handful of such claims and concluded, in all cases, that the witnesses were unreliable. It wasn't a case of the witnesses lying – not intentionally – but a case of hypnotic regression being rather untrustworthy. There were so many details of alien abductions in the public sphere that almost anyone could invent a scenario in their heads and – quite unwittingly – mislead the hypnotist.

And now…and now, aliens were real.

He looked up at the darkening sky, with stars starting to appear high above, and wondered. There had always been a number of UFO reports that had never been explained. Could they have been real alien spacecraft? It crossed his mind to wonder if it was all an exercise, but that seemed impossible. No one would waste so much effort on a handful of people from disparate organisations. No, it had to be real.

For the first time in his life, Alex Midgard looked up at the stars and felt fear.

Chapter Three

Area 52, Nevada, USA
Day 3

The shaking of the helicopter throbbed through his entire body, but Alex managed to doze as the small team proceeded towards their base of operations. Anticipation had made it hard to sleep, but he had long since mastered the trick of sleeping whenever he had a chance. The blacked-out helicopter's interior was boring and none of them could concentrate on their books, or small entertainment devices. They'd have to abandon those when they arrived – it wasn't unknown for intelligence agencies to adapt a common MP3 player as a surveillance and recording device – and Alex was too keyed up to relax into a book. Sleep was the only recourse.

"Two minutes," Jones said, consulting a small terminal. The team hadn't been told precisely where they were going, although they had been told that it was somewhere isolated, just in case there was a biological threat from the crashed alien ship. Alex had read enough position papers to guess that there might be a nuke emplaced in their destination to sterilize the entire area if something nasty did pop out of the alien bodies, an insight he hadn't shared with the others. It would only have upset them.

The helicopter touched down with a final shudder and shut down its engines. The absence of the dull roar was almost disconcerting, despite the anticipation welling up within him. For the first time in his life – in all of human history, unless some of the people who claimed to have encountered aliens had been telling the truth – humanity was going to come face-to-face with intelligent beings from another world. He, Alex Midgard, was going to see an alien. His legs felt unsteady after the long trip as he pulled himself to his feet, wincing at the bright sunlight burning in through the opening hatch. The pair of soldiers outside waved the team out into the heat. It looked as if they were somewhere in the desert.

New Mexico would be traditional, he thought wryly, as he looked around. The base was tiny compared to some of the massive USAF bases he had served on throughout his career. There was a pair of massive hangars, a small barracks…and little else, apart from a surprisingly long runway. The whole area had a faintly desolate look, as if it had been abandoned for several years or perhaps placed on maintenance. Alex had been in the air force long enough to know that there were dozens of bases scattered around the country that had never been decommissioned or sold to the highest bidder, places that could be reactivated with a few months notice. Several of them had been reactivated after 9/11, but others had been kept on the sidelines. What they could see of their new home – at least for the next month – might be only the tip of the iceberg.

"This way, sir," one of the soldiers said.

Alex studied the uniform and frowned to himself. He didn't know much about the minutia of the Army, but it struck him that the soldier was an odd combination of careless and very careful. His uniform looked as if he hadn't bothered to change, his cheeks were unshaven…yet he held himself like a front-line combat soldier. Alex guessed that the soldiers were actually a crack Special Forces unit assigned to the base and ordered to pretend that they were a reservist unit; he wondered, vaguely, if they knew what they were protecting.

The air was hot enough that stepping into the hangar was something of a relief. He looked around, expecting to see a crashed UFO right in front of him, but the massive hangar was empty, although there were marks on the ground suggesting that something heavy had been dragged into the building. The soldiers led them right towards a small cubicle set into one wall and opened the door, revealing an elevator large enough to take the entire group. It was a barren chamber and Alex was glad when the doors opened again, revealing a man wearing a USAF Colonel's uniform.

"Welcome to Area 52," the officer said. "My name is Colonel William Fields, commander of this base. We have a short security briefing to attend and then I'll take you to see the big discovery."

Alex smiled to himself. He'd thought that Jones had been joking when he'd announced – deadpan – that they weren't going to Area 51, on the grounds that Area 51 was a paranoid fantasy created to hide the existence of another base, Area 52. The entire team had had enough briefings to last them for years, but there was no avoiding it. The military machine, at least in Alex's experience, preferred to repeat things time and time again, just to make sure that they were understood.

The briefing room turned out to be a small conference room. It looked surprisingly primitive, as if it had been built in the fifties and never modernized. A handful of computers, looking out of place, stood against one wall; another held a drinks cabinet and a water cooler. A third wall held a set of plans, presumably of the base itself. There was a faintly musty smell in the air, despite the efforts of a pair of air conditioners, suggesting that the base had only recently been reactivated. Alex suspected – looking at Fields – that the Colonel had either been given charge of the base as a way of keeping him away from anything important, or that he was a reservist assigned to the base, at least in theory. It must have been a shock to discover that his base had suddenly become the most important place on the planet.

"Please be seated," Fields said. He nodded to Jones. "This base, recently re-designated as Area 52, was built back in the 1960s to serve as a secondary base for U2 and Blackbird flights over the Soviet Union. It never actually served in such a role and was transformed into a small training facility in the eighties, before being placed on maintenance following the end of the Cold War. 9/11 saw the base being temporarily reactivated to serve as an emergency biological warfare centre. It would have been used as a place to hold infected personnel and – hopefully – find a cure. The base, again, never actually served in such a role and was re-deactivated two years ago."

He looked around the table. "You've all been briefed on the security requirements, and should have been stripped of any electronic devices that can be used to communicate, so I'll keep this brief," he continued. "You are here for a month, unless you receive special permission to exit early. You are not to go to Level 0 – ground level – without prior permission from Mr Jones or myself. You have clearance to visit anywhere on Levels 1 to 6; please bear in mind that Level 7 is off-limits at all times."

Jane broke the brief silence. "What's on Level 7?"

"Various things concerning the safety of the base," Fields said, curtly. "Only authorised staff members are allowed to visit Level 7."

He pointed towards the plans on the wall. "I advise you to study them carefully," he said. "Level 1 is the underground hangar; your… object of study is there. Level 2 consists of mainly biological research laboratories. Parts of Level 2 are sealed off, requiring special permission to enter, but you'll get a briefing on that later. Levels 3 and 4 are research laboratories, Level 5 is living quarters and Level 6 holds the command centre and other essentials. You'll pick it up very quickly so I won't go into more detail.

"We are under a full lockdown protocol here, so please bear in mind that every email you send will be read by Mr Jones or myself before it is allowed out of the buffer," he added. "There are no facilities for making telephone or video calls to anyone. If you have questions about any messages you want to send, run them past us and we'll let you know. The President's orders were quite explicit."

Alex listened thoughtfully. Fields had been a good choice on the part of the President, or whoever had chosen him for the role. He wouldn't allow anyone to break the security regulations and, knowing what he was sitting on, Alex couldn't blame him. Most governmental secrets were boring, or only interesting to specialists, but a crashed alien spacecraft would be of interest to the entire world. He hoped that the security teams defending the base had MANPAD units or other weapons, just in case the aliens attempted to recover their crashed ship. Did the aliens know where the human race had hidden their prize?

"Thank you, Colonel," Jones said. He grinned nervously at his team. "I think that we're ready to see the crashed ship now."

"Of course," Fields said. "If you'd like to follow me…?"

Alex couldn't have been kept away by wild buffaloes, or even armed guards. Fields led them through a set of bland corridors, without even a handful of children's pictures to brighten up the place, and into a small room. A pair of soldiers stood there and watched as Fields used a small ID card to open a heavy door and allow them into the underground hangar. The light streaming out was blinding, but Alex couldn't have turned his gaze away if he had tried. The alien craft held his attention and refused to let go.

to himself. The daze that had fallen over him since he had seen the crashed ship faded away.

He picked up the remote control and flicked on the television, wondering what might be showing. He flicked through a set of movies – he hadn't liked them much when he'd seen them the first time – and a pair of pornographic movies from one of the pornographic satellite channels. He was tempted to watch, but flicked instead to CNN, where a newsman was talking about the death of a well-known pop star. Alex watched without much interest. An old girlfriend of his had loved the star to the point where she sometimes pretended that she was sleeping with him, but Alex had rapidly learned to loathe him. The death of the pop star – a result of drug abuse – left him cold.

"…Gathered outside the graveyard to bid their idol goodbye," the newsman said. Alex remembered joking with his friends about how they could tell when a newsman was lying – when their lips moved. "The death of Eddie has been a tragedy for music lovers across the nation, who have joined together to wish Eddie a safe passage to the worlds beyond…"

"Most of the musicians play some kind of music," Alex muttered, taking another sip of coffee. He clicked the channel and moved over to Fox News. "And now…?"

"Senator Harrington today said that he felt that the President's reform campaign had gone too far and that he would oppose further reforms wherever necessary," the newswoman said. Unlike the CNN newsman, she was remarkably sexy, with long blond hair and open shirt. "Harrington refers, of course, to the controversial reform program for schools across America proposed by President Chalk. The White House has refused to comment."

Alex rolled his eyes as the news rolled on. There were more riots in Gaza, an energy crisis in Europe, more protests and demonstrations in the United States, threats of new taxes or reforms to older tax laws, economic disruptions caused by a recent default on the part of a Third World borrower, the campaign to select a new Secretary-General for the UN had bogged down… it was all so normal. It was all so…*typical*. Even the humorous report at the end – about a rabbit that had somehow managed to injure a man with a switchblade – was standard. The world had changed and no one had even noticed!

"This coffee is foul," Jones said, from behind him. Alex refused to give him the satisfaction of jumping. "Do you mind if I make a new pot?"

"Suit yourself," Alex said, glancing down at his watch before remembering that he'd left his watch behind in Washington. The clock on the wall suggested that he had been staring at the television for over thirty minutes. "Look at the news!"

Jones frowned. "There shouldn't be anything about the...ah, crashed ship in it," he said, shortly. "What's happening in the world today that compares to what we're doing here?"

"Nothing," Alex said. He changed the channel again and found a baseball game underway. "The entire world has changed and no one has even noticed!"

"That's not a bad thing," Jones said. He finished cleaning the pot and poured more water and coffee into the machine. "The longer we have to come to grips with what we're dealing with, the easier it will be to convince the public that we know what we're doing."

"We don't know what we're doing," Alex said, after a little while. "What happens when the aliens declare themselves in public?"

"We'll deal with that when it happens," Jones said. He poured himself a cup of coffee, added a surprising amount of milk, and leaned over to pick up the sugar. "What do you think will happen when Joe and Jane Public hear about the alien craft?"

He answered his own question. "Panic, Alex," he said. "They will panic. You saw how *we* reacted to the craft and we had time to brace ourselves. The public...will remember all those moments from science-fiction – the White House getting blown to bits, the massive robot shutting down the world, tripods slicing their way through a Victorian army, giant centaurs marching through Washington – and will go completely mad. We need time to prepare."

Alex shook his head. "I don't think we'll have time to prepare," he said, glumly. "We should get the panic over with now."

"The President disagrees," Jones said, mildly. "And, seeing that he's the President, what he says goes."

He took another sip of his coffee and smiled in appreciation. "Would you want to tell the public that aliens have been flying through our atmosphere for years – perhaps decades – and the only reason we even found out about it was when one of the craft suffered an accident and crashed, right in front of the most sensitive spot in the entire country?"

He shrugged. "We need to give them some hope of a solution before we take it public," he said. "The fact that we are completely naked before them will not go down well with the public, let alone the rest of the world."

Alex looked down into the dregs at the bottom of his cup. "I take your point," he said, unwillingly. "As long as we're preparing for trouble…"

"Oh, we're preparing," Jones assured him. "I don't know how much good it will do, but we're preparing."

Alex changed the subject. "I've been looking at UFO reports ever since the Foreign Technology Division anointed me Spooky and charged me with collecting and analysing them," he said. "If even a tiny handful of those reports were real alien spacecraft, the aliens have been here for decades – and, if some of the abduction reports are to be believed, have been committing acts of war against us."

He remembered, bitterly, the frustration when he couldn't solve a mystery – and the delight when he *could*. The vast majority of UFO cases were easy to crack and his clearance, allowing him access to classified files, made it easier to locate UFO reports that were caused by classified USAF aircraft. The civilian researchers might follow up their own lines of enquiry, yet lacking that access meant that they lacked Alex's insight. The vast majority of their 'unidentified' reports had been identified. Alex had come to believe that if he had been allowed to share his findings with civilian groups, the vast majority of UFO cases could be cleared. It was, like so many other things, Not Allowed. The military preferred to have UFO researchers looking at the skies rather than into secret military hangars.

"Acts of war," Jones repeated. "Do you believe the reports?"

Alex hesitated. "The early reports – people like George Adamski – were mainly nonsense," he said. "Their reports of what there was in space – they claimed cities on the Moon or Venus – were disproved by our own space program, although it is possible that the aliens lied to them. They rarely stood up well to serious researchers and most of them have been forgotten now. The later brood – the abducted humans – claimed that they'd been taken by the aliens and used for medical research. There were plenty of similarities between the different reports and…well, most of the victims went through a great deal of trauma…"

He shook his head. "But hypnosis is unreliable," he continued. "Anyone who has studied the issue – like me, or even an avid watcher of *The X-Files* – would know enough to construct a scenario that would seem convincing, without having any actual basis in reality. It's quite possible that the abduction experiences are the mind's attempt to cover up childhood sexual abuse or worse and sorting out the real cases from the downright absurd is impossible. I haven't had much direct experience, but I do keep tabs on what the civilians are doing and they're getting nowhere."

Jones frowned. "No direct proof?"

"No," Alex said. "A UFO researcher in England suggested – quite seriously – using Special Forces to watch the houses of known victims to see what happened, if anything. Researchers have placed cameras in their houses, but they always record the victims turning them off before an abduction, or they simply fail." He snorted. "There was even a weird case of an abduction that was supposed to have been witnessed by the then-Secretary-General of the United Nations."

"And it never became public?" Jones asked. "No one ever followed up on it?"

"Hundreds of researchers tried to follow up on it," Alex confirmed. "They got nowhere."

He poured himself another cup of coffee. "Neil wants to get some other technical personnel involved," he said. "I want to make enquiries with my correspondents, see if there are any UFOs being reported over Colorado – or here, for that matter. I'm supposed to get copies of all UFO reports made to the USAF – that's hundreds every month – and an increase might show us if the aliens are hunting for their lost craft."

"Smart," Jones said. "We can have the reports forwarded to you here."

Alex barely heard him. "We get a handful of odd reports every year," he said. "Some radar locks that show, briefly, a solid object. Sightings made by pilots and other trained personnel. We even scrambled fighters more than once to challenge objects that vanished before we could catch them. I could account for some of them being stealth aircraft or experimental designs, but not all of them. How long have the aliens been here?"

Jones considered it. "When did the UFO craze start?"

Alex laughed. "There were reports of flying airships – the Great Airship Scare – in the late 1890s," he said. "There were bizarre reports from the First and Second World Wars. During the Cold War, we had reports of Ghost Rockets over Scandinavia – those were later explained as being Russian experimental missiles – and the first people claiming to have been contacted by aliens. And then we had the abductions and increasingly complex reports of crop circles, cattle mutilation and UFOs that killed or injured people…"

"Point taken," Jones said. "They might have been watching us for years."

"It doesn't help that for every serious UFO researcher, there are at least ten kooks and crazy bastards who think that we're covering up UFOs from Roswell and hundreds of other UFO crash sites," Alex continued. "Every now and then, someone out to make a quick buck will produce a book or documentary claiming to expose government secrets regarding UFOs. *The Day After Roswell* was a pack of lies from start to finish, claiming that the Earth has been at war with aliens since before Roswell…and that all of the vital advances made in science came from technology recovered after that so-called UFO crashed. My more…public counterparts are deluged with crazies convinced that we have dead aliens on ice somewhere and…"

Jones laughed. "Do we have dead aliens in the Pentagon?"

"Not as far as I know," Alex said. "I looked into Roswell when I took the job – no one tried to prevent me studying the crash – and discovered that it was nothing more than a high-altitude aerial balloon. It doesn't stop people trying to make money from UFOs – Roswell has a UFO festival every year – and it doesn't convince the nuts that we're not covering up anything, apart from our own secret projects. Hell, sir, some of my superiors prefer people thinking about UFOs. It keeps them from wondering just what wonders we might have hidden away at Groom Lake and other places."

"Area 51," Jones confirmed. "Do we have dead aliens there?"

Alex opened his mouth to rebut the suggestion, and then realised that he was being teased. He'd been to Groom Lake AFB several times in his career, but he hadn't been allowed into some of the more secret parts of the complex, even with his clearance. The President himself wouldn't be allowed access, unless there was some compelling reason to allow him entrance, and everyone who worked permanently at the base ended up being watched for the rest of their lives. If there were dead aliens there, no one had shown him...

And there was little point in a cover-up. The reports of a UFO crash at Roswell faltered on that alone. Why would anyone keep it secret for over seventy years? The alien threat wouldn't have gone away, or been forgotten about in that time. It would have altered the course of history itself.

"No," he said, finally. He stood up and switched off the television. "Shall we go see the aliens?"

Jones nodded. "Neil has decided to remain with the craft and plan out how it is going to be dissected," he said. "The others are trying to snatch some rest before coming face-to-face with real aliens. Seeing the craft for the first time..."

"Culture shock," Alex said. He frowned as something occurred to him. "You know, back when Cortez was invading Mexico, there were people who claimed that the Mexicans couldn't actually *see* his ships. They were so far beyond their life experience that they couldn't grasp their existence. Aliens are part of our culture, but what if...?"

"We'd recognise an alien mothership if we saw it," Jones said. His voice was doubtful. "Wouldn't we?"

"I wish I knew," Alex said. "For all we know, the aliens are hanging right over our heads, or are based on the moon...which might be a colossal alien spacecraft itself. Neil Armstrong was supposed to have seen UFOs on the moon..."

"I think you get paid too much," Jones said. He put down his coffee cup with a thump. "Come on. Let's go wake up the others."

Chapter Five

It was a more subdued group that assembled on Level 2, facing an intimi-dating sign that warned of BIOLOGICAL HAZARD and detailed, in ex-traordinary terms, the level of precautions that even casual visitors needed to take. It was a heavy door, capable of standing off an antitank missile – or so Colonel Fields claimed – and its mere presence underlined the dangers of biological warfare. Alex had read accounts of how the Russians had acciden-tally released dozens of different viruses into the local area while developing their biological warfare program. It still rankled with him – and hundreds of other Western analysts – that despite promising otherwise, the Russians had continued their biological warfare program, a program that might well be capable of exterminating the human race. It was no wonder that intelli-gence agencies spent sleepless nights worrying about terrorists gaining access to Russian biological weapons. Fanatics willing to die wouldn't hesitate to unleash a plague that even Stalin would have balked at deploying.

Alex had never been in a biological lab before, but the outline was famil-iar enough. There was an external-internal area for casual visitors, where they could observe the procedures without having to don heavy biological protection suits and other precautions, and an internal area that was sealed up tighter than a spaceship in orbit. There were no frills inside the viewing compartments, no coffeepots or other signs of human life. It was as cold and sterile as the grave. Ominous notices on the wall warned of other possible dangers and promised dire retribution to anyone who attempted to pass through the airlocks without permission. Alex took heed. He'd seen enough movies about biological warfare to know that none of the warnings were exaggerated.

"We don't have the bodies in any of the public examination rooms," Colonel Fields said, somewhat regretfully. "The NBC team that brought them here placed them in the storage room until we brought in a team of qualified experts. We'll have to suit up and go into the sealed area."

Alex heard Santini groan, but he didn't understand why until they stepped into a dressing room. It reminded him of a swimming pool changing area, except that it was clearly intended for both sexes…and there were more ominous notices on the wall, warning him to ensure that he had gone to the toilet before donning the protective outfit. Smaller notices warned him to report any cuts or damage to the outfit at once, reminding him that the sterile environment could be compromised quite easily. Alex remembered the Russian scientist who had accidentally infected himself with one of the nastier viruses and shivered. An accident could wipe out the entire team.

He kept his back turned as he donned the suit, feeling odd as he pulled it over his suit. It felt as if he should be naked – it was already feeling uncomfortably hot – but Colonel Fields was pulling it over his own uniform. He checked his pockets, but apart from a single picture of his ex-girlfriend, there was nothing that could have torn a hole in the suit. The ominous warning signs insisted that he check twice, so he obeyed. There was no point in taking chances.

"Let me check the suits," Jane Hatchery said. Alex had barely heard from her before now – she hadn't seemed very interested in the crashed ship once she had recovered from the culture shock – but now she was definitely taking an interest. Like the others, she was looking at her personal holy grail – the chance to examine creatures that had been born on another world. NASA might have claimed to have found traces of life on Mars or in a meteor – and scientists had speculated for years that there was life under the ice on the gas giant moons – yet no one had seen a real alien, until now. Alex had seen footage that claimed to be from Roswell, but he'd dismissed it. It couldn't have been real.

The suit was growing more uncomfortable by the minute – it was far too hot already and he felt sweat trickling down his back – but he ignored the sensation as Colonel Fields opened the airlock, waving them into a darkened room illuminated by dim red light. The airlock swung closed behind them with an ominous thud, leaving them in darkness. A moment later, there was a flash of brilliant light, a shower of liquid from high above, and then a hiss as air was pumped through the chamber.

"Please be patient," Fields said. His voice sounded odd through his mask. "This is the sterilisation process. The light should have killed any germs on the suits."

Alex waited as patiently as he could, feeling the suit shifting around him as the process was slowly completed, until finally the second airlock door swung open. The room beyond looked just like a hospital operating room, apart from the dim red light beaming down from high above. Alex blinked as his eyes struggled to grow accustomed to it, wondering why they hadn't used normal light. It was probably intended to help keep certain forms of life alive – bright light could kill some viruses – but it added an ominously unsettling air to the room. It reminded him of some of the odder alien abduction accounts. There were people who believed that the UFOs were operated by the government for carrying out secret medical experiments on American citizens.

Fields stepped around an operating table, nodding towards where the bullet-proof glass separating the sealed compartments from where the observation compartments had to be – Alex couldn't see out of the chamber in the gloom – and led them towards a second hatch set into the wall. He keyed a console on one side of the hatch and it hissed open, revealing a second darkened chamber beyond. There were a handful of small surgical beds, like Alex would find in a standard hospital and several machines with purposes that he could only guess at, but it wasn't them that held his attention. He found himself staring at the half-seen bodies lying on the beds before Fields waved them closer. The sense of unreality welled up again as he stepped forwards. The aliens were *real*.

He couldn't have sworn as to how he was so certain. The aliens were humanoid, yet he'd seen more *alien* humanoid aliens in countless science-fiction films. It was their very…lack of strangeness that convinced him that they were real, a faint sense that he was looking at something out of this world. Memories surfaced within his mind. He'd been nine years old on a rocky beach playing in a pool when one of the rocks had moved. In the moments between seeing the rock move and realising that he was looking at a giant crab, he'd had the sense of something truly alien. It had brought out the arachnophobia in him. Somehow, he felt the same way about the aliens. They were convincing in a way that science-fiction aliens were not.

"This is EBE1," Fields said, slowly. The Colonel sounded awed, but he'd had a day to get used to the idea of aliens. Alex couldn't have spoken for the world. The sense of something utterly alien was overpowering. "That's Extraterrestrial Biological Entity. One of the NBC team gave them that designation."

"Smart," Jane Hatchery said. She had managed to hang on to her professionalism; indeed, she sounded as if she couldn't wait to whip out a scalpel and start dissecting the alien. "I'll want those team members for the research program here."

Alex barely heard her. He was staring at EBE1.

He'd expected little grey aliens. The Greys had been so predominate among alien encounters and abduction reports that it seemed inconceivable that there was not even the slightest connection with reality. The Greys had entered popular culture; there were religions devoted to them, entire groups of people claiming to have been abducted and anally probed by them…hell, insurance firms were even offering to insure people against being abducted by them! EBE1 was smaller than the average human, but it wasn't grey. Even in the dim red light, it was apparent that it had a light yellow skin tone. It was very far from human.

It was thin, almost like a starving teenager, wearing a silvery one-piece suit that covered most of its body. Its head was massive, out of proportion to the rest of its body, with two very dark eyes and a tiny mouth. It seemed to lack both a nose and ears, or hair. He leaned closer, staring into sightless eyes, and shivered. The eyes were disturbing even in a dead alien. What would a live one look like in person? His eyes fell to the creature's hands and he frowned. They were long and thin, perfect for manipulating even the most complex machinery, yet there was something disturbing about them too. He remembered ET and realised why he saw the alien as disturbing. It might have passed for a friendly alien in bad light…

They could be the Greys, he thought, and shivered again. He knew far too well how unreliable hypnotic regression actually was. The victims of alien abductions might have accidentally misled the researchers, or drawn images from popular culture, or perhaps they'd seen the aliens onboard their ships, in bad light. They might have seen them as grey, rather than pale yellow – there was something strange about their skin tone as well – and reported them as such. If abductions were real, what else might be real too?

He wanted to touch the alien, yet somehow he couldn't bring himself to lay a finger on the dead body. It was almost like trying to touch a spider. He'd seen people who'd picked up live spiders and other unpleasant creatures, even allowed them to run around on their bodies, but Alex had never been able to do anything like that. There was something in his mind preventing him from touching the alien. It was just too different to be tolerated.

"They were carrying a handful of odd tools and other devices," Fields said, in response to a question from Jane. "We sterilised them and put them in one of the lower levels for later analysis. We haven't attempted to undress them or anything beyond the damage already inflicted on their clothing by the crash. We decided we'd wait for the experts before proceeding. However…"

He led them over to a second table. "This is EBE4," he added. "As you can see, it appears to be a different species entirely."

Alex had heard that before, from Jones, and had tended to discount it. There had been dozens of different aliens reported by humans ever since the UFO craze had begun, but he suspected that most of them were hoaxes or misidentifications. How could the Earth be visited by blonde blue-eyed Nordic aliens, small savage beasts and high-minded angelic entities, to say nothing of the enigmatic Greys, all at the same time? There couldn't be so many cultures so close to Earth, could there? SETI had never picked up an alien signal – or at least it had never picked up anything that could be proved to be an alien signal – and if there were so many races nearby, Alex tended to regard that as unbelievable. Conspiracy theorists had claimed that the Government was controlling SETI and using it to cover up alien transmissions, but Alex knew better. It was far more likely that there was only one race near Earth, if there were any at all.

The second entity put the lie to that thought. It was massive, well over six feet tall, and even dead, it looked daunting. It was humanoid, but had massive muscular arms and legs, as well as a face that seemed to be half-bone. Merely looking at the alien's face made him feel sick – it looked as if half the flesh had been melted off the face, revealing white bone – yet he was sure that was natural for the alien. It was injured – its legs looked badly damaged – but Alex had the odd impression that the alien hadn't suffered He found himself wondering if it was really dead and nearly stepped backwards before he caught himself. It *had* to be dead.

Its eyes were small and piggish, set within the bone. It had no hair – like the first alien – but there were hints of shell or bone on the back of its head. It reminded him of the crab he'd remembered earlier and the shell that protected its innards; the alien seemed to be covered in natural armour. Its hands were rough, large enough to crush his head in a single squeeze. He hadn't seen anything like that outside a handful of very tough soldiers who'd spent years building their bodies up into peak condition. The alien had sharp fingernails and tattoos on the back of its hands. There was no way to know why it wore those. He looked back at the first alien and frowned. EBE1 had no fingernails at all.

"My God," Gayle said. She sounded terrified. "I wouldn't want to meet that up a dark alley."

"There are nastier things wearing human forms up some dark places," Santini said. "For all we know, the creature is a pacifist."

He didn't seem so daunted by the alien, but then, he was one of the toughest soldiers in the world. Alex wondered if he was already sizing the alien up as a potential enemy. It was hard to imagine EBE1 posing a threat, but far too easy to see EBE4 being armed and dangerous. It could have stepped out of an alien invasion movie. All it was lacking was a heavy energy weapon.

"A carnivore," Jane said, dispassionately. "Unless it comes from a completely different evolutionary path to humanity, it evolved to rend and tear its meat, just like us. Humans have teeth evolved to eat meat and vegetables, but this alien has only fangs. I wonder what it eats normally."

"Us, perhaps," Gayle said. She still sounded nervous. "Wasn't there a movie about alien cannibals invading the Earth?"

Alex could have named five off the top of his head, but he had other concerns. "How many different types of alien were on the crashed ship?"

"Two," Jones answered. He'd taken one look at EBE4 and retreated to the corner. Alex didn't envy him. He was the one who would have to brief the President. Somehow, he suspected that the alien would make a bigger impact on anyone who saw him in person. "There were three of the first type and two like…"

He waved a hand at EBE4. "There were two like that one," he said, catching himself. His voice sounded more than a little shaky. "That proves that two different alien races are probing the Earth."

"Maybe not," Jane said. "For all we know, one of them is male and the other is female."

"They're so different," Santini pointed out. "How can they be from the same race?"

It was Gayle who answered, her voice flat and dispassionate. "On average, men are generally stronger and faster than women," she said. "When pregnant, women rapidly become less capable of looking after themselves, or defending themselves against attack. A woman goes through a rapid series of changes after she reaches maturity, but a man does not. Primitive societies tended to form communities that kept women protected as they would bear the next set of young, which they then justified with religion and other such outdated crap. The aliens may have something comparable to that in their biological heritage."

"Leave that for the moment," Jones said. "Doctor Hatchery, how long would it take you to confirm that there is no biohazard?"

"I'm not sure," Jane admitted, finally. "I can run through the standard tests, which would at least allow us to be reasonably certain that there is no danger, but these are *aliens* and they may have unexpected surprises within their bodies."

"I can give you one right now," Steve Taylor said. They all turned to look at him, his face hidden behind the mask. "What killed them?"

"The crash, of course," Fields said, puzzled. "The Base Security Team didn't shoot them down as they emerged from their craft."

Alex saw what Taylor was driving at. "The bodies are too intact," he said. "They crashed, but they should have been able to walk away from it. Instead, they all died."

"There have been cases of pilots crashing their aircraft and surviving," Taylor agreed. "There have been…incidents where pilots have been killed in crashes without apparent damage, but mostly the damage is obvious. Why were the aliens killed if their craft survived surprisingly intact?"

"I don't know," Jones admitted. He looked over at Jane. "Make finding out what killed them your second priority, but concentrate on the biohazard threat. It would be nice to know if we can avoid nuking this base to avoid a disease outbreak."

"Understood," Jane said, shortly. She looked down at the body, already dissecting it in her mind's eye. "I'll start work as soon as the NBC team is brought into the complex."

"They're on Level 4," Fields said.

"A thought," Alex said. "Do we *want* to dissect the aliens?"

Jones gave him a puzzled look. "How else do you intend to learn about them?"

"If one of our pilots was dissected, we'd be furious," Alex said. The American Public would go apeshit, although the response to beheaded hostages in Iraq and Afghanistan had been muted. "What happens if the aliens take offence at our decision to cut open their friends and peer inside their bodies?"

"Point," Jane agreed. "I'll stick to non-intrusive techniques at first, and then reconsider once we reach the limits of what they can teach us."

"Don't forget to stick a probe up its ass," Santini added. Alex couldn't help himself. He giggled, feeling the tension being slowly released. "We have not yet reached the limits of what rectal probing can teach us."

"Shut up," Jane said, not unkindly.

Chapter Six

Colorado Springs, USA
Day 6

Robin Lance was in heaven, or at least what she considered heaven, although she knew that many of her fellow teens would have considered being shut up in a military base to be a foretaste of hell. It was true that some women in the US Military had had bad experiences, but it was also true that offenders were punished harshly and most female servicewomen had no better or worse experiences than their male counterparts. She might have been in lockdown – which was a fancy term for being kept in confinement until her superiors decided what to do with her – but she'd been granted access to all of the radar data collected by the massive network surrounding the United States – and charged with detecting any further alien intrusions. It was a task she took seriously. The UFO had somehow slipped right through the electronic fence and even Robin, who paid as little attention as possible to current affairs, found that ominous. She had a nasty suspicion that the only reason it had been detected was because its drive system had failed.

Colorado Springs – the famous NORAD – had been largely deactivated following the end of the Cold War, only to be reactivated from time to time to serve as a command and control facility for various American operations. The President might no longer fly to NORAD in case of a nuclear war – the massive complex was too well known and almost certainly on the list of targets for a mass offensive – but it still served an important role. It was also the ideal place to store a handful of personnel who'd seen too much and who also needed to work on the mountains of radar data collected and stored under the mountain. Robin had been impressed with the massive computers and had examined the records carefully. Every radar record the United States – and some of its allies – had made for the last fifteen years had been stored.

One of the problems with UFO investigations – one of her briefing officers had told her – was that radar tapes had been routinely wiped, overwritten or destroyed. In the days before computers had become capable of storing so much data, there was simply too much information to be stored for long, not when the tapes were so expensive. The conspiracy theorists – he'd told her with a wink – had sweated blood over the thousands of tapes that had gone missing, unaware that they were routinely rewritten or destroyed. After 9/11, the USAF had started to store data for much longer periods, although even with modern computers there was a massive backlog for researchers to sort through. Without modern computers, Robin knew, it would have been completely impossible.

The problem was that radar tended to be an inexact science. It was quite easy to get an inaccurate reading if the radar beam passed through transient atmospheric conditions, or even flights of birds or weather balloons. The USAF joked about the kids who'd launched balloons into the air and triggered off a major security alert, but Robin no longer saw the funny side. A transient contact, one that appeared and then disappeared, might just be written off, rather than being investigated. The problem was that there were so many transient contacts on the records that, if all of them were assumed to be alien spacecraft, literally *billions* of UFOs had visited the Earth. Robin knew that the simplest explanation – that the contacts were actually random weather conditions or flights of birds – was far more likely, but she couldn't rule out a single contact. Going through all of the contacts would take years.

She stared down at the keyboard and considered. NORAD was equipped with quantum computers that were at least two generations ahead of civilian models, but even with the fantastic levels of computing power at her disposal, there seemed to be no way to speed up the process. Or perhaps there was. She knew when *one* alien spacecraft had visited Earth – the UFO that had crashed – and if there was anything odd on that day, it *might* signify a way of tracking the UFOs.

"Run program," she said, as she tapped the final key. It had taken nearly an hour to program in the search patterns. A general search would have revealed thousands of false trails – laid by civilian and military aircraft – yet tightening the search patterns too far would have risked ignoring vital information. It was a reverse of the standard search pattern, used to track aircraft back in time, and it was far more complex. She couldn't afford to ignore any possible contacts. Tired, she stood up and staggered off towards the bathroom. She needed to splash water on her face and perhaps drink a lake of coffee.

The program was still running when she finished washing her face and combed her hair, so she went down to the cafeteria to have a snack. The quality of food in Cheyenne Mountain was somewhat variable - Schriever Air Force Base had had better food – but at least it beat MRE packs. She took a plateful of eggs and bacon and found an empty table to sit at, ignoring the handful of young male officers who tried to draw her into conversation. She could make a radar system sit up and beg, but a social life had never held much interest for her. Besides, in her experience men wanted to talk about sport, guns and how great they were…and *none* of those were interesting. She had never met a man who was her intellectual equal.

She finished the food, placed the dishes in the washing pile, and walked back to her office. The program had finished, she was relieved to see – even quantum computers had their limits – and she poured herself a mug of black coffee before sitting down and studying the results. They were hardly a surprise. There were *thousands* of transient contacts that had appeared, disappeared, and never been seen again. One of them – she hoped – had to be the alien ship. It was quite possible that *many* of them were the alien ship. How fast could it travel?

Her fingers danced over the keyboard, looking for patterns. She'd spent two days learning everything she could about UFOs and radar and she was attempting to duplicate a trick that a British UFO researcher had developed. He'd taken a UFO report and a set of radar contacts and put them together, revealing that *something* had crossed the British mainland at a speed of around Mach Nine. It was fast enough that Robin guessed that the whole thing had been written off. As far as she knew, there was nothing in the American or British military that could move at such a speed, with the possible exception of the space shuttle. The unknown craft remained a mystery.

The patterns slowly developed in front of her. Robin's talent wasn't just operating radar – anyone could do that, with the right training - but in seeing patterns that few others could see. It wasn't easy and she found herself wondering if she was imagining things, but as she studied the pattern, it became clear that there was a *succession* of odd contacts, coming in from the East Coast and arcing over towards Schriever Air Force Base, where the craft had met its fate. Her fingers tapped in new commands, trying to refine the data. It looked as if the craft had registered and then…simply vanished. It was no wonder that the USAF hadn't launched interceptors to challenge the mystery craft. No one had realised that it *was* a craft.

Robin had seen radar data recovered from the Iraqis after Baghdad had fallen. The city had been hit heavily by F-117 stealth fighters – somehow, the degree of effort put into degrading the Iraqi air defence network had slipped out of the public mind – yet the Iraqis *had* achieved some level of detection. The aircraft had been briefly visible when they'd opened their bomb bays and released their weapons. A more alert radar team and properly calibrated air defence weapons might have cost the United States dearly. An F-117 was naturally stealthy. The alien craft – assuming she was actually looking at a real pattern – seemed to flicker between stealth mode and being visible. It made little sense to her, yet…

She pulled up the data and, having refined her program, let it loose on the data from the last ten years. It took nearly an hour for the program to complete itself, but she didn't waste the time. She had to define ways to actually achieve a more permanent contact, maybe even deny the aliens one of their tricks. When she looked at the data, she muttered a curse under her breath. It was impossible to be *sure,* yet it looked as if the aliens had been probing American defences for years. It could have been paranoia, she knew, yet she'd programmed the computers to be quite careful. There was an entire series of transient contacts that seemed to fit the evasive pattern.

On impulse, she brought up the data from the rest of the world. Few people comprehended just how much coverage the United States and its allies had built up, sharing information through the wonders of secure computer networks. American, British, French, German, Italian, Turkish, Israeli, Australian and Japanese radar networks shared data on a daily basis, allowing them to peer far into China, Russia and other hostile nations. No aircraft could move over Iran or Venezuela without being detected and tracked. The other powers howled that it was another example of Western Imperialism, yet there was no way to prevent it. Radar pulses were no respecters of borders.

She looked down and bit off another curse. The pattern suggested that *all* of the major powers had had their alien visitors, although some of those powers' radar systems were more primitive than what America would deploy. Worse, the Deep Space Tracking System reported odd bursts of high-temperature emissions at the edge of space, bursts that corresponded with possible alien contacts. She almost couldn't believe that no one had noticed the pattern sooner, yet it was easy to understand. Everyone had vague contacts and, if they weren't behaving like predicable aircraft, they tended to be ignored. It was a mistake that might have disastrous consequences.

A nasty thought occurred to her and she did what she should have done in the first place. Six days had passed since the alien spacecraft had crashed – what had happened since then? The radar data, newly collected and collated, formed in front of her and a frightening pattern emerged. A handful of new unidentified contacts had been detected at Schriever Air Force Base – her former home – and others had been detected towards Washington. She wished that UFO reports were sent to Colorado Springs – it would have been interesting to compare them with her radar reports – but there was no time. She had to kick this upstairs to her new superior officer. It changed everything.

She picked up the phone and dialled a number from memory. It was oddly primitive technology in a place that had once been called the Crystal Palace, but anyone with the right equipment could hack into a wireless conversation, or even tamper with it. The landline might be primitive, yet it was much harder for hostile powers to intercept and tap, even though the alien capabilities were completely unknown. For all she knew, they could read over her shoulder as she scrolled through the data on the computer screen.

"General?" She asked. "I think you'd better get down here. There's something that you should see."

———

General Gary Wachter was a short burly man with a shaven head, although Robin privately conceded that he had a really nice smile. He reminded her of her grandfather before he passed away. He might have been an Army General, an officer in the 3rd Infantry Division as well as a training officer before accepting the position of Chairman of the Joint Chiefs of Staff, but Robin knew better than to underestimate him. He was far from stupid. One of her former USAF commanding officers had once told her that while the Russians or the Chinese were the air force's opponents, the Army, the Navy and the Marines were its enemies, competitors for a shrinking budget doled out each year by the Government. Robin didn't care as long as she got to work on her radars, but she did wonder if the General would listen to her. She was only a junior officer, after all.

The General had been appointed supervisor of the whole operation by the President, something that made him one of the most powerful men in the country, with authority to call on assets from all of the different departments and forces. Those in the know conceded that it was vitally important that everyone worked together, but privately feared that their departments would wind up being slighted or pushed out of the way. The internal politics had already turned violent and metaphorical blood was on the walls, but Robin had heard that the President had made it clear that anyone who wasted time would find themselves on the bench, or sent to the most isolated posting he could find. There was no time to play politics with an alien force probing Earth.

"Don't worry about the formalities," Wachter said. Robin had had problems saluting him, let alone trying to remember what kind of protocol applied to a General. She had never worried about the formalities before and her former superiors had made exceptions for her. "Just tell me what you've got."

Robin was uncomfortably aware of just how thin her evidence was, but she stumbled through the explanation, trying to ignore the sensation of his eyes on her. It wasn't a sexual interest, but something more fundamental; he was judging her and her competence. Stung, she outlined the basics and then started detailing the problems, treating him to a highly-technical report that covered all of the contacts, ending with the current transient contacts. Wachter just listened.

"I see," he said, finally. Robin wasn't sure that he did. Most people's eyes started to glaze over as she outlined the technical issues. "Tell me one thing. Are you sure that the contacts are real?"

Robin hesitated. "I think that most of them are," she admitted, finally. "I've actually excluded transient contacts that don't reappear, or don't seem to follow a pattern. There might be many more contacts that…don't appear on my lists, or far fewer. I don't think that the data can be refined any further without a careful look at the craft."

Wachter nodded. "And no one is responding to this?"

"The data shows that most of the contacts are keeping well away from the aircraft we have on CAP," she said. The USAF had kept several dozen aircraft in the air for the past week, in position to respond to any serious threats, yet the pilots didn't know what they might be facing. It made Robin uncomfortable. There were three Sentry aircraft in the air and she knew some of their crews personally. They might run into trouble that they were mentally unprepared to handle. "All of the contacts are very vague, sir. I don't blame the pilots for not responding to them."

"*I* do," Wachter snapped. "I'll see to it that they're ordered to respond to *any* contact, no matter how flimsy."

Robin said nothing. The alien craft, if some of the data were to be believed, would have no difficulty breaking contact with even the fastest aircraft in the USAF's arsenal. No one knew if they carried weapons, or if they would stand and fight instead, but with so many contacts, most of them had to be false positives. It defied belief that *thousands* of UFOs were probing American airspace.

"And they're watching Schriever," Wachter continued. "Do you think that they are looking for their missing craft?"

"I think so," Robin said, slowly. She hadn't been emotionally aware of it until he'd spoken, but now a shiver ran down her back. "They may well know where it went down, even if they don't know why. Most of the new contacts are hovering over Colorado and watching us. The others seem to be skimming over the entire country and further away, north to Canada and south to Mexico."

"So they don't know where the craft is now," Wachter mused. Robin said nothing. *She* didn't know where the craft was either, although she suspected that it had been taken to Wright-Patterson Air Force Base. The headquarters of the Air Force Materiel Command was also the home base of the 445th Airlift Wing of the Air Force Reserve Command, which flew the C-5 Galaxy heavy transport. They could have taken the crashed ship anywhere from there. "That's good news, I suppose."

He cleared his throat. "Can you work out a way to refine the contacts and actually track them permanently?"

"Perhaps," Robin said. "It won't be easy. We could track stealth aircraft by setting up a network of AWACS and ground-based stations, even tying in civilian and commercial stations, but the evidence suggests that the alien craft are...odd. There are times when they're stealthy and times when they're detectable."

"Work out an operations plan," the General ordered. Under normal circumstances, someone as lowly as Robin would never have been asked to draw up an operations plan, but this was far from normal. "Once you have it, send it to me and I'll see to it that it gets implemented. The exercise we're preparing – we *were* preparing – will give us cover for all kinds of military moves, without having to tell people what they might be encountering."

He didn't sound as if he believed his own words. "Yes, sir," Robin said. "It would help if I had access to the reports from the study team."

"You'll get them," Wachter promised. He grinned at her. "I'll speak to the President about it this evening. I'm sure that he will have no objection. Keep up the good work."

Chapter Seven

The conference room on the base looked a little more comfortable after a week, although that might have had something to do with the fact that the teams working to reactivate the base had finally had a chance to clean it out and redecorate. A set of coffeepots – the base couldn't have operated without coffee on demand – dominated one wall, while the other two were covered with plasma screens and an image of the crashed alien ship. It had been taken before it had been transported away from the crash site and, somehow, had an impact beyond the obvious. Alex knew that teams had scoured the crash site of everything even remotely useful, but he did wonder if the crash site would show signs of what had happened, even to an unsuspecting eye.

He scowled down at the table, seeing his reflection scowling back at him, as the other prime team members came in. Part of him felt as if he had been sidelined – the teams looking into the craft itself and the dead alien bodies had brought in additional manpower from all over the black community – but the remainder of him was grateful for the chance to think. He could contribute almost nothing useful to the study of the crashed ship and bodies, even though he liked to think that he would have great insights. He'd spent most of the week gathering UFO reports, comparing them to the odd radar traces discovered by Cheyenne Mountain, and reading through science-fiction at an astonishing clip. Every old alien invasion book had to be re-read, looking for insights that could be used in their current situation, and even though some of them hadn't aged well, it was still fascinating – and depressing. The hard science-fiction novels suggested that humanity would be curb-stomped by an advanced alien enemy.

Jones had suggested, after looking at the pile of books that had been delivered by Amazon to one of the USAF bases that served as a clearinghouse for mail, recruiting science-fiction authors to assist in drawing up contingency plans. He'd been so pleased with the idea that Alex hadn't had the heart to tell him that Larry Niven and Jerry Pournelle had beaten him to it, never mind the authors who'd written themselves into their books. It wasn't a bad idea and he'd been drawing up a list of possible authors, yet only a handful already had any form of security clearance and – with the project so highly classified – it would take months to clear people who had never been through even a standard security vetting. Alex would have felt better about it if he'd thought that they had time, but the UFOs being picked up over Colorado suggested that time was in short supply. The aliens were hunting for their missing craft.

Alex had given considerable thought to what the aliens would do next, for a handful of American bases were well-known in UFO lore. Wright-Patterson Air Force Base was supposed to house alien craft in Hangar 18 – it didn't – and there were a handful of others that were name-checked more than once. The aliens might attack an airbase to recover their craft, yet they had to know that the odds of hitting the right base were fairly low – there had been no radar traces near Area 52. The base's defences had been augmented by a handful of Special Forces personnel with handheld antiaircraft weapons, but Alex rather doubted that they could stand off an alien attack. He'd insisted that they store data outside the base, just in case the base was destroyed by the aliens, or the experiments with the alien craft, yet the security requirements were getting in the way. It was hampering exploration of the alien craft, let alone the overall situation. The aliens weren't going to go away just because the vast majority of humanity didn't even know they existed.

Jones tapped the table for attention. "Good morning," he said. He looked surprisingly clean and well-pressed for a man who'd spent the last week on a military base - *and* he'd somehow dug up a suit from the base's stores. Alex, who wore a basic USAF uniform, wanted to hate him for it. It was as if he was drawing a line between the civilian and military worlds. "As you will have heard, the radar contacts over Colorado and the surrounding states have only intensified; although so far there have been no successful interceptions. A handful of aircraft have been routed to challenge the mystery craft, but they have always declined contact and vanished. We do not, however, have much time. I will therefore waive the formalities and get right down to business."

Alex rolled his eyes as Jones continued. They didn't have time for even a handful of formalities. "We need information as quickly as possible," Jones added. "Neil, please would you tell us what you have discovered so far."

Neil Frandsen looked annoyed at having been dragged away from the hangar deck – he'd set up a camp bed there just so that he could remain near the alien craft – but he managed to keep his voice level. The forty engineers, researchers and scientists who had been brought into the project tended to have different opinions about the alien craft. Some wanted to remain near it at all times, others could barely wait to get away from it, back to their homes and the comfortable familiar worlds they knew. A scientist had almost collapsed and had had to be transferred to another base, where he remained in lockdown and under observation. It might have been the culture shock, or it might have been something more serious. No one knew for sure.

"It would be easier to tell you what we don't know about it," Frandsen said, carefully. "As I warned you at the beginning, there is no way that we can give you a timetable for when and how we will unlock the secrets of the alien ship. We have made several interesting discoveries, yet we have also discovered hundreds of new questions and mysteries. We may not succeed in unlocking all of the craft's secrets for a very long time."

He leaned backwards and continued in a bored monotone. "The pieces of debris have been analysed carefully," he said. "The tests revealed a mixture of four different metal alloys, including two that we have been unable to identify. The interesting point is that the craft's hull appears to be incredibly conductive, yet also surprisingly strong. It may have been held together by the craft's power source – hence the glow emitting from the craft – but as yet no one has been able to prove or disprove it. The important news from a military point of view is that while the hull is strong, it should be unable to withstand a missile hit, or cannon fire. If we could track them, we could hit them, and if we could hit them, we could bring them down."

"Good," Santini said, shortly. "Have you unlocked the secret of their radar-avoidance technology?"

"Not really," Frandsen said. He looked over at Jones. "We have been unable to determine how the craft flew, but some of the researchers from the Advanced Propulsion Research Centre believe that the craft had a limited reactionless drive field that would have given it astonishing speed and manoeuvrability. One of the functions of such a drive field might have been to absorb radar energy – and other kinds of energy – but there is no way to know for sure until we actually manage to duplicate the drive. That could take years.

"On the other hand, the hull does absorb low levels of energy," he added, "so it's quite possible that radar pulses are simply absorbed directly into the hull. That's actually old news, as far as the stealth community is concerned; stealth coatings have been around for years. There are ways to track such aircraft, but without knowing more about how the alien vessels operate, it might be difficult."

"Very difficult," Santini agreed. "I was on the mission into Saudi Arabia three years ago. We just flew past their defences without impediment, as if they couldn't see us at all."

"Which is what we might be facing ourselves," Jones confirmed. "What about the remainder of the craft? Do you know why it crashed?"

"No," Frandsen admitted, reluctantly. "The rear area of the craft is almost completely inexplicable, for the moment. We've been probing it very gently, but parts of it appear to be fused, or perhaps that's actually its normal configuration. The bottom line is that we have no idea exactly what the craft did to fly, although we have dozens of possible theories. As for why it crashed…"

He scowled. "It looks as if they suffered a major drive failure," he concluded. "That's not actually uncommon for us. An aircraft launched from a USAF base might suffer any one of hundreds of possible equipment failures that would force it to return to base without actually engaging the enemy or completing its mission."

"I don't know about you," Alex said, into the silence, "but I find that rather reassuring."

Frandsen nodded. "The interesting part is that their computers may be semi-compatible with some of our own advanced systems," he added.

He held up a hand to forestall a series of astonished protests. "I'm not talking about them coming equipped with USB ports and Windows Whatever, but a certain…shared understanding of how computers work. It may take years to learn how to hack into their computers, but the specialists I've had brought in are confident that eventually we will be able to extract data from their records. Understanding it, of course, might be difficult."

Gayle Madison nodded. "I've been studying the alien markings on the craft," she put in. "They're completely beyond our understanding at the moment. It is quite possible that we will never decipher the data without their assistance, willing or otherwise."

Jones nodded. "I take it that the craft can't actually fly?"

"I don't think we'll be flying it up to the mothership to upload a computer virus," Santini said, with an evil grin. "Is the craft actually dead?"

"We don't know," Frandsen admitted. "There are very definitely traces of power left within its systems. It may be absorbing power from the surrounding area. However, if it is broadcasting for rescue, we have been unable to pick it up. It shouldn't be able to get a signal out using any tech we're familiar with, but if it can generate a stream of neutrinos, for example…"

Alex nodded in understanding. Neutrinos went through almost anything. The hangar was surrounded by all kinds of jamming equipment, but they couldn't stop a neutrino emission or something so fantastic that it was beyond even the imagination of science-fiction writers. The only sign that the craft wasn't screaming for help was that none of the UFOs had visited Area 52, as far as they knew. The aliens might have adjusted their stealth systems to remain hidden as they scouted out their target. It wasn't a pleasant thought.

"I'll forward your report to the President," Jones said, finally. "That leads us directly to the aliens themselves. Jane?"

Jane looked tired, but happy. Like Frandsen, she had been spending most of her time in her department, although she hadn't been sleeping with the aliens. The regulations forbade sleep within the biological containment area and insisted on everyone rotating out every few hours, just so fatigue wouldn't lead to tragedy.

"My team has been studying the five alien bodies carefully, although we have limited ourselves to non-intrusive probes until we know how the aliens treat their dead," she said, carefully. "The first priority was to ensure that there was no biological threat from the alien bodies – they might be friendly, but their bacteria might have other ideas – and we carried out every test in the manual, as well as several we made up specially. As far as we can determine, there is no biological hazard at all. I've kept the bodies under heavy isolation and I certainly do *not* advise throwing open the airlocks and inviting in the entire world, but I feel that the danger is minimal, if it exists at all."

Jones frowned. "Are you certain of that?"

"The aliens have a completely different biology to us," Jane said, firmly. "It is highly unlikely that any of their diseases could make the jump into humanity, or vice versa. There are some disease – Bird Flu, for example – that move between species, but they all came from Earth. The aliens did not."

"So much for any *War of the Worlds* scenarios we might have been hoping for," Santini said. "Can they live on Earth without protection?"

"I believe so," Jane said. "Their blood carries definite traces of oxygen, suggesting that they are oxygen-breathers. I won't know for sure until I have a live one to examine, but I believe that they won't have any problems spending time on Earth, or living permanently on the planet. Their bacteria and fungi – to say nothing of higher life forms – could probably find a niche here."

She picked up the remote control and flashed an image of EBE1 onto the display. "The first really interesting thing about the aliens is that they are definitely from the same planet," she said. "Their biology may be different from humanity, yet EBE1 and EBE4 share too many common points to come from two different planets. They're also all male, I believe. We have been unable to locate any wombs or egg sacs, while we have come up with good candidates for testicles and other male organs. The second really interesting thing about them is that their brains appear to be liquid."

"That's impossible," Gayle said. "They can't have liquid brains."

Jane's face darkened. "That was my thought as well, when we x-rayed their skulls," she said. "It took several attempts before we realised that the aliens all had tiny implants buried within their skulls and we suspect that those implants killed them. The bodies, as Steve mentioned days ago, were suspiciously intact, yet they were dead. I believe that the aliens committed suicide to avoid being captured – or were killed by their superiors. The implications are…disturbing."

"They didn't want live aliens to fall into our hands," Alex said. Jane was right. The implications were very disturbing. It didn't suggest a friendly motive for visiting the planet. "Why didn't they destroy the bodies completely?"

"Unknown," Jane said, flatly. It hadn't been a fair question. How could she have known the answer? "The first subgroup of aliens is smaller and weaker than the second, yet it definitely possesses a greater degree of manual skill and very manipulative fingers. There were a handful of other implants embedded within their bodies, but without surgery I am unable to remove them or speculate on their purpose. I have teams trying to construct computer models of how the aliens might move, yet without a live one…well, such procedures can only go so far.

"The second type of alien is…odder," she continued. "It is definitely stronger and probably faster than the first type, with natural armour growing out of its skin. There are sacs of chemicals within its body, near the bloodstream, with an uncertain purpose. There are no implants at all apart from the one embedded in their skulls. It has tattoos and markings that the first type of alien lacks. We don't know why."

She hesitated. "It's odd, but…when I was younger, I used to design monsters for fantasy games to put myself through Med School," she said. "If I'd been designing a monster to serve in the ranks of the Dark Lord, I might have come up with something like the second group of aliens. Their strength and endurance might be well above the norm for their race; hell, they might well have been designed to serve as soldiers. I'm not sure I like the implications of that either."

Santini frowned. "Designed?" He asked. "How?"

"People have been talking about using genetic engineering to produce soldiers with superhuman attributes for years," Jane said. "None of the various research programs ever got very far - public opinion was always very strongly against it – and mostly it flopped. The aliens, on the other hand, might have engineered themselves a warrior caste, or perhaps it evolved naturally. The two groups of aliens definitely come from the same stock."

Jones looked stunned. "It sounds crazy," he muttered. "Why would anyone do that?"

"Better soldiers," Santini said. "To think what I had to go through to earn my wings…"

"It's not unknown in nature," Jane added. "There are dozens of different breeds of dog, yet they're all the same species and they can crossbreed. I find it hard to imagine an advanced race that exists like that, but there's no reason why one cannot develop somewhere else."

"I see," Jones said, finally. He sounded oddly rattled. "Do you have anything else to add?"

"It's all in my report," Jane said. "We cannot say much more until we dissect one of the aliens to see how it all goes together, but…"

"We still don't know how they treat their dead," Alex reminded her. "The last thing we want to do is give unintentional offence."

"They crashed outside one of the most secure areas in the United States," Santini pointed out. "They're watching us even now. They have either evolved or designed a warrior caste. I think we're far beyond worrying about giving unintentional offence."

Jones was about to reply when Colonel Fields entered, without knocking, and passed him a PDA. "Shit," he said, reading the message. Alex had a premonition of disaster before Jones could say anything else. Had the aliens finally commenced the invasion? "Everything has changed."

He looked up, into Alex's eyes. "We just picked up a message from the aliens," he said. His voice was stunned, disbelieving. "They're asking for a meeting. They want to meet with the President himself."

Chapter Eight

Washington DC, USA
Day 9

"There is not going to be any debate about this," President Andrew Chalk said. "I'm going."

He stood at one end of the Oval Office, facing his inner circle. Only a handful of his Cabinet even knew about the crashed alien ship, let alone the UFO reports and the message from the stars. His inner circle all knew and had been briefed, including his Vice President, who was in a secret command post. If something happened to Washington, the President had decided on his first day in office, it wouldn't be allowed to break the command-and-control links that bound the US Military together.

Andrew Chalk had gone into the Army during the Clinton years and had rapidly been promoted until he reached Colonel, within the famed 3rd Infantry Division. He'd taken part in the march to Baghdad and developed a reputation as a tough but fair commanding officer. He'd had his doubts about the aftermath of the invasion from the start and, following Washington's reluctance to realise that the United States was caught up in a counter-insurgency campaign, he'd resigned from the army and gone into politics. He'd appealed to both right and left – the right because he had genuine military experience and was also a moderate; the left because he'd resigned in protest against Rumsfield – and his campaign had been planned with military precision. He'd crushed the challengers for the Republican nomination – his main challenger had largely been running on the grounds that he wasn't the incumbent – and then defeated the Democrats to become President. His bluff, no-nonsense manner had won him friends and allies in disillusioned politicians and citizens, although the cliques in Washington opposed him at every turn. They suspected, quite rightly, that President Chalk intended to restore honesty and openness to the Federal Government.

"This is not something we can pass on to an Ambassador or a Special Representative," he added, knowing that his Cabinet wasn't convinced. He'd chosen most of them partly on the grounds that they wouldn't hesitate to tell him if they thought that he was wrong. The worst problem politicians had was being surrounded by people who told them what they wanted to hear. "This can only be handled by the President himself. The buck stops here."

There was a long silence. "Mr President," General Gary Wachter said finally, "this is *not* beyond debate."

The President frowned. General Gary Wachter had been his commanding officer several times, to the delight of some media personages who talked about the General being the power behind the throne, or perhaps being abused in revenge for putting the President through hell as a junior officer. They couldn't have been more wrong. The President trusted Wachter completely and expected him to be as honest as he had been as a younger officer, supervising a new and very inexperienced officer.

"We don't know anything about them," the General continued. "They might be sincere about wanting to talk to you, but what happens if they kill you, or simply keep you onboard their ship?"

"That would be an act of war," the President pointed out. "Jacob" – Vice President Jacob Thornton – "becomes President and we're at war with an alien race."

"But we'd also be hamstrung," Wachter insisted. "What happens if they keep you for longer than a day, or maybe two days? We'd have to cover for your absence. The strategic defence systems require authorisation directly from the President to fire. This wouldn't be a case of you being assassinated, or suffering a major heart attack, but a case when no one knows what the *fuck* is going on. The risks are too high, Andy."

"The risks of *not* going are also too high," the President said. "They lost a craft near one of our most vital military bases. I can't help but agree with the analysts who find that ominous. If there's a chance that we can open relationships with them, in light of the latest demonstration of their capabilities, then we have to take it. We're naked and almost defenceless against a foe that controls the high orbitals."

They shared a grim look. The alien message had been inserted – somehow – into the Majestic Satellite Communications Network, a highly-classified system used for top secret discussions between the President, the Pentagon and the commanders in the field. It was so secret that no one outside the Federal Government was supposed to know about it and, indeed, most of the Government *didn't* know about it. The aliens had not only uploaded a message into the network, but they'd encrypted it using one of the latest American encryption protocols, generated by a quantum computer. The President wasn't blind to the significance of the gesture. The aliens had not only shown that they knew who to approach for a meeting, but that they could hack into American secure communications, the most secure in the world, at will. The entire secure communications network could no longer be trusted.

"There is another issue," Hubert Dotson said. The Secretary of State looked grim, but intensely focused. "How do we know that we're the only nation to have a crashed ship, or to have been approached by the aliens?"

The President looked at Tom Pearson, the CIA representative. "As you know, sir, we attempt to track the location of all of the world leaders," he said. "There are apparently no plans for any of the major world leaders to vanish from sight in the next few weeks, although I should stress that such information is often hard to obtain. The more…paranoid a regime is, the more likely it is to keep the location of its leader secret, or keep moving him around to avoid being pinned down. We know that the KGB and their successor, the FSB, looked into the UFO mystery during and after the Cold War, but if they found a craft, we don't know about it."

"I see," the President said. He'd cleaned house at the CIA after assuming the Presidency – he had never forgiven them for their failures in Iraq – but even he had to admit that intelligence work was never cut and dried. The United States hadn't enjoyed real penetration of any of its major opponents during or even after the Cold War. The CIA's reputation for leaks – which got sources killed – worked against it

"But Hubert is right," he continued. "The last thing we need is the aliens approaching the Russians, or the Chinese, or anyone else."

"They may approach us," the Secretary of State warned. "If they knew that we had a crashed ship, they would demand that we shared our research with them, or else."

"Or else what?" Wachter demanded. "There's very little that they could do to us that wouldn't rebound worse on themselves."

"They might need the information if the aliens did turn out to be hostile," Pearson pointed out, coldly. "We might need their help."

"I doubt it," Wachter said. "The entire massed force of Earth couldn't mount an offensive beyond Low Earth Orbit, if that."

"That's something we will have to look at," the President said. His voice was very cold. "What about our current defence deployments?"

Wachter looked down at his secure Blackberry. "We're proceeding through the exercise now and using it as an excuse – along with terrorist threats – to make all kinds of military deployments," he said. "We have fighter jets on patrol and ground-based surface-to-air missiles deployed at sensitive locations. The UFOs have not attempted to challenge them, Mr President, but no one expects that to last."

He hesitated. "We need to brief in more people, yet every time we do that we make a leak more likely," he warned. "We're effectively operating with one hand behind our backs. I've passed orders along for local radar operators to take a closer look at transient contacts and dropped hints about stealth aircraft testing the defences, but our people are not prepared – not mentally – for possible hostile action."

"Another good reason for me to meet with them," the President said. He wouldn't have admitted to the thrill of excitement he felt, not even to Wachter, yet the life of a President was a little like being in prison. There was nowhere for him to just be himself, even in the White House. He'd seen movies where the President fought hijackers who had hijacked Air Force One, or even flew a fighter plane against massive city-destroying UFOs... actually, that one hit a bit too close to home. "We want to avoid a confrontation if possible."

"Yes, Mr President," Wachter said. He looked down at his Blackberry. "We'll officially announce that you will be visiting Camp David for talks with foreign ambassadors and allow the Press to go nuts speculating on who you're seeing and why. We'll fly you to Schriever Air Force Base in a more private aircraft and accommodate you in one of the officer's quarters until the time of arrival. The base commander isn't happy, but he does understand what's at stake."

The President nodded. "And then?"

"Their message says that they will pick you and one other up from the crash site, two days from now," Wachter said. "I imagine that they'll transport you to a secure location for the talks and then – I hope – return you intact. The analysts, however, have all kinds of worries…"

"I know," the President said. The Secret Service – those who knew about the new threat and why the White House guard had suddenly been tripled – had thrown a collective fit at the mere thought of the President leaving an area they didn't have under complete control. They got nervous every time the President left America, even to Britain or another state with reliable security; they had argued against the President going to an alien craft. "Some of them would obviously make great science-fiction movie writers."

Wachter smiled dryly. The analysts had wondered about the President being implanted with a mind-controlling implant and sent back to order immediate surrender, or being replaced by an alien doppelganger, or being probed, or having his mind read by telepathic aliens, or…they'd come up with hundreds of scenarios, each one more unlikely and outrageous than the last. The analyst who'd come up with the scenario about the President being anally probed probably needed therapy.

"The risk needs to be accepted," the President said, firmly. "Now… what might the aliens want?"

The analysts had gone through that as well. One line of thought was that the aliens were friendly and wanted to establish a covert line of communications before they revealed themselves to the entire world. Another was that the aliens were hostile and intended to demand immediate surrender before they started throwing asteroids. The only common ground between most of the different possibilities was that the aliens would demand their missing craft back – as the US had demanded the crashed F-117 back from the Serbs. No one was quite sure what the US should say in response.

"They might see returning the craft as a gesture of friendship and goodwill," the Secretary of State said, "but that would deprive us of our chance to study their technology any further."

"On the other hand, if they demand it back, we might have no choice but to comply," Wachter countered. "What happens if they threaten to vaporise a city every day until we return the craft?"

The Secretary of State nodded. The President had worked hard to reform the State Department, clearing away the debris of years of neglect and the result was a revitalised department serving the country. The State Department's analysts were capable, but those who had been briefed on the crashed ship knew that the human race had only limited means of taking the war to space. It was far more likely that the aliens would stomp on humanity as hard as possible.

"We'd have to give up the ship," he said, finally. "What other choice would we have?"

The President said nothing. There was something to be said for standing up to an opponent and daring him to do his worst, but not when the entire human race was at stake. It was often said that the President was the most powerful man on Earth, yet how powerful was he compared to the aliens? A race that could step between stars wouldn't be impressed by the pitiful human space force, such as it was.

"None," he said, finally. "General, you have my authorisation to bring in other planning teams and get them working on what kind of hardware we can deploy to even the odds as much as possible. We'll keep the lid on as much as possible, but it's probably time we started looking at emergency measures. This problem is not going to go away."

———

No one would have believed that Pepper Reid was a fully-trained bodyguard. She looked about eighteen years old, wearing a very short skirt and a tight shirt, with long red hair that she'd tied back in a ponytail. The men who tried to hit on her each night in bars would have been astonished – and intimidated – to know that she'd gone through some of the most fearsome training the United States could provide, before being transferred to the Secret Service and being assigned to the Presidential Protective Detail. It was one of the most important – if not *the* most important – bodyguard positions in the world – and she took it seriously. It helped that no one on the outside took *her* seriously.

A Secret Service agent was generally assumed to look rather like the Men in Black; black suits, black tie, black jacket, white shirt and dark sunglasses. It was true that some members of the President's protective detail were so obvious – to deter nervous assassins – but others were less than obvious. Pepper – whose friends and fellow agents called Pepper Pot – had arrested several would-be assassins over the last year, who hadn't realised that the cheerleader slipping closer to them was far deadlier than they could ever have hoped to be. It was in one of those encounters that she'd lost her eye.

She'd feared that would put an end to her career, but her superiors had recommended her to DARPA for a highly-classified experiment. Her right eye was replaced by an artificial eye that not only worked almost as well as the real one – although it did itch at times, which the doctors assured her was psychosomatic– but also recorded everything she saw for later down-load. It had its disadvantages – it was something she could never quite tell a succession of boyfriends – yet if she saw a threat, she could instantly trans-mit an image back to the office, before moving to intercept before it became lethal, or even noticeable. The Secret Service preferred to keep attempts on the President's life quiet. It was meant to discourage others from trying.

"Pepper, come in," her superior said. Pepper had been on one of her off-days – the Secret Service didn't keep anything as mundane as a week-end – and had been surprised to be called into the office. "I have a special task for you."

He leaned forward. For the first time, Pepper saw the dark circles under his eyes, signifying lack of sleep. She'd been trained to watch for hundreds of telltales on faces – from hints that a boy was cheating on her to a suicide bomber nerving himself to hit the trigger and detonate the bomb – and her superior looked worried. It wasn't a cringing fear, but something more fundamental, the look of a man who worried that he wouldn't be believed.

"It's also highly classified," he continued. "I can't tell you about it until you agree to take on the mission. I should warn you that…it will be danger-ous, perhaps more dangerous than anything else you've ever done for us.

If you decline, it won't be held against you and it won't even be on your record."

"You don't have to insult me," Pepper said. She wanted to joke, but there was something about his attitude that quelled her attempts at humour. She'd faced the prospect of putting her body between the President and a bullet before and had come to terms with it. It wasn't as if she'd been drafted into the Secret Service against her will. "It sounds interesting."

"You don't know the half of it," her superior said. "Will you take on the mission?"

"Yes," Pepper said, without hesitation. "What do you want me to do?"

"Sit down and listen carefully," her superior said. Pepper did as he said and listened with growing disbelief as her superior outlined alien contact – and a crashed alien ship – and a message inviting the President to meet with extraterrestrials. It was beyond belief, yet she watched her superior carefully and there was no doubt that *he* believed it. "The aliens have invited the President and one other onboard their craft. We need you to be that other."

Pepper felt her head spin. It crossed her mind that it could be a hoax or a test, but if that were the case, it was a bizarre one. She'd been tested many times since she'd qualified, yet all of those tests had revolved around mundane threats and possibilities. Aliens hadn't even been mentioned, apart from late-night movies with the other trainees. No one had seriously considered the possibility that the President would have to visit an alien ship, almost alone.

"One agent won't be enough to protect him," she said, finally. She would have preferred a full team, or even a Company of Marines. "Can't we...?"

"Apparently not," her superior said. "We also need you to record everything that happens on that ship."

"You just want me for my body," Pepper said. It was a weak joke, but she needed to let the tension flow out, somehow. "What about weapons and more...obvious equipment?"

"We've prepared a briefing for you," her superior said. He stood up and held out his hand. "Good luck, Pepper. Don't fuck up."

Chapter Nine

Schriever Air Force Base, USA
Day 11

The day was bright and clear, but Robin didn't notice, shut up in the base's main radar room. A handful of security-cleared personnel had joined her in the base, but the vast majority of the base's personnel had been warned to stay in their barracks, or redeployed on short notice to other bases. Robin didn't particularly care about the security problem – she had always seen such issues as getting in the way of her main job – but it had caused a staffing shortage. The base – and the two AWACS orbiting the base at a distance of ten kilometres – had only limited numbers of cleared personnel.

She smiled to herself as she checked the network she'd established to track the alien craft when it arrived. The addition of other specialists – including some working in exotic areas such as gravity-wave detection – had added a whole series of other sensors to the radar network, including infrared and gravimetric sensors. When Robin had checked with NSA – or, rather, the General had checked with them after they'd tried to stonewall a mere junior officer – they'd reluctantly confirmed that their orbiting satellites had briefly tracked strange heat patterns near where the alien craft had entered the atmosphere. One of Robin's superiors had pointed out that the craft should be red hot from entering the atmosphere – and trailing sonic booms all over the country as they moved at hypersonic velocities – and she was at a loss to account for their absence. The best that anyone had been able to establish was that the alien craft somehow moved without disturbing the air, or somehow baffled the sonic boom before it could spread. Civilians thought of a sonic boom as a once-off event, but they trailed behind any supersonic aircraft… apart from the UFOs. It didn't quite make sense.

Robin had been given access to all the data from the crashed ship – apart from a single piece of data; its current location – and she'd used it to enhance her tracking programs, linking in with the Deep Space Tracking System and the US Space Defence Operations Centre, which handled all ABM systems. The handful in the know at those centres had been horrified at the thought of alien craft – or any kind of craft – slipping through the detection network and had worked to enhance their own systems. In theory, they could have tracked an object the size of a golf ball orbiting the Earth – and had done so, on occasion, when debris had been released from the International Space Station – but in practice, the UFOs were clearly hard to detect. They emitted almost nothing in the way of radiation and seemed to move completely silently. The only signs of their existence were odd radar traces and heat bursts as they entered the atmosphere.

And one of them was coming to pick up the President.

It was an opportunity too good to be missed, Robin knew. The sheer vagueness of most of the radar data was frustrating, if not actively misleading. She thought that she had tracked UFOs moving at speeds in excess of Mach Nine, but she knew all too well that she could have mistaken a natural event for an alien craft, or seen two echoes instead of one. The chance to take readings when there was a genuine craft in the air was too good to pass up, even though her superiors had talked at some length about the possible implications. They had effectively asked the President to come alone – a single bodyguard wouldn't be much help if the aliens had bad intentions – and that, her superiors had said, didn't imply friendly motives.

Robin didn't care. She rarely gave any thought to politics, although she'd voted Republican because the Democratic Candidate had pledged to cut the military budget, which would have included scrapping new toys the USAF needed – now more than ever. If the President was willing to take the risk of stepping onboard an alien craft, she was sure that he had considered all of the possible dangers – and decided that the risk was worth it. She would have given anything – even her brand-new brevet promotion to Second Lieutenant – to go with him. The chance to ask the aliens about their drive and propulsion systems – and how they spoofed American radar systems – would have been worth any risk.

Her console chimed and she peered down at it. A single target had appeared out of nowhere in the midst of United States Space Surveillance Network's area of responsibility. She wasn't used to thinking in such terms, but the target had appeared high over the base, diving into the atmosphere. It seemed to shimmer in and out of existence as it flew lower, slowing somehow despite following a direct flight path, yet she saw the burst of heat as it entered the atmosphere. She keyed a command into her console as the unknown craft passed out of the Space Surveillance Network's ken, and down into the domain of her enhanced radar network. The base had to be alerted before she did anything else.

She dimly heard the klaxons warning of the arrival of the alien craft through her concentration. The craft didn't seem to be perfectly solid. It crossed her mind that it could be phasing in and out of reality, but she couldn't even begin to think of what kind of tech would be required to do that. Some radar stations reported a solid contact while others seemed unable to even begin tracking the craft. She combined the radar sensors with the gravimetric detectors and hit pay dirt. The craft could be tracked through its odd gravity-wave emissions. It was impossible to be sure, but it seemed likely that the alien drives used focused gravity as a means of propulsion, allowing them to reach impossible speeds. It might even account for the absence of a sonic boom…no, that didn't explain it. It had to be something more complicated.

"Robin?" Technical Sergeant Dave Heidecker asked. He hadn't been promoted, but he didn't hold it against her. He'd once told her that higher rank was boring. The number of USAF senior officers with grey hair ahead of their time was shocking, or so he had claimed. Robin didn't care either way. "What do you have?"

"Visitors," she said. The shock of seeing an alien craft swept over her, along with an insane urge to giggle. "We have visitors."

The craft should have slammed into the ground hard enough to create tremors on the Richter Scale. Instead, it was slowing down, coming to a hover high over the base, before it started to lower itself the rest of the way. Robin had no idea what kind of technology could do that, not even an advanced helicopter. The sheer power the aliens were showing off was overwhelming. Robin regarded it as a challenge, rather than something to intimidate her, yet even she was not unmoved. The aliens were making a show of strength.

"They're about to land," she said, turning her eyes to the live feed from the base's security cameras. Whatever happened, the entire event would be recorded and studied for years to come. "Landing…now."

———

Master Sergeant George Grosskopf hadn't been happy since he'd been first on the scene when the alien craft crashed. The day had become nightmarish, first in trying to cobble together a plan to get the alien craft somewhere well away from the base – the base commander had ended up combining plans to deal with a terrorist NBC strike with plans to pick up crashed Russian satellite debris – and then in spending a week in a quarantine unit at the nearby NBC centre. The doctors had poked and prodded at him and his men every day, trying to determine if they'd been infected by any alien viruses…and, just incidentally, keeping them firmly out of the public eye. The days had been unpleasant and the nights had been worse. All of his men, George included, had had nightmares about the crashed ship and its crew. The culture shock had nearly torn them apart.

George remembered spending time staring at the television and trying to come to terms with the way the world had changed. Returning to the base after the doctors had finally conceded that the security team were probably uninfected with anything apart from boredom had been a surreal experience. Those in the know had kept their mouths firmly shut. Those who were not privy to anything beyond rumours had carried on their normal lives with a blindness that stunned George, even though he knew that they didn't know what had happened. Who cared about the death of a well-known pop star when aliens had been discovered? Who cared about who was fucking who when the world might be on the brink of interstellar war? He'd hoped that he would be assigned to protect the crashed ship, wherever it had gone – the possibility that the aliens might attack the base to recover their craft had not gone unheeded – but instead the base commander had assigned him to overhauling the defences. A dozen new antiaircraft missile batteries had been assigned to the base; along with additional handheld weapons that might add some extra punch if the aliens came back. He'd prepared as best as he could, yet…

He unhooked his binoculars and peered into the air. The alien craft was supposed to be on final approach, yet he could see nothing, apart from the clear blue sky. The movies had had massive alien ships descending on military bases – he'd watched *Close Encounters of the Third Kind* when he'd been a kid – but there was no reason to believe that the aliens would send an entire mothership, or a City Destroyer. The thought made him scowl. They'd watched *Independence Day* two days after they'd been returned to duty and one of his men had put a foot through the television screen, raving about aliens and monsters. Rumour central had had a field day with that one.

His radio crackled. "It's coming down towards the crash site," the dispatcher said. "Do you have visual contact?"

George tilted his binoculars. The guards were stationed near the crash site, but not right on top of it. It gave his men chills to be too close to it, although no one had any idea why. Men in NBC suits had gone through the entire area with metal detectors and recovered everything they could, including several hundred bullets from a live-fire security drill the base had conducted years ago. They'd used flamethrowers to clear the remains of the crash site – and put an end to any possible biohazard – yet…no one wanted to go too near it. It made no sense to him.

"No, sir," he growled. He paused as something caught his eye. There was a shiny speck in the distance, falling rapidly towards them at a colossal speed. "Correction; I have one craft…"

The alien craft rapidly took on shape and form. It wasn't the silvery almond of the first craft, but something different, a silvery egg-shaped craft barely larger than a van. It seemed to glow with a pearly light, but there was no sound, apart from a very faint bass humming. George had expected a noisy aircraft – the noise of a helicopter squadron had to be heard to be believed – yet the alien craft was almost soundless. It seemed almost to suck up the sound waves and absorb them.

He keyed his radio, linking to two of his men, who carried cameras and other recording gear. "Make sure you get damn good shots," he ordered.

There were hundreds of cameras deployed, from the most modern NSA-designed digital cameras to old-style chemical cameras from the past, just in case the alien craft's emissions screwed with the more modern systems. "Check weapons; keep them on safety until I authorise otherwise."

The question of arming his men had been hotly debated. One of his superiors had wanted the men to go out entirely unarmed, without rifles, pistols or grenades. Another had wanted them to go out armed to the teeth, adding Stinger missiles and Abrams tanks to their arsenal. They'd compromised by issuing standard weapons – and keeping substantial forces in reserve on the base itself – and ordering all weapons to be kept safe unless the shit hit the fan. A rogue shot that killed an alien, or even damaged their craft, might start a war. Looking at the alien craft, hanging almost effortlessly in the air, George understood their point. A war with a race that could do that might well be lost very quickly.

"My God," he heard someone say, behind him. "It's beautiful."

As if it had wanted the humans to get a good look, the alien craft slowly lowered itself towards the ground, the pearly white glow slowly fading to a more sickly yellow. It threw the area into odd relief, casting odd shadows around the craft, before it faded, revealing a silvery hull. Three legs seemed to *grow* out of the underside of the craft, spreading out to form a tripod, before it lowered itself the rest of the way and came down exactly where the previous craft had crashed. If there had been any doubt about the aliens knowing what had happened to their missing craft, George reflected, that settled it. The aliens knew exactly what had happened to it.

A low hum seemed to echo in the air for a long moment as the craft opened a hatch, the flowing metal somehow parting to allow light to shine out onto the ground. George had half-expected to see a spindly grey figure standing there against the light, but nothing emerged from the craft. Instead, a ramp grew out of the side of the craft and reached down towards the ground. Its arrival completed, the craft just stopped – and waited.

George's mouth was dry and he had to swallow twice before he could talk. "Sir," he said, keying his radio, "I think it's waiting for SOLDIER BOY" – the code name for the President – "now."

"Understood," the reply came back. The dispatcher sounded even more nervous than George, even though he was safe in a bunker back at the base. "Hold position and wait."

George looked up at the alien craft. Now that it had landed, it seemed to extrude an air of glowing perfection, as if it was beyond anything humanity had even dreamed of creating. An F-22 was a piece of junk compared to the alien craft, the overworked and overused heavy transports little more than barges from ancient canals…there was something chillingly inhuman about its perfection. The aliens might have grown the craft rather than built it. It looked almost natural, and yet…the situation was so strange that it was almost beyond comprehension. The USAF had been wise, he decided, to charge George with greeting the alien craft. Someone who hadn't seen one of the craft before, and the alien bodies, would have become a gibbering wreck.

His radio buzzed. "The principles are on their way," it said. "Stand by."

———

Pepper had been horrified when she'd heard the truth about where she was going, even though she had to admit that she was definitely qualified for the task. Quite apart from her artificial eye, she had had considerable experience in operating in other cultures, even as a Secret Service Agent. She'd served the President in Japan, India and Saudi Arabia, wearing a mixture of native clothes for each event. The Saudi one had been particularly revealing. Who would have thought that you could conceal a huge arsenal under a *burka*?

But aliens? She had no illusions about her task. If the aliens wanted to hurt the President, or brainwash him, or something so alien that humans couldn't comprehend it, there would be nothing she could do about it. She'd finally elected to wear a standard black suit and carry a handful of weapons, some obvious and some not, but she knew better than to think that she could protect the President. Her mission might suddenly become one of killing a handful of aliens before she was killed herself, if they could be killed, or simply being killed before she even knew she was under attack. She'd seen images of the aliens from the crashed ship and the warriors – if they were warriors – looked nasty customers. She wouldn't want to face one of them in single combat.

"Come on," the President said. Unlike her, he seemed completely calm. It was easy to believe that he'd been a decorated soldier in his time. "Let's go, shall we?"

Pepper took the lead as they walked out of the armoured vehicle towards the UFO. It dominated the surrounding area, even though it was tiny, smaller than a tank or the other crashed ship. Its entrance gaped invitingly, leading them on, but she wanted to run and hide. She had faced her own fear hundreds of times before, yet this was something different, something unworldly. It would have been easy to believe that it was all a trap, that the aliens were hostile, that it was merely the first shot in a war…

And yet, what would it gain them? The President had transferred his powers to the Vice President before travelling to the meeting. There would be no delay in America's response to any alien attack, although Pepper had no illusions. A race that could build the craft ahead of her would smash its way through the USAF with ease.

She stepped onto the ramp and felt it move slightly beneath her feet. It was hard to walk up towards the hatch, but the thought of all those watching eyes propelled her forward. The alien craft…she was right in front of it! There was a faint haze of heat around the craft, but not enough to prevent her from stepping through the hatch. She held up a hand, eyes scanning for danger, but saw nothing. A moment later, the President followed her.

Behind them, the hatch melted closed.

Chapter Ten

The Alien Mothership

Day 11

The President had pushed the thought of the cameras out of his mind. He knew – from long experience – that thinking about the cameras was what led to pratfalls and worse on television. For some politicians, including several who had insulted the voters by accident, it had been the end of their careers. Instead, he was concentrating on the mind-numbing series of briefings he had had to hear before he boarded the alien craft, including hundreds of different possible outcomes. Some of them – actually, most of them – had been stolen from the unpaid imagination of countless science-fiction writers, but they all agreed on one point. The aliens wanted something. They had gone to considerable trouble to get the President to talk to them and no one would have put forward that kind of effort without some expectation of reward.

He'd seen briefing papers that suggested everything from a demand for immediate surrender to an attempt to rent the remainder of the solar system, or perhaps somewhere in the middle. There were too many possibilities and, despite the number of briefings he'd absorbed, he knew he would have to play it by ear. Oddly, he felt rather less nervous than he had the day before America invaded Iraq, although that might have had something to do with the sheer unreality of the scene. The aliens might have wanted the President so they could talk to the man making the decisions, the man who led his country, but they probably wouldn't kill him. That would be an act of war.

The interior of the alien craft was rather disappointing, perhaps more mundane than he had been expecting. It was a perfectly circular compartment, barely large enough for two people to sit in reasonable comfort, ringed by a sofa. The President sensed rather than saw the hatch closing behind him and sat down on one side of the sofa, motioning for Pepper to take the other side. There was no sign of a pilot and he doubted that there was room for one in the remaining unseen compartments of the craft, suggesting that it was operating on remote control. A faint shudder ran through the entire craft and then the hull started to go transparent, revealing that they were already far above the base and climbing steadily upwards. There was no sense of acceleration, nor was there any sense of how the craft was powered, but the President had never been in anything that moved so fast. Perhaps the Space Shuttle or one of the advanced fighter jets could match the alien craft's acceleration, yet there were only two shuttles left in existence, and both of them required months of preparation before they could fly. The aliens were doing it casually. The sheer level of power that implied was terrifying.

He leaned back against the clear hull and watched as the blue sky faded to darkness, all the stars shimmering into existence, staring down at the tiny alien craft. They weren't twinkling at him, which puzzled him at first until he realised that there was no longer any atmosphere to cause the appearance of twinkling. The stars burned coldly in the vacuum of space, leaving him to wonder which one had given birth to the aliens. The Deep Space Tracking Network would attempt to follow the ship carrying the President and his sole bodyguard, but the President had no illusions. Wherever the aliens were taking them, they would be beyond all hope of rescue. It was equally unlikely that they would be able to avenge their deaths.

Earth itself seemed to shine in the distance, a blue-green globe hanging in space. It was easy to see why so many astronauts became religious, or embraced environmental causes; from space, there was no sign of the wars and conflicts that plagued the human race. Nothing human could be seen on the surface of the planet – there were no lights, no aircraft, no hints that humanity existed down there – and the image had a purity that contrasted oddly with the reality. A thousand years ago, Earth wouldn't have signalled the existence of an intelligent life form to the stars, but now…had the aliens found them by homing in on Earth's radio transmissions?

"There are no satellites," Pepper said. She sounded more than a little dazed; truthfully, the President felt dazed as well. "Mr President…"

The President followed her gaze and saw the Moon as the alien craft swept past it. It had taken the Apollo astronauts three *days* to reach the moon, but the alien craft had done it in…he looked down at his watch, timing the entire journey, and realised that it had done it in barely three minutes. He looked back at Earth, now a tiny blue-green sphere in the distance, and felt cold. They were further away from the planet than any human had ever been before.

To boldly go where no one has gone before, part of his mind whispered, reminding him of a handful of *Star Trek* episodes he'd watched as a teenager. There had been a girl he'd known who'd been into the series and made him watch it with her before she would put out…that had been years ago and he couldn't even remember her name. Captain Kirk and his successors had had their starships, with technology they understood, but it bore no relationship to reality. The truth was that he was on an alien craft under alien control and no longer had any control over his own fate. His survival was completely dependent on the aliens.

A massive fist clenched in his chest and he found himself gasping. The sensation ended as quickly as it had begun, but the after-effects left him feeling weak and fragile. He looked up towards Pepper and realised that she was suffering as well, her normally bright face pale and wan. Her green eyes met his for a moment in shared understanding. Whatever the aliens had done to them, it had affected them both.

He looked past her and almost swore. Where Earth had been, there was nothing but cold stars glowing in space. The aliens, it seemed, possessed some kind of FTL drive, kicking them out far beyond Earth. He looked around, wondering if they were in another star system, but the naked eye revealed nothing, not even a hint of another planet. Instead, they were rushing towards a dark shape, which rapidly took on shape and form, a colossal cylinder floating in space. It was so large – he estimated that it was over a hundred miles long, even though he had nothing to use to deduce its exact size – that it was beyond his comprehension. It swelled until it dominated the sky, glittering with ominous lights, and it was *still* growing! It was almost a relief when the craft's hull darkened and cut off their view of the outside universe. The President knew, intellectually, that the aliens wouldn't want to crash them into their massive ship, but it had been hard to convince himself of that. The hindbrain had been screaming at him.

The gravity field seemed to twist, drawing his attention back to the deck. It hadn't even occurred to him to question the gravity field, yet they hadn't been floating in zero-gravity, or smashed to a pulp by the force of the heavy acceleration. It was evident that the aliens could generate and control gravity at will, which provided a possible explanation for how their craft operated. A race that could control gravity would have no difficulty getting out of the planet's gravity well and expanding across the universe.

There was a brief final tremor running through the craft, and then the hatch melted open, allowing a warm gust of air to flow into the ship. The President had been told, in the briefings, that there was no biohazard – but all that really meant was that there was no *known* danger. The alien atmosphere might be poisonous, or it might carry germs and bacteria, or the wrong levels of oxygen and nitrogen...he was breathing it! He braced himself for sudden suffocation, but instead there was only a vague taste of something spicy, right on the tip of his tongue. He gathered himself, shot Pepper a reassuring look, and stepped up to the hatch. The alien mothership waited for them.

Their craft had come to rest in the middle of a vast shuttlebay, or perhaps it was a flight deck, although the President mentally compared it to a hangar on an aircraft carrier. There were hundreds of other craft, parked in neat rows, in the hangar, following several different designs. One of them was clearly the same design as the craft that had crashed eleven days ago and he hoped that Pepper had the presence of mind to record it. The people studying the crashed ship would find the recordings interesting and perhaps useful. He looked straight down the ramp and almost stopped dead. Two aliens were standing at the bottom, waiting for them.

He'd seen the images of the two types of aliens who had died when their ship crashed – although there were several unanswered questions about *why* they had died – and had thought he was prepared to meet either of them. The aliens facing him now were a *third* type of alien, leaving him wondering how many different types of alien there were. How many different forms of intelligent life could evolve on a single planet?

The aliens stood tall, taller than him, although not by much. They were painfully thin, with very skinny bodies and long, inhuman fingers. Their heads were featureless, apart from two massive black eyes and a tiny mouth, almost as if it were no longer needed. They looked remarkably fragile – the President half-feared that if he shook their hands, he would pull their arms right out of their sockets – yet they both had a quiet air of competence, and authority. It reminded him of something, but it took him a minute to place it; the aliens were *born* to their authority. He reminded himself that he was dealing with aliens. His impressions might be completely wrong, yet they refused to fade from his mind.

He reached the bottom of the ramp and halted. The aliens seemed completely unmoving, as if they lacked nervous tics or involuntary movements. The President knew from his own military experience that remaining completely still was hard for anyone without proper training, yet the aliens seemed to remain still naturally. It was impossible to shake the air of…unreality that had settled over him, yet he *knew*, beyond a shadow of a doubt, that he was looking at aliens. They were no hoax, no man dressed in an alien suit, but real aliens. It was almost like looking at a snake poised to strike.

One of the aliens stepped forward quickly, almost jerkily. "Mr President," he said. The voice was very…human, warm and welcoming. It didn't suit the vaguely sinister body at all. "Thank you for accepting our invitation."

"Thank you for inviting me," the President said, gravely. The sense of being completely out of his depth was only growing stronger. Normally, before he met another world leader, there would be briefings on protocols and discussions between junior staff – who could be disowned if necessary – before the world leaders actually met. "It was a remarkable trip."

The second alien stepped forward. "We speak for those on this vessel," he said. The President decided to assume that they were both male until there was evidence that suggested otherwise. There were no breasts – or, for that matter, signs that either of them had a penis. "We wish to welcome you onboard."

"Thank you," the President said, again. His mind was racing. What role did the aliens play in their society? Were they elected leaders, dictators, representatives…or what? He had to remind himself – again – that aliens might not play by human rules and that the rules he knew might not apply to the aliens.

"We wish, also, to show you around our vessel to assist you in understanding our nature," the first alien said. The double act was confusing. Which one of them was the senior, or were they equals? What protocols did they use? In Japan, the senior man would often say nothing and allow the juniors to handle the negotiations. In the Middle East, nothing important would be done until the negotiators had chatted about trivia such as the weather and the health of their families. "We believe that you will find it interesting."

The President and Pepper exchanged glances, but there was really no choice. The aliens led them from compartment to compartment, showing hundreds of spacecraft webbed up within the bowels of the mothership, to strange machines that seemed to bear little resemblance to anything humanity had ever built. There were vast gardens that grew food for the aliens, massive chambers that housed hundreds of aliens and even what the President suspected was alien entertainment. The tour seemed focused on the military aspects of the ship – they looked in at another hangar deck containing hundreds of tiny craft – and he started to understand. In their own quiet way, the aliens were making a very clear threat.

He found himself beginning to lose track of how far they'd travelled, or even where they were within the ship. The sight of its exterior hull had suggested that it was massive, yet the interior was so confusing. They could not have found their way back to their craft if they'd fled the aliens, and even if they had, what then? They were completely at the mercy of the aliens. Will Smith had flown an alien ship out of the mothership and escaped, but he'd had the greatest ally of all – a patriotic scriptwriter.

"This is the Medical Bay," one of the aliens said. They were effectively identical, so similar that the President had lost track of which was which. They hadn't even shared their names. "The medical science on this vessel is far superior to that on your planet."

It was another frustratingly vague comment. The aliens spoke only in generalities, never specifics. The President had asked probing questions, only to hear them deflected with vague answers, or a promise that all would be explained in time.

"Using this equipment, we could prolong your life for many hundreds of years," the alien added. "We could wipe out the diseases that affect your kind. We could ensure that the standard of living on your planet is vastly improved."

The President asked a sharp question. "How long have you been watching us?"

"Long enough," one of the aliens said. It was – again – a very vague answer. The President wasn't blind to the underlying threat, either. Their advanced medical science could be used, just as easily, to create a biological weapon to wipe out all life on Earth. The President had read enough scenarios about what terrorists could do if they accomplished their aim of creating a real biological WMD and the aliens, with their technology, could spread it far further. "Your race is of interest to us."

The President leaned forward. "Why?"

"Because you are there," the alien said. They walked down another long corridor and into a massive room, housing hundreds of the warrior-aliens. They ignored the humans and their companions, running through something the President had no difficulty in recognising as a weapons drill. They had looked bad enough as dead bodies, but living…they looked formidable. They were far stronger than humans and seemed to move quicker.

One of the aliens seemed to slip closer to the President. "They are preparing for all eventualities," he said. "They expect everything and nothing."

"Everything and nothing?" The President asked. "Are you expecting a war?"

"We expect everything," the alien replied. They seemed to share a long glance. "Follow us."

The President glanced back at Pepper as she brought up the rear. Her eyes were wide and staring, glancing around from side to side as she tried to capture everything. The President felt a moment of sympathy for her; he could talk to the aliens, but *she* could do nothing, but record it all. He reached out and squeezed her hand gently, before winking at her. Whatever else happened, they'd have a record to show the folks back home, where it could be analysed carefully. Perhaps the aliens wouldn't be so intimidating after all.

They reached a small chamber, illuminated only by a soft green light. A single alien sat in the centre of the room, staring down at nothing. He looked up as they entered, dark eyes peering at the humans. The alien looked...old, somehow. The other two aliens gave off no sense of age, but this one seemed centuries old. The President remembered the comment about extending the human lifespan and wondered if the aliens had such tech for themselves. Why wouldn't they attempt to develop life-extending tech that worked for them?

"Welcome onboard our vessel," the alien said. His voice was whispery, feather-light. One thin, utterly inhuman hand waved the President and Pepper to a chair. "I am Ethos. I speak for those onboard this ship. We wish to have converse with you, Mr President."

The sense of age only grew stronger as the President took the seat. The other two aliens had smooth skin, but Ethos – the President suspected that it was an assumed name, chosen deliberately for the impression it would make on the humans – was wrinkled. The massive dark eyes looked dimmer. They were, the President realised, completely lidless. The aliens slept – if they slept at all – with their eyes open.

"We must talk openly, you and I," Ethos whispered. "We must discuss facts bluntly. We must share without fear. We must talk freely. No offence must be taken. We will be open with you. We ask that you do the same."

"I understand," the President said. He risked a direct question. "What do you want?"

The answer was immediate. "We want your planet."

Chapter Eleven

The Alien Mothership
Day 11

The words seemed to hang in the air.

The President held himself together by sheer force of will. He'd been in diplomatic meetings where phases like 'give us what we want or we'll beat the hell out of you' were replaced by soothing phases that still meant the same thing, yet the alien had defied human convention. Diplomacy existed so that the nations involved could save some face and avoid being pushed into a corner where they either had to submit completely or fight – and, the President considered, avoid having to do their duty to their people – and there were strong reasons for it. Were the aliens so strong, he wondered, that they could issue a simple demand and enforce compliance? They had to be entirely confident that they could crush any resistance and take Earth. Nothing else could explain their approach, the subtle intimidation and, finally, the clear statement of intent.

He'd been briefed on the possibility, yet somehow he hadn't quite believed it, even though the aliens had clearly been scouting out the human defences. Why would an advanced alien race want to conquer Earth? They had access to the boundless resources of interstellar space and technology to make planets like Mars and Venus habitable. They could have traded with Earth for whatever they needed – every nation on Earth would want access to their technology – but instead...it dawned on the President that the aliens might not trust the human race and want it kept firmly under control. The Solar System might not be big enough for both races after all.

"Why?" He asked, finally. It wasn't diplomatic, but the alien had made it clear that they would be moving beyond diplomacy. "Why do you want our planet?"

Ethos seemed to lean back slightly. Unlike the other aliens, he moved with slow deliberate movements, rather than quick jerky motions. "We departed from our homeworld unaware that there was an intelligent race living on your world," he said. His soft whispering voice couldn't hide the impact of his words. "We loaded a microcosm of our society onboard this vessel, believing that we would arrive at a world we could inhabit and spread our race across the stars. The discovery of your race was an unpleasant surprise."

The President wasn't sure if he believed him. The human race had been transmitting radio signals towards the stars for over a hundred years, which meant that anyone within a hundred light years of Earth would know that they were there...or would it? Some of the briefings had suggested that the radio waves would fade out against the background noise, or perhaps wouldn't be recognised as the product of intelligent life. The President, who tried to avoid reality television and soap operas, tended to agree that most races wouldn't consider them the product of intelligent minds. Even so, the aliens might well be lying, or...what?

"We studied your race carefully, using scout ships to move between this ship and your world at speeds beyond your comprehension," Ethos continued. "We observed your people at war and peace, absorbed your popular culture and studied your art, science and literature to understand what made your race tick. You are very different from us and yet there are odd similarities. You have sparks of greatness and yet they are pulled down by the mundane nature of your culture. Your...most advanced societies seem driven more by the need to maintain the status quo than to reach for further greatness; your less advanced societies are feeding on themselves, tearing themselves apart rather than claiming the heritage of any intelligent race."

The President said nothing. "Your race is in serious trouble," the alien continued. "You are caught in a sociological trap that you cannot easily escape. The resources on your world are running out, or used as tools to further distort your society, while you lack the technology or the mass mindset to reach for the infinite resources of outer space. You have the technical ability to settle the Moon and mine asteroids for resources, yet you have chosen to turn your backs on space – and the danger that might come out of it. If an asteroid were to impact your planet, you would be unable to stop or deflect it before it struck, exterminating most of your population in a single blast. Your race knows nothing of it, yet you are standing at the edge of extinction.

"It grows worse. You allow deadly memes to propagate throughout your society, killing any hope for a better future. Your world is infested with people who hate for the sake of hating, religions that preach hatred for all other religions, people who fear and hate the technology that might get you out of the trap and seek a return to a simpler life that only existed in their imaginations. The rich are concerned with hoarding what they have, and preserving it from legal thieves rather than using it to create more wealth, while the poor are determined to strip the rich of their wealth. Your political systems are becoming increasingly snarled up, rendering you even less able to tackle these problems, while the fear and hate and violence grows ever stronger. Your race is on the verge of destroying itself."

The President took a breath. "I will not deny that we have problems," he said, remembering the fights he'd had with Congress over the reform program and the endless frustrations of trying to change a nation that didn't seem to want to be changed. "I will not deny that there are…significant inequalities on our planet."

"And yet your ability to tackle them is limited," Ethos said. There was no tone of condemnation in his voice, but that almost made it worse. "Your race is tearing itself apart while endless wealth and safety awaits, if only you made the investment that would open the vistas of space to you. Instead, you decay, leaving us with a problem. We need your world to survive."

The President lifted an eyebrow. "This ship was not designed for permanent occupancy," Ethos explained. "The awakening proceeds on schedule, which means that we will eventually exhaust the resources on this ship. We need to transfer as much of our population to Earth as we can before the ship finally collapses on us and sentences us to death. Your culture seems to spend most of its time denying reality. Ours – based in the cold hard realities of deep space – does not allow us that luxury. There is very little time."

"I see," the President said. "And you want to settle on Earth?"

"Yes," Ethos said. "There is no other choice. This ship is incapable of reaching another star system before it collapses. The other worlds in your system would require a massive terraforming process before they could be made habitable, which wouldn't be completed before we run out of time. We require access to your world."

The President gathered himself. "You bring advanced technology from another world," he said. "We could trade technology for land quite easily. How many of you are there?"

Ethos ignored the question. "You misunderstand," he said. "Your race is historically unkind to immigrants, even those who bring gifts and skills you desperately need. You have enough problems dealing with immigrants from your own race and develop racist feelings when they have different skin colours, or cultures, from your own. If such tiny differences make such an impression, what will happen when your people are confronted by a race of immigrants who cannot interbreed, or do not share even the same basic requirements for life, or are so…alien as to be beyond understanding? I could not leave my people to the mercy of yours."

The alien had a point, the President knew. Anti-immigration behaviour had been sweeping the American south for years – but that was different, surely – and Europe had been having its own problems, with yearly riots in major cities. It was yet another problem he had sought to reform, yet the levels of entrenched resistance to any change had shocked even him. Even the expansion of Mexican drug cabals and violence to America's border hadn't forced rapid change.

And yet…he remembered one of the briefings, comparing the alien visitors to the Europeans who'd visited America, centuries ago. They had been more advanced than the natives and had rapidly taken their land, forcing the Native Americans further and further back until they were confined to a handful of reservations. There were plenty who beat their breasts over what their distant ancestors had done, but it made no difference to reality. The Indian culture, such as it was now, existed only on sufferance. Was that what the aliens had in mind for Earth?

"If we are to integrate into your planet, it must be on our terms," Ethos said flatly. "We could not risk losing control over our destiny for the sake of your people's fear and stupidity. We could overwhelm your defences with ease, yet some of us believe that it would be better to make your people an offer first."

The alien leaned forward. "We are coming to your world," he said. "There is no way you can prevent us landing. We will settle your world and integrate your people with ours. We care nothing for your borders or the political structures you have created. We do not wish, however, to crush your people if it can be avoided. We intend, therefore, to make you – the President of the most powerful nation on Earth – an offer."

"An offer we cannot refuse?"

"True," Ethos agreed. The dark eyes seemed to glimmer in the dim light. "We propose an alliance. Your assistance in…subduing the other nations on Earth would be invaluable. You have the bases and equipment to be of great service to us. In exchange, we will respect your independence and offer you technology that will assist your people in climbing out of the cultural and political trap you have created for yourself. We will even respect your Monroe Doctrine and establish no settlements on the American continent, leaving it all for you."

The President stared at him. He had never been under so much pressure before, even as a young officer. He understood, now, why the aliens had wanted to talk to the President, the only man who could agree to such an alliance, yet it was abhorrent. American soldiers, sailors and airmen were not mercenaries who could be spent at will, or sent into battle on behalf of some foreign power, even one from beyond the stars. He could not have sold such an alliance to Congress, or the Senate, or – most importantly of all – the people. It was a betrayal of everything America stood for.

And then there were the allies. American credibility had been damaged almost beyond repair by a succession of Presidents who had ignored the concerns of their allies, or had been heedless of the message they were sending, the suggestion that American guarantees were valueless. President Chalk had sworn that it would be different and had spent considerable effort on mending fences, all of which would be swept away if he abandoned the allies to alien domination. There would be a political firestorm if details of any such deal leaked out to the public…

And then there was the most important question of all. Could the aliens be trusted?

There was no way to know. The aliens might mean every word and it would still be unacceptable, or they might intend to stab America in the back after they had subdued the rest of the world. Their technology was formidable enough that it would take years to duplicate it, yet the aliens might not be willing to allow them years, or perhaps even actively prevent them from developing the new technology. How many aliens were there in all? What did they *really* want?

"It will have to be considered carefully," he said. There were some foreign leaders – dictators, mainly – who saw the American President as being unencumbered by restraints on his power. They would expect him to sign at once without consulting his Cabinet or Congress. Ethos didn't seem to want immediate agreement. "How many of you are there onboard this vessel?"

"We have a population of one billion," Ethos said. The President stared at him. He hadn't realised that the mothership was that large. No *wonder* they wanted to offload some people as soon as possible. "We understand that you will have to consult with your government before accepting our offer."

The alien reached down to a table – the alien arm flexed in an utterly inhuman manner – and picked up a small black object. "This is a communicator capable of reaching our position," Ethos said. "You may use it to make contact with us after you have made your decision. It is powered by a tiny power cell and will continue to operate for some years."

He passed it over to the President, who examined it carefully. It was about the size of a cigarette box, with a single pair of buttons set within the plastic – he thought it was plastic – casing. One of them was marked, in English, PUSH TO TALK. The other was unmarked. He passed it to Pepper, who put it in one of her pockets, and looked back at the alien.

"We have also prepared this gift for you," Ethos said. He picked a second object off the table and passed it to the President. It was a featureless black box, apart from a USB slot at one end. "It should be compatible with your systems. It contains medical data and certain computer models that we have provided as a gesture of good faith. You will be able to use it to develop cures and vaccines for all of the diseases infesting your planet, wiping them out completely, and develop new medical techniques that will improve the quality of life for your entire race. The computer models analyse your global society in detail and provide warnings of the threats you are currently facing. You will come to understand that the only hope your race has is working with us to avert a shared disaster."

Ethos stood up and the President did likewise. "The Talkers will accompany you back to your craft," he concluded. "Thank you for coming."

———

The journey back to Earth passed in silence. The President barely had eyes for the view, even though it was even more spectacular on the return trip. He was concentrating on studying the two devices the aliens had given them and mulling over what they'd been told. Now that he was away from the alien, and the faint sense of unreality pervading the entire proceedings, he found himself beginning to get angry. Did the aliens really expect him to hand over the rest of the world on a silver platter?

Earth swelled up in front of them and he braced himself as the craft rocketed down towards North America. Now that he was prepared for the view, he found it astonishing – and terrifying. The continent seemed tiny from space, yet it grew larger until – finally – the hull turned grey again. It was something of a relief. He caught his breath as a faint tremble ran through the craft, followed by a dull thump. A moment later, the hatch hissed open and air – blessed Earthly air – came in to the craft.

It was still light outside – the entire trip had taken barely three hours – and somehow seeing the light galvanised him. He allowed Pepper to precede him out the hatch and down onto the ground, becoming aware, for the first time, of a strange gravity field. The aliens seemed to like a heavier gravity than Earth, which suggested that the smaller aliens might be stronger than they looked. There was no way to know.

The decontamination procedure had been worked out before they'd departed and they stepped into the two vans that had been driven near the craft. The President looked behind him and realised that the craft had vanished. It had taken off without them even being aware of its departure. He stepped into the van – Pepper would go into the other van – and placed the two alien devices in a sealed box. They'd be taken somewhere to be studied before they were used for their intended purpose.

"Welcome back, Mr President," the doctor said. He was one of the foremost experts in biological warfare, even though he had admitted that aliens were somewhat out of his sphere. "If you'll kindly strip for me…"

The procedure was long and uncomfortable. The suit he'd worn for the trip would be incinerated completely, just in case of contamination, or to destroy any surveillance devices that the aliens had managed to attach to his clothes. The CIA had developed bugs so tiny that they couldn't be seen with the naked eye and the aliens, probably, had more advanced technology. They could have slipped a device into his body, or his clothing, without him ever being aware of what they had done. The more paranoid fears – that he would have been returned under mind control, or perhaps replaced by an alien – also had to be checked, although personally he doubted that the aliens were *that* advanced. If they could do that, why would they bother negotiating at all? The more he thought about it, the more he suspected that the aliens weren't as strong as they claimed. There was no point in talking if they could overwhelm Earth with ease.

"You're clean, Mr President," the Doctor said, finally. "No bugs, no germs and you are unquestionably human, not a lizard in drag."

"Good," the President said, ignoring the weak joke. He needed sleep and a chance to think. He wasn't going to get either. They needed to get back to Washington as quickly as possible. "Contact my Cabinet and tell them that I'll see them in Washington tomorrow. We have some decisions to make."

Chapter Twelve

Area 52, Nevada, USA
Day 12

Alex Midgard grinned to himself as he put down the book and made another series of notes in his computer file. The project of mining every science-fiction novel that even remotely touched on the subject of alien invasion was one of the most interesting tasks he'd had to do – and he even got paid for enjoying himself! He hadn't realised how many alien invasion novels and films there were out there and digging through them all was a long process, yet it was fascinating. The authors all had a remarkable imagination. HG Wells had created the first real alien invasion book – although the Martians had actually been a metaphor for British colonialism and the effects it had on the locals – but hundreds of others had followed in his footsteps. Some were hard science-fiction, some involved made-up science…and some were just plain weird.

The alien invasion movies had been different. American alien invasion movies tended to be ruthlessly heroic, with a clear threat, a clear enemy and a united response. British science-fiction tended to be more covert, with an enemy that was only seen in flickering shadows and hints of their existence, although there were many examples of other threats. *Independence Day* and *Mars Attacks* might have settled into the public mind, yet Alex privately doubted that they could serve as a guide to any real alien invasion. He'd watched the video from the alien mothership carefully – leaving others to do the real analysis – and retreated to his room. The aliens had given the President a very careful set of messages, but what did they all mean?

He stood up, saved his work on the secure computer before shutting it down and heading out of his room. The base had become a great deal livelier now that other researchers had been brought in to work on the alien craft and bodies, although Alex suspected that there wouldn't be many more results in a hurry. A handful had been summoned to another complex near Washington to examine the data and artefacts the President had brought back from the mothership, perhaps cursing the orders that took them away from the find of the century. There wasn't a scientist in the world who would refuse the chance to study the crashed UFO.

The community room had been expanded with all the additional people; it now had a second television, a stack of DVDs and hundreds of books, as well as a buffet table and several coffeepots. Alex, who was used to the USAF's attitude that people would eat what they were damn well given, found the attitude of some of the civilian scientists rather amusing. They wanted their comforts as they worked on the craft and, by and large, they'd got them. The base might not have been designed to serve as a home for the President in the event of nuclear war – and thereby lacked basic luxuries – yet Fields had brought in more personnel and upgraded the facilities. It was creating a security nightmare – if the aliens were tracking human aircraft, they might deduce the location of the crashed ship – but keeping the scientists happy was important. They were the only hope of unlocking the alien secrets before one billion aliens arrived on Earth.

He poured himself a mug of coffee and then realised that he was not alone. Jane Hatchery was sitting in a comfortable armchair, rocking backwards and forwards as she clasped a mug of coffee to her chest as if it were a comforter. Her face was very pale and her eyes were tired, as if she hadn't slept for a week. She might have been having nightmares – many people on the base were reacting badly to the presence of the alien craft, although there was no evidence that the craft was causing it – or perhaps it was something more serious. Alex picked up his own mug and stepped over to her.

"Jane," he said, softly. "Are you alright?"

Jane looked up at him blearily. He had seen her before, but he hadn't realised how attractive she was outside of her working clothes. Her long dark hair, which hadn't been touched by a brush for hours, framed a vaguely oriental face and dark eyes.

"Do I look alright?" She demanded. Her voice was weak, but growing stronger. "I think I'm in shock."

Alex blinked. "I could take you to the medical bay," he offered. The base's doctor had been handing out more antidepressants, sedatives and suchlike in the last few days than he would normally distribute in a year. It was a matter of some concern to Colonel Fields and his staff. The base had never held a vast supply of anything beyond the bare essentials. "Or I could escort you back to your room."

"Not without dinner and flowers," Jane said. She smiled, weakly, as she pulled herself up. "I just keep having nightmares about the aliens."

"We're all having them," Alex reminded her. The base didn't have a practicing psychologist – an oversight no one had bothered to correct – but the doctor had deduced that most people were suffering from stress and culture shock. He'd given Alex a list of examples from more mundane cultures on Earth, yet he had had to admit that they had all been human. The aliens were from somewhere else entirely. "I could buy you dinner and flowers, if you would like…?"

"Get stuffed," Jane said, with a wink. "Where could you take me on this base anyway?"

Alex had to agree. The dining hall was massive and served the same food to everyone, regardless of rank or position. It was an equality he rather felt Marx would have found amusing. There were few places they could go to be alone, or just enjoy themselves, not with the alien craft looming in the background. The vast majority of people on the base hadn't seen it after their first visit, yet they all knew that it was there.

"I just keep thinking about what this all means," Jane said, when Alex said nothing. He had heard that the best way to get someone to talk was not to fill the air with nonsense, or useless blether. "What does it mean for us that aliens exist?"

Alex considered it, as if he'd given no thought to it at all. "We're not alone any longer?"

"Exactly," Jane said. "We can no longer pretend that we're alone in the universe. What will that do to our society? What will happen when Joe and Jane" – she smiled wryly - "Public learn about the crashed ship?"

"People have been watching movies and television series about aliens for years," Alex said, thoughtfully. "There might not be so much panic or fear."

Jane waved a hand towards the television. "We were watching *Independence Day* last night," she reminded him. "The vast majority of movies concerning aliens have the aliens as implacable enemies, enemies that we have to kill before they kill us. I think that we'll be lucky if we only have mass hysteria or complete panic. Tell the average person that aliens live around a distant star and they might just shrug and decide that it's none of their business, not when they have a mortgage to pay off and three screaming brats to put through school, and it might not make much of an impact. Tell them that the aliens are touching Earth, even with a single ship, and there will be complete panic. Tell them that a billion aliens are coming to Earth and the entire world will go mad."

"I know," Alex said. The alien statements the President had recorded were chilling. He couldn't blame the aliens for wanting to control how they landed on Earth and integrated into human society, but there was something chilling about it, even without considering the military aspects. The other nations of Earth wouldn't accept alien domination tamely. The Russians and Chinese still maintained vast nuclear stockpiles and a limited ASAT capability. The war could get very bloody. "But…"

"I was thinking about the Native Americans, the Indians," Jane continued, as if he hadn't spoken. "They were utterly unprepared for the Europeans when they arrived and the results were…unpleasant."

"Without that, you wouldn't be here," Alex said. "It didn't have such a bad result."

"I wonder if that's the justification that the aliens will use," Jane said. "All the suffering, all the *human* suffering, will have a good result in the end as two cultures get fused together, the best of both passed on to later generations."

"If you believe them," Alex said, flatly. He wasn't sure how much of the alien statements he believed. The aliens might believe everything they'd said, as vague and uninformative as most of it had been, but that didn't guarantee understanding. Americans had problems understanding the Japanese or the Arabs and *they* were human, with a shared biology. The aliens might look at humanity and misinterpret everything they saw. "Their studies of Earth might have been imperfect…"

Jane looked up at him. "They didn't get everything wrong," she said, coldly. He heard an undertone of fear in her voice. "They copied me in on the medical data the aliens gave the President and I went through it with my team. It was…accurate. It was surprisingly accurate. Maybe not absolutely perfect – few medical research papers are completely perfect – but very good. I could put it through the harshest peer review process in the world and it would pass."

"Bully for them," Alex said. "I don't understand the point."

"If you asked me, now, to come up with a cure for the five aliens we have in the quarantine centre, ignoring the fact that they are dead," Jane asked, "do you think I could do it?"

"…No," Alex said.

"Exactly," Jane said. "We understand next to nothing about their biology or how it all really works. Without dissecting the bodies, or obtaining live specimens to study, I don't think that we are going to get much further in a hurry. We're still studying their body chemistry and trying to figure out where there is such a high degree of dimorphism between the three observed types of alien. I'm pretty sure they all come from the same origin world – they share too much in common for it to be anything else – but why they're so different…"

She shrugged. "Give me a few years, a research team and no worries about their treatment of the dead to worry about, and perhaps – *perhaps* – I would be able to come up with something they could use," she continued. "I wouldn't be confident of success, but I should learn something, if only by trial and error. They, on the other hand, provided us with cures we could put into production and start distributing right now. The implications are disturbing."

"Every year, thousands of people go missing," Alex said, slowly. He'd studied alien abductions, or the reports of alien abductions, and knew that some researchers wondered if the aliens sometimes took people permanently, without returning them to Earth. There were thousands of unsolved missing people cases, from all walks to life. Runaways, kidnap victims…had some of them been taken to space and dissected? "Are you suggesting that the aliens abducted humans after all?"

"They couldn't have done it in another way," Jane said. "There's no way that they could have produced such data without a very sophisticated understanding of the human body. I doubt that they managed to obtain such information from the Internet or the crap we broadcast into space every day. I think that they almost certainly took a few people from Earth and studied them carefully. It would make sense for other reasons as well. They'd be worried about a biohazard, just like we were. Taking a few humans would allow them to ensure that no threat existed."

"Important, if they mean to settle Earth," Alex said. "Wasn't there a movie about a planet that killed nine out of ten people who settled on it?"

"There are probably a dozen of them," Jane said, dryly. "There is another implication from all of this, one I didn't include in my report." She held his eyes as she spoke. "I used to work in a biological warfare lab. We didn't call it that, of course, we talked in terms of finding a defence against a biological attack. The problem with biological weapons is that an attack and a defence are often the same thing. In order to produce a defence, we have to produce the weapon and figure out how and why it does what it does – and what can be used to counter it. It's not as easy as the media makes it look, Alex. A virus that is so deadly that anyone who catches it drops dead in twenty minutes isn't going to spread very far."

She ran her hands through her long hair. "The idea behind creating a biological weapon is to combine deadliness with delay, a weapon that will be contagious days – weeks – before it actually kills the host. The real nightmare is something that doesn't show itself for a year, yet is contagious – start it anywhere and it will spread around the entire world before it strikes, killing the entire global population. Anyone who could produce such cures could probably produce a bioweapon capable of doing just that."

"Jesus Christ," Alex said. "Are you saying that the aliens might…?"

"I doubt He wants anything to do with this," Jane said. "The aliens could certainly produce such a weapon. One could be being distributed now."

"Oh, fuck me," Alex said. "Is there anything we could do if we knew that there was such a weapon being deployed?"

"I don't think so," Jane said. She gave him a humourless smile. "We might have to blow up the world and call it a draw."

Alex stared down at her. "They could just hold it over our head forever," he said, finally. "That's a very cheerful thought."

"It is, isn't it?" Jane said. "Shall we change the subject?"

"When I get out of here, I'm going to take you to the finest restaurant in Washington," Alex promised. "You'll love it."

"It's a date," Jane grinned. "Remember – dinner and flowers. And you'll probably have to get me drunk first."

Alex laughed.

———

An hour later, he found his way back to the hangar that stored the crashed UFO. Like the entire team, he had clearance to visit everywhere on the base - apart from the ground floor and mysterious bottom level - and he tried to visit the UFO every day. Just looking at it reminded him that the world had changed forever, even though the vast majority of the world's population knew nothing about it. Their ignorance, Alex suspected, would come back to bite them on the behind. They wouldn't be taking any precautions against alien invasion, but then, the United States Government wasn't taking enough precautions either. The vast majority of the military personnel involved thought that it was all a drill.

"Hey, Alex," Neil Frandsen called. The advanced propulsion specialist waved at him from his position under the alien craft. Seven researchers were poking and prodding the hull with an entire arsenal of devices that had brought in from research labs all across the country. Alex knew that several devices had been requested from Japan and Europe, but Jones and Colonel Fields were still worried about the secret getting out. "Come and see what we've found!"

Alex followed him into the craft and stopped dead. The hull had been blank grey metal before, but now it was covered in strange alien writing that seemed to be somehow translucent, as if it wasn't quite there. He reached out and touched the hull softly and felt something almost rubbery. The *skittering* sensation from the outer hull was absent.

"Strange," he said. "Can we have a word?"

Frandsen allowed Alex to lead him into one of the small offices attached to the hangar. "Sure," he said. "What's up?"

"A question," Alex said, seriously. He rather envied Frandsen. He had useful work to do, while Alex…could only study alien invasion books and compose reports trying to predict what the aliens could do to the human race. "Have you found anything that could be used as a weapon on the alien craft?"

"Not yet," Frandsen admitted. "We have been looking for a weapon or a weapons system, but we haven't identified one. Given that we are dealing with alien technology we might not recognise a weapon if we looked right at it, at least until we manage to trigger it by accident. They might have everything from lasers to charged energy beams, but…"

"I'll tell you one thing," he added. "That hull of theirs is capable of absorbing energy, so my guess is that they will have some kind of energy weapons in their arsenal. The defence doesn't make sense unless they figure on facing an enemy armed with such weapons. I think that a missile would break it, yet we don't know if they have force fields or other technology straight out of science-fiction. We're still studying the drive, but we're nowhere near figuring out how it does what it does."

"Thank you," Alex said. "Can you tell me…?"

"The data from the President's trip was very helpful," Frandsen continued, interrupting him. "We don't have the slightest idea *how* they do it, but it looks as if they have some kind of gravity drive. The good news is that now we know that, we should be able to track them because of gravity distortions near their craft. It might also explain how they avoid creating sonic booms and other issues."

"I see," Alex said. Frandsen could get too enthusiastic if given half a chance. The level of technobabble was beyond his understanding. "You'd better work on finding out how to track the bastards. I have a nasty feeling we're going to need it soon."

Chapter Thirteen

Washington DC, USA
Day 12

"Thank you, Bob," Abigail Walker said. "I'll see what I can do."

She put the phone down with a puzzled frown. Something was clearly up in official Washington, yet no one seemed to know what it was, or – if they did know – were willing to talk to her. That was unprecedented in her seven years as a reporter, digging up scoops that were the envy of many other reporters; someone was *always* willing to talk. A Congressman or Senator could normally be relied upon to give out information – and, if not them, there were the hundreds of people who worked under them. It was very hard to keep something a secret in a modern society unless the number of people who knew it was very small…and this, whatever it was, seemed to encompass thousands of people.

The notepad lay open in front of her, mocking her. The handful of lines she'd written didn't add up to anything, apart from a mystery. Thousands of reservists had been called up for an exercise – their employers were making a terrible fuss to their congressmen and getting nowhere – and the exercise itself, planned for several months, had been brought forward at short notice. Abigail knew little about the military, but she did know that exercises were normally planned months in advance, just to ensure minimal disruption. Bringing it forward had probably cost the government a great deal of good-will. The other aspects of the mystery seemed even stranger. Last night, according to several reports, the President had transferred his powers to the Vice President and dropped out of sight. Officially, he had gone for a medical check-up, but the staff at the hospital claimed that he had never arrived there, or been seen by any of the doctors. It was possible that he had gone to a secret location – the Secret Service hated the President being anywhere publicly known – yet even that made little sense. Why would the President vanish for a few hours in the middle of an exercise?

And then there were the military bases. Security around America's military bases was tighter than it had been in years – President Chalk was a firm believer in security – but their security had suddenly been enhanced, without explanation. There were thousands of reports of a possible terrorist attack floating around the net, yet nothing had materialised, as far as Abigail knew. The guard patrols had been enhanced, the security perimeters had been expanded and aircraft were flying patrols over all the major cities…for what? There had to be thousands – tens of thousands, hundreds of thousands – of people involved, yet no one had breathed a word of what was going on. That, in itself, was odd. Matched up with the rest of the data…

Abigail looked through the glass transparency into the World News Network office and frowned again. She would have preferred to work for Fox or CNN, but her *asshole* of an ex-husband – she'd known that it was a mistake the day after they married, even though they'd stuck it out for several years before divorcing – had taken the chance to badmouth her to his employers at CNN, making it harder for her to find employment. She was a researcher, not some piece of candy to be stuck in front of a camera to read the news while taking deep breaths, and employment had been hard to find. The World News Network had hired her without hesitation – it had taken her a year to discover that the executive who'd hired her detested her ex and discounted everything he had ever said – and given her a new purpose. She liked to think of herself as having repaid their trust, but she knew that reporting was a harsh business. The day she stopped bringing in the goods was the day she would be out on the streets.

She caught sight of her reflection in the glass and pulled a face. At twenty-nine years old, she was pretty rather than beautiful, with long brown hair falling over a short body. Her husband had been heard to remark that she was too short to be a good reporter and she should leave the business to him, but she'd ignored him. The World News Network might not have the vast penetration that CNN or Fox enjoyed, yet it was building a reputation, fighting back subtly against the big boys by improving the quality of its reporting and carving out a niche for itself. They were growing more prominent, but the two big boys still enjoyed considerable influence and they wouldn't hesitate to squash the interloper if they could. She needed to crack the scoop before one of their reporters – who were probably putting out for some congressman's aide – broadcast it to the world.

Some reporters preferred to use computer records, but Abigail preferred to keep her private stash of contacts in a little black notebook she carried with her at all times. Over the years, she had built up an extensive network of people who would talk to her, on and off the record, a network she had kept to herself. Knowledge was power in the world of reporting. Every reporter with a gram of sense made their own contacts, whatever it took – Abigail had lost track of the number of times she'd taken her contacts out to dinner, or spent hours drinking with them in bars – and kept it private, even though it was a common joke that a source, once bought by one reporter, would often sell themselves to others as well. It was a little like prostitution, but dirtier. She had never slept with a contact, but she knew reporters who had, just to get a scoop. The bitches didn't care about their professional ethics as long as they beat their competitors.

She'd encoded the names and numbers, although she had few illusions about what would happen if a code-breaking team from NSA – or even from one of her competitors – went through it. It was quite possible, if one played around with a number long enough, to discover that they'd found the number of a famous or connected person, yet an investigative team would probably not see it as a coincidence. She'd transposed the digits according to a scheme she kept in her head, using a common set of numbers she could easily recall, but the best defence was never losing track of the book. She kept it with her at all times.

Her fingers danced over the phone's keypad, dialling the number of a prominent Senator. Senators, in her experience, would do almost anything to get into the media – and sometimes they came to regret it – and Senator Hamlin had been very helpful when she'd broken the story about two Senators and a Congressman who'd travelled to Thailand to sample the food and the sex industry. They'd lost their seats and had been jailed for years, a disgusted public turning against them in droves. She rather liked

Hamlin. He might have been a Democrat, but he had few links with the power brokers in the party and tended to vote his conscience.

"Hello, Senator," she said, when he picked up the phone. Every politician had a public line and a handful of private lines. The public had to talk to his staff before they could speak to the Senator, if they got to speak to him at all. Abigail had always had mixed feelings about that. The idealist in her wanted the Senator to talk to each and every member of the public who wanted to talk to him; the practical side of her nature knew that if the Senator talked to every one of them, he wouldn't have time to do his job. "I'm sure that you recognise my voice."

"Abigail, my dear," the Senator said. His voice was warm and welcoming and she found herself smiling. Senator Hamlin was homosexual, something that displeased the more conservative side of the country, and charming. He would have had no difficulty picking up any girl he wanted, had he played for that team. "It's been a long time."

"Indeed it has," Abigail agreed. "I'll make this quick, Sam. I've been hearing rumours about something…unexpected happening and…"

The sudden change in the Senator's voice was shocking. "What have you been hearing?"

Abigail hesitated, and then decided to be honest. "Very little," she admitted. "I've just been hearing fragments from here and there, odd suggestions that something is going on, yet no clue as to what it actually is."

"Good," Hamlin said. "Abigail, take a word of advice from this old queen. Don't push it any further. Leave the story alone."

"But I…"

"I could offer you a dozen other scoops if you're interested," Hamlin continued. "I could tell you about a Congressman whose stance on a certain issue is at variance with those who put him in power, or a Senator who has his hand in the till, but not this. The Majority and Minority Leaders both warned us not to discuss the matter any further. Let it go."

Abigail stared down at the telephone, wishing that she could see Hamlin's face. "But Senator, the people have a right to know…"

Hamlin laughed at her. "You mean, *you* have a right to know," he said, "and that is debatable. I've enjoyed your company in the past, my dear, so trust me on this. Let it go for now. Please."

"I understand," Abigail lied. "Thank you for your time."

"My pleasure," Hamlin replied. "When this is all over, I'll take you to dinner somewhere and you can pick my brains then. I might even tell you something. Good day."

She heard the phone click down and the line disconnect, trying to understand. She knew Senator Sam Hamlin fairly well and he was no pushover. He'd been in the Army before he'd been pushed out of the closet – no one had asked, he hadn't told, but somehow the Army had found out in a way it couldn't ignore – and had picked up several medals for bravery, and a Purple Heart. He'd joked about it to her – he'd told her that he'd forgotten to duck one day in Afghanistan – but it more than proved his bravery. He was a keen supporter of the military, a person hardly unwilling to challenge the President...and yet, he was silent. Someone – the Majority and Minority Leaders – had convinced him to keep his mouth shut. How had they done that?

It made little sense. Herding politicians was like herding cats, only these cats spat venom, and if the leaders annoyed too many politicians, they could be booted out so quickly their bottoms would be aching years in the future. If they had told a politician to keep his mouth shut, he might have blabbed about it at the earliest opportunity, just to teach the impudent leaders a lesson. Somehow, they had convinced Hamlin – and the others, she assumed – to keep his mouth shut. Hamlin; a Senator who called it as he saw it. Hamlin; a man of his word...

Understanding dawned. They hadn't used threats or blandishments, they'd *convinced* him to keep his mouth shut. They'd told him what was going on, or a cover story they'd invented to provide concealment for something else, and it had been good enough to convince him to remain silent. The secret, whatever it was, had to be something *really* big.

She looked down at her notebook again, trying to see the pattern. Investigative journalism had a great deal in common with intelligence work – indeed, Abigail knew that footage streamed from reporters in foreign countries had been used by the CIA and the other intelligence agencies from time to time – and it was impossible to say which piece of information would allow her to pull the whole story together. One of the most famous scoops of her generation had come when a reporter had taken a very careful look at the hundreds of disparate pieces of information and realised that they added up to a secret deal between the US and Iran. There was a pattern in front of her – she was sure of it – yet without the key, she couldn't pull it all together.

Perhaps I aimed too high, she thought to herself, and searched through her notebook for another number. She thought highly of the American military – when she thought about it at all – but she had no illusions about it. The vast majority of soldiers, sailors and airmen were proud of their service and did an excellent job, but there were always those who thought that they'd been given a raw deal. The man who thought that he had been denied promotion, the woman who felt that her sex worked against her, the rear-echelon mother fucker who thought that the troops on the front line were overpaid and oversexed, the volunteer who'd thought that he was volunteering for something else...there was no shortage of dissatisfied people.

Sergeant Danny Kyle worked at Andrews Air Force Base, near Washington. Abigail had encountered him quite by accident, but it hadn't taken long to realise that he was a gold mine. He worked as part of the ground crew on the base and loathed the fighter pilots with a passion that seemed surprising in such a short man. Kyle believed that he was constantly passed over for promotion, while the fighter jocks took all the local women and poured scorn on the heads of the people who kept them in the air. Abigail had courted him, promised to run interviews exposing the true nature of the USAF – at least as Kyle saw it – and picked up a handful of useful titbits from him. She consulted her other notes and confirmed that Andrews Air Force Base was one of the bases that had been given expanded security – and, one report suggested, additional antiaircraft units. It was almost as if they were expecting an attack on the base, but that was impossible. The United States Navy ruled the waves. No one could slip a carrier into attack range without having it detected and unceremoniously sunk.

"Hey, Danny," she said, when he picked up his cell phone. Kyle lived on the base and, sometimes, he didn't pick up her calls. He was a rat, plain and simple, with a rat's gift for hiding his activities. He would have made a competent motor mechanic, but Abigail wouldn't have wanted to fly in any plane he'd serviced. To hear him talk, the ground crew were permanently on the verge of accidentally-on-purpose sabotaging the aircraft that flew from the base. "How's it hanging?"

Kyle's voice was nervous. "Abby?" He whispered. Abigail had only given him the short version of her name because she had no illusions as to how long he'd hold out if Base Security interrogated him. It wasn't as if she were doing anything illegal, but it would be embarrassing to be discovered and her other sources would dry up. "What are you calling me for?"

Abigail frowned. Kyle had never sounded *scared* when talking to her before. He'd been a bombastic rat, bragging about his accomplishments at the same time as he bemoaned the USAF's talent for ignoring his greatness. He'd hit on her gracelessly more than once and he had enough arrogance to pass for one of his hated fighter jocks. He sounded as if someone had terrified hell out of him.

"I need information," she said. Kyle was predicable enough. She had slipped him enough money, over the years, to pickle his liver, or spend hours with the prostitutes that served the base and preyed on American servicemen. He'd tell her what she wanted to know. "Something odd is going on and I want to know what's happening."

"Look," Kyle whispered. He didn't sound reassured. "You don't understand. Stay away from this…"

Abigail blinked. For the second time in the day, she had been surprised by one of her contacts. Anger raged up within her. "Danny," she said, as seductively as she could, "tell me what I want to know and you'll have a big reward."

"No," Kyle hissed. He sounded absolutely terrified. "Never call me again. I never want to see or hear you again. Go find someone else to suck dry."

The phone went dead. Abigail stared at it, dazed. She hadn't even realised that she'd been sweating until she felt the dampness on her back. It was unbelievable. The reason Kyle had been denied promotion by the USAF – she knew, even if he didn't – was that he couldn't keep a secret, or remain reliable over long periods. They'd been quite right. Kyle had quite happily told her things that should have remained a secret for much longer, even though much of what he'd told her had been useless. The thought of him concealing something…

He didn't have the will to break off contact with her either, not unless someone had really put the frighteners on. She couldn't believe that the USAF had trusted Kyle with the real secret, whatever it was, but he might have worked it out on his own. He did have a certain level of intelligence, after all, and he might have deduced the truth. If it had been frightening enough to scare him…Abigail wondered if she should be scared too. Had Senator Hamlin been scared?

The door opened and Cindy stuck her head into Abigail's office. There was one of her in every office, a girl without a single cell in her head, yet hired because she caused blood to drain away from the interviewer's own brain. She was blonde, stacked, and beautiful enough to make Abigail feel rather dowdy. As far as Abigail could tell, she didn't even have a life outside the office. She barely knew that she'd been born.

"Hey, Abigail," Cindy said, with a smile that would have seriously tested Senator Hamlin's homosexuality. Abigail scowled at her. She had long since given up trying to teach the girl proper formalities. "I got an interesting thing for you."

"Really," Abigail said. The editor – who happened to be a woman – had given Cindy the Kook Desk to run, on the theory she couldn't screw that up. Abigail privately thought that was overoptimistic. "You'd better give it to me then."

"I was talking to one of the UFO researchers, you know, one of the *serious* ones," Cindy said. Abigail rolled her eyes. The number of cranks who sent information to the station seemed to increase every year. "He said that there'd been an increase in UFO sightings, everywhere."

Abigail stared down at her notepad. That couldn't be right, could it? Did the military think that it was going to encounter UFOs?

Chapter Fourteen

Washington DC, USA
Day 12

"I do not believe that it is an exaggeration," the President said, "to say that this might be the most important meeting in the history of the United States, if not the world. We need to make a decision, and fast. We do not know how much time we have before the aliens take matters into their own hands."

He looked around the table. The secure conference room, deep under the White House, was as secure as human ingenuity could make it, yet there was a big question mark over the capabilities of the aliens. Could they read information right out of secure computers at a distance? Could they use spy rays to probe the secret meeting and listen to the President's words? Had they managed to affix a surveillance device to the President despite all the precautions? There wouldn't ever be an electronic record of the meeting. The only transcript would be taken by the President's private secretary, who would make no copies and secure the original well away from the public eye. They might be being paranoid, the President knew, but what other choice did they have?

The Vice President sat at the other end of the table. The President would have preferred to use the secure videoconferencing network to ensure that the Vice President survived any strike on the White House, but the aliens had proven that they could decipher the most secure codes the NSA had created for America. The NSA was still in denial over what the aliens had done – they had sworn that the codes were unbreakable – yet until they could produce new codes and secure the infrastructure, it couldn't be trusted. Quite a few orders would have to be hand-carried, raising other security issues, just to ensure that the aliens didn't eavesdrop. There had been no protests. Everyone in the room knew what was at stake.

"You've all seen the recording," the President said. He had braced himself for disappointment – the aliens could have interfered with Pepper's magic eye, or perhaps the nature of the mothership itself would have prevented it from working properly – but the entire video had survived intact. There were some odd flickers of static and a couple of places where everything became distorted for a few seconds, yet it was usable. Some of the more paranoid Secret Service agents had raised questions about what had occurred in those seconds, but all agreed that it wasn't long enough for something bad to have happened. "You know what they're offering."

He met his Vice President's eyes. "They're offering to ally with us and work with us to occupy the rest of the world," he said. It had to be spoken aloud, just to ensure that everyone knew what was going on. "In exchange for our assistance, we maintain our independence and gain access to some of their technology. If they are to be believed, they *need* Earth quickly. They cannot hold in orbit while we make preparations for their arrival and accommodation. They want – they need – a large degree of political control. In effect, they're invaders, here to take the entire planet.

"The question is simple," he continued. "Do we accept their offer?"

There was a long pause. "My analysis team admits that the ultimate question of what we are to do is a political decision and must remain that way," Jones said. The President had ordered him flown from Nevada to Washington in a fighter jet, risking the discovery of the location of the crashed ship. "That said, they have made some observations that must be discussed. The interesting part is that the aliens went to some lengths to try to convince you that they didn't really *need* our help. I find that rather reassuring. Why would they bother trying to convince you to help them if they could just overwhelm the entire planet?"

The President had had similar thoughts. "You're saying that they might not be as strong as they claim?"

"Precisely," Jones said. "The teams working on the crashed ship haven't been able to duplicate it, but they are confident that we will be able to understand and copy their science, perhaps within a decade or two. It appears to be magical to us, yet it is rooted in hard science and they obey the same natural laws as us. Unlocking their secrets will take time, yet it can be done. We should not allow the mere fact that they are aliens to blind us to the fact that they have limits as well."

He paused. "That said, we have been unable to identify any weapons on the crashed ship," he added. "They may not have armed the ship, or they may have armed it with weapons we haven't been able to recognise as weapons, at least not yet. We don't know exactly what they're capable of doing to us, but we believe that it would include advanced lasers, coherent energy weapons, plasma cannons and other weapons, all borderline-possible now. They would also be able to use the high orbitals against us. They could drop rocks on our cities and military forces, smash us back to barbarism before they landed…there are too many possibilities.

"Yet they want Earth and, if they are to be believed, they *need* Earth. They cannot destroy the planet without condemning themselves to die as well. My analysts believe that they will refrain from wrecking the planet or pushing us into a corner where *we* will wreck the planet and call it a draw. It would be comparatively simple to damage Earth's biosphere to the point where it could no longer support life."

"We cannot plan to destroy our own world," the Vice President said. "Destroying a planet – our planet, along with our entire race - to win a war is no victory."

"We believe that it would deter them from trying to wipe us out," Jones said. "We must not misunderstand this point. They have formidable powers and they *could* wipe us out completely, if they chose to do so. The only counterpoint we have is that we could render Earth completely useless to them. It is not something to be cheerful about, but it is something to bear in mind."

The President said nothing. It was commonly said that the American President was the most powerful man in the world, yet few really understood the scope of that power, or its limits. On his own authority, the President could send America's vast military might into battle, or launch a nuclear strike against any target on Earth. And yet, that authority had limits. The Presidency sometimes meant being a bull in a china shop, remaining very still to avoid breaking the china. He could wreck most of the planet on his own authority and, in doing so; destroy the nation he had sworn to serve.

"So," Hubert Dotson said. "Our choices are simple. Give them what they want – an alliance – or tell them no. What will they do then?"

"We don't know," Jones said. "They may approach another world power and make the same offer, but there isn't another power with the same level of deployable military force as we have. The Russians and Chinese have formidable difficulties in deploying their forces outside their borders. I can't see the Europeans agreeing on anything, let alone an alliance to split the world between them and an alien race. No one else really matters on this scale.

"Or they may move ahead on their own," he added. "We just don't know."

"There might be advantages in dividing the world between us," Tom Pearson said. The CIA Director looked down at the table, tapping absently on it as he spoke. "God knows, we have too many problems coming from parts of the world that most of our population don't even know exist. If the aliens settled in the Middle East, or Africa, or Russia and China…they'd have far more problems than making our lives difficult."

"And we'd have to dominate the American continent," the Vice President pointed out, acidly. "Does anyone else remember the exercise we ran a year ago, when it looked as if Mexico was going to collapse into civil war and send chaos flying north into the Border States? The conclusion was that it wouldn't end well. I doubt that the aliens would allow us to leave those states nominally independent and we really wouldn't want them on our borders…"

"They don't need to be on our borders," General Wachter pointed out, dryly. "Their technology could get an attack force from Africa to Washington within minutes."

"There is much to say for removing the problems from the rest of the world," the Secretary of State put in, "but it wouldn't be the end of our problems. I can't see the American population going for an agreement that cedes the rest of the world to the aliens, even if we benefit. We have lobbies here for dozens of nations that would be horrified. What would the Israeli lobby say if we sold out Israel to the aliens? What would the Polish lobby say if we sold out Poland…?"

"They already say that we sold out Poland," Pearson said. "Does their opinion really matter?"

"Yes," the President said, flatly. The Secretary of State was right. Ceding half the world to the aliens would probably cost him the next election, if Congress didn't outright impeach him. Briefly, he considered allowing it to happen so that he took the blame personally, before pushing the thought aside. It wasn't just his career on the ropes, but the future of humanity itself. "I could name at least twenty senators who'd have a heart attack at the mere thought of abandoning the rest of the world."

"And all the lobbyists would tear into them," the Vice President added. "Every country in the world that wants influence in Washington has its own team of lobbyists working here. They'd all go mad trying to prevent the aliens from landing, or push us into taking the lead against them. The political chaos could tear the country apart."

The President scowled. He'd done his best to clean out the State Department, removing people who had been – to all intents and purposes – bribed to serve another country, not America, but it was a nightmare. High-quality people, the people the country needed, wanted higher salaries, leaving public office to those who – sometimes – didn't hesitate to form alliances with representatives of various nations. It was a major problem, yet it wasn't one that could be handled easily, not when there were hundreds of entrenched interests fighting to maintain the status quo.

"There are also the economic issues," Dahlia King said. The Secretary of the Treasury smiled at the President's expression. "I know, the economy is one of the last things you want to think about, but it is a serious concern. If we lost our links to the rest of the world, the effects would be devastating to the American economy. They'd be unpredictable, but... millions of people would become unemployed, the value of the dollar would plummet and thousands of businesses would go out of business. The remainder of the world's economy would be devastated as well."

"They'd probably have other concerns," Pearson said, darkly.

"The introduction of alien technology would also cause economic unrest," Dahlia added, flatly. "If they replace...for example, the oil industry, millions of people will find themselves out of work. Their cures alone, assuming that they work as advertised, will cause another chain reaction and put millions more out of work. They may have decided not to attempt to invade us because they know that invading the rest of the world – and giving us a poisoned gift – will ruin us for the foreseeable future anyway."

"That's a dark thought," the President said.

"Yes, Mr President," Dahlia said. She had clawed her way up from poverty to reach her position and she had an understanding of exactly what poverty meant. It was one of the reasons he'd given her the job. "I would be fundamentally opposed to their offer on moral grounds, but the practical issues defeat it."

"I do not believe," the Vice President said, "that we are considering withholding their gift from the public. Is it all that they said it was?"

Jones nodded. "My analysts confirmed that the cures they gave us are legitimate," he said. "We could eradicate AIDS within the year if we produced the cure and vaccine, and then started distributing it to everyone within and outside the country. We could rid ourselves of cancers and hundreds of other threats…"

"And wreak huge damage on the economy," Dahlia reminded him. "There would be a sharp drop in demand for medical supplies, causing more economic unrest."

"Jesus," the Vice President snapped. "I cannot believe that you are proposing that we withhold cures that people *need*!"

"I am not proposing anything of the sort," Dahlia snapped back. "I am pointing out that using their gift will have more effects on our society than the obvious. They chose their gift carefully. If we use it, we have to handle an economic storm. If we don't use it, we have to weather a political storm instead. They chose it very carefully."

The President tapped the table. "General," he asked, "what's your opinion?"

Wachter considered it. "In my role as Chairman of the Joint Chiefs of Staff, it is my duty to inform you that occupying the entire American continent will be difficult," he said, carefully. "We would need to increase the size of our deployable units rapidly before we could contemplate any such action. That said…

"The aliens want us to abandon our allies," he added. "The aliens want the rest of the world. It is my belief that they will eventually turn on us after we have betrayed everyone who might help us. I do not believe that we should accept their offer."

"That does raise another question," Pearson said. "If they launch an invasion, could we beat them off?"

"Perhaps," Wachter said. "I think that if we refused to go along with them, yet offered them another deal, they might agree to it. Their desire to have us as allies does suggest that they are weaker than we thought."

"There's another point," Jones added. "They *didn't* ask for something they should have asked for – they didn't ask for the ship back. Why not?"

The President leaned forward. All of the analysts had suggested that the aliens would demand their ship back, yet they hadn't; they had issued no demands about the ship at all. It was an odd oversight; the more so because the aliens very definitely knew where the craft had crashed and which government had it. It made no sense.

"Why not?" He asked. "What do your people believe?"

"The craft is something that we wouldn't give up easily," Jones said. "It's our key to understanding their technology. They should have demanded it at once, yet it's something that we would resist returning, and so they would have to force us to hand it back. Why wouldn't they demand it back…unless they couldn't carry out their threats?"

"You're saying that they might be *far* weaker than we believe," the Vice President said. "You're suggesting that they couldn't just *take* the craft back?"

"They're not gods," Jones said. "They're advanced, yes, and they can do things that we can't do – yet – but they're not gods. I think that we can resist them, perhaps enough to get a better deal for humanity out of them."

"The current deal is unacceptable," the President agreed. He looked around the table and saw no dissent. "Do you have any suggestions as to what we *should* offer them as a counter-proposal?"

"There's quite a bit of empty space on this planet," Jones said. "We could offer them temporary accommodation in flyover country, and perhaps help them buy land elsewhere. We could help them to resupply their craft and perhaps extend its life…"

"All in exchange for their technology, of course," Pearson injected.

"Of course," Jones said. "We'd also want to inspect their craft and ensure that they are actually telling the truth. They could have lied through their teeth and we'd have no way of knowing, until we board their ship."

"I don't want to rain on your parade," Dahlia announced, "but they claimed that they have one *billion* aliens on that ship. That is not a small number. I doubt that we could accommodate them all on CONUS. We might have to take land for them from another country, or barter with them – or perhaps the aliens would barter with them. I cannot see it as being anything other than very disruptive…"

"It's going to be very disruptive anyway," Wachter pointed out. "Even here, I doubt that we could clear a vast area for them without protest. We might end up driving people off their land for the aliens – which would cause a political firestorm, perhaps even civil war."

"I think we have to face one fact," Jones said. "The world is going to change remarkably. Whatever we do, whatever we decide, the world is never going to be the same again."

"We'll make our counter-offer to the aliens," the President said. "Perhaps we can find a compromise that would be acceptable to all parties."

On that note, the meeting ended.

———

The President's wife had died while he'd been a junior officer and he'd never remarried, making him the first President in over a hundred years to lack a First Lady. His detractors had made much of that when he'd been running for office, claiming that he had no one who could advise him late at night, but the President had never even thought about remarrying. His wife had been something special and he'd never met another woman quite like her. The times when he wished he had found someone else were few and far between, but that night he wished he had a close confident. Only a handful of people could see him as anything but the President…and most of them couldn't give real advice. The buck stopped with him.

He had never felt the weight as strongly as he did as he lay in bed. No other President had faced such a decision. Lincoln had faced his own demons and forces that sought to tear the nation apart, Roosevelt had struggled to fight a war on two fronts, Bush had confronted a whole new type of war, yet none of them had faced aliens. None of them had faced a foe who could exterminate the entire human race. None of them had risked the destruction of the entire world.

It was a long time before he knew sleep.

Chapter Fifteen

"Mr President, sorry to disturb you, but we may have had a security breach."

"We may have had?" The President repeated. He didn't have time for this. "What happened?"

Janine Reynolds' took a deep breath. "As you know, Mr President, we have agents within the majority of the UFO organisations within the country," she said. "It was a precaution against their seeing something we didn't want them to see, a secret project rather than a UFO. One of them reported that the World News Network has been in contact with them about the increased number of UFO sightings and how it may connect to our military preparations."

"That's rather thin," the President pointed out, mildly. "Does it connect to something they can actually run without looking barking mad?"

"We're not sure," Janine admitted. "There are more and more people every day privy to at least some aspect of the secret. They may have figured out enough to patch the rest together, but we won't know for sure unless we increase our surveillance and hack into their computers."

The President considered it. He doubted that the media knew enough to run with the story – he knew what he would say to anyone who brought him such a story and no editor would want so much egg on their face – but the secret, any secret, would start to fray if the media kept poking away at it. How much did they actually know? If they were just probing at random, it could be safely ignored, but if they had linked it all together…

"See to it," he ordered. The NSA had a wide remit for keeping an eye on the media. "Try and figure out how much they know as soon as possible, but don't show them that we're interested. That might as well tell them that everything they suspect is true."

"If they suspect anything," Janine said, frankly. "I'll get back in touch, Mr President."

"And speak to the Director of the FBI," the President added. "If someone leaked, I want their ass in jail. No one should be privy to even the outermost aspects of the secret without having signed any number of security agreements and they've clearly been broken."

"Yes, Mr President," Janine said. "I'll see to it at once."

The President put the phone down. "I'm sorry, General," he said. "You were saying?"

General Sandra Dyson was a tall powerfully-built woman wearing her dress uniform. As Commanding Officer of the United States Strategic Command, she was the senior female General in America and quite possibly the most powerful woman in the world. The United States Strategic Command, which had responsibility for space defence and protecting the United States against strategic threats, was a relatively new command, but it was at the forefront of current events. Sandra was young for her rank, yet there was no doubting her competence. She'd even worked to pull all of the different space-based defence systems together, defying interservice disputes and disagreements to create a network that should have provided protection against a rogue state with nuclear weapons and the ballistic missiles required to deliver them.

"No problem, Mr President," she said, in her thick southern drawl. The two colonels she'd brought with her as assistants nodded in unison. "I was briefing you on the status of our space defence systems."

The President nodded. Two weeks ago, no one could have proposed a defence system designed to fight off extraterrestrials without being laughed at, if not escorted away by the men in white coats. Now, there was a genuine extraterrestrial threat and the United States had been caught with its pants around its ankles. The President knew that the analysts were in agreement that the aliens were weaker than they seemed, yet it could only be a relative measure…and the aliens still held command of space. If it came to a war – and the aliens had not responded to his counter-offer – it might be the first war in history that the United States fought and lost. Vietnam didn't count, as the United States had given up.

Sandra hadn't brought a PowerPoint, knowing that the President detested them. Instead, she spoke from memory. "Our defences start in orbit, with a handful of killer satellites and older stockpiled Brilliant Pebbles," she said. "The killer satellites were designed to fire slugs of metal into enemy satellites, which tend to follow predicable courses, and even a relatively tiny amount of damage could prove fatal. The Brilliant Pebbles have tiny thrusters and use them to manoeuvre into the path of incoming ballistic missiles. They were designed during the Cold War, but they should still be useful today, once we put them up. We've held both shuttles on the ground and are rapidly reprioritising so that we can make the best use of our craft."

The President nodded. NASA had thrown a collective fit at the thought of holding one of the shuttles – which had been scheduled to launch two days after the UFO crashed – but it had been rapidly squashed. There were only a handful of people at NASA privy to the information about the UFO and those who knew nothing were screaming their heads off, complaining that the military had pre-empted their missions in favour of something militaristic.

"The problem is that we don't believe that they will be particularly effective against the alien craft," she continued. "They were designed to attack targets that didn't dodge – or fire back, for that matter – and we don't have very many of them. Due to various political decisions, we were never allowed to orbit many KE-ASAT – that's Kinetic Energy Anti-Satellite weapons – to provide coverage of the entire world. The aliens – like the Russians or the Chinese – could simply overwhelm our defences by firing hundreds of missiles in one mass attack. The killer satellites may be even less useful. We have no hard data on how much damage their craft would suffer from a relatively low-powered weapon."

She shrugged expressively. "We're also retargeting our ICBMs to be fired upwards and detonated in orbit," she added. "The bottom line, however, is that the enemy will definitely see them coming and probably either take countermeasures of their own or simply avoid them. They were never designed for use against attacking alien spacecraft, but rather for targeting other states on Earth.

"Medium-range, we have a sizable number of missiles capable of engaging targets in low orbit or entering Earth's atmosphere," she said. "We have ground-based THAAD – that's Terminal High Altitude Area Defence missiles – which we can use to target satellites and other threats in space. We intended them to intercept incoming missiles, but they can be retargeted on alien craft if necessary. We also have RIM-161 Standard Missile 3, a ship based anti-ballistic missile fired from Aegis ships. The Aegis Ballistic Missile Defence System proved its worth against crashing satellites and should be capable of being retargeted against alien craft.

"We also have aerial systems, including the Boeing YAL-1 Airborne Laser, deployed from USAF-modified Boeing 747-400F. They fire laser beams at their targets and the system has been quite successful in tests, but they require considerable time on target to be effective and the aliens can probably manoeuvre away from the beams or deploy countermeasures. There are also a handful of air-launched ASAT missiles that can be deployed against targets in low orbit, but we never stockpiled very many of them."

The President frowned. "Why?"

"Political reasons," Sandra replied. "Congress didn't like the program very much and placed restrictions on it, encouraged by the telecommunications lobby who had billions in orbiting capital at risk. The project was closed down for years and only reactivated after the Chinese deployed a comparable system. We had several other systems underway at the time and so the USAF program was never given priority.

"Finally, we have ground-based systems, ranging from Patriot and Arrow missiles capable of engaging incoming targets, to lasers and other beam weapons mounted on the ground," she concluded. "My teams have studied the reports on the crashed ship carefully and they have concluded that a hit from a Patriot would be sufficient to destroy the craft, unless it is protected by a force field or some comparable system out of science-fiction. We could be reasonably confident of giving them pause if we knew the weapons would be completely effective, yet we know nothing of the sort. We don't even know what weapons *they* can deploy."

She winced visibly. "The major problem is that we only have limited numbers of these systems, Mr President. We could start mass production now, but it would take years to produce a sizeable number of such weapons and deploy them, and we may not have that much time. There are concepts on the drawing board that might help tip the balance in our favour, but even if we got the funding out of Congress, it would take years to build workable hardware."

"I see," the President said. "What about other nations?"

"The Russians have their operative Gorgon and Gazelle systems," Sandra said. "They're both ground-based systems and they have comparable weaknesses to our own, although we assume that the Russians have plans to upgrade the system in a hurry if necessary. They also have their own air-launched missile systems and ground-based beam weapons, although our data suggests that their operational status is…not good.

"The Europeans, Indians and Japanese have some access to Patriot missiles and a handful of concepts that could be turned against targets in Low Earth Orbit, but they haven't moved ahead to any deployable hardware. Both Iran and North Korea claim the ability to shoot down satellites in orbit, but our analysis suggests that the systems are unreliable, if indeed they work at all. Hard data is lacking.

"The Chinese are the joker in the deck," she concluded. "They have ground-based and air-launched weapons, as well as beam weapons they learned to make from the Russians. We don't know how many deployable weapons they have – their claims range from a mere handful to the capability to provide total protection against ballistic missile attack – yet they definitely have enough to be taken seriously. If we could negotiate the use of their weapons, it would certainly give Earth some additional punch."

The President looked down at the table. "That might not be easy," he said. The State Department was trying to set up a meeting between the President and the other major world leaders – the four other permanent members of the United Nations Security Council – in hopes or organising a coordinated response to the alien threat, yet without providing some clue about the agenda, it was hard to coordinate a meeting. The President's brief absence from power had been noticed. The absence of all five Security Council members would definitely be noticed and the media would draw all kinds of conclusions. "How would you rate our chances?"

"Lousy," Sandra said, honestly. "Our capability to take the war to them is effectively non-existent."

"I see," the President said. "Can we change that in the very near future?"

"Probably not," Sandra admitted. "I have teams working on possibilities, everything from Project Orion to the Alcubierre Warp Drive, but unless we have a very lucky breakthrough I doubt we'll have workable hardware in less than a decade. Orion is theoretically possible, yet we would have to take years to produce a working spacecraft…and then the environmentalists would go berserk. I'm not sure I would blame them. The costs, both in dollars and in environmental damage, would be considerable. We cannot even produce new space shuttles – God knows, NASA dragged its feet so much that we don't even have a replacement coming within the next few years. All of the pretty pictures they produced turned out to be little more than that.

"One of my teams did dig up an old concept for a orbital laser battle station that could be deployed in orbit, either on its own or mounted to the proposed *Freedom* space station," she added, thoughtfully. "The concept was never taken beyond the planning stage, but we *could* mount weapons on the shuttles and the International Space Station, although I'm sure that there would be international protests if we armed the ISS. Practically speaking, I don't think that it would do much good. The station is a sitting duck to almost any determined attack."

The President nodded slowly. One of the scenarios he'd seen during his inauguration briefings had been a terrorist-launched missile bringing down the station, destroying billions of dollars worth of hardware at a cost of a few hundred thousand dollars. The North Korean leadership had sometimes threatened the station – and China, of course, had long refused to accept that spy satellites could fly freely across its territory. The Chinese were rational, at bottom, but no one would say that about the North Korean leadership. Kim's replacement was even more insane than he had been and some of the reports from refugees had been horrific.

"That's something to discuss when I meet the world leaders," he said. He opened a drawer and pulled out a single sheet of paper. "This National Security Directive, issued with the full understanding and consent of the Cabinet, the Majority Leader and the Minority Leader places *all* space-capable defence assets under your command. The United States Strategic Command will take the lead in defending us against the aliens, when or if they choose to engage us in battle. I want you to implement the defence plans as quickly as possible. I also want you to submit funding requests we can rush through Congress and start producing usable hardware as soon as we can."

He saw Sandra wince and smiled to himself. With the consent of the Majority and Minority leaders, Congress wouldn't raise an effective fuss, but those who did complain would turn it into a real political catfight. The Joint Chiefs would have a collective fit as well. Each of the services had its own space-capable system, in defiance of logic, and they would resent giving it up, even temporarily. In the battles for budget, having such capabilities helped attract more funding. It wasn't something to mock in the current economic climate. The last thing the United States needed was a sudden new drain on its resources, but what other choice did they have?

"Yes, Mr President," Sandra said. The two colonels were staring at the paper as if it was a map to hidden treasure. "Ah…has there been any reply to your message?"

"Nothing from the aliens at all," the President said. It bothered him. The techs had suggested that the aliens lacked FTL communications, even though they had calculated that the craft that had carried him to their mothership had moved faster than light, and that the message was still heading out to the alien ship, but the President doubted it. The aliens had kept an eye on America – and were still flying their craft through restricted airspace, mocking the defenders, those who knew they were there. They could have easily picked up the message and transported it to the mothership on one of their smaller craft. "They may be still thinking about their response."

"Or they may be talking to the Russians, or the Chinese," Sandra pointed out. "If we rejected their bargain, they might have moved on to someone else."

"I know," the President said. The Russians had been manoeuvring for years to reassume control over Eastern Europe. The aliens could offer them that on a platter. The Chinese wanted Taiwan back, and then perhaps most of the surrounding countries – and the aliens could give them what they wanted. Would they accept a deal that condemned the rest of the world to alien domination?

The analysts hadn't been able to decide. The CIA and the other intelligence agencies had been watching for signs of alien contact, but so far they'd found nothing, not even a vague rumour. The Russians and Chinese were far better at keeping secrets than the American Government and it wasn't as if they were short of uninhabited territory that could be used for a secret meeting. The National Reconnaissance Office had been studying satellite footage from the last week, trying to see if the aliens had landed within their territory, but it was useless. The aliens would know when the Americans weren't watching – if they cared enough to try to hide. It was impossible to prove or disprove one way or the other.

"There are some advanced concepts I'd like to see get funding, but I doubt we could fund all of them," Sandra said. "I mean, we could build railgun systems capable of hitting targets in orbit without giving them so much advance warning, yet we haven't even moved on to producing usable hardware, apart from a test model. I don't even know how well our fighters stack up against the alien craft, or how they will engage us – or even if they will engage us at all. If they have high-powered lasers, more powerful than our own, they could wipe out the entire USAF in a single afternoon."

The President could see it in his mind's eye. A beam of light flickering from aircraft to aircraft, leaving explosions in its wake as fuel overheated and exploded, or the beam burned through the cockpit and killed the pilot before he could eject. It wasn't the most depressing possibility, either. Another one had come right out of *Independence Day*, with human fighters trying desperately to escape invincible alien spacecraft, protected by invulnerable force fields. Somehow, he doubted that a mere computer virus would bring down real aliens.

"We have to try," he said. "Tell anyone who argues about the command to come see me and I'll read him the riot act. We don't have time for petty disputes, General. The fate of the entire world is at stake."

"Yes, Mr President," Sandra said. She stood to attention. "We won't let you down."

Chapter Sixteen

SETI Institute, California, USA

Day 20

It always disappointed visitors – just as it had disappointed Karen Lawton on her first day – that the headquarters of the SETI institute were so mundane. There were no massive radio telescopes staring into the heavens – they were located out in the desert, or in other countries – or images of extraterrestrials, only a set of computer banks and a handful of technicians to keep an eye on them. Karen, like the others in the massive chamber, was on her internship, unlike the handful of True Believers who ran most of the organisation. If she decided she liked the work, she could apply to SETI for a permanent position, but she'd decided long ago that the work was largely boring. She'd trained as a radio expert and had gone into astronomy because it seemed interesting, but SETI wasn't the place to make great discoveries. If there were aliens out there, they were keeping very quiet.

She looked down at the console and scowled to herself. The morning shift was just like any other shift to her, as dead as the grave. The vast majority of the work was automated, or handled by thousands of volunteers across the globe who donated some of their computer time to studying the endless input from the stars. The heavens were ablaze with radio signals and howling static, yet all of them had a natural cause, apart from one. She'd studied the odd WOW signal picked up years ago by SETI, but the cause remained unidentified and, as human understanding of the universe deepened, she suspected that it would turn out to have a natural cause. The interstellar navigation beacons SETI had picked up had turned out to be quasars, stray signals had turned out to come from lost or damaged satellites and every hopeful they'd found had had a natural explanation. Even if they did pick up something – anything – there was no guarantee that they would be able to understand it. A lifetime spent in a mixed family had left her convinced that there were cultural barriers even among humans that could never be broken. An alien race might have completely different concepts of how the universe actually worked.

It had been hard, but she'd already made up her mind to quit at the end of her internship, perhaps even see if the NSA would take her on. She'd been approached by a recruiter before accepting the position at SETI, but as a committed antiwar activist she could hardly have accepted the position at No Such Agency. Her last boyfriend would have had a fit, although seeing as she'd dumped him for trying to cop a feel in the middle of a movie they'd watched together, she found it hard to care about his opinion. He probably hated her now anyway. She hadn't castrated him, but it hadn't been for lack of trying. She'd been lucky not to be arrested for assault.

Ping!

She blinked in disbelief, which was rapidly replaced by cynicism. The computers scanned every incoming signal, looking for odd patterns that might indicate the presence of alien life, and alerted their human operators to anything interesting. It had been exciting, the first time, until she'd been told that there were hundreds of alerts every month, even with the best filtering software thousands of volunteers could produce. No one, apart from the young and naive, even got interested any longer. How could they when the dream of locating an alien civilisation had been replaced by a desperate struggle to keep being funded, knowing the odds against success?

Karen leaned down and tapped a pair of keys, putting the incoming signal through a verification process. It compared the signal's point of origin to any known satellite or chunk of space debris, anything that could serve as a transmitter. SETI had had some excitement three years ago when a dead Russian satellite had suddenly come alive for twenty minutes and started spewing out gibberish – no one knew why or how – that had passed for an alien signal, until someone had verified it as being manmade. The media had made fun of it – and a pair of hoaxes someone else had created – and further dented SETI's image as serious science. It didn't help that thousands of UFO reports were forwarded, every year, to SETI. Most of them, too, were hoaxes.

The signal refused to vanish. Puzzled, feeling an odd trembling deep within her chest, Karen ran through the second set of verification procedures. The signal was coming from deep space! It was unbelievable and she ran through the verification procedure again, yet it was undeniable. The source of the signal was on the very edge of the solar system! She checked again, using the incoming feed from several different telescopes to triangulate the source of the signal, and discovered that there was no mistake. The Voyager and Pioneer space probes had drifted out of the solar system years ago, yet they'd been on a completely different heading. The source of the signal couldn't be manmade, could it?

Wonder warred with fear in her chest. Wonder won. She picked up the phone and tapped in a number, half-nervous that one of the others would see her discovery before she had a chance to claim it as hers. SETI was very competitive. Anyone who located an alien signal would instantly become the most famous person on the planet and there were hundreds of True Believers and even Lukewarm Believers who wouldn't hesitate to try to steal the credit. She copied the data into an email and forwarded it out of the Institute, sealing her claim.

"Ah, Director," she said, when the Director finally answered. "I think you should come see this. I've got something very interesting on my computer."

————

Director Daisy Fairchild had been born to a mother – her father remained an unknown, much to her relief – who had fallen in love with the hippy lifestyle so prevalent among her fellow teens. She had followed her calling and moved to live with a naturalistic commune outside San Francisco where they engaged in free love, took as many drugs as they wanted and generally tried to stay away from real life. Daisy had been born on a muddy field and would have grown up with the commune if her grandfather hadn't taken her away from her mother shortly after she'd been born. A muddy field, her grandfather had said, was no place to bring up a baby and he'd been right. Daisy's mother had kept her faith and, after the Courts had ruled in her favour, had tried to convince Daisy to remain with her, but Daisy had refused. The hippies were growing older and looked more pathetic every year. Many had left the commune for jobs, marriage, and a life more ordinary.

It was an irony that her mother's connections – as a true believer, she had the ear of some quite powerful people – had helped her to obtain the position she held. SETI had plenty of enthusiastic volunteers who were willing to assist with the project, but it had lacked a trained manager who could bring in funding and public support. Daisy had revamped the system completely, banging on as many doors as she could for funding while developing public displays that brought in more funding and lecture opportunities, even though she didn't really believe in SETI and its mission. Her mother might have talked about aliens coming to save Earth or beaming the chosen up to the mothership, leaving the rest of the human race to wallow in filth, but it had never happened. It was just a job, as far as Daisy was concerned, one that she was good at handling. Who *cared* if there was alien life or not?

She walked down the long corridor, silently cursing the intern under her breath. SETI relied upon them and so she couldn't give them the thrashing they deserved, every time they saw something and thought that it was the big one. Daisy's predecessor had quit over a report of alien contact that had been proven – too late – to be a hoax signal. The media had picked up on it – someone within SETI had alerted the media without checking the signal – and he'd become a laughing stock. It had been his own stupid fault for believing that the Men in Black were on their way to close SETI down and conceal the truth about alien visits. Daisy suspected that the Men in Black needn't have bothered.

"All right," she said, as she strode into the radio chamber. She'd found it somewhat disappointing at first too, but the original planners had reasoned that keeping SETI as a distributed system made it harder for the government or anyone else to interfere. "What do you have?"

The intern was dark-haired, pretty enough to be a cheerleader…and grinning from ear to ear. Daisy had only seen her once before and then only from a distance, when she'd welcomed the new interns to SETI, knowing that most of them would be gone within six months. She couldn't remember the girl's name. If it hadn't been on her nametag, she would have had to ask and reveal that she neither knew nor cared. Or at least she hadn't cared. If Karen had found something real, she would be turned into the most famous person in the world. SETI would promote her and, in doing so, promote the mission. The funding opportunities would be considerable.

"A signal," Karen said. "It's coming in on the hydrogen band wavelength, from a source on the edge of the solar system."

There was more technobabble, but Daisy tuned it out as she examined the display, trying to think. She had to admit that the signal looked convincing – none of the Senior Astronomers in the room were trying to squash Karen – and there seemed to be no reason to believe that it was a hoax.

"We've got confirmation from three different observatory stations," one of the Seniors said. His face was flushed with excitement. As a True Believer, the prospect of alien contact was wonderful. He'd often spoken of how important it would be to greet the aliens peacefully, although Daisy got nervous every time he spoke to the media. He looked like a mad scientist and sometimes talked like one. "It's real, Director! We've found alien life!"

Daisy ran her hand through her hair, trying to think. The vast majority of SETI scientists would want to proceed with a news release, either to prevent the Men in Black or some other delusional nonsense from preventing the public from being informed, or – more practically – to prevent someone else claiming credit for the discovery. The news would be flashing through the SETI community already and someone might just jump the gun…and, as the world turned, other telescopes would pick up the signal.

And yet, if it was a hoax, how could her career survive?

"Check it," she ordered, shortly. "Are we entirely certain of the source?"

"Yes," Karen said, flatly. The intern looked as if she'd just had a massive orgasm, Daisy reflected, sourly. She probably had. She didn't know if Karen was a True Believer or not, but her discovery had catapulted her to fame and fortune. She was pretty enough to be a natural on the talk show circuit. "There is nothing that could have produced such a signal."

Daisy mentally ran through the briefing papers in her mind. SETI was signed up to a variety of international agreements concerning the detection of an alien signal, yet none of those agreements had any legal power and no one had any illusions as to how well they'd stand up after the discovery of real alien life. The Declaration of Principles Concerning Activities

Following the Detection of Extraterrestrial Intelligence was written by True Believers, yet on the verge of the greatest scientific discovery of the century, no one would bother to go through the entire procedure. They'd just shout the news to the skies.

Her cell phone vibrated. "Director," her secretary said, "I've just had a call from CNN. They've heard a rumour that we've picked up a signal."

Daisy felt her gaze sweeping the room. Someone had sent a note to the media. They probably wouldn't take it entirely seriously at first – or perhaps they'd run it with a few disclaimers so that the blame would fall entirely on SETI – but the more they pried, the more they'd learn. They'd eventually seek to take control of the dissemination and that could not be allowed, not when SETI had just proved its worth to a universe of doubting sceptics.

She looked up at an image of ET someone had hung on the wall and made her decision. "Tell them that I will be holding a press conference later today," she ordered, smoothly. "We'll hold it…three hours from now. Until then, we'll hold our cards close to our chests and wait."

The connection broke and she smiled at Karen. "My congratulations," she said, calmly. "You're about to be famous."

Karen blushed. "Thank you, Director," she said. "Can I call my parents?"

"If you wish," Daisy said. She looked around the room, mentally matching names to faces. "I want a formal notification sent to everyone on the list that we have detected a signal of unknown origin. Get them to start checking the signal and confirming its source. The senior staff will compose a press release that we'll issue at the press conference later today. Karen, you're going to have to get ready to face the baying pack of newshounds. The rest of you, start working on the signal so that I have something to tell the reporters when they arrive, and keep me informed."

"Director," one of the juniors said. "What about the source?"

Daisy blinked. "What *about* the source?"

The young man held his ground. "It's within the solar system," he pointed out, very calmly. His face was pale. "We checked it six ways from Sunday and found nothing that could have generated it – nothing human, that is. The source is within the solar system. Director, we could be on the verge of actually meeting the aliens, face-to-face."

Daisy stared at him. She'd always assumed that SETI would pick up signals from another planet light-years away, even though she knew that the vast majority of signals that Earth beamed out were too weak to be detected even by a SETI-like project on the nearest star. She'd always considered it a good thing, or at least she had when she'd bothered to think about it at all, for an alien race that watched most of what passed for human entertainment would probably get a very distorted idea of humanity. An alien starship in the solar system was outside her league. The entire world would change overnight.

"Get me some confirmation on that," she ordered, thinking hard. Would it be wise to announce that at the press conference? What would the Government say? It wouldn't remain a secret for much longer anyway. Every observatory in the world would be looking for the signal's source. "Email it to me through the intranet. I'll have a look at it once we've made the first announcement."

She stepped out of the radio room and suddenly felt weak at the knees, as if she were going to faint. She hadn't really taken her job seriously, not as anything more than just another job. If SETI had succeeded, if a radio signal had been detected from another star, it wouldn't have made that much difference to Earth. It would be years before humanity could send a reply, or get a message back after they replied, but an alien starship in the solar system was something else again. The world was going to change. She glanced around her, taking in the hundreds of fantasy aliens displayed on the walls, and realised for the first time how silly most of them looked. The entire world looked increasingly surreal.

Carefully, she pulled herself forward until she could walk normally again. She had a job to do and she wasn't going to faint, not until afterwards. SETI needed her to remain on top of things until her job was done.

———

Karen endured a series of hugs from the other interns — most of whom were nerds who had never touched a girl in their lives — and the older researchers before escaping back to her console. Her mind kept humming a single thought — *I'm going to be famous* — yet she was scared. She'd known that the source was within the solar system, but she hadn't thought about the implications until Mickey pointed them out. The aliens weren't just saying hello to Planet Earth, they'd invited themselves over for tea. It was beyond belief. It couldn't be happening. Part of her just wanted to crawl up in a corner and hide, or find proof that her signal wasn't alien after all, even if it meant that she would become the laughing stock of the world. It couldn't be happening…

But it was.

Slowly, she started to key in commands into her console. The alien signal was using a rotating modulation, perhaps to add a random variable that would make it out as being of artificial origin, but there were very definitely patterns in it. They'd repeated something ten times, then something else another ten times, and then something else again. She deduced that it was a simple case of them repeating the signal to ensure that nothing was lost in transmission – a common problem in space – and it suggested that the aliens wanted their signals to be understood. Carefully, she started to examine the signal.

All of the experts agreed that deciphering an alien signal could take years. Aliens came from completely different cultures and building up a common understanding would be extremely difficult, even with both sides trying their hardest to understand one another. She'd read papers that suggested that Dolphins and Chimps were actually intelligent, yet the surest proof that they were not was that they had never attempted to communicate with humans, if only to tell them to stop mucking up the oceans. The signal should have taken years to decipher.

She succeeded on her very first try.

Chapter Seventeen

SETI Institute, California, USA
Day 20

Abigail caught her breath as she pushed her way into the lecture hall. It had been sheer luck that she'd been in California when the alien signal had been detected – she'd gone to Camp Pendleton in hopes of tracking down a source who had implied that he would tell her more in person, only to refuse to even meet her when she had arrived – and, just for the moment, she hated it. The room was normally sparsely populated – SETI just wasn't very important in a world that held pop stars and other more newsworthy items – but today it was standing room only. She recognised some famous media faces among the gathered crowd, all chatting away excitedly. They knew that something was up.

The news had broken only two hours ago, after someone had released a statement onto the World Wide Web. The media hadn't taken it seriously at first until reporters with links to SETI had picked up on the story, followed by bloggers with a reputation for getting their facts right. Abigail knew that both Fox and CNN had been seriously embarrassed by bloggers from time to time – they'd published inaccurate information and bloggers had caught them at it – yet she knew better than to dismiss them as unpaid amateurs. There were reporters who regarded their career as just a job, compromising their principles to fit in with the editorial slant of their organisations, but the bloggers did it as a labour of love. They were more trusted by the news-reading public than either Fox or CNN – or, for that matter, the World News Network. It was humiliating to admit to how badly the media had lost the public's trust, but Abigail's superiors had seen it as an opportunity, helping to sort out the trustworthy bloggers from the net's hordes of liars and uninformed. If most of the bloggers believed something to be true, it probably was…although even they had been fooled from time to time.

She found a corner and pulled out her Smartphone, checking the feed from her superiors and three different blogs. Radio telescopes covering the side of the planet facing the signal's source – the bloggers were already claiming that the source was within the solar system and therefore had to be an alien starship, although a sizable minority were under the impression that it was a lost human probe – had not only confirmed the signal's existence, but that it wasn't coming from any known human satellite or probe. The mood in the astronomical community was one of cautious interest. SETI had been a bastard child for so long that it was a little late to be hopping on the bandwagon, although Abigail was pretty sure that universities would be trying to use it to gain more funding for their own space studies departments. It could revitalise space exploration.

The bloggers seemed to share the same opinion. Many of them had pointed out that if the aliens actually did have a starship within the solar system, it would mean that humanity would be talking to the aliens in person, perhaps within as little as a week. Others wondered if it was the opening moves in an alien invasion, although they were dismissed as roundly paranoid. Skywatch – the under-funded organisation charged with watching for asteroids that might impact the Earth and ruin humanity's day – hadn't picked up the alien ship before it had started sending the signal. Why would anyone, the bloggers asked, bother to announce the invasion before launching the attack? The paranoid ones countered that perhaps the signal was a challenge to do battle and the discussions had rapidly degenerated into flame wars. Abigail couldn't decide what she thought, personally. A million light years seemed a long way to come for a fight.

She looked over at the cameras the Fox Network had sent along and concealed a smile. The networks – and the streaming video that would be sent over the net – had argued over how many cameras should be placed within the chamber. They'd finally conceded – Daisy Fairchild, whatever else she happened to be, was a formidable negotiator – that all of the networks would have immediate access to the footage shot by one team, chosen by lot. WNN would be watching Fox like a hawk, suspecting that a quick-thinking newsman might conceal footage to give Fox an exclusive, but it hardly mattered. The press conference would be going out live.

"If I could have your attention, please," a voice said. Abigail turned her head to see Daisy Fairchild standing on the stage, projecting her voice over the crowd. She was clearly an old pro at holding press conferences, for she ignored all of the shouted questions and waited patiently for them to settle down. It made a change from the normal pushy – if not downright rude – behaviour that most people allowed reporters to get away with, but then, Daisy had something they wanted desperately. "I have a short statement and then I will answer questions."

The room became quiet as the reporters settled down to listen. "Three hours ago, a signal of unknown origin was detected by one of SETI's researchers," she said, very calmly. Abigail could tell that she was delighted, and scared. "The signal was put through the most extensive verification procedure we have developed in order to confirm its origins. We were able to triangulate the source of the signal and confirm that it did not originate from any known space probe launched from Earth."

There was a chilling, pregnant silence. "We have confirmed our results with hundreds of other observatory stations around the world," Daisy continued. "There is no longer any room for doubt. The signal is coming from an extraterrestrial source."

Abigail winced as the room erupted in uproar, with reporters shouting questions at Daisy, and then yelling at each other to shut up and let her answer their questions. Daisy waited, apparently untroubled by the roar of the crowd, until the sound slowly died away, allowing her to speak again. She seemed more amused than anything else.

"The signal may take years to decipher," she concluded, "but one thing is clear. From this moment on, the human race is no longer alone."

The reporters kept shouting out questions, drowning each other out in an echoing tirade. Abigail half-covered her ears to block out the din, knowing that Daisy wasn't speaking, but waiting for the noise to die down again. Some of the reporters seemed to be in flat denial and were howling accusations that SETI was telling lies as a publicity stunt, or that it was covering up the true nature of the aliens. Abigail didn't believe either theory. Even if some madman at SETI had come up with a plan to fake an alien signal, she couldn't see every other observatory in the world going along with it, particularly not to please SETI. Plenty of scientists regarded SETI as an upstart and would have been quite happy to put the boot in. As for covering up the true nature of the aliens…well, unless SETI had already deciphered the signal, how could they have even begun a cover up?

"So," one of the reporters managed to say, finally. "Does that mean that they have a ship in the solar system?"

"It is one possibility," Daisy acknowledged. "There are others. We could be dealing with some alien version of the Voyager or Pioneer space probes" – Abigail was unsurprised to see that most of the reporters looked blank at those famous names – "or perhaps we're picking up an alien signal coming out of a wormhole, or a space-time distortion. We have been unable, as yet, to get any confirmation from either orbiting or ground-based telescopes. They've been booked up for the next month and untangling them is proving to be a hassle."

One that might be resolved just by dropping that comment in the midst of the media's feeding frenzy, Abigail reflected, and then a nasty thought occurred to her. The alien signal wasn't coming from another star, but from an alien starship, one that had somehow stumbled across Earth's solar system. The timing was suspicious, to say the least. Seventeen days ago, the United States had begun what looked like a covert military mobilisation, as if the government expected big trouble. Had they known that there was an alien starship in the solar system?

The thought seemed ludicrous, yet it made an alarming amount of sense. The increased number of reservists being called back to duty, the sudden changes in military patterns, the deployment of antimissile systems all across the United States…and, strangest of all, the recent changes in the military's organisation. There were ten uniformed commands under the Department of Defence, including the United States Strategic Command, the Air Force Space Command and United States Northern Command, all of which held some degree of responsibility for space defence. The latter, in particular, was closely linked with Canada. If the reports were to be believed, the United States Strategic Command had effectively taken over the other two, with nary a protest. It made no sense to her.

She knew, from an old source that used to work for the USAF, that all ten of the uniformed commands regarded each other as bitter enemies, particularly when it came to funding. Any attempt to merge the three should have resulted in a particularly nasty political catfight – there were plenty of politicians with an interest in keeping all three commands operative – and yet, no catfight had materialised. Her source had said, quite clearly, that the junior and middle-ranking levels were angry and suspicious, but the senior levels had moved rapidly to squash protests and relieve people who refused to play ball. There hadn't even been a whisper out of the politicians, which was even stranger. The only politician who could keep his mouth shut was a dead politician. Why had they suddenly abandoned such pork barrels?

Another reporter shouted out a question. "Do you believe that the aliens pose a threat?"

Daisy waited until the new uproar had died down. "There is no reason to believe that the aliens present any kind of threat," she said, carefully. "They've come a very long way to say hello to us. We could at least treat them with some dignity."

She leaned forward, looking into the camera. "I appeal to all of humanity to refrain from sending any signals back to the alien spacecraft," she said. "We need to agree on a unified response from the planet. This is too important to allow nationalism and our petty regional bigotries to get in the way. The alien message is meant for all of humanity."

"Take it to the UN," someone shouted, provoking another argument. Some reporters agreed with the unknown speaker, while others pointed out that the aliens would be dead of old age before the UN ever came to a decision about what to send back to the alien ship. Abigail had covered the UN's operations in some parts of the globe and hadn't been impressed. They'd probably send the aliens a message so condescending that the aliens would immediately declare war. Why not? They'd done it in Africa and the Middle East in the past.

"The key question of how we are to respond will have to be debated worldwide," Daisy agreed. "I do not know how the governments will respond."

She seemed to smile at the reporters. "And now I would like to introduce the young woman who was responsible for this great discovery," she said. "Please allow me to present Karen Lawton to you."

Abigail smiled at the girl as she stepped nervously onto the stage. She didn't look old enough to have a period, let alone work away from home at SETI. Part of her pitied the girl, for she was about to discover that her life was no longer her own, but the rest of her mind envied her. Karen was going to fly high in the new world order. The President himself would want to meet her, the Secretary-General of the UN and the Pope would want to shake her hand…hell, and she'd probably serve as a centrefold for the sexy side of science. The fame and fortune would destroy her. Abigail had seen it before, when people won the fame lottery, or even just millions of dollars.

Poor girl, she thought, tightly. *Poor little girl*.

Silently, she composed her story in her head. It would probably be presented on the net first and only then on television. The reporting cycle was so tight these days that it was no wonder that the bloggers found so many mistakes to point out – and gloat over, as if the media had made them deliberately. Who had time for fact-checking these days?

The questions rolled over Karen, who looked as if she wanted to flee. "What will you do now? What does the alien message say? Do you have a boyfriend? What do you do when you're not at SETI…?"

Very poor girl, Abigail thought.

———

Only Daisy's hand on her arm stopped Karen from fleeing at once. Modern technology might have partly eliminated the need for flashbulbs, but several camera men were still using them, making her blink every time they took a photograph. Her legs wobbled alarmingly and she could barely look down at the eyes following her every move. It felt as if she was being studied, dissected, stripped bare and then filmed in intimate detail, leaving her a shivering wreck. There were people who loved being the centre of global attention. Karen almost wished, now, that she'd allowed someone else to claim the credit.

Her mind was spinning, as if she was slightly drunk. The alien message kept echoing in her brain. They'd *wanted* it to be understood, she knew; it was the only explanation that made sense. She'd once watched an episode of *The Simpsons*, where a weird green alien had announced that he was actually speaking his native language, but by remarkable coincidence both his language and English were exactly the same, yet that was extremely unlikely in real life. She'd worked on the assumption that it would take years to decipher the message; hell, she hadn't even told Daisy what the message said.

She somehow steadied herself and looked down at the reporters. It was a mistake. Their sheer presence overwhelmed her, leaving her mind staggering as they called out question after question, all blurring together into one ghastly noise. Her mind snatched out individual questions and recoiled. She would have understood questions about the signal, or about SETI itself, but who *cared* about her personal life? What right had they to demand that she shared intimate details with them? She recoiled and felt Daisy's hand, as hard as a pair of handcuffs, keeping her in place. She *hated* Daisy at that moment, hated her and hated herself for agreeing to be interviewed in the first place. She should never have agreed to face the baying horde. It was worse than being raped.

"Babe," one of the reporters shouted. Karen allowed herself to believe that he was from one of the tabloids, or some other newspaper that made its money from exploiting people. "Are you well?"

"No," she said, wrenching her arm away from Daisy and running off the stage. The handful of security guards Daisy had placed in the room to keep the reporters under control – "animals," she'd called them, and she'd been right – didn't attempt to prevent her leaving. She ran through the door, into a small waiting room that was normally empty, and collapsed into a comfortable armchair, sobbing. She'd been a fool. She shouldn't have tried to be famous.

She felt a light touch on her shoulder and looked up. Daisy was standing there, her face twisted into a sympathetic smile. She was the last person Karen wanted to see at that moment – if ever – but there was no way to escape, short of running out of the building and mailing SETI her resignation in the mail. The Director looked oddly compassionate, yet Karen couldn't forgive her for putting her in front of the reporters.

"I suppose you're here to spank me," she snarled, finally. It was easy to be angry at Daisy. The Director was probably hacked off about the ruined press conference and mad at her too. "What did you tell the bastards?"

"I told them that they'd pushed you too far and that perhaps there would be a private interview later," Daisy said. "It wouldn't go down very well if they caused you to collapse in public. You're hot stuff, girl. Taking your jeans down and spanking you would look lousy on my resume."

Karen couldn't believe it, but she actually laughed, as if it were funny. She hadn't even realised that she could destroy Daisy's career, just by saying the wrong thing to a reporter, or someone else now that she was famous.

"I'm sorry about that as well," Daisy admitted. She reached out and put a hand on Karen's shoulder. "I should have prepared you more to face the animals. I just thought that they would show a little more decency to you. I should have known better."

Karen shrugged, dislodging Daisy's hand. She'd grown up in a world where everything from the President's bowel movements to what underwear the rich and famous were wearing was public knowledge. She'd seen how reporters could destroy lives with ease. They'd destroyed Princess Diana and her family, hounded every sitting President until the day he'd left the Oval Office and wrecked countless lives with false charges. The cost of fame was that her life would never be the same again.

"You should have," she said, bitterly. "There's something else."

Daisy frowned, but waited for her to speak. "I took a look at the alien message and tried to decipher it," she said. "I managed it easily. The message is in English."

She looked up into Daisy's eyes. "It was easy to understand," she said. "They're asking for a meeting."

Chapter Eighteen

It was perhaps the most famous broadcast in history. President Roosevelt had spoken to the country in the days after the attack on Pearl Harbour and President Bush had spoken just after 9/11, but how could the two most infamous sneak attacks in history compare with the announcement that aliens existed. Indeed, not only did they exist, but they were also on their way to Earth. Alex didn't envy the President at all. He had to reassure the people and try to prevent panic, yet also warn them that there might be dark times ahead. The Tiger Team had gathered in the communal lounge to watch the address.

The President stood in front of a podium in the White House Press Room, flanked by two of his most senior Cabinet members. The Secretary of Defence looked grim as ever, while the Secretary of State was smiling nervously. Alex knew that planning cells within the State Department had started looking seriously at the implications of contact with aliens – particularly the long-term contact that the aliens had promised – and he'd seen some of their projections. Very few of them had been cheerful. Even if the United States was not invaded directly, the loss of much of the rest of the world would be devastating. The United States, like it or not, was heavily interlocked with the entire world – it was hard to find a place where the US had no interests – and the aliens would cause chaos by landing anywhere, even the South Pole.

"My fellow Americans," the President said. President Chalk wasn't known for long speeches, to the dismay of some of his political advisors and the glee of his opponents. He'd had the last laugh as the American people had evidently felt that electing a blunt, plain-spoken ex-soldier was better than electing a smooth-talking snake oil salesman. "I must confirm that government stations have detected an alien signal from space, transmitted by an alien spacecraft approaching the Earth. The human race is no longer alone."

Alex watched the reporters in the room staring at him. Many of them had clung, against all logic, to the belief that the alien spacecraft was a giant hoax. They knew better now, for there was no way that President Chalk would lie to the entire country about aliens. The panic was already setting in all over America, although it hadn't turned violent, apart from a spat of nasty incidents. People were stockpiling food, supplies and weapons, often in defiance of calls for calm. Alex privately suspected that it would get worse when it settled in that a massive alien starship was approaching the planet.

"There is no need for panic," the President continued. "The aliens have asked us to meet with them to discuss the future. There are few reasons to believe that the aliens pose any kind of threat. However, in order to take proper precautions, I am – with the full concurrence of Congress – declaring a full mobilisation and recalling all reservists to their duties. The National Guard will be federalised and brought to full strength and we will consider recalling troops from overseas. If there is any threat, no matter how minute, we will face it as a nation of civilised people, not as savages who are afraid of the dark."

Alex scowled. He'd advised Jones to advise the President to admit the full truth, to tell the world how the aliens had invited him onboard their craft and offered to divide the entire world with him, but the President had rejected the advice. He could see the President's logic – admitting the truth would cause a global panic, as well as destroying any hope of reaching a global agreement on how to counter the aliens – yet he had a nasty feeling that it would come back to bite them on the behind. The only advantage was that the President could take the mobilisation into the open and they would no longer have to worry about a reporter putting all the pieces together.

"The orbiting space telescopes are attempting to obtain pictures of the visiting spacecraft now and we will make them public as soon as possible," the President concluded. "This is a great nation, and humanity is a great people, and we will welcome our new friends to Earth together. I have faith that we will all meet the new challenge of encountering life from beyond the stars. I will now take questions."

Jones snapped the television off as the reporters began to ask questions. "The President will be busy with the scum of the universe for the next few hours," he said, sharply. Alex smiled. If there was a life form lower than a reporter, it probably wasn't on the approaching alien mothership. "He will want to confer with us as soon as he escapes the zoo, so we need to have something to tell him. Alex, what do you make of the message?"

Alex looked down at the USAF-issue PDA in his hand. "It's very informative and, at the same time, it tells us nothing," he said. "Listen. *To the people of Earth, we come in peace. We bring you greetings from a far star and offer you gifts to facilitate your entry into the wider community surrounding you. We ask that you allow us to speak with your United Nations as soon as it is convenient. We await your reply and look forward to a long and productive association between our races.*"

He put down the PDA and looked up. "That message was very clever," he admitted. "First, the delivery; the message wasn't just sent in English, but in Russian, Chinese and French as well. It can't be a coincidence. That's the four languages spoken by all five members of the United Nations Security Council. The message isn't just intended for wide distribution around Earth, it's a subtle warning that they know us very well and won't be fooled if we try something clever, like trying to mislead them. They also knew, I suspect, who would pick it up. Even if SETI had been closed down in the wake of the crash, other radio telescopes would have picked up the signal and it would have been out. They wanted the message to be detected.

"Second, the message itself," he continued. "They tell us, directly, that they come in peace. That very phase is part of our culture – *we come in peace* – and, again, it shows how much they've studied us. They tell us nothing about what they're bringing, or what they want, but they promise introduction to a wider community, hinting that they're not alone either and that there are other alien races out there. It may be true or false – we don't have any way to tell. They phrase it as a request, rather than a demand, increasing the chances that we'll accept their message without demur. And, finally, they put the ball in our court and ask us to reply."

Jones spoke into the silence. "The President has been talking with various world leaders, but some groups have already sent messages back to the aliens, hitting them with everything from promises of worship to demands that they back off and withdraw from the solar system," he said. "They're looking at ways to prevent others from trying to communicate with the aliens, yet he wasn't optimistic. It won't be long before lunatics like Iran's leaders or Chavez start sending their own messages to the aliens."

"They're probably going to be very confused aliens," Santini said, lightly. "I had to spend a few months reading through NSA's signal intercepts and much of it was the most boring old crap imaginable. If every nut with a CB radio starts trying to transmit to the aliens, they're going to start thinking that we're a planet of idiots, or fools."

"I've been looking at the text of the signal," Gayle said. "They've given us nothing that we can use to speculate effectively – we don't even know what they intend to speak to the UN about."

"A demand for surrender, perhaps," Alex said. He'd been wondering about the same thing. "The offer of gifts will be attractive to many nations."

"Quite," Jones agreed. "Gayle, you saw their computer models of human behaviour. How well *do* they know us?"

Gayle looked down at her hands. "It's hard to answer that question with any degree of certainty," she said. "Humans have been attempting to model their own behaviour since the science of psychology was…"

"Brought out of nothing by overpaid headshrinkers," Santini said, coldly.

Jones silenced him with a glance. "Carry on, Gayle," he said. "I'm sure we can refrain from further interruptions."

"It rarely worked," Gayle said. "In fiction, psychologists developed Psychohistory, the science of human behaviour in large numbers, to allow them to model out and influence the development of humanity for thousands of years into the future. The real world isn't so neat and tidy. Even Asimov, the founder of the concept, admitted as much when he created the Mule, who wrecked the Foundation and the Seldon Plan. A low-probability event allowed a new tyrant to come to power and reshape the galaxy to his will, not that of the Foundation. It happens in real life as well.

"Hitler was one such example, a person we were required to study carefully," she continued. "Hitler was born in a world that could have avoided the First World War, yet chose to fight it instead. He moved to Germany to avoid serving Austria-Hungary, yet ended up in the German Army. He showed considerable physical bravery and narrowly escaped death when he was gassed. Germany lost the war – if Germany had won, Hitler might never have been anything more than yet another Corporal – and he found fertile ground for his poisonous ideology. The Great Depression comes along and provides him a boost forward, yet if a handful of German politicians had shown more backbone, or determination, he might never have risen to power.

"And even then, he made decisions that could not have been predicted. It was Hitler, more than anyone else, who drove the world into war, yet what would have happened if he'd made the rational decision at any number of decisive moments? Or what if he'd been killed in one of any number of assassination attempts? Or if Japan hadn't gone after us, therefore allowing Hitler to avoid deciding if he should declare war on us as well? I submit to you that the aliens do not have a valid science."

She ran her hand through her hair tiredly. "There are two problems they would have had to overcome," she explained. "The need to predict irrational decision making and the need to account for every possible variable. The absence of the latter makes irrational – at least from their point of view – decision making more likely. I highly doubt that their models are as good as they claim. My own analysis suggests that they may have a point in the short term, but there are already feedback trends working to correct some of our problems. They may not have accounted for them."

"I think we're getting a little off-topic," Jones said, finally. "Should we agree to meet the aliens at the UN?"

"I doubt that we have a choice," Alex pointed out. "I don't think that the President could order the UN to refuse to meet with the aliens, if they chose to do so. We could argue against it, but…hellfire!"

He scowled down at the table, composing himself. "They've put us in a position where any attempt to refuse to meet with the aliens will become a political liability," he said, angrily. "The offer of gifts…well, the aliens could give us something that would really upset the economy, so *naturally* the Evil American Government will want to prevent the rest of the world from getting their hands on it. It will make us look like the bad guys to the rest of the world."

"I see," Jones said, slowly. "Why would they bother trying to make us look like the baddies?"

"It splits up any potential alliance against them," Alex said. "NATO is supposed to react as a group to any attack on any individual member nation, yet if the aliens convince the world that we're the enemy, the other nations may refuse to become involved with the war. The problem with democratic politicians is that they won't do anything they think will be unpopular… and helping us, if we're seen as the bad guys, will be very unpopular indeed."

"It may not matter," Santini pointed out. "What could the rest of NATO do to help us even if they wanted to? We're not talking about the War on Terror or a skirmish along the Mexican Border, or even an outright invasion of Europe by Russia. We're talking about an alien invasion force using advanced technology and a billion aliens who want to settle on our world. If they concentrate merely on us – on America – what can Europe do to help us?"

"Very little," Jones said. He shook his head. "Leave it for the moment. What other gifts can they offer us?"

"Superconductors," Neil Frandsen said, suddenly. He smiled at their expressions. "My team has been working away at the alien craft ever since we brought them into the base and one thing we've managed to identify is a working super-efficient superconductor system. I won't go into details – I know you hate technobabble – but it should be fairly easy to duplicate and we're working on building up experimental models that can be developed at another location. If we manage to get them to work, we could change the world – again - within a couple of years."

"Through superconductors?"

"Oh, yes," Frandsen said. "You see, with a really efficient superconductor, we could create – among other things – very good batteries, storing vast amounts of power. We could fit them into cars and cut our need for gas radically, or load them into tanks and other military vehicles. The pollution count would go down sharply, pleasing the greens, while the whole oil dependency would just vanish, pleasing the right. Most interestingly of all, a working superconductor could be used for a surge output, which could be used to power lasers vastly more efficient than anything we can deploy today. It seems a simple concept – batteries are hardly warp drive or matter transmission – but the effects would be radical."

He leaned forward. "And that wouldn't really alter the power balance between us and them," he added. "Even if we learned how to duplicate them for ourselves, it wouldn't be something we could use immediately to build our own spacecraft or weapons. We're still no closer to figuring out how to duplicate their drive, although we do have working computer models of their gravity fields now, allowing us to track their craft with greater efficiently. We couldn't take what they gave us and use it to knife them in the back."

"Lasers," Santini mused. "Could they have high-powered lasers as well?"

"Almost certainly," Frandsen said. "I would be surprised if they didn't have them, although I don't know if they use them as weapons."

"They probably would," Santini said. He hit the table in sudden frustration. "Why are they just playing with us?" He demanded. "Why don't they just invade?"

"Perhaps because they can't just overwhelm us like *that*," Alex said, snapping his fingers. He was surprised that it was Santini who was showing signs of stress – his career had included dozens of secret missions in places most people would be surprised to learn that American forces had operated at all – but cabin fever was getting to them all. "It's something to hope for."

"We've got the latest images of the mothership," Jones said, in the uncomfortable silence. He clicked a remote control and put up the first image. It looked like nothing more than a handful of stars, were it not for the arrow someone had drawn on the image, helpfully pointing out the alien mothership. Jones clicked again and again, bringing the mothership into view. It was massive, yet somehow it was hard to make out real detail. "The best that NASA can suggest is that the spacecraft is surrounded by a force field that makes taking photographs of the hull tricky. No one has any idea of how they're doing it or how to compensate for it."

"They're using their drive field," Frandsen said, with cool certainty. "They're warping the fabric of space itself around their vessel."

Jones blinked, but waved the matter aside. "NASA was able to come up with some figures," he said. "The mothership is *big*, the size of a large asteroid. It's quite easy to believe that there are over a billion aliens on that motherfucker."

"No wonder they're running out of resources," Alex commented. "It might explain why they tried to bargain with us and then launched this… psychological warfare offensive. They simply don't have time for a long struggle for dominance and they can't risk destroying the Earth. They need the planet as much as we do."

"I hope you're right," Frandsen said. "It would be easy enough for them to establish bases on asteroids, on Mars, even on the Moon. They've certainly got the technology. And there's something else to think about."

He smiled, without humour. "If the mothership was to be destroyed in orbit, the results would be unpleasant," he said. "I read an article that stated – quite rightly – that the destruction of the Death Star in *Return of the Jedi* would have exterminated the little furry creatures on the planet below, with the wreckage falling into the atmosphere and striking the surface. We're in the same boat. If that ship were to be destroyed…we'd all die too."

Jane spoke into the silence. "You're all forgetting one detail," she said. "They're coming here. How long do we have?"

"Not long," Jones said. "The ship may alter its speed, but if there's no significant change, in six weeks that bastard will be orbiting the Earth. Just six weeks…"

Chapter Nineteen

Area 52, Nevada, USA

Day 25

"I've got the popcorn," Alex said. "Did you bring the wine?"

It was probably the oddest date he'd ever been on, but as long as they were not permitted to leave Area 52, there was little choice. He'd convinced Jane to watch the World News Network's *In Focus*, a weekly show that focused on the issues of the day. Inevitably, the WNN had chosen to focus on the arrival of the alien mothership - and the alien request for a meeting.

"Only a single bottle of crap I borrowed from the dispensary for medical reasons," Jane said, with a wink. Alex chuckled as she passed over the bottle of cheap wine and two glasses. "I don't know if we can get drunk on that stuff, but we could have a lot of fun trying."

"How true," Alex said, flipping through the channels until he found WNN's live feed. The introduction music was already playing as the screen focused in on a woman holding a microphone, facing four guests who looked uncomfortable under the cameras. Alex recognised one of them, another was wearing a General's dress uniform – and a beard, in violation of regulations – but the other two were strangers. "Here we go."

"Welcome to *In Focus*," the woman announced, as the camera closed in on her. It was probably just a coincidence that she was showing a remarkable amount of cleavage. "I'm your host, Mariko Tam. With me tonight are former General Dave Howery, US Army, Father Andrew, Chairman of the American Interfaith Relations Congress, Thomas Anderson, the well-known science-fiction author and Doctor Gary Young…"

"*Professor* Young," Young injected.

"A leading researcher into UFOs and alien contact," Mariko concluded. "Later, we will be looking into Congress's hearings on NASA's failure to deliver a working space program and rumours of who will be chosen to meet the aliens. First, however, a brief rundown on everything that's happened since the world turned upside down."

Alex snorted as a brief montage of news clippings, from the SETI press conference to the President's speech, played as the narrator explained everything that had happened since the first signal had been detected. It sounded bland to him – it only included information that was in the public domain – but it allowed Jane a chance to pour the wine. Alex took a sniff, considered suggesting that it should be poured back into the horse, and then decided to drink it anyway. In his experience, news shows involving UFO researchers tended to get exciting.

Jane touched his shoulder as she sat down next to him. "Do you know him?"

"Gary Young?" Alex asked. "Only by reputation. I was never allowed to go public as the Air Force's man on UFOs. He's got a reputation for being a sober researcher, not a crackpot, but he firmly believes in Roswell and dead aliens in the Pentagon."

"It's not as stupid as it sounds," Jane pointed out reasonably. "We do have dead aliens in this complex."

Alex shrugged as Mariko turned back to her guests. "Mr Anderson, as a well-known science-fiction author," she said, "what do you think this means for us?"

Anderson was a young man, around thirty, Alex decided. He had short dark hair and a goatee. When he spoke, it was with a distantly English accent. "Everything will change," he said, firmly. "The discovery of alien life alone would reshape the world, but the aliens are coming here, for good or ill. The aliens say that they come in peace, yet they cannot help but have a massive effect on our society. The entire world will change when they land."

Mariko smiled at him. "Do you believe that they are hostile?"

"There's no evidence one way or the other," Anderson said. His voice sounded oddly stilted, as if he didn't quite believe his own words. "It may not matter. The first contact between the Europeans and the Indians – the Native Americans – were devastating for the Indians. They never really recovered from the shock and ended up marginalised on lands the white man didn't want to take. The white men didn't always mean ill – there were missionaries who wanted to convert the Indians to the Christian faith, believing that without conversion they would go to hell – yet it hardly mattered. The impact on their culture was staggering.

"These days, when we locate a tribe that may have remained unaware of the wider world, we try to leave them alone, or introduce ourselves to them gently," he continued. "The effects can still be staggering. We may find ourselves in the same place even if the aliens mean well. If they're hostile, of course, all bets are off."

"It seems unlikely that an advanced race – and they must be advanced, because we can be fairly sure that they didn't come from our solar system – would harbour hostile intentions," Gary Young pointed out. He was a balding middle-aged man, but there was a spark of vindication in his eyes. Alex knew that the UFO Community had been indulging in gloating and claiming that the discovery of the alien mothership proved that they'd been right all along. "The more advanced a society becomes, the less likely it is to be so…undeveloped as to harbour hostile intentions."

"Human history says otherwise," General Howery said, sharply. "Who put a man in space first? The Soviet Union, a state that was a prison camp above and a mass grave below. There's no iron law of history that says that an advanced society must have advanced morals – or even that we will agree on the same morals."

"True," Anderson agreed. "The Spanish had brutally simple intentions when they probed Spanish America; they wanted gold, gold and more gold. They destroyed two mighty civilisations in the process. They were more advanced than their opponents and crushed them with ease."

"And let us not forget that terrorists used advanced technology, technology we take for granted, to start a war with us," General Howery said. "The aliens might have stolen the technology off another race or a subgroup of their own race. We dare not assume that they're friendly just because they are more advanced than ourselves."

"They came all this way," Young countered. "Why would they have done that unless they wanted to trade? I doubt that interstellar conquest is cost-effective."

"We know nothing about their technology," Anderson said. "We do not know how much it cost them, relatively speaking, to launch that ship at us. We may be looking at a project so expensive that it bankrupted an entire solar system, or something that cost them the equivalent of a handful of dimes. In the time of Queen Elizabeth I, sending a ship to Asia or America cost plenty of money and the results were sometimes unrewarding. Two hundred years later, travel all around the world was commonplace and the British Empire was built on trade. The advancement of technology propelled America forward and turned the world into a smaller place.

"We know nothing about the economics of interstellar travel," he added. "They may be interested in trading, or they may be interested in invasion, or they may just want to say hello. I believe that it is dangerous to assume anything until we know for sure."

"How true," Mariko said, into the silence. "Gary, what is the UFO Community's reaction to the discovery of a *genuine* alien ship?"

"There had actually been an upsurge in UFO reports for the three weeks *prior* to SETI's announcement," Young said. "The reports literally skyrocketed after the announcement and…well, most of them were fakes. There was a man who claimed that he'd been taken onboard a flying saucer by two women with pointy ears and invited to have sex with both of them." There were some chuckles from the audience. "It's always been hard to separate out real reports from fakes and the discovery of a real alien craft has only made our task harder. We do believe, however, that the upsurge in reports before the craft became public knowledge is indicative of alien interest in our society. They certainly knew who to talk to."

"They did," Mariko agreed. "And what do you people feel that the aliens have in mind?"

"The UFO Community is split on the issue," Young admitted. "There are some who believe that the aliens are friendly and welcome the chance to meet with them. There are some who have drawn up elaborate scenarios featuring alien abduction and crossbreeding and fear that the aliens are hostile. There's no consensus and probably never will be."

"Oh?" Anderson asked. "I used to read a lot about UFOs. The little grey aliens were supposed to have abducted thousands of people and put them though humiliating and painful medical examinations. If those reports were all true, surely it suggests that the aliens are hostile? They certainly seem to show a frightening lack of concern for human feelings."

"That is something that the UFO Community has debated for years," Young said, slowly. "We may well have misunderstood what the aliens were doing. Let me give you a simple example. I went to my doctor for a full check-up and he gave me a full examination, which was rather humiliating although not that painful. I couldn't help feeling violated when he examined my delicate parts even though I *knew* that he meant no harm. It was very different from being arrested at an airport and strip-searched – perhaps even cavity searched – by a security guard. In one, it was a medical procedure that you would consent to; in the other, it was a procedure forced upon you out of suspicion. The procedure is not that different in the two cases, but you didn't consent to be searched and would have found it humiliating – and it would have made you furious.

"Abductions – the reports we find creditable – tend to take place at night, when the victim's mind is often hazy and tired," he added. "It is quite possible that they gave details that their mind made up – not lying, but sincerely believing their own words – or that the experience was less frightening than they believed it to be. Worse, most of the details of abductions have fallen into the public mind and victims, under hypnosis, have constructed stories that are far too similar to *real* accounts."

Alex nodded in agreement - he'd made the same point - as Young launched into a lecture on the problems associated with hypnosis. "He's one of the people who believe that aliens are good and people in the government have been covering up their visits," he said, taking another sip of his wine. It didn't improve with age. "He generally gives the aliens the benefit of the doubt."

"He does have a point," Jane said. "There are medical procedures that are frightening even when you're fully informed."

"True," Alex agreed. He winked at her. "The problem is that if you added up all the different types of alien reported by witnesses, you might well end up with over a thousand different types of alien. They can't all be real. The discovery of the mothership and real aliens doesn't mean that everything ever written about UFOs and alien contact is real. One of my predecessors used to wonder if the aliens were deliberately sowing false information to confuse the human investigators."

"Why not?" Jane asked. "*Our* aliens are doing the same thing."

"If we assume that the alien abductions are real," General Howery was saying as Alex looked back at the television, "we have to accept that the aliens have repeatedly committed acts of war. The purpose of the military is to defend the citizens of the United States. Taking civilians from their homes for medical experiments – *abducting* our citizens – is very definitely a hostile act. We would have to assume that massive ship is carrying millions of invaders and treat it accordingly."

Mariko spoke before Young could protest. "Do you believe that the aliens pose a direct military threat?"

"There is no way to know," Howery said. "The President's decision to mobilise is a simple – and very wise – precautionary measure. If the aliens are limited to moving only at slower-than-light speeds, it seems unlikely that creating an interstellar empire would be a viable task. We didn't develop empires until we developed the ability to keep the colonies together – and we revolted and threw off the yoke of Britain, despite Britain having far more military power than the Thirteen Colonies. Waging war at such a distance was an impossible task.

"If the aliens *can* move at faster-than-light speeds, it is quite likely that interstellar empires – or political structures – can and do exist," he added. "We will have to wait and see."

"And if it does come down to a fight," Mariko said, "could we win?"

Howery's face went blank. "You should know that I couldn't speculate on that," he said, coldly. "You never know who might be listening to this broadcast."

"Smart man," Alex commented. He'd placed General Howery now. "It's almost a shame that he had to retire."

"We have not yet heard from our religious representative," Mariko said, carefully. "Father Andrew, what is your position on alien contact?"

"We're all very excited," Father Andrew said. He looked like an older version of Father Ted. "The Church has long accepted the existence of other forms of intelligent life – angels and demons being among the most prevalent – and the thought of sharing information with religions that developed on another planet is fascinating. I understand that some of the more fundamentalist believers are questioning the…humanity of the aliens, or claiming that they pose a threat to human religions, but I like to think that they merely pose a challenge, one that we will overcome."

Mariko smiled. "A challenge?"

"We are told that God created man in his own image," Father Andrew said. "The aliens, however, might look nothing like us. Are they too created in God's image?"

He leaned forward. "Some of my fellows believe that the aliens will have holy books akin to our own," he added. "Others believe that the story of Jesus will have its counterpart among alien religions. Even more believe that the aliens will have no religion and we have a duty to bring them the Word of God. Learning the truth and then deciding how to act on it will be a new challenge."

"You've used that word twice, Father," Anderson said. "Has it occurred to you that the aliens might attempt to impose their religion on us?"

"Humans have long attempted to force their religions on other humans, and so you may well be right," Father Andrew said. "We could hardly complain if the aliens treated us as we treated each other. I believe, however, that the alien religion would find no fertile ground on Earth – assuming, of course, that it even exists – and I don't think that the aliens will attempt to try. It would be uncivilised."

"Human history is also full of humans who have acted against their religions in the name of what they believed was a greater good," Anderson added. "The aliens may see it the same way."

"They may," Father Andrew agreed. "I do not believe, however, that God will ask us to undertake an impossible task."

Anderson snorted. "Ah, but who decides that the task is impossible?"

"Thomas, you gained renown with your *Moonstruck* science-fiction series and your *There'll Always Be An England* alternate history series," Mariko said, quickly. "How do you believe science-fiction will respond to alien contact?"

"We've been planning it for years," Anderson said. There were some chuckles from the audience. "I do not believe that there is a possible scenario that hasn't been explored by one writer or another. Yes, a great deal of quality science-fiction will be invalidated at a stroke, but that doesn't mean that science-fiction will be useless. We have writers who have explored the uses of new metals and materials without ever seeing them developed; books we can use to plot out the colonisation of the solar system. Classics such as *Footfall* or *Higher Education* will still have relevance even after alien contact."

He paused. "There is a more interesting development," he added. "The entertainment industry pumps out hundreds of old movies a week. The Sci-Fi Channel was due to show *Earth Versus The Flying Saucers* on Tuesday, until they pulled it and replaced it with *ET*. I had a look through the listings for the next week and there's no *Independence Day*, no *Alien*, nothing involving hostile aliens or alien invasion at all. What do you think that means?"

"Perhaps the executives believe that the aliens will be annoyed by alien invasion movies," Young said. "I believe that movies concerning the Nazi Period in Germany were pulled from overseas broadcasts for the same reason."

"They'll probably find them laughable," Anderson said. "I do think that someone is trying to shape public perception and portray aliens as being friendly."

Mariko leaned forward, exposing the tops of her breasts. "Do *you* believe that they are friendly?"

Anderson considered it. "The aliens may be more like us than they seem," he said. "They may not be wise monks or savage warriors, but *people*. They may have their hopes and fears, their heroes and their villains, their…"

"But do you think they're friendly?"

"I believe that they will want to deal with us on the best terms possible, to them," Anderson said, shortly. "Gary had a point. They may feel that they're doing the right thing and we may feel that we're being cheated. We may find ourselves selling Manhattan Island for a handful of beads. We have to deal with them carefully and watch our backs."

General Howery smiled. "And we need to avoid giving offence," he added. "They have space superiority by default. They won't need antimatter bombs and nanotech to seriously damage Earth. We may have to adjust to living in a universe where the real powers are alien races born on a dozen worlds thousands of light years away."

"And if the aliens are truly hostile," Mariko asked, "will we fight?"

"Yes," Howery said, flatly.

"But there is no reason to assume that they are hostile," Young said. "We shouldn't greet them at gunpoint."

"Human history suggests that any contact between an advanced and a primitive society will end badly," Howery said. "We need to make preparations before it is too late."

Chapter Twenty

The Oval Office was supposed to be soundproofed, but the President could hear the chanting of the protesters outside the gates, demanding that the alien contact be as peaceable as humanity could make it. Thousands of protesters had made their way to Washington and the FBI was reporting that tens of thousands more were on their way, protesting against the military preparations to greet the aliens. He'd watched footage earlier of protest marches through Memphis – calling for the aliens to bring back Elvis, of all things – and other, similar protests in a dozen world capitals. The general mood on the streets seemed to be a demand for a peaceful solution and the President almost envied them, the young men and women who thought that they could change the world. They didn't know about the UFO crash or about his flight to the alien mothership or – for that matter – the alien statement that they wanted the Earth. The protesters were being told all kinds of New Age bullshit about how the aliens would bring paradise to Earth, yet the President thought he detected a note of fear under the howling. A fear that the military-industrial complex would find a way to cheat humanity out of its glorious destiny among the stars, or, perhaps, a fear that the government would start a war. It didn't matter that both beliefs were insane. All that mattered was that people believed it.

"We do not have much time," he said, shortly. Now that his entire Cabinet knew about the approaching alien mothership, he'd decided to brief them on the crashed UFO and his later meeting with the aliens. It had prevented a nasty crisis when some of his handpicked Cabinet had attempted to propose reasonable solutions, unaware of the information that drove the President's decision-making. "I have to meet the other permanent members of the United Nations Security Council in two days. What do we tell them?"

"The truth," Jones said. The little man was an old friend, someone who formed a bridge between the civil and military administrations. The President tended to trust his advice. "We don't know if any of them have been contacted as well, so we lay all of our cards on the table and warn them that the aliens aren't coming in peace. They're not this new…Third World Alliance, Mr President. They know that we wouldn't lie about something like this."

The President scowled. A day ago, Iran, North Korea and Venezuela, in a joint statement, had announced the creation of an alliance between various developing nations to speak to the aliens in the name of humanity. The major nations hadn't signed up to their alliance – the leaders of the alliance had been struggling to outdo each other in their condemnation of Western Imperialism – but the President was reminded of an old military saying. Quantity had a quality all of its own. It was an unwelcome truth that the United Nations couldn't prevent any of the major nations and most of the minor nations from going their own way, yet the aliens had insisted on speaking to the UN and the Third World Alliance would control a significant number of seats. It could have unpleasant implications for the future.

"If we tell them the truth, if we tell them about the crashed ship, they will demand that we share access to the ship," Tom Cook said. The Secretary of Defence leaned forward. "The nation that first manages to unlock the secrets of interstellar travel will be the most powerful nation on Earth for a very long time. They will have no choice but to demand access, because their own futures would be at stake. If we refuse to grant that access, they may feel that they have to take decisive measures."

Jones frowned. "You mean they may launch an attack on the base?"

"Impossible," General Wachter said. "They must know that we would retaliate."

"They wouldn't have to launch an attack," the Secretary of State pointed out. "All they'd have to do is tell the aliens where the craft is hidden. We think that the aliens aren't strong enough to just take the craft back, but we might well be wrong and the aliens might just be unable to locate it. We'd be left without the craft and a bloody nose."

"Assuming that they know where the craft is," the President said. "Do they know where the craft is?"

Richard Darby, the Director of Homeland Security, winced. "The Russians and Chinese have always placed a much greater focus on human intelligence – HUMIT –than we have, for various reasons. We had several very high-profile spies during the Cold War and afterwards; we even discovered a long-term Russian sleeper agent a couple of years ago. They may not know where the craft is hidden – we took precautions to prevent even vetted personnel from leaving the base or even learning their exact location – or they may know exactly where it is. They probably know our secret installations far better than the aliens do and might put two and two together if they realise that a base has come back online."

"We have been reactivating facilities all over the country," Cook pointed out. The President nodded. The expense was already considerable, even though much of the groundwork had been laid before the alien mothership had been detected. "They may not be able to pick out the one housing the craft."

"With all due respect," Darby said, "it might not be wise to bet the farm on it."

The President gazed around the table, his eyes silently quelling the argument. "What do you advise?"

"A half-truth," Cook said. "We tell them that you were contacted and taken to the alien ship. We show them the recordings as proof."

"They never mentioned the crashed ship," Jones said, excitedly. "We could give them the raw footage and let them study it for themselves."

"They may not be impressed," Janine Reynolds said. The NSA Director looked down at the table. "You would be astonished at how many utterly convincing faked photographs there are out there. We actually used to create faked photographs of terrorist leaders in Iraq to humiliate them in front of their followers. They might well conclude that everything the President shows them is a fake."

"That would be an insult to the Office of the President," Wachter said, stiffly. "No one would tell a lie on such a scale."

"The Big Lie is always easier to believe than the small petty lies," Janine pointed out. "It helps if people want to believe that the altered image is actually their favourite actress in the nude, or a terrorist leader kissing another man, or…hell, a flying saucer hovering in the sky. They may believe the President wouldn't lie about something like this, but they may not believe the aliens, or what the aliens told the President."

"And there are already accusations that we knew about the aliens for a long time before SETI picked up the signal," Darby said. "The World News Network ran an expose claiming that we were making military preparations long before the aliens were actually picked up, although they didn't release anything about the crashed ship. They left the exact question of *how* we knew as an open issue…"

"We can just say that we picked up the mothership on advanced optical sensors mounted on classified satellites," Janine said. "Everyone knows that the NSA orbits quite a few classified satellites each year. We even got the first images of the alien mothership from one of them. It would even be relatively true."

The President tapped the table. "Very well," he said. "We will tell them about our contact, but not about the crashed ship, or what we've discovered from it. Tony, where do we stand on security at Area 52?"

Jones took a moment to gather his thoughts. He was a civilian and military affairs meant little to him, yet he had been given considerable power to direct military operations – a power, the President reflected, that was always given to civilian politicians. It looked different; he had to admit, when he was sitting in the Oval Office, facing decisions that were daunting in their scope. Obama, Bush and Clinton had had it easy, although he couldn't understand how Clinton had found time to have oral sex in the Oval Office. There was just too much to do.

"We have two companies of soldiers from Camp Pendleton on exercises at an abandoned base ten kilometres from Area 52," Jones said. The President silently identified them as Marines. "They have transports that could get them to Area 52 within fifteen to twenty minutes, where they will reinforce the soldiers on duty at the base. We've armed them with MANPAD weapons as well as their standard equipment, but if the aliens come calling I don't know if they'll be able to stand them off in time for help to arrive.

"There's nothing visible on the surface at all apart from a handful of dusty buildings and a chain-link fence, with no locals around for dozens of kilometres," he added. "Colonel Fields suggested pushing out the security perimeter and detaining anyone who wandered into the area, but I decided that would call unwanted attention to the base, particularly as we would have no legal grounds to detain them. The base itself is secure and anyone who attempts to break through the fence will be arrested.

"The nearby communities have received agents who will inform us if something changes," he concluded. "We had some panic when a Russian dance team drove through Nevada, but it turned out that they actually were dancers showing off their skills to the children from various schools. There shouldn't be anything to alert unwanted visitors."

The President nodded. "Good work," he said. Colonel Fields was an old lush – that was why he'd been effectively exiled to Area 52 in the first place – but he was shaping up nicely. Besides, Ben Santini was watching over his shoulder. He looked down at the image of the alien mothership. "I take it that there have been no new developments?"

"We can't get decent images for some reason," Janine said. The NSA had taken over the orbital telescopes and pointed them all at the alien ship. "We can tell you quite a bit about the craft – we think that it could probably hold a billion humans if they were packed in like sardines – but nothing specific. We're still picking up hints that the aliens are watching us by sending other craft into our atmosphere, yet the telescopes are not seeing them being launched from the mothership. NASA thinks that the ship is being propelled by a drive field – a nice term for something they admit they cannot even begin to duplicate – and that the field is causing our optical difficulties. We don't know for sure.

"That said, the team at Area 52 were right," she added. "If that ship were to explode while it was in orbit, the results would be devastating. Earth would become uninhabitable."

The President nodded. On his desk was a proposal to reopen and expand the bomb shelter network – such as it was – that had been created during the Cold War. The planners wanted to spend billions of dollars on trying to protect humanity from alien attack by creating hardened shelters, yet the President had no illusions. No amount of bomb shelters could protect the majority of the human race. Thousands of citizens weren't waiting for the government to do something about it and were busy purchasing or building their own, along with guns, food and other supplies. There were reports of shortages of all essential items right across the country. There had been panic-buying riots in every city in the United States as people fought desperately for items they desperately needed – or thought they did. The National Guard had been called out to a dozen cities.

But none of it would matter if the aliens were bent on human conquest, or extermination. The President had met the aliens and talked with them. He'd had a long career in politics after he'd left the army and he was a fair judge of people. The aliens, he was sure, had meant what they'd said. It was easy to believe – to allow himself to believe – that he'd misread the aliens, who weren't human after all, but he doubted it. They had meant what they'd said and that meant that they intended to invade the Earth. The protesters outside knew nothing about it.

Lucky protesters, he thought, sourly.

"We'd better not destroy it then," he said. He'd read reports on the teams working to retarget the ICBMs so that they could be launched against targets in orbit, but Janine was right. Quite apart from the moral issues – there were a *billion* aliens on that craft – it would be the most self-defeating victory in history. There would no longer be history on Earth. "I have a more pleasant duty to perform now, so if there's no other business?"

On that note, the meeting ended.

———

Karen had never been to the White House, or even to Washington, before she'd detected the alien craft and deciphered the message. It had seemed absurd to even think that she would go, unless she went with a school trip or a tourist group. The invitation to meet with the President had been a surprise – the media hadn't been happy at how she'd fled their press conference – but it hadn't taken her long to decide to accept, along with her family. They were now quartered in one of Washington's more expensive hotels, courtesy of the Secret Service, and being shown around the city by a tour guide. Karen herself had been invited directly to the White House.

There'd been a quick briefing on protocol, but she'd been too nervous to take it in and she'd just kept nodding. The President wasn't a king or a dictator; he wasn't someone who would lop off her head for daring to ask questions or for some minor breech in protocol. The President's Personnel Secretary – a long-legged blonde who kept smiling at her in a faintly disturbing manner – escorted her through the building and provided a running commentary on each of the portraits and artworks lining the walls, before escorting her in to the Oval Office itself. Karen had seen pictures, of course, from when she was very young, but they all paled compared to the room itself. History had been made in the Oval Office. The ghosts of former Presidents seemed to look down on their successor, watching in silent judgement and perhaps shaking their heads in dismay. The United States had evolved since its foundation and some of the former Presidents would have found it a very alien place.

The President himself was a surprisingly handsome man in person, even though he had to be in his late forties. Karen tried to figure out how old he was and failed, although she knew that he'd been an adult during the Iraq War. The media might refer to him as the ugliest President ever to sit in the Oval Office, yet up close he had a rugged charisma that seemed to transcend his appearance. She reminded herself of what Daisy had told her - that the President was a consummate politician who would try to present himself to her in the best possible light - yet she was awed by his presence. He shook her hand firmly and she almost forgot to let go of it.

"Please, sit down," he said, waving her to the sofa. He didn't go back behind his desk, but took the comfortable chair facing her. "I will be greeting you formally later this evening" – Karen winced at the reminder she would have to face the press, if only a handful of reporters, again – "but I wanted to meet you in person first and extend my congratulations."

Karen almost melted. The President of the United States was congratulating her! "Thank you, sir…ah, Mr President," she said. She felt herself flushing and wanted to flee, but somehow held her ground. "It was sheer luck."

"Perhaps," the President said. His face didn't change at all. "Ninety-nine percent of great events and decisions happen because of luck. You also cracked the alien message and that wasn't luck."

161

"It wasn't meant to be hard to decipher," Karen said. She'd made that point to Daisy, but she didn't know if the President knew. Why should the President take an interest in SETI – apart from the obvious? A week ago, no one had known that aliens existed and Daisy – Director Fairchild – had been struggling to gain enough funding to continue operations. Now, everyone and his dog wanted to offer SETI money and Daisy was already looking at expanding the array network, perhaps even bringing the Square Kilometre Array online before the intended date of 2020. "Mr President, that message was intended to be easy to crack."

The President's eyes seemed to narrow as she stumbled through an explanation, painfully aware that she was talking to the President as if he were an ignorant child, even though Daisy had warned her that most politicians knew nothing and desired to know less. He didn't interrupt her, or ask questions; he just listened. Karen knew that Daisy and the other Senior Astronomers at SETI had placed their faith in a peaceful contact, yet there was something vaguely sinister about the whole affair. There was something that didn't quite add up.

"I see," the President said, finally. There was something…odd in his tone. Karen remembered skimming through a brief biography on the President and noting that he wasn't fond of dissembling. "We'll talk about this later."

His words hung in her mind even after her parents arrived in the White House for a brief photo opportunity and a handful of questions from selected reporters. It was easier than facing a mass of reporters again – it helped that they couldn't decide if they should be taking pictures of her, or the President, or both – yet her brain refused to let it go. What had the President meant?

———

They met later in the Oval Office.

Karen had been warned, in no uncertain terms, that the President only had a few moments to speak with her – he was a very busy man – but he showed no sign of urgency as they talked briefly about her life and SETI. She recognised the tactic as one designed to put her at her ease and encourage her to talk freely, yet she had to admire the President's skill. He didn't give any hints of falsehood or deceit, even though she knew that all politicians developed such skills as a matter of course.

"You had...issues with the signal," the President said. "Would you care to tell me about them?"

"They spoke to us in English, then other languages," Karen said. She wanted to explain all her concerns, but time pressed and she kept it simple. "They couldn't have picked all that up from radio transmissions alone."

The President said nothing, encouraging her to continue with a single raised eyebrow.

"We...ah, SETI studied the problem extensively over the last few years and all of the experts agreed that it would take aliens years to learn even one of our languages," she continued. "We expected that we would be reduced to the level of building up a shared language piece by piece, learning the alien terms for 'yes' and 'no' or 'true' and 'false,' yet the aliens were able to compose a message and speak to us perfectly. It defies belief."

"A great deal about this whole situation defies belief," the President pointed out. "Who would have believed, in the final years of the twentieth century, that human affairs were being watched from the timeless realm of space?"

It was a misquote, but Karen understood. "Yes, Mr President," she said. "They've been watching us for a very long time."

"Perhaps," the President agreed. There was...something in his expression, as if he wanted to say something, but couldn't – or wouldn't. "Do you feel that the aliens are trustworthy?"

"No," Karen said, flatly. "I think they have an agenda of their own."

"True," the President said. There was an odd note in his voice. "I feel the same way. Hard times are coming."

The President's aide popped in to say that time had run out before Karen could answer and ushered her out to where her parents were waiting, leaving her with one thought. The President knew more than he'd said aloud. It had been, she decided, an oddly unsatisfying meeting. She thought, briefly, about sharing her thoughts with Daisy, before deciding to keep them to herself.

Daisy didn't need to know.

Chapter Twenty-One

Colorado Springs, USA
Day 28

"I think you need to see this," Robin said, into the phone. There was a pause as she listened to the voice on the other end. "Yes, of course I'll wait."

She put the phone down and smiled to herself. Now that other radar technicians were involved with tracking the alien craft, she could follow up her own lines of inquiry rather than watching over their shoulders. She had been looking at the alien flight paths, convinced that there was a pattern there if she looked hard enough, and she'd finally stumbled over the key. In hindsight, it was brutally obvious, but she simply hadn't been thinking along the right lines. It was an error she intended to correct.

General Sandra Dyson strode into Robin's compartment as if she owned the place, which in a sense she did. Cheyenne Mountain was coming back online rapidly now that the alien mothership had been detected and the world knew that alien contact was just a handful of days away. Robin had little interest in the political situation, but even she understood that the world was already changing and that the aliens might present a new and dangerous challenge. She had no intention of allowing the aliens and their undeniable superior technology to defeat her.

"General," she said, managing to remember to salute this time. She rather approved of Sandra Dyson, who happened to be tolerant of nerds and geeks in the USAF. There were some, mainly pilots and ground crew, who had no tolerance for the technicians who made it all work, but the truth was that the USAF couldn't have fielded a modern fighting force without them. The technology was no longer as simple as it had been back when the

USAF had confronted a foe on equal terms. Now, a multi-million dollar gadget could determine the fate of a fighter jet that cost billions of dollars to produce, or prevent cheap and nasty enemy missiles from landing on their target. "I was looking at the aliens we were tracking and I found something interesting."

The irritating thing about tracking the aliens, at first, was that they only appeared as transient radar contacts, if that. It made it hard to tell if she was looking at a genuine radar contact, a flock of birds or a glitch in the machine. One of her former colleagues had drawn a series of cartoons in which the target had been identified as a piece of fluff inside the radar system, but it was no laughing matter. Launching a missile or deploying interceptors on the strength of a transient contact could have resulted in disaster.

Now, however, they could track the alien craft to a high degree of certainty and she'd noticed a pattern. "The aliens have been maintaining a series of high altitude overflights – not just over here, but over most of the rest of the world – but they haven't been landing anywhere in America, as far as we can tell," she said. "I noticed, however, that many of their tracks seemed to lead due south, right towards Antarctica. I called the NRO and got them to re-task a stealth satellite to fly over the continent and look for anything unusual. The alien tracks seemed to terminate at a single location."

She saw Sandra's smile, but she didn't understand it. It hadn't occurred to her to question it; yet no mere Second Lieutenant could have talked the NRO into altering one of their satellites before, even if the fate of the world rested on the decision. The President had ordered the NRO to comply without hesitation to any request for intelligence coming from NORAD and they'd re-tasked the satellite without demur.

"I couldn't make heads or tails of what they'd sent, so I asked them to have their analysts take a good look at it," she continued. "They found... this."

She put the image up on the screen. There was a tiny fraction of the icy continent that was warmer than it had any right to be. If that wasn't enough of a giveaway, there was a single image of an alien craft on the ground, floating into shadow. She knew they'd been lucky – normally, she suspected that the aliens kept their base well out of sight when a regular satellite was directly overhead – yet the implications were disturbing even to her. The aliens had established a base in one of the most inaccessible areas on the planet.

"You're certain of this?" Sandra asked. The General leaned forward, as if she could pick out more detail just by staring at the image. Robin knew that she wouldn't learn anything else; the NRO hadn't been able to tell them anything about the size of the alien base. If it hadn't been for the location, Robin would have wondered if an alien craft hadn't crashed there as well. "That is definitely an alien base?"

Robin grinned. The General *believed* her! "I compared the location to the files," she said. "It's actually in the midst of an area notorious for bad weather and…ah, what the researchers called electromagnetic interference. Any aircraft that flies into the area risks losing their navigation systems and other electronic devices. The researchers used to speculate that there was a large deposit of magnetic material in the area, but no one sent in a team to explore. The whole area is listed as an Area of Inaccessibility and off-limits to everyone. It's actually quite some distance from McMurdo Station – the closest human outpost – which might be why no one has followed it up."

"Antarctica is known for bad flying conditions," Sandra mused. The problem, Robin knew, was that so many tales grew in the telling. The aliens might have deliberately done something to conceal their base from prying eyes, or the interference might be natural and the aliens had merely taken advantage of it to keep human interlopers away. "Why would they establish a base there, of all places?"

Robin had been giving the matter some thought. "It's not an easy place to reach," she said, slowly. "There are no large military forces stationed in Antarctica, even with the disputes between the various nations that have claims to parts of the continent. I doubt that there are even a hundred soldiers in all on the continent. The aliens wouldn't have wanted a base we could reach easily."

"I've been reading up on UFO contacts," Sandra said, slowly. "The aliens were supposed to have established a network of bases on Earth, perhaps even on the Moon."

She shook her head. "Do you have any details about how many craft are based there, or the exact size of the base?"

"No, General," Robin said. "I asked one of the analysts to keep working on it, but he said that the base is very well concealed and if we'd looked an hour or so later, we'd have seen nothing. We only got lucky because we were tracking an alien craft on its way to the base."

"An entire alien base, just waiting to be stripped of its technology," Sandra said. Robin had to agree. It was the opportunity of a lifetime, one that could not be allowed to just slip away. "Don't speak to anyone about this – in fact, give me the details of the NRO analysts you spoke to and I'll have them warned as well. They'll have been thoroughly vetted if they work there, but there's no point in taking chances."

She smiled wanly. "And the other alien contacts?"

"Just high-altitude recon missions, as far as I can tell," Robin admitted, reluctantly. "I've been using them as tests for the new tracking system. I could have fed the data to a THAAD launch site and attempted to engage the alien craft."

"Try to hold your fire," Sandra said, dryly. "In five days, the aliens will present themselves at the UN. We don't want the war to start until after that, do we?"

Robin decided she was joking and shook her head. "No, General," she agreed. She didn't want there to be a war at all. She wanted the chance to examine the alien technology herself. She was sure that humans could find more uses for the alien tech than the aliens themselves had found. "What do you want me to do now?"

"Continue tracking the alien ships and inform me at once if anything changes," Sandra ordered, flatly. "I need to speak to the President and then to the Chairman of the Joint Chiefs of Staff. We need to start making preparations to take that base off their hands."

———

"Further protests are expected in seven other cities later in the week," the FOX announcer said, "despite the breakdown of one protest into a mob of violent thugs. The New York Police Department announced that they'd arrested over four hundred people, most of who would be released without charge, although the City of New York intends to bring charges against various rioters. Mayor Hundred announced two hours ago that anyone who committed an act of violence in the course of the riot would be charged and brought to justice. Various legal watchdogs, including the ACLU, have charged the NYPD with excessive violence and mass arrests, sweeping up the innocent as well as the guilty, and have promised to bring suit against the City Government. In a speech in New York, Mayor Hundred had this to say…"

Captain Philip Carlson looked away from the television as a young man looked into the room. "The General will see you now," he said. He looked far too young to serve at the heart of America's defences. "If you'll follow me…?"

Philip left Mayor Hundred prattling on about how law and order would be maintained in New York and followed the young man though a series of slightly musty corridors, finally entering an office overlooking the Situation Room. NORAD might have been officially decommissioned and put on standby, at least until the alien mothership had been detected, but it had had the best technology available at the time and it had even been updated over the years. One massive display showed the entire might of America's military power, a second showed a live feed from an orbital telescope, revealing the alien mothership. He felt something inside his heart break as he studied the massive ship. The people who had built it had nothing to fear from humanity.

"Captain," General Sandra Dyson said, as Philip snapped to attention. "Please take a seat. I'll be with you in a second."

Philip nodded. It didn't take a genius to know that the meeting was about the aliens and their mothership, not after NASA had been unceremoniously ordered to halt the countdown and hold *Atlantis* on the surface. The shuttle, one of the two remaining shuttles in American service, had been scheduled to make a supply run to the ISS and launch a pair of commercial satellites into space, but it had been pulled from the launch schedule on short notice. The astronauts had been furious about that decision. The competition to fly shuttle missions was intense and the scheduled pilots had been disappointed. Few of them believed that NASA would ever get its act in gear and start building new spacecraft.

The alien mothership mocked NASA, as Congress hadn't hesitated to point out. Senator Sam Hamlin, a space-booster since he'd been a kid, had savaged NASA in front of a special committee, calling for the entire senior staff to be ruthlessly sacked, if not transferred to Leavenworth and left there to rot. He hadn't minced his words and had castigated NASA for everything, up to and including high treason. Congress seemed to agree. In the interests of showing that they were Doing Something, they had already authorised vast new space programs and projects, most of which wouldn't produce usable hardware for at least a decade. NASA spent most of its funding on bureaucracy, public relations, and legal affairs and popular programs. There was little left for actually launching men into space.

"We should have met the aliens in orbit around Jupiter or Pluto," Hamlin had pronounced, speaking in front of Congress. "We might have earned a little more respect!"

"Captain," Sandra said, closing the file on her computer. "I'm sorry about the delay, but we've just had a small upset here."

"No harm done, General," Philip said, forbearing to mention that if a General wanted a meeting with a mere Captain delayed, she'd get what she wanted. "I'm not expected back at the Cape for another week."

Sandra's lips twitched. "You're going to be going up in *Atlantis*," she said, flatly. He had the impression that it had already been arranged and forced down NASA's collective throat. "You and another military crew will be taking weapons to the ISS and mounting them on the station. *Atlantis* herself will be armed and serve as a space fighter if necessary."

Philip stared at her. It was true that he was one of NASA's military-cleared astronauts – and therefore flew many of the classified military operations, mainly launching satellites for the NSA – but he hadn't expected to be given command of an armed shuttle. There were international treaties *against* permanently placing weapons in space! NASA was a mostly-civilian agency and they'd have a fit when they realised that they'd suddenly become an arm of the USAF. The idea of arming the shuttles would be horrific to them.

"Yes, General," he said. It was a new challenge – and a chance to fly in space. How could he refuse? "I should point out that the shuttle is not a space fighter in any sense of the word."

"I understand," Sandra said, seriously. "We are almost certainly sending you to your death if it comes down to a fight. We'll try and get the other shuttle prepared in time, but I doubt that we'll have her ready to fly by the time the mothership enters orbit. The alien craft seem to fly like…well, craft out of a science-fiction movie. We gave serious thought to just evacuating the ISS and abandoning the station, but some analysts figured that arming the station might give it a chance."

"Not much of one," Philip said. He hadn't served a term on the station – another position with more volunteers than there were places – but he'd seen it on shuttle flights and knew how fragile it was. A single missile would rip it apart. "Do we have any weapons that can be deployed against an alien threat?"

"Some," Sandra said. She looked him in the eye. "I won't lie to you. The odds of surviving this mission are very low. If you want to decline it, let me know now and it won't be held against you later and I'll find another pilot."

Philip grinned. He'd flown JSF fighters for the Navy before transferring to NASA, always looking for another challenge. NASA had talked about using the shuttle to make bombing raids over Moscow, but the Cold War had ended and such missions had never materialised. There had been proposals to deploy a Project Thor system from the shuttle to help win the war on terror, but Special Forces and USAF aircraft had started to win that war before NASA had even finished the paper studies. There would never be another opportunity like this…and, of course, if he declined it, he would never have another chance. He'd be lucky to fly again.

"I accept," he said, simply. "What do you want me to do?"

————

General Sandra Dyson had grown up as a tomboy, the youngest child of a southern man who'd had five sons before she'd been born. His wife had died giving birth to Sandra and she'd grown up with six men, without any feminine influence. Her father had been a soldier, four of her five brothers had gone into the Army…and Sandra herself had joined the USAF. It had been a long climb up to the highest levels, yet it was something she was proud of. Her father had been a patriot and he'd taught his kids that while America wasn't perfect, and it did have flaws, it was still far better than most of the rest of the world. Sandra had deployed to countries where freedom of speech, religion and almost anything else was a joke. She had no doubts about her own loyalties.

She wished that she could have flown the shuttle instead. She'd flown into danger before, but then that had been against a known danger, one that could be countered. The USAF was the finest air force in the world and had known it, known that it would never face a superior foe – until now. The aliens, if they chose to invade, would enjoy massive superiority. She was sure that she had sent Captain Philip Carlson to his death, yet she had argued for the mission, in hopes of giving the aliens something else to worry about. Their actions suggested to her that they *weren't* capable of simply overwhelming the human race, but they still had superior technology. If it came down to a war, the death toll would be massive. The war might well be lost.

It was easy to stare down at the big screens and accept that they were just numbers; that the men and women who served in America's armed forces were just figures that could be dismissed at will, but she knew better. They were living breathing humans, with hopes and dreams and fears of their own, each one with a family and friends who loved them. It had never been easy to send men and women into harm's way, expecting – knowing – that some of them would get hurt or killed, but they'd volunteered. She'd volunteered to serve, yet she had to remain in the rear. A General had no place leading the charge.

She composed herself and returned to her computer. She couldn't afford such worries, not now. There was a war to plan.

Chapter Twenty-Two

Fort Benning, USA
Day 29

"Welcome to Fort Benning," the guard said. Lieutenant-Commander Nicolas Little shrugged. He hadn't visited the Fort since he'd been part of a six-man SEAL team sent to test the defences. "I have orders to escort you to your destination."

"Thank you," Nicolas said.

He kept his voice even with an effort. It wasn't the guard's fault that he'd been summoned away at very short notice from the Little Creek Naval Amphibious Base, not when he'd been training with the remainder of his unit for a possible new deployment to the Middle East. The SEALs – along with hundreds of other Special Forces units – had been instrumental in hunting terrorists and convincing various local governments that harbouring terrorists would get them nothing but pain. Few people recognised the value of borders now, allowing the Special Forces to stage raids on terrorist bases, wherever in the world they might be. Nicolas had served in so many different countries that he'd lost count and had been expecting to take command of a new deployment when he'd received new orders.

They walked in silence. There was no point in pestering the guard; he was just a messenger. The orders had been vague - that was par for the course in Special Forces - yet he didn't know who had summoned him to the Fort. Fort Benning was overcrowded as thousands of reservists were recalled to their units and prepared for a possibly hostile encounter with aliens, but at least the security was good. Terrorists had staged attacks on army bases in the Continental United States before and few people took any chances any longer. Fort Benning, the home of the United States Army Infantry School, was where new recruits underwent their Basic Combat Training and Advanced Individual Training, before being deployed as trained soldiers. Nicolas had good memories of his time there. He'd thought that it was a harsh program until he'd gone through the SEAL training program, which seemed excessive to the point of sadism. It hadn't been until his first deployment that he'd understood the purpose of the course. SEAL teams operated away from support that ordinary soldiers expected as their right and they had to be among the toughest soldiers in the world. They had no other choice.

The office was bare, clearly opened for just one visitor. Nicolas snapped to attention, wondering why it had been a surprise. He'd known General Gary Wachter from a shared deployment in Iraq. He might have been an Army General, but he'd understood how to use Special Forces and deployed them with a fine understanding of their capabilities…and limitations. The other man, standing in the corner, was instantly recognisable as the base's CO. He'd known him as a younger officer.

The CO leaned forward. "Do you recognise me?" Nicolas nodded. "The General here has a mission for you, one so highly-classified that only the President and a handful of others know that it is even being considered. *I* do not know what the mission is, but it comes directly from the National Command Authority. You will have wide latitude to carry it out, with a direct link to the General and overwhelming authority. Do you understand?"

"Yes, sir," Nicolas said, tightly. He'd had briefings like that before, when a dangerous mission was in the works and information was being tightly controlled. The CO's job was merely to verify the legitimacy of the orders. "I understand."

"Good," the CO said. "Good luck."

He saluted and slipped out of the office, closing the door firmly behind him. "At ease," General Wachter ordered. Nicolas knew better than to relax completely. "Do you know what you're doing here?"

"No, sir," Nicolas said. "Why have you summoned me here?"

"Someone told the President that you were the best damned SEAL in the world," Wachter said. His face twitched into a humourless smile. "And now you have the chance to prove it."

Nicolas kept his face blank with an effort. The *President* had been a soldier and he knew the value of Special Forces. He'd ordered them deployed to hundreds of trouble spots since he'd been elected. If the President had ordered the mission personally, it had to be something interesting, perhaps vitally important.

"Yes, sir," he said. Overconfidence was a weakness, but the SEAL teams were almost as good as they thought they were. "What do you want me to do?"

Wachter told him.

"Sir," Nicolas said, "with all due respect, you have to be fucking joking."

"I'm not," Wachter said. "Nor is the President. We're putting this together on the run and you'll have to iron out the details – the Commandant wasn't joking when he said that you would have considerable latitude; if you want to hire prostitutes on Uncle Sam's dollar, you can – yourself. Under ideal circumstances, we'd have weeks or months to prepare for the mission, but these are far from ideal circumstances."

He looked down at the map he'd placed on the desk. "Do you believe the mission to be impossible?"

Nicolas hesitated. He'd done things that most people, even most soldiers, would have dismissed as suicide. SEAL teams had done the impossible time and time again, even though there had been near-disasters in dozens of missions. He knew that some of the training officers worried that the SEALs were losing their edge – terrorists were hardly trained enemies and most of them were cowards – but he didn't share their feeling. The entire mission... might just be possible.

"No," he said, finally. "You do know that this could be considered an act of war?"

"We know," Wachter said. "Your team will be positioned to strike, if necessary. We may recall you without striking if the situation changes, but frankly...the evidence is that we're staring down the barrel of an alien invasion. Your mission might change the course of the war."

"If it is a war," Nicolas pointed out. "They might change their minds if they realise that we're prepared to fight."

"Maybe," General Wachter agreed, "but the President would consider that wishful thinking. We don't want this fight, but if we have to engage them, perhaps we can give them a nasty surprise or two. Good luck."

"Thank you, sir," Nicolas said. "We're going to need it."

——

Alex had never been to Fort Benning before, although he'd visited several other Army bases in the course of his career. Fort Benning's role as a training centre allowed it to conceal various other purposes under the vast numbers of men and women who swarmed around the base, being trained in infantry combat and related skills. The USAF had given him some training, but it had been nothing compared to Basic Infantry Training, let alone the heavy training that Special Forces units routinely underwent. Looking down at the two hundred soldiers who filled the lecture hall, he felt distinctly unhealthy, even intimidated. There were fewer bodybuilders than he had expected, but the men shared the same attitude of sheer determination and violence, patiently waiting to be unleashed.

"I've never seen anything like this," Ben Santini said. Alex remembered that he was a former Special Forces soldier himself before he'd been tapped for the Tiger Team, with experience in a dozen different countries. "They've got SEALs, Force Recon Marines, Delta Force, Ranger Pathfinders and Air Force Ravens...*and* units that never should see the light of day. That group there is from the Wrecking Crew – I'd stake my life on it."

Alex had to smile. It was lucky that they were standing behind a one-way window, because he didn't want to *think* about what the human wolves would make of Santini's words. They were chatting in small groups – there seemed to be friendships that crossed rank and unit barriers – and bullshit-ting about what their mission might be.

"They're dangerous," he said, finally. He wanted to run, not go down and meet them. Leaving Area 52 hardly seemed worth the encounter. He'd dealt with Air Force Ravens before, but the others were new to him. "They look as if they could kill me with a single punch."

"If any of them couldn't kill you with a single punch, they'd be thrown out in disgrace," Santini said, with a wink. "They're trained in a hundred ways to kill people with their bare hands, and each and every one of them is a rated expert in all kinds of weapons. I've seen groups run out of ammo, pick up AK-47s and use them to carry on fighting. We used to run groups through army bases just for the sheer hell of it and see how many they could mock-kill before the guards got their shit together and took us out. Believe me, those guys are the survivors of a very harsh training regime. They're the best of the best."

He smiled at Alex's expression. "What those protesters on the streets don't realise is that men like them are what keeps them safely in their beds, living comfortable lives, lives so comfortable that they don't realise that they're very fragile," he said, seriously. "I always thought of them as people who ate sausage, but didn't want to know how the sausage was made and maybe even believed that it materialised out of nowhere. Those men down there" – he jerked a thumb towards the window – "are the sausage-makers. They're the butchers who allow the bakers and the candlestick makers to get on with their lives."

"You two, come on," Nicolas shouted. Alex was on his feet like a shot and Santini followed at a more sedate pace. "You don't want to miss the briefing, do you?"

Santini snorted. "Not since we're giving it, no," he said. Nicolas had recognised him at once, much to Alex's dismay. Was there a security breach underway? "Lead on."

A Sergeant bellowed for attention as Nicolas strode in, followed by Santini and Alex. "At ease," Nicolas said, as he took the stand. The assembled Special Forces soldiers stared at him. "You've all volunteered for a mission, without knowing who you're going to be working with, or what you're doing. I know that none of you will want to back out once you know. I will not tolerate, however, any disputes between the different units. We have barely enough time as it is to prepare."

His gaze swept the room. Alex was amazed by how…ragged the assembled men seemed. Some were watching Nicolas like a hawk; others were sitting as if they didn't care, staring at the ceiling rather than at their commander. Santini had told him that the Special Forces were generally more informal than the regular army – every man had been tested under fire numerous times – but it was still astonishing. He hoped that Nicolas's words were not falling on deaf ears.

"We will be briefed here, and then we will take over part of the base to train as a group," Nicolas continued. "In four days, we'll be on our way. Some of us have worked together before, but others have not. We're going to be working our butts off to make this group meld together. Anyone who doesn't give me a hundred percent effort will spend the rest of his life regretting it. Alex?"

Somehow, now that he'd been called forward, it was easy for Alex to step up to the stand. "You will all have heard about the alien starship approaching the planet," he said. It would be old news by now. The dangerous men staring at him, no doubt wondering what he was doing there, would have considered facing an alien threat. "What you will not have heard is that the story doesn't begin with SETI's discovery of the alien ship."

He ran through a brief outline of everything that had happened, from the crashed UFO to the President's meeting with the aliens. "We have discovered evidence that there is an alien base on the surface of this planet," he continued. "This, added to the other evidence, suggests that the aliens are far from friendly. The mission – your mission – is to be in position to threaten and take the base, should the aliens launch an invasion of Earth."

It grew easier to speak once he had pushed through the first part. "The alien base is located in Antarctica," he said. There were no gasps, no cries of shock, but a ripple ran around the room. Alex knew – they did not – that the vast majority of the team had been chosen because they all had experience operating in such conditions, either in Antarctica or the Yukon. "We know its location, but we know nothing else about it, not even how many aliens are stationed there. There have been hundreds of reports of UFO encounters in the surrounding area and we must assume that the base has been active for quite some time. They may have based an entire army under the ice."

The UFO Community certainly believed that the aliens had bases all around the world, and Antarctica was named as one of the prime locations. In 1946-47, the United States Navy had launched a research mission – including nearly five thousand men, thirteen ships and multiple aircraft – that had scouted out the area. Operation High Jump – as it had been termed – had provided fertile fields for all kinds of conspiracy theories, suggesting everything from hidden Nazi bases to alien contact – or even a hole leading to an 'inner Earth.'

"There are two objectives of the mission if it comes down to a fight," he concluded. "The first is to obtain as many samples of the alien technology as possible. The second is to destroy the base and deny the aliens the ability to use it against us."

"Thank you," Nicolas said. There were no claps. "In four days, the Navy will be flying in the regular supply transports to McMurdo Station, a research base in the Antarctic. This time, they will be transporting us and our weapons instead. Once we're on the ground, we will put the entire place into lockdown and evacuate as many non-essential personnel as we can, before sending recon teams to pin down the location of the alien base. If we receive the order to attack, we will move out using the base's transporters and attack as soon as we reach the alien base.

"I'm sure that I don't have to tell you how many unknowns there are," he continued. "We know nothing about their strength or numbers, or what we will be facing when we break into their base. They may have forces already on route from their mothership to reinforce the base, or they may have stationed ground-attack craft at the base. We will be playing it largely by ear. Luckily, we're trained to improvise when necessary.

"The *George Washington* is currently engaged with exercises with the Royal Australian Navy and, quite by coincidence, will be returning along a path that will bring it near enough to support us. We will also be moving up three modified *Ohio*-class submarines that will serve as transports for moving anything we capture out of the area. They are also armed with Tomahawk missiles that can provide additional fire support if required. I don't need to tell you, I suspect, that the second part of the mission is not going to be easy.

"We have no way of knowing what surveillance capabilities the enemy possesses, but it stands to reason that they will be monitoring the surrounding area pretty closely," he concluded. "We're trained to sneak through the most heavily-guarded areas in the world and we will have to apply the same principles to the alien base. They may even have surveillance technology that we've never even heard of!"

He smiled, tiredly. Alex couldn't understand it. He was listing problems and it shouldn't have been inspirational, but somehow he knew that the men in the room were inspired by his words. It dawned on him suddenly that tackling the alien base was a real challenge, something even the best Special Forces agents would never have done before, and they *wanted* the test. They wanted to pit themselves against the aliens and see who the best was.

"If any of you want to back out, let me know privately after this," Nicolas said. "PT in the gym in ten minutes and God help any of you who've forgotten your stuff!"

The sergeant called them all to attention again and they filed out of the room. "Not a bad briefing," Nicolas assured Alex. "We've had briefing officers who never quite got to the point."

"Thank you," Alex said. He still couldn't get over the experience of meeting so many Special Operations men at once. "Good luck."

"We make our own luck," Nicolas assured him. He saw Alex's expression and smiled. "Hey, it could be worse. If it does come down to a shooting war, we can at least assume that everyone in that base is hostile." His smile grew wider. "Do you know what happened to us in some dirty little Iraqi town?"

Alex shook his head. "Oh, we had a lead on this fucker of a bomb-maker," Nicolas said. "Dude didn't have the stones to go out and actually lay the bombs, but he was damn good at making them idiot-proof so even kids could go emplace them in our path. We all wanted to kill him or sweat him of everything he knew and then kill him, so when we got a tip, we pulled out all the stops.

"It was one of those indistinguishable Iraqi houses, but there was this van parked in front of it and we thought, you know, that it was a car bomb or perhaps how the bombs were being transported around the country, so we slipped up to it while we were scouting out the area. Team One goes into the house, Team Two watches the escape routes – they lost the coin toss – and Team Three goes into the van. We sneak up to it, brace ourselves because we can hear noises from inside the van, and yank open the doors. What do we see?"

He laughed. "There was this boy of around seventeen and this girl of around fifteen, both naked, in the middle of having sex," he said, between chuckles. "They were just staring at us – I think they thought that we were their parents or someone – and we were just laughing our heads off. Someone had the decency to give them their clothes while we searched the van, poor kids. They didn't have anything to do with the terrorists; they'd just come across half the town to have sex in private. We didn't report them because we knew what her fucking family would do to her. Poor girl."

Alex watched as he strode off, leaving the two of them alone. "Ben," he said, slowly. "Most of those men are going to die, aren't they?"

"Yes," Santini said. "I'm very much afraid they are."

Chapter Twenty-Three

Near Reykjavík, Iceland
Day 30

Geography, the President reflected, had not been kind to Iceland. Located as it was in the middle of the Atlantic Ocean, it was of great military significance and would have been one of the battlegrounds of World War Three, had the Cold War ever turned hot. Its membership in NATO had been a matter of great domestic concern and after the end of the Cold War; most foreign military units had been pulled out of the country. Iceland's own tiny military – too small to guarantee its independence against anyone who really wanted the country – had been redeveloped to counter the threats of the post-Cold War era. The country might still have been a NATO member, but it was effectively neutral, a neutrality that suited others very well.

He watched from his seat as Air Force One drifted out of the sky towards a former American air base located near Iceland's capital city. The base had never been decommissioned completely, but had instead been revamped at considerable expense to serve as a meeting place for the senior world leaders. The Icelandic Government provided local security and a guarantee that reporters – and protesters - wouldn't be allowed past the chain-link fence that composed the first line of defence. Having to provide so much security was something of a sore point with the locals, but the inner lines of defence had authorisation to shoot to kill, without asking questions first. The dire signs surrounding the base might be ignored by reporters seeking the scoop of the century, or locals protesting against the base's mere existence, even though the base was an economic net gain to Iceland. It also helped ensure that the country's neutrality would be respected by all sides.

Air Force One touched down with the faintest of bumps and taxied to one end of the runway. A RAF plane occupied one of the hangars, informing him that the British Prime Minister had already landed, but the Russians, French and Chinese leaders were still on their way. By long custom, there would be no prior engagements anywhere else on Iceland, or any announcement of the agenda, although it wouldn't take a genius to guess that the meeting was connected to the aliens. There were only three days until a genuine alien spacecraft landed in New York City and the world was waiting anxiously to see what the aliens had to say.

There was no point in leaving his seat until the Secret Service had checked the security arrangements surrounding the plane and the residential areas. The Icelandic Police had responsibility for the general security – no other world leader would trust his safety to the American Secret Service, nor would the Secret Service be happy with entrusting the President's safety to someone else – but by long-standing agreement, the Secret Service got to look over their shoulders. The other protection services would be doing the same, which would only make the experience a trying time for all concerned. The world leaders might not plan to kidnap each other – that only happened in bad movies – but all five nations had spied on each other from time to time.

"Mr President?" Pepper asked. She wore a more conventional suit than her standard outfit, but she still looked attractive. The experience of meeting the aliens hadn't fazed her, even though she'd endured a week of testing in the Naval Hospital, just in case she'd picked up any alien bugs. "They're ready for you now."

"Good," the President said. He put down his newspaper – the reporter writing the article had managed to get the names of half the world leaders wrong, he'd noticed with some amusement – and stood up. "Any problems on the ground?"

"It's bitterly cold out there, Mr President, but nothing else," Pepper informed him. "The locals say that there haven't been many protests near the base, even though the fact you're coming here is no longer a secret. They've been concentrated in the cities."

"It's too cold to protest," the President said, wryly. "Lead on."

Two more Secret Service Agents fell in around him as he walked through the massive aircraft and down the steps. The chill hit him at once, bringing with it a faint aroma of aircraft fuel and something he couldn't quite identify. The base had housed overnight conferences before, but he didn't intend to stay to eat with the other leaders, not with an alien spacecraft bearing down on Earth. They'd all made similar plans. The aliens – if they launched an attack on Iceland – could wipe out all five of the most significant world leaders at a stroke.

The interior of the conference chamber was luxurious, to the chagrin of various protesters who thought that the millions of dollars spent on the complex could have been better spent on feeding the poor. For once, the President was inclined to agree. A life spent in the military had taught him that luxury, while never to be despised, was always something a man could do without, certainly if his own life was at risk. The ornate chambers, the carefully-concealed electronic infrastructure and the catering staff – each one a five-star master chef – cost more than he cared to think about. It served a vital role – the five permanent members of the United Nations Security Council needed to talk in private – yet it was expensive. There were times when he thought that all such meetings should take place in the open. They would at least have gone quicker.

"Welcome back, Mr President," a woman said. The President recognised her as Vigdis Branson, the Manager of the Complex. "Do you wish to be shown to your rooms at once, or introduced to the British Prime Minister?"

"The rooms, please," the President said, gravely. "Please inform me when the other three arrive."

It was nearly two hours before everyone was assembled and the conference could begin. By agreement, there were no private secretaries or aides in the room, merely a single recorder making a copy of the conversation. The President had brought along a very old-fashioned tape recorder on a hunch, suspecting that the aliens could read information stored on humanity's computers at will. It would have the added advantage of being difficult to copy, either by reporters or foreign spies. The other world leaders thought that the President was being paranoid, but after they had been promised a full transcript produced by the Manager, they relented.

There was no need for formality or precedence, the President knew, and they spent the first twenty minutes chatting about families and other topics that didn't impinge upon their responsibilities. The President found it rather relaxing. The other world leaders might not possess the same degree of power as the President of the United States, but they were the closest things he had to peers, men who wielded vast power over their nations. They might be political enemies in public, yet in private they had a great deal in common. There were people in all of their nations who would have been horrified to see them cracking jokes and exchanging information, but it help to grease international diplomacy.

The State Departments and their counterparts *hated* such talks, of course. They could never trust the world leaders to stick to their scripts and concentrate on the topics the departments considered important. Worse, insults exchanged between world leaders could be considered an act of war, while an Ambassador could be recalled home in disgrace and made to carry the can for a diplomatic spat. The wonders of international telecommunications made Ambassadors less important than they had been a hundred years ago, yet there was still a place for them. The President had personally chosen the Ambassadors for significant countries and appointed men who could be trusted to serve American interests. His predecessors hadn't always been that lucky.

"And then they discovered that she was in the laundry," the Russian President concluded, having outlined a raunchy tale centred on a diplomatic reception in the Kremlin. Evgeny Vikenti, President of the Russian Federation, was one of the President's old acquaintances, even though there had been considerable friction between America and Russia over the past few years. Russia's increasing assertiveness in Eastern Europe was damaging the balance of power. "There she was, completely naked – and stuck! I don't know how her husband lived it down."

The President chuckled. It helped that the tale had been genuinely funny. "We do have an important matter to discuss," he said, opening his briefcase. "There is the minor matter of a genuine alien starship approaching the Earth."

He spread the images, the latest taken by a series of orbiting space telescopes, on the table in front of them. The Chinese President picked up the first one and examined it carefully, while the others were passed around to the other three world leaders. They would all have seen similar images from their own telescopes or through the news media after NASA started leaking images of the alien mothership, but America led the field in space-based observation systems. There were some in the NRO who had wanted to revolt at the thought of showing other national leaders the results of American research and development. The President had squashed that harshly. There was no time for a catfight over who should have access.

"Impressive," Mu Chun mused. The Chinese President was almost stereotypically inscrutable when he wanted to show nothing of his feelings. "Some of my Generals believe it to be an American trick."

"The combined space programs of the entire world could not have built that craft," Vikenti said. The Russian leaned forwards aggressively. "A ship that size could carry many millions of aliens. Why are they coming to Earth?"

"Invasion," the President said, flatly. He dropped his bombshell. "The aliens contacted me a week before their mothership was detected."

He watched the reactions. The French and British leaders looked surprised, and outraged. The Russian and Chinese Presidents looked more contemplative. The President wondered if that meant that they had been contacted, or if they thought that the Americans were lying. He found that thought rather insulting, even though he had long since come to accept that lying was a fundamental part of international – and probably interstellar – politics. The aliens had definitely lied at least once.

"Outrageous," President Vincent Pelletier said, finally. The Frenchman made his *pro forma* protest. "You should have informed us at once."

The President shrugged. "Speaking bluntly," he said dryly, "would you have informed us if you had been contacted?"

There was no reply. "That leaves us with a single question," the President added. "Were we the only ones to be contacted?"

"There has been no contact between the aliens and any member of my government, to my certain knowledge," the Chinese President said, finally. The others nodded in agreement. "It seems that America was the only nation singled out in such a manner."

In public, there would certainly have been outraged protests. In private, they could accept it and move on. "They have certainly studied us for longer than they admitted," Arthur Hamilton said. The British Prime Minister shrugged. "You said they were intent on invasion. What did they say to you?"

The President produced a set of four folders from his briefcase and passed them around, noting in passing how…normal each of the folders seemed. There was no clue on the covers as to the secrets they contained, or how they would change the world if they fell into public hands. The President's staff had already prepared measures to cover it up if some – or all – of the data was leaked.

"You can study the folders for yourself at leisure," the President said. The folders contained everything apart from the details of the crashed UFO. He'd been convinced to cover that up completely. Later, there would be time for a more leisurely sharing of information. "The important points are that the aliens are not coming in peace."

He briefly ran through the entire story, from the message that had brought him to a preset meeting place to the flight to the alien ship and the ominous message he'd received. He didn't leave out the details of the alien offer to America, or his own decision to refuse the offer, knowing that they would deduce its existence anyway. They'd certainly suspect if he tried to cover something up. He'd seriously considered discussing the discovery of the alien base, but a single leak would have blown the assault force's role – now on its way to Antarctica – and made the attack impossible.

"Impossible," the French President said, finally. "How could they hope to occupy an entire world?"

"They claim to have the numbers to do it," the President said. "I have no independent verification of anything they told me."

"So they could have been lying," the Chinese President said. "They may come to the UN to try to bluff us into surrender."

"Or they may intend to make a show of force," the British Prime Minister said. "I was briefed that their craft could easily throw rocks at us until we surrender."

"It's a possibility," the President agreed. "We need to come to an agreement on how to react."

"My country will not surrender," the Russian President said. "We have been invaded before, by Napoleon and Hitler. They both inflicted hideous punishment upon our land and people, yet we survived and bested them. We have called up our reserves and have been preparing for war. We will not tamely accept defeat and occupation."

"We may be unable to defeat them," the British Prime Minister pointed out. "Our capability to launch an attack on their mothership is non-existent. They can just hammer us until we beg for mercy."

"Or start selling each other out to gain favour," the French President added. "How many of us would sell the rest of the world out if the aliens offered us technology from beyond the stars?"

The President remembered the mass of data he'd brought back from the alien mothership and scowled. "That's beside the point," he said. "We need to agree on how we can respond to their threat, as a group."

He watched their reactions carefully. It was hardly politically correct, but if all five of the permanent members of the United Nations Security Council agreed on something, it would happen. They possessed the votes, the economic influence and – at bottom – the military force to shape the world in their favour. The trick was to get all five to agree and that rarely happened. The entire Iraq Crisis had blown up because the Americans and British had wanted to remove Saddam, while the French and Russians had wanted to remove all the sanctions and collect the money Saddam owed them – and the Chinese had merely wanted to avoid creating a precedent. It had been a hideous catfight and the scars were still felt over a decade later.

And then there was the problem of enforcing the UN's will. The blunt truth was that any of the Big Five could do whatever they wanted and the UN would be unable to stop them. They couldn't be sanctioned or threatened with military force, which meant that the UN only had as much authority as the member states chose to grant it. The President's strongest supporters included men and women who wanted the UN kept under strict control, but the irony was that the control was already there, just waiting to be used. Many good-natured men saw the UN as the Parliament of Man, yet it was really nothing more than a stacked deck. The Secretary-General and the entire political edifice could be ignored at will.

"I think we can all agree that invasion, even of a small part of the planet, is unacceptable," the French President said, finally. "Even if they only landed in…say Africa and Australia, they'd still have a massive effect on the balance of power."

"And yet they are going to have to land somewhere," the President pointed out. "If they were telling the truth about their ship, they're right at the end of their endurance and they will *have* to unload some of their people."

"Here's what we do," the British Prime Minister said. "We tell them that we intend to allow them to settle in land we'll sell to them, in exchange for their technology shared between us all as a group. We insist on having our own people on the mothership so that we know exactly what we're dealing with…and so we have options if things go badly wrong. Between us, we can offer them a choice between getting what they want for free or facing a hostile world armed with nuclear weapons."

"Assuming they're daunted by nukes," the President pointed out. "They might not care about our nuclear weapons at all."

"If they're unaffected by nukes, we might as well get started on our surrender terms," the French President said. "The world is going to change. If we can get them to settle here on our terms…well, it's worth the risk of displeasing the rest of the world. It's better than fighting either the aliens or your country."

"I refused their offer," the President said.

"So you say," the Russian President said. The President couldn't blame him for being paranoid. In his place, he would have wondered if a deal had been struck after all. "I agree to the British Plan."

The discussions went on for several more hours, with a brief pause for cups of tea and coffee, before the various world leaders boarded their aircraft and returned to their respective countries. The main body of the shared plan would remain secret, but they'd prepared a joint press release that would be non-committal, informing the world that they'd agreed to meet with the aliens in New York. The President allowed himself to sleep on the flight back to Washington, but sleep didn't come easy. His thoughts kept jumping from point to point.

He had the nasty feeling that the aliens weren't through with their surprises, not yet.

Chapter Twenty-Four

Someone had vandalised his locker.

Captain Philip Carlson wasn't entirely surprised. The Space Shuttle had been scheduled to be retired from service in 2010, but NASA had kept the two remaining orbiters flying until – some said – they crashed or exploded on the launch pad. There were dozens of trained men and women who could fly the Shuttle, but simple odds meant that they would only get one or two chances to actually fly before they grew too old and had to be retired. There were astronauts who had never actually flown in space, growing older and older – and bitter, bitter at NASA and at the military astronauts who had flown dozens of missions. There were men who expected to die of old age before man built a base on the Moon, or sent a mission to Mars, or even deflected an asteroid before it hit the Earth. They took what refuge they could in picking on the military officers.

He shook his head as he checked the contents, before relocking the locker and heading off to the preparations room. He and his co-pilot had been separated from the standard NASA protocol for pilots on the verge of a flight – another source of tension between the other astronauts and the military pilots – although they'd still found time for the traditional breakfast of steak and eggs. The vast majority of the launch preparations were hardly necessary anyway, they'd just been added to try and avoid legal liability for any accidents that happened along the way. Philip – and all of the astronauts, military or civilian – had long since accepted the possibility of a sudden explosive death and bitterly resented the bureaucrats who insisted on covering NASA's collective ass where possible. After *Challenger* and *Columbia*, they'd taken over and imposed regulations designed to strangle any hope of initiative from the pilots. The result had been a massive collapse in morale.

The roar of the crowd could be heard even at a distance as he was escorted out of the building towards the massive shuttle, standing on its rear end and pointing towards the skies. Someone at NASA, either a frustrated pilot or a civilian bureaucrats, had leaked the fact that military pilots were flying the shuttle mission and the media had drawn the correct conclusion. The protesters carried signs imploring the pilots not to fly weapons into outer space, or prepare for war with the aliens, believing that there would be a peaceful solution to the crisis. Some of them were just plain dumb, accusing NASA of having been in contact with the aliens for years, or even having kidnapped Elvis and a thousand other missing people. At least one protester was under the impression that the moon landings had been faked; his sign demanded that NASA admit to the massive hoax. He, at least, was amusing. The remainder of the protesters were just…stupid. Did they really believe that NASA would abort the launch just to please them?

He paused under the gantry to stare up at the shuttle. *Atlantis* was massive, larger than many civilian airliners and merely looking at the shuttle shocked many people into silence. It was a wonderful craft, despite its limitations, but it never went anywhere. The shuttles went to orbit, bussed people to the International Space Station or launched a handful of satellites into orbit, and then landed at the runway, only a few miles away. It never went to the Moon, or Mars, or any other brave new world. That, Philip suspected, was what had killed NASA. It simply didn't do anything that attracted the public's imagination.

Philip, like all of the shuttle pilots, was a big space buff. If the human race had developed space the way they should have developed space – the way the aliens had definitely developed space – it would have solved so many of the Earth's problems. There were billions of tons of raw materials floating around the sun, waiting to be picked up and used to build space habitats in orbit. The energy crisis could be averted by developing space-based sources of energy, mainly collecting solar power and beaming it down to the Earth. Pollution could be cut back sharply with factories and other industries moved into space…the list went on and on, yet NASA didn't even *try* to do more than create useless visual images that were somehow never translated into reality. There were all kinds of theories, but Philip suspected the truth. NASA was simply too big to handle something as important as space.

His co-pilot was waiting for him at the bottom of the elevator. Felicity Hogan was younger than him by seven years, a former navy pilot who had transferred to NASA when the Ares or Orion looked as if they were going to be flying in a few years. She was dark-skinned and attractive enough to serve as a centrefold in a pornographic magazine, although she'd once told him that she'd sooner show them photographs of space. She'd been briefed on the mission and had volunteered without hesitation. Like him, she'd flown JSF aircraft from aircraft carriers, even if she'd never been tested in serious combat. That might be about to change.

They rode up to the shuttle's cockpit in silence and patiently endured the ground crew's endless series of tests, before they were allowed to enter the shuttle and take their seats. The crew fussed around them while others performed a final series of checks on the shuttle itself, looking for problems that could impede their mission. NASA, after two embarrassing disasters, had imposed a zero-tolerance program for any faults; if there were a single problem, the mission would be scrubbed until the fault was found, corrected, and then reported in triplicate. Philip had lost count of how many pilots had been poised in the cockpit, waiting for their first launch, and then discovered that there was a tiny fault and the mission had been cancelled. Some of them had never flown either. He smiled to himself. A number of former astronauts had been summoned to Washington to face Congress and the Special Enquiry into NASA's failure and perhaps retribution would be at hand.

"This is Launch Control," his radio buzzed. "All systems check out A-OK. I repeat, A-OK. Launch in ten minutes and counting."

Philip let out a breath he hadn't realised he'd been holding. With so many people at NASA adamantly opposed to launching weapons into space on a Space Shuttle, it hadn't been beyond possibility that one of them would have committed an act of minor sabotage. They would probably never have been caught – so many things could go wrong so easily – even though Philip would have torn the ground crews apart to find the culprit. They would never even have known if there was a *real* culprit or if it had been a genuine accident. A single screw loose could have forced the cancellation of the mission until well after the alien mothership arrived in orbit.

"Thank you, Control," he said, exchanging a glance with Felicity. She winked back at him. There were only two of them on the flight – the shuttle normally carried a full crew – and they had a moment of privacy. "It's too late to turn back now."

Felicity gave him a sharp look. "I volunteered for this, sir," she said. "I know the risks."

Philip looked at the countdown. "They don't," he muttered. The early stages of the shuttle's launch were all automatic. NASA had never developed the Shuttle-C concept, but in his view they needn't have bothered. The shuttle pilots were barely needed until the craft reached orbit. "They don't know anything at all."

———

Armed Marines secured the perimeter around the base and the shuttle's launch site, Abigail saw, as she shifted around to gain a better perspective. The Marines were polite, but very firm. No one was going to be allowed through to see the shuttle at close-range, unless they wanted to spend the rest of the day in jail. NASA's security team and officers from the Florida Highway Patrol had been rousting protesters all day, including a team that had planned to sneak inside the launch site and stuff cardboard up the ship's thrusters. It was the kind of idea that would only appeal to someone who didn't know much about the shuttle – Abigail suspected that the shuttle's engines would fire and simply burn the cardboard away – but it hardly mattered. The seven protesters had been cuffed, arrested, and escorted away in a pair of black vans. The remainder were standing in front of the Kennedy Space Centre Visitor Complex and the surrounding complex, shouting their heads off.

She relaxed as she found a place to watch without having to keep pushing others away. The lunatic fringe was out in force, screaming their protests from a safe distance, demanding that the mission be cancelled. Abigail couldn't blame them for their feelings; ever since the news had broken that the shuttle would be carrying a military payload, the nation had been buzzing with rumours that it was a weapon intended to attack the aliens. The protesters were screaming and chanting, but she could detect a hard edge of fear under their words. The massive shuttle was puny compared to the alien mothership. It was little more than a joke in poor taste.

"Warning," a voice proclaimed. "Shuttle launch in three minutes. I repeat, shuttle launch in three minutes."

The protesters shouted and jeered longer, shoving at the Marines and Police Officers in front of them. It looked for a long moment as if a full-scale riot was going to break out, but somehow the Marines held their ground. Abigail glanced behind her and saw reinforcements – both police and military – arriving in a large convoy. Perhaps the protesters realised that the soldiers wouldn't allow any of them to press through to the shuttle, although anyone stupid enough to be under the shuttle when it launched would deserve everything that happened to them. Abigail doubted that the investigators, afterwards, would find anything of them apart from a charred afterimage burned into the launch pad. The unlucky protesters would end up as candidates for the Darwin Award.

She studied the shuttle as the countdown ticked towards zero, once again awed by its massive size. It was larger than most airliners, or military aircraft, and it had an aura of restrained power, just waiting to burst out of its drives. It was fantastic…and yet, it was boring. The shuttle she was staring at was older than she was, reaching the end of its long career…and NASA was risking everything by keeping the remaining two shuttles in service. A third major shuttle accident would be the end of NASA, if Congress didn't pull the plug soon. The Special Enquiry was gaining steam.

The noise – a dull roar – struck her ears before she saw the smoke, flowing out of the shuttle's rear end. She looked at the timer and saw that it was ticking down the last few seconds. The shuttle seemed to be shaking very slightly, just before a brilliant yellow-white glow appeared under the craft. Slowly, agonisingly slowly, the massive craft seemed to start grasping for air, propelled forward – she could see now – by two external boosters, not its main thrusters. It seemed to be permanently on the verge of falling back to the ground and exploding – she couldn't remember how long it took before a shuttle could no longer be landed safely during launch – yet it kept moving, staggering upwards towards space. The noise seemed to fade – or perhaps she was growing used to it – as the shuttle picked up speed, racing faster and faster as it rose towards the heavens.

The protesters were silent now, watching as the craft gained height. There was something undeniably majestic about the sight. Even the Marines and Police Officers were watching as the external boosters separated from the main craft – which was now propelled by its main thrusters – and fell back towards the ground. They'd land somewhere in the ocean and be picked up and reused. The shuttle was hardly a working SSTO – the dream of space enthusiasts for years – yet it could be reused, apart from the external tank. That would burn up in Earth's atmosphere.

"Launch successful," someone announced. The shuttle was now nothing more than a light in the sky. Abigail shielded her eyes with her hand and tried to follow it as it rose ever higher. She envied the pilots and their chance to go to space, even as she feared for their future. WNN had taken an official position of neutrality on the alien contact, but Abigail knew that if the military was launching an armed shuttle, they had a suspicion that trouble was coming. "Launch successful."

"Good luck," she whispered. She pulled her notepad out of her pocket and started to make notes, but her mind was elsewhere, following the shuttle. "God bless."

The protesters were starting to disperse now and the cops let them go. A handful who had acted up badly and been cuffed and left to sit on the ground were loaded into vans and taken away, although Abigail knew that they'd be out within a few hours. There had been violent protests all across America – all across the entire Western World – and while thousands had been arrested, they couldn't all be charged. The police had settled for charging the ones who had committed violence and releasing the others with a stern warning. It hadn't stopped them from being threatened with over a thousand lawsuits.

She shook her head as she picked herself up and headed towards the car park. WNN had allowed her to go in person to watch the shuttle launch, but she had been ordered to be in New York by tomorrow. The aliens were going to land in New York in two days and WNN intended to have a full crew on the ground, recording everything that happened. CNN, Fox and hundreds of television networks from around the globe would be competing for ratings – there would literally be nothing else on television. The entertainment channels had already announced that they intended to run nothing but repeats – all movies involving friendly alien contact. The irony wasn't lost on her.

Her cell phone buzzed as she left the complex, informing her that her apartment in New York had been prepared for her, a rather unsubtle way of telling her to get to the city quickly. She laughed, put the cell phone back in her pocket, and looked up towards where the shuttle had been. It was gone.

———

It had been a year since Philip had flown in space, but it was something no one ever forgot. The absence of gravity suggested that people could be truly free in space, but the truth was that space was a realm where the iron laws of physics held total sway. A single mistimed burst from one of the thrusters could force them to abort their mission, or – if they ran out of fuel – they'd drift through space forever. He'd heard that some astronauts had seriously considered hijacking an orbiter and flying to the moon – it was theoretically possible – but no one had ever taken such a risk. It might delight the public, but NASA and his fellow astronauts would have crucified him. They already had to ask permission for almost everything they did in space. No one wanted to have to endure even more supervision from the ground.

He checked the shuttle's guidance systems and allowed himself a sigh of relief as they slipped into the correct trajectory for gliding towards the ISS. The station floated in a stable orbit around the planet, allowing the shuttle to catch up with the station, match course and speed, and then dock without problems, but an error would be expensive to correct. It hadn't escaped him that the alien craft seemed to operate without regard for the laws of physics and *Atlantis* was pretty much a sitting duck as far as they were concerned. He'd put on a brave face for General Dyson, yet…now, floating in space, he knew the immensity of what he'd agreed to try. The odds of success were minimal.

"Captain," Felicity said suddenly. She was looking down at the Near-Orbit Monitoring System, a low-level radar system designed to watch for pieces of space junk that might harm the shuttle. Philip had been onboard a shuttle when a tiny piece of junk had starred the forward cockpit window and he'd nearly wet himself in shock. A tiny bit more force and the entire shuttle would have been wrecked. The return to Earth had been touch and go. "We've got company."

She pointed out of the cockpit. "Look."

Philip followed her gaze. Normally, despite the increasingly large amount of space junk orbiting the Earth, it was rare to see anything with the naked eye. A satellite – even the largest humans had built – was tiny compared to the planet below. Now…he could see a craft orbiting beside the shuttle, a craft that was clearly not of human origin. It was so close that he could make out details. It was a glowing almond, shimmering in space…

He recognised it. It was the same design as the craft that had crashed on Earth, nearly a month ago. He'd seen the images from the crash and read the reports from the study team, but none of them had conveyed the sheer impact of the craft. Just hanging in space, pacing the shuttle effortlessly, it was terrifyingly intimidating. It was in no one's interest to start a war with the aliens.

Felicity's voice seemed to echo oddly in his ears. "Sir…Philip…what the hell do we do?"

Philip considered the weapons that had been loaded onboard the shuttle, but knew that they would be useless. "Nothing," he said, shortly. The alien craft was showing up clearly on radar. It wasn't even *trying* to hide. It could pace them all the way to the ISS, or…for all he knew, it could be in a galaxy far, far away in a split second. "We're just going to ignore it and pretend it's not there."

Felicity snorted. "Easier said than done," she said. "If they can build a ship like that, one that makes *Atlantis* look like a matchbox toy, what the hell do they want with Earth?"

Chapter Twenty-Five

New York, USA

Day 33

"Shadow Lead, we have a contact," the AWACS said. "Do you copy?"

Captain Will Jacob glanced at his HUD. It was a clear day, perfect flying weather for the two F-22 Raptors stationed in orbit around New York. All civilian air traffic for a hundred miles around the city had been grounded and a total air exclusion zone had been declared – in hopes of keeping out aircraft piloted by reporters intent on the scoop of the century – leaving only a handful of military aircraft in the sky. The live feed from the AWACS was shockingly clear. A new contact had entered the atmosphere and was flying towards New York at Mach Four.

"We copy," he said. "Shadow Lead, moving to intercept."

The Raptor was the finest fighter jet in the world, outclassing its nearest American, European, Japanese and Russian rivals, but even it couldn't maintain a speed of Mach Four. It wouldn't have to, he saw; the alien craft was rapidly decelerating, showing a shocking disregard for the laws of physics. Bull sessions back at the base had gone over and over how the alien craft might be powered, but looking at the contact now, the best that Will could suggest was a form of reactionless drive. The alien craft seemed to have no difficulty in performing the impossible.

He tensed as the contact rocketed towards the pair of Raptors, still decelerating. There was no reason to expect trouble, but the two pilots knew that they were far too exposed out here, away from the hundreds of military jets orbiting on the far side of the exclusion zone. It would take precious minutes for help to arrive if they ran into trouble…and the ROE were strict.

They were strict at the best of times, not always for the right reasons, but they'd been told in no uncertain terms that they were not to engage the alien craft, or even light it up with their onboard targeting systems, unless it gave clear proof of hostility. If the aliens had advanced lasers or other superweapons from science-fiction, the Raptor pilots wouldn't even see the proof of hostility before it blew them out of the sky. The Dark Shadow pilots had been joking around, acting like Will Smith and other movie star pilots, but the joke wasn't so funny now. The aliens were powerful enough to make the entire USAF look primitive.

"I have a contact," he said, as the alien craft blinked up on his HUD. It was glowing brightly in infrared, but cooling rapidly, somehow dispersing the heat of re-entry. "Contact is now moving at Mach One and proceeding towards New York. There are no IFF signals" – not that he'd expected any – "or other signs of trouble."

"Understood, Shadow Lead," the AWACS controller said. "Keep us informed."

Will snorted to himself as the alien craft came into view. The pilots had speculated endlessly on what the alien ships might look like – if they didn't have to worry about aerodynamics, their designers could go nuts if they wanted – but his first sight of the alien craft was somewhat disappointing. The craft was shaped like a giant egg, barely twice the size of a transport helicopter, with no visible drive system. It was as smooth and pristine as a bowling ball. For a moment, he felt a flicker of envy. The Raptor was a wonderful aircraft, but the alien ship outmatched it and made it look like a child's toy. It seemed to be cooperating, slowing to a speed the Raptors could match with ease, yet it could accelerate at any moment and leave them eating its dust. The lesson wasn't lost on him.

If it comes down to a fight, they can run rings around us, he thought. It wasn't something he dared say aloud. They'd been warned that the aliens might be able to intercept their radio transmissions, even decrypt transmissions that were supposed to be secure. It wouldn't be the first time the military had been humiliated by someone cracking unbreakable codes, but this one could have more disastrous consequences. They'd agreed on a series of code words for sensitive situations, yet Will was all-too-aware that it had limitations. They would have to wait until they returned to base if they encountered something they couldn't communicate safely through the radio.

The two Raptors banked in a perfect display of synchronised flying and matched course and speed with the alien craft, which showed no sign of being aware of their presence. Will glanced over at it and felt a shiver running down his spine. The Raptors were normally never as close to potential targets as they were now. The USAF – and every other advanced air force in the world – had been looking for ways to kill their enemies from further and further away, not to close in with the enemy planes for a high-tech dogfight. The F-22s were just too expensive to be thrown away like that. The aliens made a mockery out of all of their preparations. The F-22s might simply be swatted like flies if they had to fight the alien craft.

He glanced down again in surprise as he realised what was missing. The alien craft had been coming in at a terrific speed, fast enough that it should have been creating an air stream that would have bounced the two human aircraft around, perhaps even forced them to maintain their distance. The alien craft seemed to move without disturbing the air around it, leaving no visible trail of its presence. The AWACS was sending a live feed, but he'd already realised that the alien craft was hard to track on the most modern sensors the USAF possessed. If it hadn't been for the ground-based systems, the alien ships might have been impossible to track with any certainty.

"New York," his wingman said. Will looked down and nodded. Manhattan Island was rising out of the country ahead of them, a daunting tribute to humanity's greatest achievements in bending the world to their will. It was the skyscrapers, standing proud against the skyline which defined America far more than anything else; a credit to the land of the free. No wonder that the enemies of freedom had aimed their blows at New York's proudest monuments. They'd been striking right at the heart and soul of America itself. "Sir…?"

Under normal circumstances, Will and his wingman would have guided the alien craft in to land, but these were far from normal circumstances. The briefing had said that space had been cleared in front of the UN Building, with the crowds and politicians kept well back in case the alien craft happened to be radioactive or otherwise dangerous, and that the craft should be capable of landing like a VTOL aircraft. Will wasn't sure how they were so certain, unless the aliens had informed them in their second message to the world, but he knew enough to trust his superiors. The entire American military had been showing a remarkable unity in response to the alien contact – and possible threat.

"Stay on our flight path," he ordered, looking down at the city below. They had slowed to below Mach One and would no longer be producing a sonic boom, but the roar of their engines would be scaring people down below. Will was old enough to remember the eerie silence in the air after 9/11 and how the first aircraft flying afterwards had scared people, convincing them that another terrorist attack was underway. "They know where they're going."

The alien craft started to sink towards the ground, creating an impression that it was being *lowered*, like some demented puppet craft on a string. There was no hint of acknowledgement, no hint that it had even noticed the Raptors during the brief moment when they flew alongside the alien craft, nothing. It didn't even seem aware of the missiles slung under the fighter's wings, or of any possible danger. No one was sure what would have happened if a missile had been loosed, but everyone agreed that the consequences would have been bad. There had been a serious line of thought that the Raptors should have gone up completely unarmed, a debate that had gone all the way up to the President, who had ruled that the aircraft were to be armed. It was a trust that Will appreciated. If they'd run into trouble, unarmed aircraft would be sitting ducks.

He watched as the alien craft drifted towards the marked landing pad, feeling another flash of envy, this time for the men and women on the ground. They would *see* live aliens for the first time, while Will and his fellows would have to catch repeats, later. The AWACS crew were probably peeking at the live broadcast from the ground, but there were no facilities for television on the fighters. It had never occurred to him to regret that before. Besides, the CO would have had a fit if he'd caught his pilots watching television when they were supposed to be flying.

Smiling, he twisted the fighter away from Manhattan and headed towards the orbiting tankers, protected by a swarm of Raptors and F-18 Super Hornets. Once they'd refuelled, their orders were to join the other military aircraft on stand-by, just in case anything happened. There were enough military assets on alert to conquer a small country or destroy the Warsaw Pact armies in their prime, yet what he'd seen had convinced him that it wouldn't be enough if the aliens turned hostile. The world had already changed – the mere announcement of alien contact had changed the world – but meeting aliens with such superiority would alter the way the human race looked at itself, forever. He remembered meeting people from societies that had never caught up with the changes sweeping the globe and shivered. Was that the fate in line for humanity?

———

Mayor Michael Hundred allowed himself a smile as the alien craft slowly started to fall towards his city, a shining egg hanging in the air. Part of him had been braced for disappointment – the city had been hoaxed before – even though pretty much every government in the world had confirmed the discovery of an alien craft. The world was too mundane, too *spoiled* to allow the presence of something as wondrous as another intelligent race. Hundred had been a science-fiction fan long before he'd run for Mayor of New York and knew that science-fiction's visions of extra-terrestrial life had never become reality. The interstellar navigation beacons had turned out to be quasars, NASA's pretty pictures of interstellar spacecraft had never left the drawing board and civilians didn't get to fly to the Moon for a holiday. There were no longer any dreams in the world.

But now the universe had come calling and the Big Apple would greet them with open arms. Hundred had fought savagely against both the UN and the Federal Government for control of the landing site, disliking both of them for different reasons. The UN had a long history of clashes with New York, normally over offences committed by UN diplomats with diplomatic immunity – everything from unpaid parking tickets to rape and murder – and there was no way Hundred was going to allow the UN to control the most important event in the city's history. The Feds had been even more impractical – they'd wanted to evacuate the entire city and station military forces all around the UN – and it had been easy to play them off against one another. The prospect of a political catfight in public view, where the aliens could see, had daunted even the UN.

Hundred had made his own preparations for the alien landing, using advice from the Feds and even the UN. A large space had been cleared for the alien craft, surrounded by hundreds of New York's Finest. All police leave had been cancelled and hundreds of additional officers had been drafted in from the surrounding area, causing a massive drop in crime. Hundreds of known hardcore troublemakers – men and women who went to protests and turned them into violent riots that had to be dispersed by the police – had been swooped on and preventively arrested, held in custody until the aliens were well away from the city. It would probably result in hundreds of lawsuits, but Mayor Hundred didn't care. The troublemakers wouldn't have a chance to ruin Earth's first meeting with representatives from beyond the stars.

He cast his gaze towards the crowds and winced. The troublemakers might be cooling their heels in jail, or lying very low somewhere away from the landing pad, but the remainder of the lunatic fringe had turned out in force. They dressed as aliens from various television shows and movies, carrying signs welcoming the aliens to Earth. The NYPD had orders to confiscate any threatening or unpleasant signs – he'd made a special request that people refrain from doing anything the aliens might interpret as threatening – yet he knew that the whole display could collapse into chaos at any moment. It was bad enough to know that a dozen different government agencies had set up detectors looking for radiation – or any other unpleasant surprises – but it was worse knowing that armed soldiers had been positioned nearby, just in case something went wrong. He hadn't had it all his own way.

A deafening racket split the air as several school bands burst into tune. No one had been able to agree on a shared tune, so Hundred had ordered the use of the *Star Wars* theme tune, one he'd enjoyed as a kid. That had lasted twenty minutes before someone had pointed out that *Star Wars* wasn't exactly about peaceful alien contact and it might be better to use one where the view of aliens was more positive. The shortage of movies involving friendly aliens – *ET* or *Close Encounters of the Third Kind* had been rapidly dismissed – had led to a suggestion that the national anthem should be played. That, in turn, had led to an accusation from the UN that America was trying to monopolise the coming talks. Someone else had pointed out that the aliens might not like band music and everything had broken down from there. The Mayor had finally ruled in favour of a simple tune that couldn't cause offence and everyone had breathed a sigh of relief.

The alien craft hovered into view and the bands broke down as their players – all children or teenagers – forgot their notes. The Mayor sympathised with the irate bandmasters – he saw one of them screaming unheard abuse at a blonde girl with spiky hair who played the saxophone – but he couldn't blame the children. There was something about the alien craft that pulled the human eye towards it. The bandmasters slowly gave up the fight and the music died away, replaced by a hum that the Mayor *felt*, rather than heard. The alien craft grew a set of tripod landing struts and gently settled down to the ground.

Hundred watched as the reporters snapped photos, transmitting them through the satellite network back to their organisations. The Mayor had been told that every news station in the world was going to be covering the alien landing, apart from a handful from the more repressive countries who didn't want their people aware of the existence of alien life. A thousand commentators were babbling away, expounding on the Meaning Of It All to their viewers, all of who probably wished that the reporters would shut up and get out of the television. They wanted to see the aliens and their craft, not someone who would be gone when someone younger and prettier came along.

A faint ripple, like ripples in a pond, seemed to rush across the alien craft. Hundred watched, for once lost for words, as part of the craft seemed to extend down towards the ground, forming a ramp for the aliens to walk down to Earth. Another ripple marked a hatch forming out of the craft, marring a perfect hull to allow the aliens to leave their ship. Hundred had heard of memory metal or nanotechnology, either one of which could have produced such an effect, and he found himself wondering which one the aliens used. If they'd developed programmable metal to a level far in advance of human technology, it could be used for all kinds of projects that had only been dreams before, dreams in the mind of science-fiction writers. Humans had spent so long considering the uses of materials and technology they'd never invented – not yet, anyway – that he was sure they could have shown the aliens a few new tricks.

Humanity's export to the stars, he thought wryly. *Science-fiction and imagination.*

He heard the Secretary-General praying very softly in Arabic. Hundred didn't get on very well with the Secretary-General of the United Nations, who had the unpleasant duty of telling him that the accused often had diplomatic immunity and the worst they could do was throw him out of the city, but he felt a moment of sympathy for the man. He'd been placed into his position as a placeholder, nothing else. He'd never expected to be greeting aliens in real life. He probably hadn't even given any thought to the possibility. Hundred, at least, had the advantage there.

"Don't worry," he muttered. The existence of aliens meant that differences between humans were no longer important – at least, that was what most science-fiction novels claimed. Others had been more depressing. "They're probably not hostile."

The Secretary-General shot him an irritated look. Hundred smothered a chuckle as the first alien appeared in the hatch. His attention was riveted by the creature as it stood there, allowing the humans to get an eyeful. It was humanoid, but it was undeniably alien. Hundred felt a cold chill running down the back of his neck as he came face-to-face with something *other*, something so *different* that it was beyond his comprehension. This was no actor in a mask, no product of CGI, but something new and terrible.

"Come on," he whispered, as the alien began to descend the ramp. "We have to greet him formally."

Chapter Twenty-Six

New York, USA

Day 33

Secretary-General Abdul Al-Hasid found himself staring as the alien walked down the ramp, every step careful and deliberate. In the two years he'd served as Secretary-General, he'd looked into many eyes, the eyes of men who were willing to compromise and men who intended to die for their faith. They'd all been human, however, and the aliens were anything but. The big dark eyes were completely unreadable and very inhuman. The being gave off a sense of great age, a sense that it was very far from home, yet even for an experienced diplomat, there were no tells to work from. Al-Hasid found himself mentally floundering, driven on only by his duty – and a desire not to let the Mayor of New York outshine him. He wanted to run and hide, cursing the day he'd accepted the position. It had been the greatest mistake of his life.

There were books and television programs that depicted the Secretary-General as the effective ruler of the planet, but Al-Hasid knew that was a lie. The best that could be said for the role was that the Secretary-General served as an umpire and a neutral arbitrator, yet even that was somewhat untruthful. The UN was staffed by men and women whose first loyalty was to their home country, not to any transnational institution, and the powers of the Secretary-General were sharply limited. He had no armies to send to enforce his will, no prestige that could be used to shame someone into standing down, often the best he could do was convince a would-be murderer to rape instead. It was such compromises – if compromise was the right word – that had sapped the UN, destroying any hope it might have had to become something more than a debating chamber. It very definitely was not the Parliament of Man.

Up close, there was a faint spicy aroma around the alien being. He - Al-Hasid decided to assume that it was a he until there was a reason to change that assumption – stopped a metre away from the two politicians, appraising them silently with his big dark eyes. Al-Hasid wondered, suddenly, if the alien was trying to decide which of them was which. He sometimes had problems telling the difference between some humans and the aliens probably had similar problems. They might find all humans identical, or they might have intercepted transmissions discussing one of his predecessors and expected to meet him. He plucked up his courage and stepped forward.

"In the name of the United Nations of Planet Earth, welcome to Earth," he said. The protocol experts had gone crazy trying to decide what the Secretary-General should say to the aliens. Popular perception aside, high-stakes diplomacy rarely took place in public. No one even knew if the aliens spoke English, although the one message they'd sent to the planet had been in English.

"And welcome to New York," the Mayor added. Al-Hasid felt himself overwhelmed by a sense of the absurd. "We wish to show you around the city."

"Thank you for your welcome," the alien whispered. His voice was slow and sibilant, echoing oddly around the silent city. Even the ever-present roar of cars had faded away. "We come in peace."

The crowds went wild, cheering loudly, even throwing hats and signs into the air. Al-Hasid looked at the alien and saw him flinch slightly under the racket, the first truly human sign he'd seen from the alien. It was probably lucky that the bands had been silenced by the craft, he decided. Welcoming the aliens was a task probably better suited to a group of trained diplomats rather than an entire city.

"We have important matters to discuss," the alien continued, so softly that Al-Hasid could barely hear him. "We must address your United Nations at once."

"Of course," Al-Hasid said, barely aware of the Mayor's displeasure. Accidentally or otherwise, his city had just been snubbed. "They are eager to hear from you."

The alien bowed, lowering his great head for a single moment. Al-Hasid took it as his cue and beckoned the alien forward, inviting him to walk with him. A moment later, two more aliens – both smaller and slightly different than the first alien – appeared from the craft and followed them. Al-Hasid glanced at them, puzzled. They seemed too different from the first alien to come from the same roots, or were they female? The aliens might have been humanoid, but it was clear that they were far from human – and they certainly shared little with humanity. The tales about Ancient Astronauts were almost certainly nonsense.

He was reminded, suddenly, of an old story that had been circulating around the UN since 1990. Secretary-General Javier Perez de Cuellar had not only seen a UFO, but he had witnessed, along with his bodyguards, a woman being abducted by little grey aliens. No one knew for sure if the story was true - Javier Perez de Cuellar had never confirmed it publicly – and he'd taken the secret to his grave. Al-Hasid wondered if his predecessor had shared the same sense of growing unreality, or if it had all been a hoax. There was no way to know.

The alien showed no reaction to the lines of NYPD officers and UN Security Staff, or the shouted questions hurled by the reporters on the other side of the barriers. Al-Hasid allowed himself a moment of relief – some of the questions were downright imprudent, if not outrageous or stupid – as they reached the Main Entrance. Normally, anyone going into the building would go through a security check – the UN was a prime terrorist target – but it had been decided to allow the alien through without any checks. Attempting to search the alien would have probably been taken as a hostile act.

His lips twitched. One of the contingency plans the Americans had hastily drawn up had included confiscating the alien craft until a NEST team could examine it to confirm that it posed no threat, something that would *definitely* have been regarded as an act of war. *He* wouldn't have been too happy to have his private jet confiscated.

"We have prepared rooms for you," he said, remembering his duty as a host. "Do you require time to rest?"

"No," the alien whispered. Al-Hasid smiled to himself. The diplomats would have quite happily waited for hours for the alien. No one wanted to miss this meeting. "We can speak at once to the assembled diplomats."

Al-Hasid smiled as the alien was led into the United Nations General Assembly. Normally, it was rarely more than half-full, but now it was standing room only in the observation gallery. Almost every reporter in the world had demanded admittance, but only a handful could be permitted entry. A quota system had been established, and the live footage from the meeting would be shared with all television networks without charge, but some networks were already screaming about having been denied access. Al-Hasid was quietly rather pleased with Al Jazeera's absence, even though he knew he'd pay for it later. Al Jazeera had been something of a nuisance ever since it had published a report claiming that Al-Hasid was on the American payroll. It was completely inaccurate, not least because the Americans hardly needed to bother.

He watched as the alien walked right towards the podium, as if he was already familiar with the chamber. He had already decided to dispense with protocol, but Al-Hasid knew that no one would care. The impact of the alien's presence was such that he could have recited nothing more than the names of stars, or countries in the United Nations, and they would have listened raptly. The two smaller aliens took up positions behind their leader – at least, Al-Hasid assumed that he was their leader, although he had to remind himself not to take anything for granted – and waited. The entire chamber fell silent.

———

Abigail had been lucky. WNN had pulled every string and called in every favour it was owed and had obtained one of the coveted places in the General Assembly. All three of the main American networks were represented, along with representatives from the BBC and various other famous networks, covering almost the entire world. The alien message, whatever it was, would be going out to the entire world. No government – at least not in the West – could avoid broadcasting it, not when it was going out on the Internet and the satellite network. Censorship on such a scale was simply impossible. The Internet, as the saying went, treated censorship as a malfunction and rerouted around it. Even the Chinese were allowing the broadcast to go out without hindrance. Trying to keep it from their people would have provoked massive unrest.

Her gaze swept the chamber as she tried to look away from the sheer overwhelming presence of the alien. The UN was normally organised by alphabetical order, but there had been some changes, marking the nations that had signed up to the Third World Alliance. In the General Assembly, where each nation had one vote, they might carry the day, even though Abigail had heard that the United Nations Security Council intended to take a hard line with the aliens. The smaller nations, the ones with least to lose, had been putting out stories about the end of poverty and massive wealth redistribution on a global scale. There was no proof that the aliens intended to do anything other than say hello to Planet Earth, but it hadn't stopped the propaganda machine from talking about a new world the aliens would create, one where the Evil First World Nations could no longer exploit the poor and weak.

Privately, Abigail doubted that it would be anything as simple as they made it sound. In magic, she'd been told by a former boyfriend, merely declaring a thing a thing made it that thing, which probably explained why magic didn't work. Declaring a dead horse a live one wouldn't bring it back to life, nor would branding a state a People's Democratic Republic magically transform it into a place fit for human occupation. Her one trip outside the United States as part of the Peace Corps had been to the Sudan, where she'd encountered corrupt officials and a mindset that ensured that people would continue to starve, no matter how much food and aid was poured in from the West. The aliens might not be able to improve the world, even if they wanted to help humanity out of the hole it had dug for itself.

There was a tradition that a Special Session of the United Nations General Assembly was always opened by a Brazilian, but they'd allowed that right to lapse in the face of the alien presence. No one knew what the alien wanted to say, but no one wanted to sit through hours of meaningless generalities before they got to the point. The eyes of the world were watching, something that rarely happened unless there was a war on or a big human disaster that had penetrated the news. It was easy to be cynical. WNN had a better reputation than either Fox or CNN for impartial reporting, but how could they report everything? The American public was more interested in which supermodel was being screwed by which sports star than how many children were starving to death in Africa.

"Thank you for allowing us to address this gathering," the alien said. Its voice was soft, almost a whisper, but the microphones picked it up and broadcast it around the world. "We have travelled far in search of other intelligent races. There are so few intelligent races in the galaxy that the discovery of a new race is a rare event. It is never ordinary, or common, to meet a strange new life form. The discovery of Earth was a matter for great joy among my people."

A rustle swept around the chamber. They hadn't realised, perhaps, that they might not have been the first race the aliens had encountered. Statistically, one of WNN's pet scientists had explained, the odds of any given star harbouring intelligent life were low, but on a cosmic timescale many of them might develop life. Another had put forward a tougher argument. There were hundreds of thousands of known stars like the Sun, yet only one of them had been examined in detail – the Sun itself. The Sun had given birth to at least one living planet – Earth – perhaps two, if the speculations about life developing on Titan were accurate. Logically, it was at least possible that the other Sun-like stars had intelligent life of their own.

The debate had torn apart the Drake Equation and the Fermi Paradox. Frank Drake had attempted to calculate the number of intelligent races in the galaxy at any given moment, yet the figures suggested far more races than humanity had evidence existed. The Fermi Paradox was more confusing and suggested that humanity *should* have picked up evidence of alien life and, therefore, the aliens didn't exist. Humanity was alone in the galaxy – or, more worryingly, someone out there was wiping out intelligent life forms before by could develop the technology to protect themselves. Other scientists had claimed that the paradox wasn't a paradox at all and produced their own mathematical models to demonstrate their points, although Abigail tended to lose track of the debate. She didn't have a hard science background, but it struck her that if the scientists didn't know what the numbers actually were, their fancy equations were really nothing more than talking points.

"We studied your world carefully, over a long period of time," the alien continued. "You are a remarkable people, yet you are trapped in a socio-political trap that you cannot easily escape. You have denied yourself access to the vast resources waiting for you in space, even to the point of denying yourself any defence against falling asteroids striking your planet. Indeed, we deflected an asteroid that would otherwise have struck your world and exterminated your people. We did it only because you had no way of protecting yourself."

A second rustle ran through the chamber. Abigail wondered if the alien was telling the truth, for it was impossible to verify. If they had saved humanity's collective butt, the human race would be grateful, yet there was no proof. It might have been a convenient lie just to make the human race feel grateful – and inferior. She remembered her own thoughts when *Atlantis* had rocketed into orbit – and how outmatched the shuttle was compared to the alien craft that had landed in New York. There was no denying that the aliens possessed awesome technology.

"You have also refused to develop the technology that could be used to save you," the alien continued. "You preach a return to a simpler world that could not possibly support your entire population. You flinch from technologies that could save your race and clean up your world, the world you have desecrated because of an outmoded economic structure that penalises advancement and rewards stasis. You allow the most horrific acts to go unpunished and treat national leaders who should be removed as honoured guests. You are rapidly approaching a point where your world will tip into an abyss of pure chaos as your societies break down and fragment. Your world is on the brink of catastrophic collapse.

"We can help you.

"We *will* help you.

"Our race has not flinched from advancement, from claiming our destiny, a destiny your race should share," the alien said. The chamber was deathly silent. "We are prepared to use that technology to help you. We have power sources that will not pollute the planet you have abused any further. We have technology that will bring life back to the deserts and allow you to clean up the worst of your polluted areas. We have technology that will assist your race to develop its own space-based industry and remove factories from your lands. We can place human colonies all over the solar system and beyond, ensuring that the human race can no longer be destroyed by a rogue asteroid – an asteroid that would not have been beyond your ability to halt, had you bothered to develop your facilities in space.

"We can help you to develop new economic models that will ensure that all of your children have enough to eat, a distribution of resources that will make sure that no one goes without food, or the bare necessities of life. We will assist you to clean up areas dominated by terrorist governments, where people are held in bondage for being the wrong sex, or the wrong religion, or the wrong skin colour, or perhaps just because they dared to speak truth to power. We will show you how to reshape your world and claim a destiny among the stars, a destiny that all intelligent races aspire to from the moment they first look out at the land and realise that they can reshape it at will."

There was a long chilling pause. "But there is a problem," the alien said. "This was not our first attempt to approach your people and your leadership. We sent a single ship into your atmosphere to make contact with the American Government, believing that they would be receptive to our offer. The ship was shot down by the American military and its pilots were killed. The data unit we gave the crew, as a symbol of our goodwill, was confiscated. They have not even attempted to put the data to use to improve your world.

"We request, we *demand*, the return of that ship and crew," the alien concluded. "We demand that American preparations to meet our ship with aggression are halted. If these demands are not met, within five of your days, we will be forced – more with sorrow than with anger – to reclaim the ship and halt your preparations with deadly force. Then, and only then, can we offer you a brave new world for your children, one that you can be proud of creating."

The chamber erupted into chaos.

Chapter Twenty-Seven

"Well…shit."

There didn't, Alex decided, seem to be much more to say. The live feed from the UN General Assembly showed the delegates shouting their shock and outrage, blurring together into a single howl of rage. The Secretary-General, looking pale and terrified, was banging for silence, but no one was paying attention to him. The reporters were on their feet, shouting questions at the American Ambassador, who looked disbelieving. The entire session had degenerated into chaos.

The three aliens, having delivered their speech, turned and walked out of the chamber, followed rapidly by the Secretary-General, babbling away to them. There was no way to know what he was saying to the aliens, but Alex suspected that it didn't matter. The aliens had delivered their ultimatum and now intended to depart before their ship was seized. He considered picking up the telephone and urging that the ship be captured before it could depart, but it would have been too late. Besides, the President would almost certainly have balked at a direct act of war.

"Those filthy fucking sons of bitches," Santini erupted from his chair. "They've stuck a knife in our backs!"

Alex could only agree. The aliens had just blown any hope of a unified response out of the water. Even the other members of the United Nations Security Council would have problems working with America if they – or their people – believed that the United States was responsible for starting a war with an advanced alien race. The leaders might know better…except they might not. They hadn't been told about the crashed ship and would react angrily to having that information kept from them, suspecting – correctly – that America had intended to develop the alien tech for its own use. They'd certainly place a high price on any aid they sent to the United States, if they could send any help at all. America's great geographical advantage over the other four UNSC members had just become a weakness. They *couldn't* send much in the way of help, even if they wanted to help. America would be standing alone.

"They know us too well," he agreed, ruefully. He should have seen that coming, but they'd all been blindsided by the apparent alien willingness to work with the United States, rather than start a war. No *wonder* they had never mentioned the crashed craft! It would have been inconvenient for their plans if the United States had returned it ahead of time. "Now half our own people are going to think that we're the villains."

The scenario unfolded in his mind. The opinions of much of the rest of the world could be discounted, as politically incorrect as that was. The opinions of much of the American population could not be discounted, or there would be a political crisis. If the public were strongly against keeping the craft and telling the aliens to go to hell, it wouldn't be long before Congress tried to impeach the President, or force him to return the craft at once. Either one would trigger a massive political crisis that would paralysis the American Government when it needed to be working as a smoothly-functional machine. It wasn't just the mob of protesters who protested everything from climate change to foreign aid to unpleasant regimes, but the silent majority who cast their votes in elections, for Congressmen, Senators...and Presidents. The hordes of protesters could do nothing more than make a loud noise, yet if the silent majority agreed with them...the President might stare down the protesters, but what about the rest of the country?

"Fuck it," he said, as he realised that the aliens were in a stronger position than they knew. "How the hell do we prove that the craft crashed without help?"

Santini looked over at him. "We show them the damaged hull?"

"Someone who didn't know much about missiles would think that was inflicted by a missile," Alex pointed out. "We can't *prove* that it wasn't shot down by the defences around the air base – hell, it's even a reasonable assumption that it *was* shot down. It's not as if we make a habit of allowing unidentified aircraft to fly through secure airspace without challenging them. Someone could quite easily buy that we didn't know what it was when we fired on it, but also that we certainly covered it up afterwards."

"I see," Santini said. He sounded doubtful. "No one would fall for that."

Alex put on his best impression of Tommy Lee Jones. "A person is smart, but people are dumb," he said. It had been one of his favourite scenes in the movie, for it was entirely accurate. A single person might appreciate the subtle points and nuances of any given situation; a group couldn't see anywhere beyond the surface, if that. "You go out and tell a group of people who grew up in a paradise that the United States is the source of all evil and the enemies of the United States share their vision of what is wrong with the United States and you'll have nine out of ten of them convinced that the United States is in the wrong to go over there and kill those fucking medieval monsters who kill women for wearing make-up and men for daring to kiss other men.

"They don't know, deep inside, the truth about the universe. They think that the aliens are certainly friendly, because an advanced race has to be too civilised to think about war and conquest. They think that the distance between us and the aliens lends enchantment to the aliens, because they're wondrous creatures so unlike humanity. They're going to be *certain* that we shot down the craft because...hey, that's what the Evil Military-Industrial Complex *does!*"

He shook his head slowly. "They played us," he said, bitterly. "They told us all the harsh truths about our planet we didn't want to face, they offered us the way out, and then they kicked us in the teeth. The entire planet is going to think of us as the bad guys. Our own population, for daring to shoot down an alien craft; the rest of the Security Council, for not telling them about the crashed ship; the rest of the world, for depriving them of the redistribution of wealth and resources they so desperately need. They wanted to isolate America and they succeeded. It was brilliant."

Jones came in the door, pale and sweating. "I have to visit the President in two hours to consult with him," he said shortly. He didn't look keen on the idea. It meant a flight in a military fighter and that was always uncomfortable for the passenger. "What the hell do I tell him?"

"They played us," Alex repeated, and ran through his brief conclusions. "I cannot help but feel that the second set of demands is the important one. They want us to shut down our defences and allow the mothership to enter orbit peacefully."

"So that we don't blow it up and die like those little furry creatures from *Return of the Jedi*," Santini added, dryly. "They must know that we'd be aware of the consequences if we took out the mothership."

"They don't think very highly of our space program," Alex pointed out. He shrugged and returned to the topic on hand. Jones had heard too much about NASA's flaws and how new hardware had to be created from scratch over the last two weeks. "They wouldn't go to all this trouble unless they needed to force us to stand down."

"Or unless they want to provoke a fight anyway," Jones said. He nodded towards the television screen, where a dark-skinned announcer of barely legal age was declaiming rapidly on the Meaning Of It All. Alex suspected that most people watching the broadcast were watching her and barely listening to the words coming out of her lips. "The President wants options!"

"They lied to either the President or the United Nations," Alex said. "The simplest solution – which is normally the correct one – is that they lied to the United Nations. Their claims were too grandiose to be completely true – hell, much of it was out of bad space movies where the Elder Aliens come down from the heavens and end war, poverty and a new age dawns over the planet. I think the evidence suggests that we are facing an invasion and the aliens are softening us up to make us easier to take."

"They don't need to bother," Santini pointed out, dolefully. "All they have to do is hurl rocks until we bend over and spread our legs for them."

"That would also damage the planet badly," Alex said. "If they need to unload their people as quickly as possible, they're not going to want to ruin Earth."

"Perhaps we could threaten to ruin Earth," Santini suggested. "We could threaten to detonate a nuke or two in Yellowstone and cause a massive volcanic eruption, or perhaps start a massive war with dirty nukes…"

"The President would refuse," Jones said, tightly. For the first time, Alex realised that Jones was scared, almost out of his mind. The prospect of alien invasion was far more real to those who had studied the alien craft and bodies. "Even if we tried, the aliens would know that we were bluffing."

"They wouldn't have a choice but to call our bluff," Alex agreed. He ticked off points on his fingers. "The first choice is to accept their terms, return the craft and stand down our defences. That probably puts off the invasion, perhaps until the aliens can think of more demands, perhaps permanently. The downside is that we will lose any chance of deciphering more of their technology and perhaps building our own weapons using their tech. The second choice is to refuse to return the craft, on the grounds that it crashed on our territory, but to offer to return the bodies."

"I don't think they'll go for that," Santini said. "The bodies aren't important unless we manage to figure out something we can use as a biological weapon against them and poison them all. It's the craft and its technology that is the real prize here."

"The third option is that we refuse to return the craft until we have a full accounting from the aliens," Alex continued. "We tell the world everything that happened, from the moment when the UFO crashed outside one of our most classified locations, to the President's visit to the alien ship. The other United Nations Security Council members will back us up on that one. They all saw footage of the aliens before they landed in New York and no one – officially – knew what the aliens looked like until then. We refuse to stand down and render ourselves defenceless until we know for sure exactly what we are dealing with."

"And then the aliens start hurling rocks," Jones said, acidly. "It wouldn't take many rocks to mess up our country, would it?"

"No," Alex said. He felt helpless, stumbling through a long dark passage. The light at the end of the tunnel might just turn out to be an oncoming train. "I don't know what else to suggest."

"I have a suggestion," Santini said, suddenly. "Nicolas and his men are in Antarctica, so have them move up the attack schedule and hit the alien base now. They can show the world that the aliens had a secret base on our planet long before we ever knew of their existence, which doesn't suggest friendly motives, does it?"

Alex shook his head. "No," he said, "but legally…it's tricky. The aliens aren't based in territory we claim – hell, we don't have any claims, apart from the research stations. Launching an attack without very clear proof of hostile intent would set off a diplomatic crisis…and perhaps trigger a war with the aliens. We'll look like the people who fired the first shot."

"I cannot believe that we're worried about a diplomatic crisis now," Santini snapped. He nodded towards the television, where the reporter had been replaced by a diplomat from Germany, who was expressing his shock and outrage over the entire crisis and calling on the American Government to return the alien craft at once. "We already have a diplomatic crisis on our hands."

"And the last thing we need is to trigger a war while we still have room to negotiate," Alex said, carefully. He looked away from the television and down at the table. "They may be bluffing, sir. There's no reason why they would go to all this trouble unless they feared our ability to resist. We can make a counter-offer in front of the entire world and see how the aliens respond to that."

"They're not concerned about public opinion," Santini said. "Why should they care?"

"We're facing an invasion," Alex reminded him. "We have to show that we've done all we can to avert it – and to prepare to fight it, if it does come down to war. If we stand down the defences now, we will be in a weaker position when we finally have to fight, even if we get a chance to fight. We have to convince our own people that we're not only doing everything we can, but that the aliens are being unreasonable and deliberately provoking a war."

"I'll take your advice to the President," Jones said. He sounded tired and worn down. "He'll make the final call about what we say in response. Keep working on possible options if it does come down to war."

Alex sighed as Jones left the room. There were no more possible options until new hardware could be designed and built, and even producing test models would take longer than they had before the mothership entered orbit. It was bitterly frustrating; without NASA's dead hand, they could produce all kinds of experimental craft, yet none of them could match the known capabilities of the alien craft. In the future, those secrets would be uncovered – knowing that it was possible to do something was half the battle – but would it be in time? The human race's ability to wage war against the aliens was very limited. The aliens had to know that…

"They have to come within range of our weapons if they want to settle the planet," he mused, as Santini got up and left as well. "They have to be afraid of what we could do to them, or they wouldn't bother playing political games."

He looked over at the display, a live feed sent through a secure landline direct from NORAD. The defences looked ready, yet he was chillingly aware of how flimsy they actually were against any advanced opponent. The Russians could have launched a full nuclear strike and would probably have landed enough nukes on American soil to put an end to America's existence as a coherent nation. The aliens would probably be untroubled by half of the American defences and laughing their collective ass off at the remainder.

"Ben said you were depressed," a voice said, from behind him. "You look as if you've just had a nasty shock."

"The entire world has just had a nasty shock," Alex said, as Jane settled down next to him. The Doctor looked tired herself. She'd been concentrating on trying to unlock more secrets from the alien biology without cutting into or dissecting the bodies, not an easy task. "The aliens have blown the secret wide open."

"And everyone is now scared to death," Jane agreed. Her eyes followed yet another television star explaining – again – what had happened, as if the entire country hadn't already seen the scene in New York. The schools and colleges had been closed to allow their pupils to watch the alien landing. The vast majority of employees had been given the day off; drills and endless exercises in military bases had been halted to allow the soldiers to watch television. The only people who wouldn't have seen it live were people in essential positions. "What happens now?"

Alex shrugged. He didn't feel like discussing it.

"The President comes to a decision and then we know what we're facing," he said, tightly. His face twisted into a bitter grimace. "We might be at war by this time tomorrow." He struck a dramatic tone, aping an actor from one of his favourite television shows. "Ladies and gentlemen, Planet Earth is at war."

"It might not come down to that," Jane said, reassuringly. "They don't want a wrecked planet any more than we do."

"They want to take our planet," Alex reminded her. "The human population might be surplus to requirements. What happens if they just decide to exterminate us?"

"Then we die," Jane said, practically. "Now shut up and watch television. You're depressing me."

"Yes, mother," Alex said, dryly.

"Crowds have already been gathering outside the White House and a dozen other sites in Washington," the announcer said. The television showed thousands of people standing outside the White House, looking towards the building and waiting. It wasn't a violent protest, or even a peaceful – if noisy – demonstration. It was more like a vigil, praying for peace and clarity. "The President has not yet responded to the alien claims, but sources inside the Pentagon confirm that the United States is ready and able to repel an alien attack."

The camera panned over the crowd. "These people have come to offer their strength to the President and to pray that he will make the right decision, whatever it may be," the voiceover continued. "The entire world is hanging on his words. Whatever is going on inside the White House today may decide the fate of the entire world."

"What a melodramatic asshole," Alex said, shaking his head.

"He has a point," Jane pointed out. Her voice was soft, but Alex could hear the undertone of fear, the fear he shared. "Whatever choice the President makes *will* determine the future of humanity itself."

Chapter Twenty-Eight

"As yet, there has been no response from the White House to the alien demands," Shelia Hetman said. Standing close enough to the blonde bimbo to hear her every word, Abigail rolled her eyes, silently thanking God that the network executives didn't consider her photogenic. There was something about staring at a camera that killed off the brain cells. "With two days remaining before the alien deadline runs out, massive crowds of demonstrators have arrived in Washington to demand that the alien craft shot down by the USAF is returned at once."

Abigail let her eyes wander away from Shelia as she continued to blether on, prattling about how brave the protesters were to have come all the way to Washington. It wasn't as if they were Chinese or Iranian pro-democracy protesters, who faced beatings, rapes and jail sentences when the authorities cracked down on them. The racket the protesters were making was shockingly loud – the sound of thousands of humans shouting together was terrifying – and she could barely hear herself think. The wonders of modern technology ensured that Shelia's words could be heard though the network, even though it seemed as if they would be drowned out by the crowd. It would, Abigail decided, have been a great improvement.

The silent vigil had been driven away by the hordes of protesters, who had materialised seemingly out of nowhere. Every organisation in the nation who believed that there was nothing like a massive public protest were rallying the faithful and sending them to Washington to protest…well, everything. The vast majority of protesters were protesting the shot down alien craft, but quite a few of them seemed to be protesting other causes as well. The old rent-a-mob network was working overtime, despite police attempts to shut down public transport and even websites that were urging people to make their feelings known by going to Washington and protesting in front of the White House. There were thousands upon thousands of protesters in the area, a sea of young boys and girls, screaming their protest into the air. It had started as a cacophonous racket of hundreds of different demands, but it had slowly merged into one.

"Return the craft," they bellowed. "No nukes! Return the craft! No nukes!"

Abigail wasn't even sure where the 'no nukes' bit came from. WNN was already planning a special report on the origin of the riots, but she'd done a little research and suspected that the answer lay in the Internet – and how hundreds of mailing lists had been used to spread the word, along with email spam and other methods. The message was mutating as it spread wider and wider, like a demented game of Chinese Whispers. The protesters screaming their heads off probably believed that the aliens had come to remove all the nuclear weapons from Earth and wanted the government to surrender them at once without a fight. There were even more outrageous beliefs out on the net, with some people believing that the aliens intended to eat the entire human race to them having built the pyramids and other mysterious structures from the past.

She scowled towards the south as she heard new sounds. Someone had been organising a counter-demonstration and had somehow managed to recruit several thousand people to their cause. There were thousands of police on the ground, trying to keep the two groups firmly separate, but the entire city had been paralysed by the protests. She'd heard that everyone who had a place to live outside the city or enough money to live away from his or her work had left Washington within a day of the debacle at the United Nations. The entire country seemed to be in the grip of an economic crisis caused by the alien demand, and the millions of people trying to flee the cities.

"The leader of the protesters has declared that he and his fellow believers will not vacate Washington until the President returns the alien craft and resigns from office," Shelia continued, drawing Abigail's attention back to her fellow reporter. "He is with me now."

The protest leader looked surprisingly normal, although he wore nothing to identify himself. That probably meant that he was well known to the police and Abigail was rather surprised that WNN hadn't found something to identify him. It was possible that he'd only agreed to be interviewed on the condition that his name wasn't mentioned on air, even though that would have surprised her. In her experience, most protesters loved having their names shouted to the skies, often in connection with words such as 'police brutality' and 'arrested on a false charge.' They believed that the correct way to get noticed was to make as much noise as possible. It annoyed many citizens, but various attempts to ban such protests had floundered on the principle of freedom of speech.

"We're going to remain here until that war criminal in the White House faces justice," he proclaimed, taking the mike from Shelia and speaking directly into it. "The people of the United States will not stand for the White House and the hordes of corrupt politicians hoarding alien technology for their own use and denying it to people who desperately need it. We knew that they were selfish bastards" – the broadcast was going out live, Abigail knew, and that wouldn't even be bleeped out – "and now this proves it. In order to keep their power, they've brought us to the brink of war with an all-powerful alien race!"

Shelia reached for the microphone, but the protest leader wasn't through speaking. "I call on every citizen of the United States to take to the streets and demand that the government return their craft," he thundered. "There's no point in talking to the corrupt bastards in Congress or the Senate, there's no point in trying to do it peacefully – get out there and get on the streets. Make your voice heard!"

He passed back the microphone and vanished into the crowd, probably wisely. The Police might have tried to arrest him for inciting a riot. Abigail watched him vanish within the teeming mass and wondered if he'd ever get out; there were so many people that she'd be surprised if some hadn't been trampled, or knocked to the ground in the confusion and crushed. Many of the protesters were teenagers, but some were older people or children. They wouldn't stand a chance if it turned violent.

Shelia recovered herself, somehow. "That was the leader of the protests here in Washington, making a statement to the world," she said, finally. She wasn't good at improvising on the fly, Abigail thought with a tiny glimmer of malice. She normally worked with a script, but now that the entire country was either out in the streets or clamouring for news, it was all hands on deck at WNN. The news business was a cutthroat one where only the fastest to the scoop survived. "I am joined now by a well-known science-fiction writer who will proceed to give us her opinion on the current situation. Jules, do you believe that we should return the craft?"

Jules proved to be a strong-looking woman with long blonde hair, wearing a biker's outfit. "No, I do not," she said, firmly. Abigail admired her courage. She was only a handful of meters from protesters who might tear her limb from limb for daring to suggest that the craft should not be returned. "There are too many unanswered questions about the aliens and their activities that need answers before we agree to place our future in their hands."

She leaned forward. "They told us a great many things, but they haven't proven a single one, apart from their mere existence," she continued. Shelia looked as if she wanted to interrupt, but didn't quite dare. Jules was quite formidable. "What do we actually *know* about them? Very little, beyond the fact that they have some kind of antigravity drive and a massive mothership that will be in orbit in less than a month – is there anything else? We know nothing about them and the protesting fools down there are asking us to trust the aliens unreservedly!"

"But," Shelia said, making a valiant effort, "you don't think that the government was in the wrong for shooting down the alien craft?"

"If they shot down the craft at all – which is something else that is unproven – the craft was certainly nosing around a defended area," Jules informed her. "We don't bother to station missile batteries in the midst of the Pacific Ocean where there is nothing to defend. If they were spying on a classified military base, for example, doesn't that open their motives to question? They might well have been taking notes before launching the invasion, or scouting out our military potential. There are too many unanswered questions to trust them, yet.

"No one would be happier than I if the aliens proved to be friendly, with gifts and technology we can use to reach for the stars, but I think that we should be more careful before we trust them. The government is a known evil. The aliens are not."

Shelia stared at her, as if she were speaking in a foreign language. "And don't you think that people have a right to protest?"

Jules looked over at the teeming mass of screaming protesters and scowled. "You don't have the right to protest effectively," she said, "if by effectively you mean harassing or even harming people who are trying to do legal things, even if you don't like them. The protesters out there are harassing the entire city, for what? They're making it harder for people to get to work! There are better ways to make their feelings known than disrupting an entire city."

She stalked off, leaving Shelia holding the microphone. "That was a well known writer," Shelia said. "We turn now to…"

Abigail sensed, rather than heard, the change in the crowd as *something* went badly wrong. It was impossible to tell what had happened, but the crowd seemed to be breaking down into panic, spreading out and clashing against the police lines. She peered down towards the barriers blocking the two groups of protesters and realised that the police had failed to keep them apart, allowing the two groups to clash with mindless violence. Both groups seemed to be coming apart, pushing the police back as they lashed out senselessly. Abigail caught her breath as she saw a young boy on the ground, bleeding from a head wound, before the panicking crowd obscured him from her gaze. The deafening chants had become howls of pain; the mob had become a wounded animal, screaming in pain. She saw a policeman shoved down and trampled and knew that others had been badly injured, or worse.

The entire scene was dissolving into chaos, thousands of protesters pushing everywhere, trying to escape or fight. She knew from covering prior protests that there would be those who had gone to the protests specifically to trigger violence, or to fight the police if it came down to a fight. They'd get hundreds of their fellow protesters injured, perhaps even killed, and just so they could get their kicks. The police would have to deal with them, but how? The police seemed to be totally overwhelmed.

"THIS IS THE POLICE," a megaphone boomed, as a helicopter orbited high overhead. Merely seeing it there was a surprise. The White House was normally secure airspace, with only governmental flights allowed. "REMAIN WHERE YOU ARE AND WAIT! DO NOT ATTEMPT TO ESCAPE!"

Someone threw a stone at the helicopter. It didn't have a prayer of hitting the craft, but it came down among the protesters, knocking someone to the ground. The cry of pain seemed to drive the mass into a frenzy, sending them running everywhere. Abigail wondered why the police hadn't ordered the mob to disperse, before realising that it would have pushed thousands of people into the side streets where many more would have been seriously injured. The only hope of preventing serious injuries was to break the crowd up slowly, but it was already too late for that. The violence was spreading rapidly out of control. Someone threw a Molotov Cocktail at a reporter's van and it exploded into a fireball, sending hundreds of people fleeing for an elusive safety. Others produced weapons and turned on their opponents, savaging them in the confusion. She flinched as a group of protesters ran past her and realised that the reporter's location – all protesters knew to leave a space for the reporters – was no longer safe. Such considerations were no longer on their minds. They just wanted to get away.

She looked up as she heard the first tear gas canisters burst. Some protesters promptly put on masks, or wrapped wet cloths around their mouths, while others threw themselves to the ground or tried to flee the gas. A line of black-clad policemen, carrying riot shields and truncheons, were advancing from one corner of the scene, trying to break the mob into smaller groups. They were followed by an entire army of policemen who secured the rioters as they were subdued. A handful of rioters tried to fight and were flattened by the police, before being arrested and dragged away…

Everything broke down into a series of confusing impressions as the rioters surged back against the reporters and their assistants. She saw a mass of people coming right at her, slamming her down, and she distinctly heard Shelia scream before she hit the ground. Her entire body hurt as the rioters pushed on past her, screaming and howling their outrage, kicking and clawing at her body. She wanted to curl into a ball, but she couldn't even do that, not with her body in such pain. It felt as if she'd broken every bone in her body and she wondered, suddenly, if it was the end. She'd thought that she would die in Sudan, after making a report that was too honest for the local government's taste, not on the streets of Washington. They'd be running red with blood after the riot…

A pair of strong arms grasped her and rolled her over onto her belly. Before she could complain, her hands were twisted around behind her back and secured with a plastic tie. She tried to kick out before realising what was going on and was rewarded by a knee in her back and a harsh voice warning her to lie still and wait. The policeman straightened up and walked on to the next person, leaving her to stare around blankly. She couldn't see much from her position, but it was clear that they were securing everyone remaining in the area, rioters and reporters alike. She managed to look over at where the vans with the cameras and other equipment had been, and bit off a curse. The rioters had completely wrecked them, along with other vehicles and lives. She heard Shelia screaming as a pair of cops tied her hands, as if she expected them to rape her at any moment, before she was unceremoniously dumped on the ground next to Abigail. Her eyes were wide with shock and fear. Shelia's world had turned upside down.

Abigail lost track of how long she and most of the others lay helpless on the ground. A medic gave her a quick check, pronounced her essentially unharmed, and left her there. A handful of seriously injured – including a reporter she knew from CNN – were carefully carried away to the ambulances, leaving the remainder alone. The area was swarming with policemen now, slowly separating out the protesters and escorting them to a series of police vans. When a policeman helped her to her feet and pushed her towards a long line of similarly-tied protesters, she didn't try to resist. There was no point in trying to resist. She took the opportunity to glance around, memorising as much of the scene as she could before she was shoved into the van, noting the hundreds of dead or seriously injured scattered around. Several of them were children, she realised, or policemen. The riot had gotten badly out of control.

"Let me go," Shelia shouted, as another policeman helped her to her feet. She had come completely apart under the stress. "I'm a reporter! I'm not involved! Let me go!"

"Shut up," Abigail hissed, taking a risk. She felt a certain responsibility to Shelia – she was young, naïve, and hadn't realised that the only reason she had the job was that she was too attractive for her own good. She couldn't be allowed to irritate the police more than strictly necessary. "Follow me and be patient!"

She ignored the odd look one of the policemen gave her, flushing slightly as she realised he must have taken her for one of the professional protesters who wanted to be arrested so that they could claim to have gone to jail for their cause. She wanted to scream that it wasn't like that, that she was only looking out for her colleague, but there was no longer any more time. The protesters were firmly helped into the van and pushed towards cold seats. There was no resistance. Those who might have fought had been separated or knocked out – or killed – during the riot. The remainder just wanted the whole nightmare to be over. They didn't even pull or tear at their bonds.

Abigail caught one last glimpse of Washington before the doors slammed closed. There were burning vehicles and bodies lying everywhere, thousands of policemen and armed soldiers littering the streets, blood and water lying on the ground, soaking into the fabric of the nation. It was something she would have expected from a Third World Hellhole, not Washington DC.

It looked very much like hell.

Chapter Twenty-Nine

Washington DC, USA
Day 37

"Seventy-one people killed, five hundred and nine injured and over six *thousand* arrests," the President said, flatly. "What the hell happened out there?"

The Director of the FBI looked uncomfortable. "The protest turned violent," he said, carefully. The President's authority over law enforcement was limited, but few would have denied the President anything if he had asked. "The riot was deliberately incited by known anarchists and troublemakers in the pack and rapidly grew out of hand. The Police attempted to break down the mob and prevent it from causing further harm and failed. Thirteen policemen were killed in the line of duty."

"I see," the President said, coldly. "And what do you intend to do with the six thousand people behind bars?"

"Rather more than that if you count the ones arrested at other protests," Richard Darby said. The Director of Homeland Security looked tired and worn. Homeland Security had received thousands of warnings of terrorist plots over the last few days, ever since the aliens had dropped their bombshell. The vast majority of them would be hoaxes, but they all had to be investigated. The signal-to-noise ratio was very low. "I think we arrested well over fifty thousand people in all."

"The ones we have proof incited the riot or committed acts of violence against the police or their fellow protesters will be charged," the FBI Director said. It was a weak answer and the President knew it. "We confiscated most of the video footage taken of the riot..."

"You mean the video footage that makes American policemen look like Nazi Stormtroopers?"

"...And we will analyse it carefully to determine who else should be charged," the FBI Director continued. "The ones we scooped up who are not going to be charged immediately will be released over the next few hours, once we have compiled a list of their names and details so we can find them again if we decide to charge them later. We'll probably discover that we did release a few hundred who should have been charged and..."

"Very well," the President said, tiredly. His eyes hurt and he needed sleep. "Can you guarantee that no further riots will take place?"

"Of course not, Mr President," the FBI Director said. "If you had spoken to the nation..."

The President scowled at him, but took his point. He *should* have addressed the nation immediately after the alien bombshell, but he'd spent the time talking to other world leaders and trying to pull the united front back together. The aliens had shattered it with a handful of well-chosen words. The world seemed to be divided; half of them believed that America had shot down the alien craft, the other half doubted the alien words privately, but had little choice but to go along with them in public. It didn't include the endless barrage of words from Tehran. The Iranian Government had informed its people that they were in communication with the aliens and with their help they would drive the Great Satan from the Middle East and establish true Islam over the Holy Cities. The President suspected that it was all bullshit, but there was no way to disprove it. America's word had been called into question too many times.

"Yes," he said, finally. "I'll speak to the nation immediately after this briefing."

He dismissed the FBI Director with a wave and turned back to his Inner Cabinet. "The aliens have been ingenious in placing us in a very unpleasant position," he said, flatly. "The other permanent members of the Security Council are sympathetic in private, but publicly...the message they're getting from their own people is leave America to face the aliens alone. We may continue to get intelligence from radar stations and other systems based in allied countries, yet there is little else they can do to help us, openly or covertly. We have one day left to respond.

"The question is simple. Do we submit to the alien demands or fight?"

The question seemed to hang in the air. "Let us be clear on this," the President said. "The very future of our existence as a nation, as a people, as a shining light on the hill is in doubt. We may be facing a war we dare not lose, but cannot win. We may be facing the first foe who can outmatch us as badly as we outmatched Saddam or any number of other Third World barbarians. Our most advanced technology might be primitive in comparison to their technology. The decision we make here might determine the survival of the human race itself."

He waited for someone to speak, wondering who would speak first.

"State has a bad reputation when it comes to considering the need for military action," Hubert Dotson admitted, finally. "We get accused of representing other countries interests more than those of the United States. We get accused of accepting unpleasant compromises to avoid having to admit that we failed. We've done our best to reform the department over the last few years, yet we still face the inflexible realities of the world. We face another inflexible reality here.

"Our great strength during World War Two was that nothing ever touched the Home Front. Our opponents and our competitors had their lands fought over, or their industries worn down by endless fighting. We were immune to the effects of the war, we became the arsenal of freedom and we turned that advantage into the world's greatest industrial superpower. We might suffer limited defeats, or stalemates, yet we never *lost* completely. The last war that could have crushed us as a nation was the Civil War, where we fought each other. No nation had the power to lay us low.

"It was also a weakness. We allowed ourselves to forget the underlying truths of war and peace and failed to concentrate long enough on any given problem to solve it. We abandoned Iraq in 1991, we abandoned Vietnam, we abandoned Korea and let's face it, we came damn close to abandoning Iraq again in 2004. The American mindset doesn't really allow for long commitments and so our allies constantly worried that we were on the verge of abandoning them. They were forced to make their own contingency plans, which put our relationship with them under stress and did immeasurable harm to our diplomatic standing. We never took war seriously. We never really believed that we could be *defeated*. We never *were* defeated. It did us no real harm, in any absolute sense, to lose in Vietnam. Our interests were not damaged.

"But this is different. We are facing a foe that can carry the war right to our homeland. The aliens have massive superiority. They can pick and choose when and how they hit us. They can break through our defences at will. We're not emotionally capable of accepting that we can be defeated, but here we *can* be defeated. If we go to war against the aliens, we may lose – and if we lose, this time it means the end. We could have survived if the Soviets had taken Europe, we could survive if the Chinese gobbled up Japan, Taiwan and all of Asia, but we could not survive defeat on our home territory."

The President leaned forward. "So you're counselling surrender?"

"If it was just me and you, I'd suggest fighting to the last," Dotson said, sharply. "It's not just me and you, it's the entire country, perhaps the entire world…and I am not going to lose all of that for a point of principle. The truth we Americans prefer to forget is that strength and the will to use it may not make right, but it determines what happens! We could lose this, Mr President, and that will mean the end of our existence as an independent nation."

There was a long chilling pause. "It seems to me," General Wachter said, "that we are looking at the end of our existence anyway.

"The aliens lied, either to us or the UN. They're untrustworthy by definition. I think we're looking at an invasion and they're launching this offensive to soften us up. They've triggered a political crisis that will ensure that we are unable to rally the rest of the world to defend the planet against the new colonists and perhaps even topple the government. They stuck a knife in our backs…and I find that encouraging.

"Why would they even bother launching this offensive if they could overwhelm us as easily as the Secretary of State suggests? I believe that they told us the truth the first time around; that they're colonists and that they need Earth as much as we do. I believe that they cannot throw rocks at us and bombard us into submission because they need a place to live too. The only explanation that makes sense is that they know we can resist and they intend to hamper it as much as possible.

"Their demands are telling as well. They're not demanding unconditional surrender, merely the return of their craft and the dismantling of our strategic weapons systems, as puny as they are. It doesn't even seem unreasonable to most eyes, yet it does tell us what they find important. The only reason to demand that we disarm those systems is to prevent them becoming a threat to the alien mothership, which means that they have to be a threat in the first place!

"We could stand down those systems, we could allow the mothership to enter orbit, we could…but that would mean placing our fate completely in their hands. They could just keep making demands until they stumbled upon something we literally *could not* give them. When that happens, they will go to war and we will not be in such a strong position to fight them. If they want war, they will have war, regardless of what we want. It only takes one side to have a war. If they want peace…we can refuse to give in to their demands and attempt to negotiate. Let them fire the first shot."

He took a breath. "The use of force is always a political decision," he said, finally. "I believe, however, that our only hope of survival as a species, the only hope of remaining in control of our own destiny, is standing up to the aliens now and telling them that we will not surrender our planet and if they want to share it, they can do it on our terms. The world will still change, but at least we will have a say in how it changes."

The President listened as, one by one; each member of the Inner Cabinet offered their opinions. Some agreed with General Wachter that the aliens had to be fought, or stated that they believed that the aliens were bluffing and they were weaker than they seemed. Others felt that the risk was too high to justify standing up to the aliens and risking complete destruction at their hands. The President said nothing of his own feelings, preferring to allow the others to talk, but Wachter was right. The aliens might have been telling the truth when he'd spoken to Ethos in person – he believed that Ethos had been telling the truth – and their motives were hardly friendly. Any alliance with them would be on their terms. The President knew enough to know that wasn't a guarantee of safety for American interests, let alone American freedom and liberty. There would be no guarantee that the aliens wouldn't turn on them in the end.

"Congress is split on the issue," Senator Hamlin said finally. The President might not always have liked him, but he respected him, even though he was resolutely independent of the Cabinet. "Some believe that we should fight; others that we should return the craft and offer to negotiate on the other issues. It's not going to end well."

The President nodded, silently thanking God that he'd had the foresight to ensure that most Senators and Congressmen had been fully briefed well before SETI picked up the alien signal. It had averted a political catfight and prevented his immediate impeachment when the aliens had declared that their ship had been shot down, but it had also torn Congress apart. A handful of politicians hadn't been briefed – they had a long history of leaking classified information to the media – and they were screaming about how they'd been kept in the dark. The protests and the disruptions they'd caused hadn't helped.

"No, it's not," he agreed. He wanted to take a vote, but there was no time. Perhaps, if things went really badly, he could be impeached and made to carry the blame, a scapegoat for alien outrage. "We have little choice, it seems. It's fight now or fight later."

He looked over at his Press Secretary. "Please inform the networks that I will address the country in one hour," he ordered. It wouldn't be hard. The White House had been bombarded with requests for information ever since New York. "We tell the aliens that we must refuse their demands until we get a full accounting of their true motives. And if we have to fight, we will."

———

Abigail caught herself rubbing her wrists where the plastic tie had dug into her skin. The police had been surprisingly gentle compared to police in some countries, but it hadn't been a very pleasant experience, even after they'd been dumped into a commandeered gym and made to wait for attention. They'd been searched, the ties had been removed, and warned to behave themselves, or else. A handful had shouted abuse at the cops and had ended up being cuffed to the railings, the remainder had just waited, all the fight beaten out of them, until the cops finally compiled a list of who they'd caught. They'd released Abigail five hours after taking her into custody with a warning that she might be recalled and rearrested at any time; Shelia, who had played a slight role in inciting the riot, had been transferred to another holding facility. WNN had sent a legal team to argue the point, but Abigail privately suspected that it wouldn't get them very far. The mood in the country wasn't very sympathetic to the protesters.

The call from the White House had been a surprise, even though procedures were firmly in place for addressing such a situation. The call had merely said that the President intended to address the nation and the various news companies were invited to broadcast the statement. The airwaves were already being covered with messages informing the nation that the President would be speaking in an hour and normal coverage would be paused to allow the President to speak. There had been riots in places where the President had spoken over a ball game or something like that, but Abigail doubted that many people would not be watching the President. The country needed reassurance and it had received precious little of that in the last few days. There were people walking around glancing nervously at the skies.

It hadn't helped that thousands of people had come forward claiming to have seen where the alien craft was shot down. There were so many people from so many different places that Abigail was certain that most of them were lying, or simply mistaken. If they were all telling the truth, it looked as if most of the country had been bombarded with wrecked alien ships, or as if the USAF had successfully repelled an alien invasion. The map of America in her office was studded with red pins marking each of the so-called crash sites, but the researchers hadn't managed to make even one of them seem realistic. There were only a handful of reports that might just be accurate, yet all of them were in very isolated areas. None of them could be confirmed and anyone who might have been in the know wasn't telling.

She rubbed her wrists again as the President appeared from a side door and walked to the podium. Normally, the reporters would have been shouting questions, but this time they were silent. They were humans too and they were scared. It wasn't something any of them were proud of, but they wanted the President to tell them that it would be all right and that there was nothing to fear, apart from fear itself. They wanted comforting words from a man many of them bitterly opposed on political grounds.

"My Fellow Americans," the President said. He looked older than usual, although it took Abigail a moment to realise why. The President hadn't put on any make-up or other preparations to go on television. "I speak to you now on a matter so grave that it affects the entire world. The fate of the entire planet is at stake.

"The aliens told you that the USAF shot down one of their craft. The aliens are lying. The craft in question crashed near a USAF military base and was recovered by a team from the base, who discovered that it was not of human origin. The craft was moved to a secure location and studied, yet before we could make any public statements, the aliens contacted the government and invited me to board their mothership and talk to them. I accepted their offer and travelled on a similar craft to the alien ship.

"They told me that they were colonists, travelling to Earth unaware that humanity existed. They offered me a deal; America would assist them in subduing the remainder of the world and, in exchange, we would maintain our political independence. They gave me data to prove their capabilities - data that proved that they have been kidnapping humans from Earth for years - and then returned me to Earth. I refused their offer and they transmitted the signal that SETI picked up. They came to New York and the entire world knows what happened then. We will release the footage of the contact to prove what really happened.

"The aliens have lied to us," he concluded. "Their scout ship was studying some of the most highly-classified and sensitive defence installations in America. Their behaviour is far from friendly. They could have levelled with us and offered partnership on equal terms. Instead, they sought conquest and now they have launched an offensive intended to force us to stand down our defences and tamely accept their domination for the foreseeable future. We dare not lower the defences until we know what they really want.

"I speak now to the alien leaders. We cannot surrender our entire planet to you. We can work with you to ensure that both races benefit from sharing technology and information. We are prepared to discuss working with you and settling you on this planet, but we will not surrender and place our fate entirely in your hands. We must reject your demands. If you wish peace, work with us. We extend the hand of friendship to you. Between us, we can build a world we can both be proud of.

"My Fellow Americans, we face the greatest challenge in our nation's long history. Let us face it together, as a united people. We will not tamely surrender to alien domination. If we are to fight alone, then we will fight for what we believe, our freedom, our liberty…and our country."

Chapter Thirty

McMurdo Station, Antarctica
Day 38

"They should have sent us in at once," Sergeant Bruce Barns muttered, in the common room. Almost the entire team had gathered in the chamber to watch the President's broadcast. "As it is, we're sitting out here freezing our butts off, for what?"

"The Force Recon dudes are freezing their butts off," a Marine Lieutenant put in. "We're sitting in here nice and warm."

"And don't forget we're a sitting target as well," a SEAL added. "They can probably pick us up from orbit on infrared and they have this place marked with a big circle entitled *hit this*."

Nicolas scowled. He tended to agree that the attack on the alien base should have been launched at once, but the orders had been very specific. Once McMurdo Station had been secured, the assault team was to probe the area for the location of the alien base and wait. The orders for the assault would be issued directly from Washington. A five-man team of Force Recon Marines were already probing towards the alien base, hunting for it in the strange Antarctic weather, but the remainder of the force was waiting. The Teams were trained to take the initiative at all times, yet no one would thank them for launching an assault without orders.

The scientists at the base had been first terrified, then outraged when the assault force had arrived and rapidly severed all communications between McMurdo Station and the outside world. McMurdo Station wasn't the only base on the icy continent, but the confused legal situation and the weather ensured that few would come to visit, if anyone did. The crew running the base had been more sedate, even though they'd been horrified to discover that they were on the front line of a war. They'd cooperated, at least. The scientists had spent most of their time composing elaborate complaints they intended to send to the President personally and one of them had almost managed to get a message out, despite supervision. Nicolas had ordered him held in a single room under armed guard and the rest had got the message, even though they looked at the soldiers as if they were monsters from another planet.

One of them had briefed Nicolas on the exact legalities of the situation, leaving him more confused than ever. The continent was divided between claims made by over a dozen nations, some dating back to before the First World War, and studded with bases of various types. America had jurisdiction over McMurdo Station and the other American bases, but America hadn't laid claim to more territory, even the location containing the alien base. The aliens could have claimed squatter's rights if they had declared the existence of the base; it wasn't as if they'd built it in Nevada or Siberia or somewhere that unquestionably belonged to a single country. The legal issues wouldn't matter if it came down to a shooting war, Nicolas had decided, even though his briefer had warned him that they were committing a war crime just by being there. That, Nicolas had decided, was definitely nonsense.

"Or perhaps we should all go out there for the exact moment when they start hitting home," another soldier said. It would have surprised civilians to know how informal most of the Teams could be. The American Special Forces soldiers spent most of their time in tiny units, or melding together with other units to form elite detachments used for a single mission, then disbanded. There was no question of chain of command or legal authority, but outside fighting, it was sometimes hard to know who was in charge. "The President told them that we wouldn't bend over and spread our legs for them, so they have to attack us or back down, right?"

"Or perhaps they're plotting something *really* clever," a Raven said. The Air Force Special Operations soldier leaned forward, taking another can of soda. "For all we know, that base could be incubating an entire army and that mothership is a hologram generated by advanced hand-waving technology. Everyone stares at the mothership, while they miss the real threat buried under the ice."

"Bullshit," a SEAL said. "They've been bouncing radar pulses off the mothership, so it can't be a hologram."

"It could be a solid-light hologram," the Raven countered. "It might even appear solid because of the hand-waving, but instead we're about to crash right into the alien army."

"It's not a good place to store an army," Barns pointed out. "Sure, they can knock out all of the bases on this continent and make a few thousand people miserable, but so what? They'd still have to get their army to Argentina or wherever they wanted to invade. We'd have problems doing that and we have the biggest navy in the world. That carrier trying to sneak over here has more aircraft than most of the air forces in the entire world."

"Most powerful navy," a pendant said. "If we count ship numbers…"

Nicolas rolled his eyes and left the room, barely aware of raised voices as the argument carried on, growing more and more elaborate. The sergeant wouldn't let it break down into a fight, although all of the men had more discipline than that. It was almost amusing how their conversation tended to revolve around the mission, or the aliens, or women. The standard joke in the Special Forces was that women were an illusion and anyone who claimed to have seen one was a lying bastard. It didn't help that many of the married soldiers had problems keeping their relationships working when they couldn't always tell their wives what they were doing. It was easy to be suspicious when a partner said nothing and few relationships could survive such doubts.

His daughter was seven years old now and he hadn't seen her in months. It was ironic, but his divorce had been surprisingly painless. It helped that he and his ex-wife had both been reasonable people and had put their daughter first. Little Nancy had been their priority and they'd both ensured that she saw her father as much as possible. The new husband had been happy to oblige – he was a decent person, even though Nicolas had wanted to hate him – and after his ex-wife had died, had continued to take care of her daughter. It had had its amusing side. Nicolas had been suspected of being homosexual after his superiors had discovered that the daughter he went to see had two fathers and no mother.

He lit a cigarette as he looked out over McMurdo Station. It was something of a disappointment to a man who had expected a lunar colony-style settlement. Dark buildings studded the landscape, marring the perfect white snow and ice, while brightly-coloured vehicles were strewn around as if the drivers had just abandoned them in the middle of their tasks. It wasn't too far from the truth. A set of long-range transports were being repainted to make it harder to see them against the snow and ice, but the others would be left at the station until the end of the mission. The Antarctic region was beautiful, but only outside the human settlements. The environmentalists might have had a point about humans despoiling the environment.

The Sergeant found him there an hour later. "No update, sir," he said, without preamble. "Nothing from Washington and nothing from the advance patrol."

Nicolas tossed away the remains of his cigarette. He hadn't expected anything from the patrol, but President Chalk had a reputation for making his mind up quickly. "We'll just have to wait," he said, shortly. It seemed that he'd spent half of his career since graduating from the SEAL training course – a hellishly sadistic course intended to weed out everyone who just couldn't hack it – waiting for orders to attack. "Keep monitoring the situation."

International Space Station, Earth Orbit
Day 38

"So what do you make of it?"

Captain Philip Carlson was not very impressed with Colonel Irving Harrows, the commanding officer of the International Space Station, but he did his best to avoid showing it. Normally, *Atlantis* wouldn't have remained attached to the ISS for long once she had been unloaded and picked up the crewmen who were going back down to Earth, but now his shuttle seemed to be permanently attached to the station. Hurry up and wait had always been a part of his military career, but it seemed that NASA had even more of it than any military service, ironic for an organisation that claimed to be completely civilian.

"I think we're going to be at war within the day," Philip said, finally. The alien spacecraft had continued their close approaches to the ISS, mocking them with the sheer perfection of their design. A single alien craft might have been barely larger than the shuttle, but it flew like a science-fiction nightmare come to life. Philip had seen American and Russian plans for space fighters and all of them had really been nothing more than miniature shuttles. They obeyed the laws of physics and flew predicable flight paths. He'd even become interested in becoming an astronaut after reading a hard science-fiction book involving fighters that couldn't have passed for aircraft, let alone flown in the atmosphere. X-Wings and Tie Fighters were about as realistic as a flying aircraft carrier, at least using humanity's technology. The aliens could probably design and build real X-Wings with *their* technology.

He glanced down at the LEO Display. The ISS maintained a permanent radar watch of the surrounding space, waiting for the inevitable moment when a piece of space junk no larger than a baseball or even a marble came right at the station. There had been a handful of chilling near-misses and the station's crew had had to deflect several items that would have ripped the station in half if they'd struck the hull, but that wasn't the real problem. The aliens were definitely monitoring the station as part of their war of nerves.

NASA's UFO files were a confused mixture, but it was undeniable that astronauts had seen and reported hundreds of UFO sightings, some of which had entered the myths surrounding the space program. Neil Armstrong, according to legend, had seen massive flying saucers on the moon – "*they're on the moon watching us,*" he was supposed to have said – and UFOs had followed spacecraft on their missions. No one was sure what to make of it and reports had diminished after NASA started removing pilots who saw UFOs from flight duty, but it was clear now that some reports had been genuine. The object holding station a bare thirty kilometres from the ISS had a profile that was growing to be chillingly familiar. It wasn't even *trying* to hide.

"And then?" Harrows asked. "What happens then?"

"We die, probably," Philip said, and launched into another explanation of how fragile the station was if the aliens decided to throw a missile at it. No one knew what the aliens used for weapons, but everyone was sure that it would be something extremely deadly. They could have thrown a kitchen sink at the ISS and taken out the entire station. "Aren't you glad you volunteered to remain on the station?"

Harrows snorted. NASA had wanted to pull all of the ISS crewmen off the station when the alien mothership arrived and replace them with a team of dedicated contact specialists. That idea had been overruled by the President and the ISS had been left in the care of a small caretaker team, while the remainder of the crew had headed down to the planet where they would be safe. It hadn't caused a political catfight with the other nations involved in the ISS Project, much to NASA's surprise, although Philip suspected that the President had been quietly keeping the other members informed of what was going on. The President's speech made it clear that the United States had known about the aliens a long time before they started contacting SETI.

"Not really, no," he said. "I should have listened to my old man."

Philip lifted an eyebrow, trying to show interest. "What did he say?"

"I don't know," Harrows said, with a wink. "I wasn't listening."

Philip looked down at the image of the mothership. The ISS only mounted one telescope – a Japanese design used for studying distant stars – but it was more than suitable to provide an image of the alien ship. He'd seen the measurements, yet it was still incomprehensibly huge, its dimensions vast beyond imagination. It was easy to believe that there were a billion aliens cooped up on that ship, eager to set foot on the Promised Land. Philip would have quite happily traded half of America for access to the technology that had built that craft; indeed, he tended to agree with the bloggers who wanted to offer the aliens Africa and the Middle East in exchange for technology. It would have been a worthwhile bargain.

"It was probably something about being patient," he said, finally. The mothership *looked* close, but it was too far away to be targeted by any of the shuttle's puny weapons. Looking at the alien contact watching the station, Philip suspected that the battle would be short and very one-sided. The shuttle had to obey the laws of physics. The aliens laughed at them. "All we can do is wait – and pray."

Cheyenne Mountain, USA
Day 38

Robin ran her hand through her hair as she sat back from the console. The President's speech might have focused a few minds outside the mountain, but Robin and the remainder of the crew bringing the base back online already knew the truth. The men and women walked around the base as if they expected the skies to fall at any moment, as if they expected the base to be targeted in the opening rounds of any alien attack. Robin couldn't disagree with that – NORAD *was* a logical target – but there was no point in worrying about it. NORAD was designed to stand up to multiple nuclear hits and if the aliens had anything more powerful than that, the war would be lost very quickly anyway.

It was ironic, but there was little left for her to do. She'd overseen the creation of new warning systems for the United States and had passed responsibility over to other radar specialists. She had been given permission to work following her own instincts, studying the alien craft in the hopes that she would discover something new, but the truth was that she rather suspected that she'd found out everything she could. There was a great deal of information on how the alien craft moved – they seemed to have problems manoeuvring at high speed, for reasons that made little sense – yet there was little she could add to it. The aliens were still watching the United States, their craft blinking in and out of existence, but they were making no hostile moves. Some of the radar technicians believed that meant that the aliens were backing down after the President had called their bluff, but Robin wasn't so sure. The contacts were high over every major military base in the world. No country had been spared.

The one question she had tried to answer was if the aliens *knew* that they were being tracked? It was hard to be sure, but she had the impression that they sometimes believed that they were undetected. She and the other radar specialists had been told not to vector interceptors towards the alien craft, yet there were times when the aliens brazenly challenged the defenders and times when they tried to be sneaky. It made little sense to her because there seemed to be no pattern…but the aliens were far from human. Something that made perfect sense to *them* would look strange to a human. Their concepts of what made a perfect military tactic might be very different from a human concept. Robin had little experience or knowledge of fighting on the ground, but she'd been told that different cultures had different ideas of war. An alien culture might make the World War Two Japanese look reasonable.

She looked back at the display as the console chimed an alert. A new target had appeared in Earth Orbit. The alien craft sometimes seemed to drift along in orbit before heading down into the atmosphere, but this one seemed more...*purposeful*, somehow. She followed it as it drifted into position; just as another contact appeared, followed by a third, a fourth, a fifth... Dozens of contacts were blinking into existence even as she watched, spreading out until they had the entire world surrounded. This was no mere recon mission, she realised in shock. There were too many craft for that. This was an attack!

Robin reached for the alert button and pressed it down hard, sending sirens howling throughout the complex. The entire sequence was carefully programmed. As soon as she pushed the key, FLASH alerts were distributed over the entire network, warning them that an attack was underway. Defence stations would be coming online, aircraft would be launching into the air to combat any alien threat and civilian aircraft would be landing at any available airport. It wasn't something to do lightly – 9/11 had cost the United States billions of dollars – but there was no choice. She knew what she was looking at.

She picked up the phone and pressed down on the emergency key. If the General was talking to anyone else, they'd just been disconnected. It wouldn't please a senior officer to be cut off by a junior, but there was no choice. The country was about to come under attack. NORAD's staff was already responding to the crisis, yet they needed political direction. The General had to clear any missile launches personally.

"General," she said, watching as more enemy icons flickered into existence. There were over two hundred alien craft in orbit now and there were more appearing every second. "I think the war is about to begin."

Chapter Thirty-One

Cheyenne Mountain, USA
Day 38

"What are we looking at?"

General Sandra Dyson strode into the Operations Room barely a minute after she'd been called. She'd been in her office doing paperwork, but the alert had brought her out in a hurry. Robin was privately impressed by how quickly the General had reacted, although she suspected that no one could have moved fast enough to matter. The alien attack might already be underway.

"We have multiple alien contacts," Robin said, as the massive display altered to show another group of alien craft appearing. They were appearing in groups of five craft now and she wondered if they were the alien version of squadrons. They certainly seemed to fly in formation. "There are around three hundred alien craft circling the Earth in high orbit. Their intentions are unknown."

"It looks pretty clear to me," Sandra said, as she took her seat in front of the big board. The massive screen at the front of the room, looming over the smaller workstations, showed the aliens settling into their flight patterns. "That's almost certainly the first move in their offensive. Do you have a precise count?"

"Negative," Robin said, slowly. "The contacts are flying in formations that sometimes register as single contacts. Their flying skills are remarkable." She paused. "They are also outside effective weapons range."

She keyed her console as the flow of alien craft seemed to halt, trying to pick up images from orbiting cameras on NSA satellites. The NSA had been reluctant to reprogram its satellites to take a look at targets in Earth orbit – apart from the handful of satellites that had been doing just that – but the President's orders had been explicit. It didn't matter anyway. The best that multi-million dollar cameras - capable of reading a postage stamp from orbit - could produce were streaks of light. The alien craft danced and weaved in a pattern Robin suspected was meant to be intimidating – or perhaps they were just showing off. There was no way to know.

"We could probably hit them with the ground-based lasers, but at that range I doubt we'd even melt their paint," she added. She had the nasty feeling that the aliens were just preparing their next move. Groups of alien craft were dancing together, seeming to merge into one contact, then separating and returning to their positions. It reminded her of something oddly familiar, but her mind refused to process the information and come up with the data. "They're free to do as they please."

"All right," Sandra said. She looked over at one of the other consoles. "Inform all parties that I am declaring an Air Defence Emergency. Tell them to pull down all civilian air traffic now – I don't care who they are or why, just get them to the nearest airport and down on the ground. Scramble the ready fighters, but hold the remainder on the ground until the attack patterns develop. Prepare a FLASH warning signal and forward it to me for evaluation."

"Yes, General," one of the other dispatchers said. "Air Defence Emergency declared."

Robin barely heard him. An Air Defence Emergency meant that Sandra – in her position as commander of America's defences – was God, as far as anyone in the air was concerned. She had the legal right to shoot down any pilots who refused to cooperate, although after 9/11, it would be a brave or stupid pilot who refused to follow orders. The priority was to get every other aircraft out of the sky to prevent the aliens using them as targets, leaving the military aircraft free and clear to engage anything in the sky. The procedures had been drafted to deal with terrorist-controlled aircraft. No one had seriously expected to use them against alien invasion.

She'd taken part in a war game once that had assumed that Castro, on the verge of dying from ill health – had launched everything he had against American bases in Florida. It hadn't gone well. USAF, USN and Air National

Guard pilots had had real problems working together, while the Air Defence System had been completely surprised by the new threat. The evaluation had concluded that the men on the ground had believed that no one would mount such an offensive and hadn't treated it as seriously as it deserved. The irony was that if the defence forces had reacted perfectly, the Cuban Air Force wouldn't have gotten within bombing range of the beaches, let alone the rest of the state. If Castro had actually tried to launch such an offensive, the results would probably not have been good. The USAF could have wrecked Cuba from one end to the other and the 1st Marine Division could have occupied the entire Island, but it would have been small consolation to the dead.

"They're coming lower," she said, as the display updated. The alien craft weren't even trying to hide any longer. They were showing up clearly on standard space-tracking radars. "I think they're playing chicken with the satellites."

She felt Sandra looking over her shoulder as the alien craft danced closer to the swarm of human satellites orbiting the planet. The aliens seemed to delight in flying right at the satellites, then altering course so sharply that humans would have thrown up, had they felt the effects of such sudden movements. She suspected, judging from the data from the crashed alien craft, that the aliens had some kind of internal compensator. They weren't *that* much tougher than humans.

"Get the Dark Sky Plan underway," Sandra said, shortly. "Warn all units that they may lose access to satellites."

Robin sucked in her breath. It was hard to remember that while *she* regarded it as a challenge and an interesting display, the General regarded it as a threat. Dark Sky was a contingency plan for losing all of the human satellites and their ability to coordinate the American forces. It wouldn't matter so much in CONUS – there were secure and shielded landlines connecting the various bases – but it would have a real impact on America's ability to operate outside North America. The United States depended so much on satellites that losing even a handful of them would provoke a major economic depression.

She nodded. "Yes, General," she said, more soberly. Losing the satellites would mean losing the ability to communicate with the assault force near the alien base. The President would have to issue the order before the aliens opened fire, if they did open fire. They could still be bluffing.

Sandra had picked up the secure phone, linking her directly to Washington. "Yes, Mr President," she said. "It looks like the opening moves of an attack to us. They haven't opened fire yet, but we believe that it is only a matter of time."

There was a pause. Robin strained her ears, but couldn't hear the President's response. "We're holding fire and I've declared an Air Defence Emergency on my own authority," Sandra added. "The majority of civilian air traffic will be on the ground in ten minutes. Understood sir; DEFCON ONE."

She glanced over at another operator. "DEFCON ONE," she repeated. "Get the signal out now. COCKED PISTOL: DEFCON ONE."

Robin felt her stomach clench, despite herself. DEFCON ONE hadn't been declared outside of exercises in living memory. The entire United States military had been at DEFCON THREE since the mothership had been detected – and unofficially working towards DEFCON ONE ever since the alien craft had crashed – and had gone to DEFCON TWO after the aliens had dropped their bombshell in Washington. DEFCON ONE meant that a war was underway or was believed to be about to begin. It was reserved for imminent or ongoing attack on America itself. No enemy nation had attacked the Continental United States since World War Two.

———

FLASH TRAFFIC CRITIC
FRIGHTFULNESS. FRIGHTFULNESS.
SET CONDITION DEFCON ONE, REPEAT DEFENSE CONDITION ONE
NORAD HAS DETECTED MULTIPLE INBOUND TRACKS FROM THE ALIEN MOTHERSHIP.
NCA HAS DETERMINED HIGH PROBABILITY THAT ALIEN ATTACK IS IMMINENT. ALL UNITS SET DEFCON ONE AND PROCEED IN ACCORDANCE WITH OPLAN 6666.
MESSAGE ENDS

———

A moment after the chilling message had flashed up on her screen, Robin blinked as a new alert tone sounded in her earpiece. A satellite had just vanished. Another vanished a moment later. "General," she said. The interrupted telemetry from the orbiting systems made it all too clear what was happening. The signals simply cut off, without warning. The radar showed no trace of what was happening to them, or what kind of weapon was being used, yet she knew what was going on. "They're opening fire on the satellites."

"Shit," Sandra said. "Mr President; they're taking down the satellites."

There was a pause. "Understood, Mr President," she said. "I'll send the signal now."

She put down the phone and looked down at the operators. "You are authorised to engage the enemy," she said, formally. "Engage Fire Plan Alpha."

"Fire Plan Alpha, understood," an operator said. "KE-ASAT units are responding. They're manoeuvring now."

Robin watched, knowing that the system wouldn't work perfectly, if at all. KE-ASAT had been designed to track and destroy enemy satellites and missiles, both of which followed predicable courses. The alien craft flew like starfighters out of a science-fiction movie. They would be able to easily avoid the KE-ASAT weapons or destroy them before they managed to get close enough to an alien craft to detonate. There was no way of knowing how much damage they'd do, either. The alien craft might be completely destroyed or they might not even notice.

"Hellfire," Sandra muttered. Robin understood. The aliens might not have realised that the KE-ASAT systems were different from the other satellites – they seemed to have ignored the stealthed satellites, which was an interesting datum – but they knew a threat when they saw it. The KE-ASAT system had never been deployed in sufficient numbers for political reasons and, even after the alien mothership had been detected, there just hadn't been the launch capability to put enough of them in space to threaten the aliens. The aliens were wiping them out one by one. "What are they firing?"

"Some kind of energy weapon," Robin said, slowly. The orbiting sensors weren't picking up much, but missiles or rail guns would have shown up on radar. The entire battle was unfolding slowly, yet she knew the outcome.

"I recommend engaging with ground and air-based beam weapons and THAAD missiles."

Sandra picked up the phone again. "Units Alpha through Gamma, you are authorised to open fire," she said. "I repeat, fire at will. Good hunting."

Newer contacts appeared on the display as the lumbering 747 laser transports moved into position. They'd been scattered around the country and based alongside the fighter squadrons that would protect them if they came under attack, yet it looked as if they'd made a serious error. The laser weapons weren't effective against hardened targets without a sustained or massed firing pattern, but that was no longer possible. The 747 aircraft were too vulnerable to risk for long and simply lacked the power to put out a coherent beam for the time required. The only advantage the lasers had was that the first warning the aliens would have would be when the lasers struck their craft.

She watched as brilliant lines appeared in front of her, marking targets. The alien craft seemed to dance away from the laser beams, yet none of them were seriously damaged. The ground-based lasers took far too long to retarget against a new enemy contact, forcing them to fire bursts at any target that happened to wander into range, yet it was becoming increasingly clear that the worst that happened was a brief burst of heat surrounded the targeted craft. It seemed far too clear that the aliens were barely affected.

"We're not making any impact?"

"No, General," Robin said. The lasers simply couldn't hit the alien craft long enough to burn through their hulls…or force shields, or whatever. "The lasers were never designed to cope with targets that could manoeuvre in space like birds wish they could."

She frowned as the first wave of THAAD missiles roared up towards the alien craft, challenging their control of the skies. For the first time, the aliens showed some real concern, dancing away from the missiles before they could get too close or shooting them down with their mysterious weapons. Robin checked the remaining orbital satellites and ground-based sensors, but was still no closer to determining what the weapon actually *was*. If it was a laser so powerful that it could burn through a satellite in a split-second, the aircraft the USAF had launched would be wiped out before they had a chance to realise that they were under attack. The only optimistic sign was that the aliens weren't engaging the 747s or their fighter escorts directly, preferring to remain in orbit.

"General, Colonel Montgomery is reporting that three of his laser units are overheating," one of the operators said, quickly. "He's requesting permission to cease fire before the laser melts."

"Denied," Sandra ordered, harshly. The lasers were making no impact at all, as far as Robin could tell, but she understood. The aliens had to be kept as far back as possible. Losing the lasers would be a small price to pay for success. "Order him to continue firing until the lasers go unserviceable."

"General, all military and civilian American satellites have been taken out," another operator said. Robin looked up at the big board. All of the satellites she had tracked over the years were gone, nothing more than space debris drifting down towards the planet. Her imagination filled out a picture of alien craft crashing into the wreckage and exploding, but she knew that it was unlikely. The main body of the wreckage was on a trajectory that would send it into the atmosphere within a few days at most. They'd be seeing spectacular firework displays in the night – if they lived that long.

"I see," Sandra said. Her ability to command her forces had just dropped a notch, yet she didn't seem very worried about it. Robin decided that it was probably because she'd planned and drilled for such a situation in the past. "What about foreign satellites?"

"They're untouched," the operator said. "They just ignored them. Didn't even buzz them as they raced past."

Robin frowned as a new point flickered up on her screen. "They're taking out dead satellites as well, from every nation," she said. Earth's human-built moons included a number of satellites that had simply failed once in orbit. Some had been repaired by the space shuttle, or brought back to Earth to be repaired, but some had just been abandoned to drift endlessly in the vacuum. "They're smashing them into pieces. I think they're clearing the space lanes, getting rid of all the junk…"

"Why would they bother?" Sandra asked. The General leaned over Robin's shoulder. "Why would they even care?"

"They want to land on this planet," Robin pointed out. "Perhaps clearing LEO of space junk helps their preparations."

"Perhaps," Sandra agreed. "Or perhaps…"

"General, General Henshaw reports that his THAAD units have shot two-thirds of their load without scoring perhaps more than one or two hits," another operator said. "He is requesting permission to hold fire and move his position before it comes under attack."

Sandra's voice was very composed. "Order him to cease fire," she said, finally. Robin caught the bitterness underlying her words and shivered. The United States Strategic Command had absorbed all of the nation's space-related assets, from orbital weapons to ground-based laser systems, and deployed them…for what? The aliens might have lost a craft or two – looking at the data, she honestly wasn't sure if one had been hit, let alone two – and in return, the United States had lost every piece of orbiting capital it had. The military results were staggering, well worth the loss of an alien craft or two, but the economic results would be absolutely devastating. Every telecommunications firm in the nation would go bankrupt. "Keep tracking the bastards…"

"Yes, General," Robin said. It was easier to track the aliens now, somehow, despite all the falling space debris. They seemed to be gathering back into their formations, preparing their next move. It was so maddeningly familiar, yet the more she worried at it, the less sense it made. Why were they flying so close to one another that their contacts merged into one?

"General, the Civil Aviation Authority is asking if the Air Defence Emergency is over…?"

Sandra's voice hardened. "Tell that stupid ass that the emergency hasn't fully begun and all civilian aircraft are to remain grounded until further notice," she snapped. Robin winced at her tone. Civilians could come up with some stupid ideas, but the unlucky idiot was about to have the skin peeled off his bones. "Furthermore, tell him that…"

She broke off as new contacts appeared on the display. "What are they?"

"I'm not sure," Robin admitted. The new contacts seemed larger than the first set of contacts, roughly comparable to the craft that had crashed… had it really been just over a month ago? They still weren't that large, but they didn't have to be massive to be potent – or dangerous. The alien craft were forming up into new formations, one high over the Atlantic Ocean and one high over the Pacific. It looked as if they were preparing to swarm down on America on both the East and West Coasts. "I think they're preparing to move into the atmosphere."

"Get the uplink to the fighter bases moving," Sandra snapped. Her voice tightened. "Launch all fighters in accordance with the Operations Plan. Inform them that the ROE are now Alpha-One."

She paused. "And tell them I said good hunting," she added. Robin nodded, watching as sudden flares of heat in the atmosphere marked alien craft swooping down towards the planet. They seemed to move with a cold coordinated precision that implied determination – and hostility. "Down in the atmosphere is *our* turf."

Chapter Thirty-Two

Atlantic Ocean
Day 38
The signal made chilling reading.

> FLASH TRAFFIC CRITIC
> FRIGHTFULNESS. FRIGHTFULNESS.
> REPEAT CONDITION DEFCON ONE, REPEAT DEFENSE
> CONDITION ONE
> ALIEN CRAFT HAVE OPENED AGGRESSIVE ACTION.
> ALL UNITS PROCEED IN ACCORDANCE WITH OPLAN
> 6666.
> ROE ALPHA-ONE: REPEAT ALPHA-ONE.
> GOOD HUNTING.
> MESSAGE ENDS.

Colonel Thomas Mandell looked down at it once, and then up at the main display. The AWACS was orbiting on a wide course that took it near several USAF bases, escorted by a swarm of American fighters and two tankers, yet he knew that it would be one of the prime targets. Intelligence had no idea what kind of weapons the aliens used – speculation ranged from heat rays to antimatter bombs, with everything in-between extensively discussed – but he was sure that they would be formidable. It was quite possible that the aliens would destroy the entire USAF within minutes of opening fire.

"Colonel," Lieutenant Rogers said, "we have multiple incoming contacts, coming in front orbit. I am picking up at least thirty alien craft on a direct course for Washington and the surrounding area, moving at Mach Six. They're shedding heat into the atmosphere as they move."

"The Global Warming freaks are going to love them," Mandell muttered. It was a pity that they didn't have a missile-armed ship directly under the alien re-entry positions, but there had been no way to predict their arrival point. Aegis cruisers had been deployed to positions where they could provide additional firepower in support of the defences, along with most of the carriers and other ships. He looked down at the signal again. ROE – Rules Of Engagement – Alpha-One allowed the American aircraft to open fire without provocation, or the enemy firing the first shot. The previous orders had had the fighters holding their fire until they were fired upon, or believed that they were under threat. "Pass the message on to the squadrons."

"Aye, sir," Lieutenant Rogers said.

Mandell nodded grimly. The problem with maintaining DEFCON ONE over any period of time was that it put colossal wear and tear on the equipment. The USAF would have had to start rotating aircraft out for repairs within a handful of days, hence the decision to remain on DEFCON TWO until the aliens made unambiguous signs of hostility. Shooting down the satellites, someone had decided higher up the food chain, clearly counted as a hostile act. The aircraft on CAP were being recalled now to form up with their comrades who were just leaving the ground, before they departed to engage the enemy. They had been far too exposed on their own.

No one knew what tactical doctrine the aliens possessed, or what they considered an acceptable loss rate, but their technology gave them a number of options denied to the USAF. One possibility was that they would lure out the air defence units and then rocket past them, heading overland and bombarding their bases before they could react. It was why Air National Guard units had been kept in reserve to shield likely targets, yet without knowing just what the aliens could do, it was impossible to know how effective any of the defence measures would be. The aliens might have weapons that could take out an entire airbase in a single shot.

"The fighter pilots are responding, sir," Lieutenant Rogers said. On the display, the handful of Raptors were racing out towards the alien craft, still dumping their heat into the atmosphere. They might even remain hot long enough for heat-seeking missiles to be used against them. "They're on their way."

There was no point in issuing any further orders, Mandell knew. The pilots knew what they had to do and issuing any other instructions would only have distracted them. The AWACS could only continue to supply information to the pilots and wait. They had orders of their own. If the alien craft came near them, the AWACS was to break contact and escape – if possible. Mandell knew that it might not be even remotely possible. No one had lost an AWACS in combat since the concept had first been developed, but there was always a first time…

———

Captain Will Jacob tensed as the Raptor lifted off from Langley Air Force base and rose into the sky. It always felt as if the aircraft was straining at the leash, yet today it felt different. The base had been preparing for war since before the announcement, but after the aliens had dropped their bombshell at the UN, non-dependents – the families of people who worked on the base – and non-essential personnel had been evacuated and moved to safer housing elsewhere. The mobs of protesters outside the base, demanding a peaceful solution – as if the pilots themselves didn't want a peaceful solution – had been told to move on, but many had chosen to remain. The base security staff hadn't pushed it. If the base came under attack, it would be their own stupid fault if they were caught up in the battle.

He checked his HUD and winced when he saw the decelerating alien craft. The radar telemetry suggested that the aliens had real problems flying in anything other than a straight line at speeds over Mach Three. A simple predictable flight path would have made them easy targets, although no one was sure what would happen when one of the AIM-120D AMRAAM missiles struck an alien craft. The pilots had argued it over time and time again, believing that the missiles would be completely effective, or that the alien craft would be protected by force fields and they'd all be killed before they could escape. The aliens seemed to be slowing down in preparation for a dogfight and, with their full manoeuvring capabilities open to them, would definitely be tough targets.

"All right, everyone," he said, knowing that the rest of his squadron would be right behind him. "Prepare to engage. Lock missiles on target."

The USAF was facing a problem it had inflicted on several nations since the Vietnam War. They were opposing an enemy force that got to pick and choose the time and place of combat. There was no reason why the alien craft couldn't come out of orbit right over the heartland of America, or enter on the other side of the world and fly right around the globe to hit their targets. The aliens could and presumably would hit American bases; the United States could not hit their mothership and take it out once and for all. It was rather like battling an aircraft carrier. Even if they took out all the fighters, the carrier could retreat, rearm and return at a later date. The only way to win the war outright would be to take out the mothership and that was impossible.

Will had never been a fan of *Star Wars*, but two of his fellow pilots had come to the USAF because of watching *A New Hope*. They'd been fans of the Expanded Universe and they'd been happy to discuss the inevitable results of the Death Star's explosion over the Forrest Moon, with the extermination of the cute little teddy bears who had somehow defeated the Imperial Stormtroopers. The results of destroying the mothership, even if it were possible, would be comparable. The human race would be exterminated.

He glanced at his HUD as the two forces converged. The strategists had spent hours arguing over what moment the USAF should open fire, but with alien countermeasures still an unknown, no one knew for sure. The USAF – like all modern air forces – had attempted to develop weapons that allowed them to engage their targets well before the range where the increasingly expensive USAF aircraft could themselves be engaged and destroyed. Yet the longer the missiles took to reach the enemy craft, the greater the chance that the aliens could avoid their fire or deploy countermeasures.

"Stand by," he ordered. The aliens were still decelerating, yet the two forces were flying towards each other at terrifying speed. He peered into the distance, but the alien craft were still out of sight. "Lock on…"

His finger uncapped the firing button. The missile was already locked onto the lead alien craft, a spacecraft of a completely new design. Will thought of it as a very odd-looking F-117, a smaller version of the retired stealth aircraft. It looked as if it was deadly enough to take out all the Raptors on its own and he felt a twinge of envy for the pilot. The aliens could have taught the human race so much, yet now they were on the brink of going to war. The President's speech had galvanised the pilots. Even though many of them were annoyed that no one had told them about the alien craft, few questioned the President's decision. It helped that the President was a military man.

The firing tone echoed in his ears. "Shadow Lead; Fox-Three!"

His Raptor jerked as the AMRAAM launched from the fighter, racing away into the distance, followed rapidly by missiles launched by the other fighters. The alien craft showed no reaction at first, and then suddenly they seemed to spring into life, dancing through the air to evade the missiles. He felt another twinge of envy – the Raptor couldn't move like that on a bet – before realising that there was another threat. The aliens had returned fire and flickering multicoloured flashes of light were racing towards the human aircraft. They moved terrifyingly quickly…

"Evasive action," he snapped, twisting the Raptor sharply. A flash of… *something* raced past the cockpit, nearly blinding him for a second. The weapon, whatever it was, didn't seem to move at light speed, but it was fast enough to be worrying. "Watchman; hit count?"

A flash of light in the distance caught his eye. Something had detonated all right. "We assess that you have three hits," the AWACS said. Will blinked. They'd fired twenty missiles at the alien craft, but only *three* hits? "The alien craft successfully evaded the other missiles."

Will cursed as he yanked the Raptor aside. The alien craft were growing closer, firing as they came. Their weapons didn't seem to be that accurate, but it hardly mattered. The amount of…whatever it was that they were firing would almost certainly guarantee a hit sooner or later. The Raptor formation was being broken apart just by the hail of incoming fire. Mutual support would soon become impossible.

"Fire at will," he ordered. He achieved a lock-on and fired another missile at an alien craft, bringing the Raptor around in a tight turn to follow the alien fighter. It dived and twisted like a living thing, but it couldn't escape the missile. It slammed home…

For a crazy moment, Will saw a flickering ball of light surrounding the alien craft; just before it exploded with enough force to shake the Raptor badly. Green-blue flickers of light raced past him as another enemy fighter rolled onto his tail, firing madly in an attempt to bring him down. He twisted desperately, seconds before one of his comrades put a missile into the alien craft, a moment before it would have had him. The alien craft exploded with shocking force.

"What the hell are they carrying?" Someone asked. "Antimatter?"

"Rubbish," another pilot said. "Antimatter would have swatted us all out of the air."

"Can the chatter," Will snapped. The entire battle had devolved into a high-tech dogfight, something that was supposed to be impossible. No one had told the aliens that. Their weapons were *designed* for dog-fighting at close range. "Cover each other and take them all down!"

An alien craft swept into view and he depressed the trigger for the Raptor's cannon, but the shells went wide, streaking past the target. The alien craft seemed to *twist* suddenly in the air and then it was coming right at him in a high-speed game of chicken. Will pulled his aircraft to one side as more energy bursts flashed past him, leaving the disappointed alien fighter to swoop around and try to fly right up his tail. Will was almost impressed. He considered himself the greatest fighter pilot in existence – a fairly common belief among fighter pilots – and the alien pilot had made him, coming within inches of blowing him out of the sky. He couldn't even think about returning fire or aiming at another target. The moment he took his mind off escape, he'd die.

"I'll cover you," another pilot said. "Hang on…"

Will saw what he had in mind and dived for the ocean. A moment later, the alien craft twisted, too late. The shockwave struck Will's aircraft and for a terrifying moment he thought he was going to be slammed right into the water before he regained control to discover that he was flying on his own. The aliens were still pressing the offensive, but they hadn't sent another of their craft after him. He pulled the Raptor up and used the moment to gain an overall picture of the battle. His situational awareness had been shot to hell by the alien craft.

It wasn't good. Radar-guided missiles seemed to be the only advantage the human race had. Eleven alien craft had been destroyed, but seven Raptors had been blown out of the air…and only one pilot had managed to eject. Perhaps he'd be picked up by a SAR helicopter or the Coast Guard, yet if the aliens chose to engage non-military aircraft he might drown in the ocean before any rescuers could find him. The Dark Shadows had considered themselves the hottest pilots in the sky and yet they could barely hold their own.

"Cannons are ineffective," one of the pilots snapped. He sounded badly shaken. All pilots had bad moments in their careers, yet no one had faced such a battle since the Second World War. "I repeat; cannons are ineffective! I just shot my wad and the bastard didn't even blink!"

"I'm out of missiles," another pilot snapped. He sounded on the verge of panic. "I need to return to base!"

"Stay where you are," Will ordered sharply. The F-22 Raptor had multiple modes, but they'd all been configured for air combat and carried the full complement of eight missiles, along with their cannons. If the aliens could evade the missiles – and it was clear that they'd been able to break the locks and escape – they might continue to harass the pilots until they'd used all of their missiles, and then moved in for the kill. "Cover your buddies!"

An alien craft loomed up in front of him and he snapped a Sidewinder away on instinct. The alien craft twisted desperately, throwing itself through a series of flips that should have torn the craft apart, but it was too late. The Sidewinder struck the alien craft's drive field – this time, Will saw the bubble clearly – and the alien craft exploded.

"Shadow-Lead, this is Watchman," the AWACS said. "We assess that you have additional enemy craft on approach vector."

Will swore as the data blinked up on his HUD. There were another twenty-five alien fighters bearing down on them. The Dark Shadows could fire off their remaining missiles and strike a target with each one without wiping out the alien force. The aliens would turn the battle into a turkey shoot, with the humans as the turkeys.

"All right, it looks like we're not welcome here any longer," he said, lightly. There were other human squadrons closer in to possible targets. They'd be able to find help unless the aliens accelerated and caught up with them. The remaining alien craft in the first wave seemed to be backing off slightly, waiting for their comrades to catch up and finish the humans off. "Prepare to…"

CHRISTOPHER G. NUTTALL

The skies were suddenly clear. "Sir, they're gone!"

Will stared at his HUD. One moment, the alien fighters had been wiping the floor with the human defenders; the next, they'd broken off the engagement and vanished. It made sense a moment later. The aliens hadn't headed out of the atmosphere, but west, heading towards the mainland. There were other fighter squadrons on defence duty closer in, but there was no reason to believe that they would fare any better than the Dark Shadows. The aliens were splitting up into smaller units now, curving their flight paths towards their targets, daring the human race to stop them. The Raptor had an impressive top speed even in horizontal flight, yet it wouldn't be fast enough to catch up with the alien craft.

He felt sweat pooling inside his helmet and cursed under his breath. They'd fought a bitter running battle against an unknown foe, and the best they had been able to do was hold their own. He twisted the Raptor around and the remaining pilots followed him, heading back to Langley. They might arrive in time to save something of their home base.

———

"They just broke through the air defence fighters," Lieutenant Rogers said. "They're coming right at the mainland!"

"I saw," Colonel Mandell said. The alien paths were predictable now. They were targeting USAF bases all along the east coast. Washington DC was in their path and it looked as if the aliens were going to fly over the city. They wouldn't enjoy the experience. The defenders had ringed the White House and the other government buildings with antiaircraft weapons. "Pass on a warning to their targets."

He checked the scopes, but it seemed as if they'd been lucky; the aliens weren't coming for the AWACS. It was an odd oversight, one that puzzled him, yet maybe the aliens hadn't recognised and understood the AWACS. It should have been easy to deduce from the radar and radio signals alone, but perhaps the aliens didn't think that it was important. It wouldn't last. Without the orbiting satellites, the USAF would be falling back on its communications aircraft and they'd become vital targets.

"Sir," Lieutenant Rogers said, suddenly. "They're heading right towards the *Ford*!"

"Shit," Mandell said. The USN had stationed a carrier near Washington and the aliens had definitely recognised *her* for what she was. The *Gerald R. Ford* was one of the most powerful ships in the world, yet she had never truly been tested. The aliens were about to give her a baptism by fire. "Warn the Navy pukes that they're about to have company."

He hesitated, looking down at the air defence aircraft scrambling to counter multiple inbound alien attacks. "And tell them that they're on their own," he added. "There's nothing left to send."

Chapter Thirty-Three

USS *Gerald R. Ford*, Atlantic Ocean
Day 38

"All hands, we have inbound multiple hostile aircraft. I repeat, we have inbound hostile aircraft!"

Joe Buckley braced himself as the words echoed through the mighty carrier. He'd never expected to be onboard when the carrier came under attack and had been looking forward to going ashore and returning to his old haunts when the alien mothership had been detected. The thirty-seven year old reporter had been embedding with the United States Navy for years and had never seen an attack on his ship. By now, he was practically one of the crew, knowing the officers and men intimately and sharing their stories with the world.

The *Ford* had been on a fireman deployment in the Mediterranean Sea and had been returning to its homeport in Virginia when the alien mothership had been detected. It had been a routine cruise – North African despots knew better than to challenge the United States and its mastery of the seas – and very little had happened of note, apart from a handful of exercises with the Israeli Air Force. Joe had covered the exercises from his position on the carrier and debunked hundreds of myths spread by various governments that were unrelentingly hostile to both America and Israel. The World News Network had been pleased and he had been promised a more sedate posting next year, before the alien mothership had cast even the *existence* of next year into doubt. WNN had asked him to remain on the carrier even after it had been rapidly reassigned to defence duties and he'd accepted. Surely, he'd reasoned, the aliens hadn't come so far to start a fight. Looking down at the display, he was starting to suspect that he'd been catastrophically wrong.

He looked over at the CAG, who was talking quietly to Admiral Morrigan. Morrigan had been the commander of the *Ford's* task force – outside movies, no American carrier went anywhere without a heavy escort of smaller ships and submarines – for as long as Joe had been embedded on the ship. A sixty-year-old veteran of Iraq and several near-skirmishes with the Chinese, Morrigan seemed permanently calm, as if he'd seen it all before. The *Ford* had been 'sunk' in several exercises after the point defence had been overwhelmed and Morrigan, instead of tearing the offender a new asshole, had calmly dissected the problem and ordered fixes. The most serious threat the carrier faced - an attack by Chinese or Russian-built cruise missiles, some of which might carry a nuclear warhead – could be countered, if the defences all worked together. Morrigan had pioneered cooperative exercises that had prepared the carrier's task force for war. They'd planned for Chinese aircraft, Russian submarines and Iranian suicide boats. Joe doubted that any of them had prepared for alien attack.

"We're shifting the CAP to intercept the incoming alien craft," Lieutenant Ho said. Ho was young enough to be Joe's son – or at least he *looked* young enough to be Joe's son – and was his official minder. Joe had had some bad minders in his early days, before President Chalk had encouraged the military to cultivate good reporters and discourage bad ones – although the training period did tend to discourage those without the stamina to sit it out – and Ho wasn't such a bad type. It helped that Joe had a generally good reputation. Men and women talked to him. There were reporters who couldn't have gotten a friendly reception even if they were buying the booze. "You did read the warning papers?"

Joe almost laughed at Ho's expression. The young Vietnamese-American looked as if he was out of his depth, terrified of getting even a single thing wrong. The incoming alien attack, after having skirmished with the Raptors and inflicting heavy losses, had concentrated more than a few minds. The operators sitting at their consoles had something to focus on, but Ho had nothing, apart from Joe. The warning papers had been read and signed long ago – basically, Joe had agreed to publish nothing without the Admiral's consent and the Admiral had agreed not to be too harsh about deciding what was public interest and what was a dangerous piece of news – and besides, Joe's ass was on the line too. The *Ford* not only held thousands of men and women, but a single reporter as well...and the aliens might not recognise his neutrality. Actually, he wasn't neutral at all. The United States had its flaws – Joe wasn't blind to them – yet he knew the enemies of his country and how even the 'good' ones were barbarians. He would have taken an American soldier over a hundred enemies any day.

"Of course," he said, seriously considering telling Ho to sit down. His career in public information had hardly prepared him for enemy attack. "Besides, what am I going to send back today?"

He ignored his minder's answer and concentrated on the big display. It changed so fast that he could barely follow it, even after watching the exercises against simulated cruise missiles. The cruise missiles had bored in towards the carrier without flinching, moving in a straight line; the alien craft seemed to be manoeuvring towards the carrier, as if they expected to be intercepted by a formidable layer of point defence. They weren't far wrong. The USN had assembled thirty-one of its most modern ships to defend the carrier and its brood – any alien craft intent on challenging the *Ford* would have to blow through a point defence network that was the most advanced in the world. The defences around Washington itself, Joe had been told, were less capable than a USN defence network.

"They're engaging the CAP aircraft," one of the operators snapped. "They're inflicting heavy losses."

Joe winced. The carrier's massive air wing included both F-35 Lightning II Joint Strike Fighters and F/A-18E/F Super Hornets, among the most powerful and deadly fighter aircraft in the world. The carrier had also deployed its entire complement of tankers and AWACS aircraft, linking the latter into NORAD's massive electronic fence surrounding the continental United States. It had fascinated him when he'd first boarded the carrier and learned that the President, in a bunker under the White House or at an undisclosed location, could see through the carrier's systems, even though he had understood that some Presidents had used it to micromanage even basic military operations. Joe himself had written several articles critical of the last President's habit of micromanaging and prided himself on the thought that he might have swung a few votes. He should have been writing demands for more air defence aircraft instead. The exact figures were heavily restricted and classified, but it didn't take a genius to guess that however many aircraft America was deploying, there wouldn't be any replacements in the time between engaging the alien craft and the mothership entering orbit.

"This is Eagle-Lead," a voice said, suddenly. Joe recognised the voice, a blonde female pilot leggy enough to be a supermodel. She'd been aggressive as hell when he'd interviewed her, claiming that it was an advantage for a fighter pilot – and a woman on a carrier mainly staffed with horny men. "The bandits are breaking through. I say again, the bandits are breaking through! They've shot down nineteen of our aircraft and…."

Her voice vanished in a sudden burst of static. "Eagle-Lead is down," a voice said. He sounded rather shocked. Joe realised that the aircraft had been destroyed and there wouldn't have been time to eject. Eagle-Lead – who'd been called Barbie when she'd been off-duty – was dead. No one had believed that she could die. "Eagle-Lead is down."

"All hands, prepare for imminent air attack," the Captain's voice said. Joe felt his chest clench, feeling as useless as Lieutenant Ho. All around him, men and women were responding to the crisis facing their ship, but he could do nothing apart from observe. He couldn't even record the battle for posterity. He'd intended to file a story without actually *becoming* the story. "Incoming hostile targets."

"Clear all ships to open fire in accordance with the firing plans," Admiral Morrigan said. If he mourned the loss of Eagle-Lead and twenty other pilots, he didn't show it. Joe looked up at the display and felt a chill running down his spine. The alien craft had left the remainder of the first CAP flight eating their dust and were rocketing towards the second flight – and the carrier below. "They may engage at will."

Joe watched grimly as the battle unfolded. The alien craft were losing height rapidly, practically skimming the surface of the sea as they closed in on their targets. The escorts were rapidly redeploying themselves to face the incoming threat, but everyone knew that the carrier itself wasn't an easy target to move. The ship was vast – it was larger than many towns – and altering course wasn't easy. The aliens could hardly fail to hit it if they closed to weapons range – whatever their weapons range actually was – and opened fire.

"*Lake Erie* is engaging the enemy," an operator said. "The remaining escorts are opening fire now."

The alien craft ducked and weaved, concentrating desperately on evading the missiles launched by the cruisers, while returning fire with their own weapons. Whatever they were shooting hardly showed up on the systems, apart from damage inflicted on the escorts as the aliens punched their way through. It didn't look to Joe's inexperienced eye if they were firing missiles, yet there was no way to know what they *were* firing. The babble from the operators as they struggled desperately to defend their ship – the carrier's own point defence weapons, including a laser system designed to serve as the last line of defence, were engaging the enemy now – rose and fell, but none of it was informative. He looked over towards a live feed from a camera mounted on the carrier's superstructure and saw a handful of weirdly shaped aircraft dancing around one of the *Ford's* smaller escorts. The escort was clearly ablaze, but still fighting...

The USS *Winston S. Churchill* blew up.

Joe stared at it in numb disbelief. The USN hadn't lost a ship since...he couldn't remember, but it had been decades ago. The USN's modern wars had all been against enemies who lacked real maritime forces – unlike the British, who'd waged war against Argentina over the Falklands and lost several ships – and more ships had been lost to the breakers than enemy action. Ships had struck mines in the first Gulf War, yet none of them had actually been lost...the camera moved to another ship, still desperately fighting as the aliens pounded her with their strange weapons. It was a battle that could only have one ending. He saw a Super Hornet duck into view, launching a missile towards an alien craft and blowing it out of the air, seconds before a hail of alien fire destroyed both the aircraft and the escort it was trying to save.

"Eagle-Eye is down," another operator said. Joe barely comprehended his words. Eagle-Eye was – had been - one of the advanced E-2 Hawkeye AWACS aircraft. He'd flown in them several times to see how the crew reacted to different situations, yet he'd always believed that they were kept safely out of enemy range. The entire situation was so horrific that it was almost surreal. He would have pinched himself if he hadn't had Lieutenant Ho watching him with admiring eyes. Joe wanted to snap at him – what was he doing that was so heroic? He was just watching disaster unfolding in front of him. "They're closing in…"

"All hands, brace for impact," the Captain's voice snapped. "Brace for…"

A series of dull thumps echoed through the ship. It seemed comparatively minor at first, until a second series seemed to shake the entire hull. Joe felt the deck shift under his feet, sending him crashing to the deck. Alarms were ringing everywhere, warning him that the carrier was in dire trouble, yet somehow his mind refused to believe it. The carrier had laughed with scorn at waves and enemy attack. It couldn't be damaged by a handful of alien aircraft.

"Mr Buckley," Lieutenant Ho said. "What are you…?"

The ship seemed to shake again. There was a weird taste in the air for a second, like charged or ionised air, and then green light seemed to flare over the consoles like St. Elmo's Fire. Joe heard screams from crewmen as consoles exploded into massive fireballs, throwing bodies left and right. The lights failed, plunging the entire CIC into darkness, before the emergency lights flickered on. They failed a moment later, but by then the fires were illuminating the compartment. They revealed a scene from hell.

Joe felt sore all over, as if his body had been put through a massive exercise period, yet somehow he managed to pull himself to his feet. He felt suddenly seasick – he hadn't been seasick since he'd been a kid sailing with his father on the Great Lakes – and vomited on the deck until there was nothing left in his stomach. It occurred to him that the Navy Crewmen would probably have a few things to say about it, as if it was the most important thing in the world, yet he knew that something was wrong. His brain ached, as if he had been concussed, and it took him minutes to realise that the ship had been attacked. The entire CIC was in ruins. He looked over at Lieutenant Ho and knew that there was no point in trying to help him. The young man, barely out of his teens, had hit his head so hard that it had crushed it like an eggshell. The sight seemed to bring Joe back to himself. The CIC should have received an emergency crew within seconds – he knew how well drilled the crew were – and yet, no one had materialised. Were they all dead?

"Help," he said, stumbling over to the nearest body. It proved to be a female operator, one of the crew who helped direct the fighters while they were in the air. She was breathing, but it was laboured and forced, leaving her on the edge of death. Joe stared at her, trying to remember what to do, but nothing surfaced in his mind. She passed away without ever regaining awareness of her surroundings. He stumbled from body to body, but it was the same story. The Angel of Death had passed through the compartment and somehow spared his life only.

The ship shook around him again, reminding him that his survival might not last. The *Ford* had a backup facility if the Bridge or the CIC had been taken out, yet that might have been taken out as well. Whatever the aliens had hit them with – the green fire, whatever it had been – might well have wrecked the entire ship. It was getting harder and harder to breath – the fires were consuming the oxygen – and he stumbled over to the hatch. Miraculously, it wasn't jammed and he staggered out into the passageway. There was no one around to help him, or anyone else. The carrier seemed to be deserted.

Slowly, he made his way up to the deck. The aliens had remodelled the interior of the carrier and nothing seemed to be quite where it had once been. There were fires burning everywhere, consuming everything…it dawned on him that there was a nuclear reactor on the ship and it might be on the verge of meltdown. The USN had taken pains to assure him and other reporters that meltdown was impossible, but alien attack and a wrecked carrier had probably been outside the testing requirements. They'd probably screwed the warranty.

He found himself giggling hysterically at that thought as he finally reached the deck. A man reached in and helped him out. Joe was so relieved to see him that he gave him a hug, to the man's embarrassment, before he recognised him. Commander Fletcher would have been on the bridge during the fighting – did that mean that the bridge was gone too? He allowed Fletcher to pull him to his feet and stared down the long flight deck. It was burning brightly; the handful of aircraft that had remained on the flight deck, having been unserviceable when the aircraft were scrambled, had already been destroyed. The carrier had been completely wrecked.

Fletcher slapped his face, hard enough to bring him back to his senses. "Joe, damn you," Fletcher was shouting. "Is there anyone alive down there?"

"They're all dead," Joe said, numbly. The carrier's crew numbered in the thousands, yet he could only see a handful of survivors, trying to get the life rafts up and running. The carrier's superstructure had taken terrible damage. He stared out over the water, hoping that he would see some ships coming to their aid, but saw nothing. The *Ford's* task force had been one of the most powerful fleets the USN had assembled and the aliens had wiped it out within minutes. It felt as if he'd been crawling through the burning carrier for hours. "I saw them die."

"Focus," Fletcher ordered, sharply. Joe realised that Fletcher was badly wounded and felt a moment of shame. He ached, but he was unharmed. "Concentrate on getting off the ship and back to land!"

"Yes, sir," Joe said. "I…"

He broke off as he saw two dark specks rapidly falling out of the sky towards him. The air seemed to be empty of human aircraft – the carrier's air wing had either been destroyed or escaped back to the mainland – and there was no mistaking the incoming craft for human. Blue-green bolts seemed to flare ahead of them, slamming down into the carrier's deck. He felt, more than heard, a dull rumble, shattering the innards of the carrier and leaving it ablaze and sinking in the Atlantic Ocean. There was no point in trying to escape. The carrier was breaking up under their feet. His last impression was of a flicker of brilliant light reaching out to take him…and then nothing but darkness.

Chapter Thirty-Four

Sergeant Danny Kyle heard the aircraft launching into the sky from his position on one corner of the massive air force base, struggling with the makeshift aircraft the USAF had liberated from the Boneyard. The Boneyard - or the Aerospace Maintenance And Regeneration Centre, as it was formally known – had been stripped of aircraft for the defence effort. Kyle and his fellow ground crew had been working their asses off to get the useless aircraft into position, just because someone had convinced the CO that the aircraft might still have a use. They might not have been able to fly – a large percentage of the aircraft in the Aerospace Maintenance And Regeneration Centre had been cannibalised for parts – but they still *looked* usable.

The concept, Kyle had to admit, was sound. The USAF had gone to war against the Serbs in 1999 and bombed them back to the Stone Age, which, in his opinion, the area had never actually left. Or so it had seemed.

The USAF had declared victory and gloated over their success until afterwards, when analysis teams had descended on the Balkans and rapidly discovered the reports of a crushing defeat had been badly exaggerated. The Serbs might not have been able to match the stunning level of technology brought to bear against them, but they'd played all kinds of tricks with their limited technology and successfully tricked the USAF into wasting expensive bombs and missiles.

Dummy tanks had absorbed antitank weapons, cheap radars had confused and decoyed the most advanced guided weapons in the inventory, dozens of dummy targets had absorbed expensive weapons and Yugoslav jets had flown combat missions over Kosovo at extremely low altitude, using terrain to remain undetected by AWACS flying radars. In short, it had been an expensive lesson in the limitations of technology, one that had largely passed most of the USAF by.

Kyle's own bitterness over his lack of promotion – his succession of supervisors and Commanding Officers had never rated him very highly – had become a general sense of disdain towards the entire USAF. The hot-shot fighter pilots had fucked up and yet they were still treated as heroes. Where was the heroism in wasting weapons that cost the American taxpayer over a million dollars per shot?

He looked up at what had once been an F-14 Tomcat. It had been stripped of engines and most of its classified systems, but the ground crews had replaced them with heat-emitters that would mimic a jet on the ground, preparing to launch itself into the air. Any tactician would know that destroying a jet on the ground – as the Israelis had done to the Arabs in the Six Day War – was far preferable to fighting it in the sky. The aliens would come to attack the air base and would see targets that would soak up some of their fire. The Tomcat might never have seen active service – there was no time to look up its lineage – but now it would definitely serve its country.

"Come on," the CO shouted. Kyle didn't like him and suspected that the feeling was mutual. He'd seriously considered simply leaving the USAF when his time ran out, yet what else could he do? His old mother loved the idea of her son, the hero, and he hadn't the heart to disillusion her. He worked on the aircraft and other preparations on the ground; others flew out to take the glory. "We have to get the other aircraft into position before it's too late."

It's too late already, Kyle thought, but he held his tongue.

Andrews Air Force Base had never been so busy before, even with all non-essential personnel evacuated and the surrounding civilian popula-tions warned to leave the area. Most had complied, but some had definitely refused to allow the aliens to scare them out of their homes, while the mob of protesters at the fence kept howling obscenities towards the military per-sonnel they could see. The armed soldiers at the fence didn't seem to be deterring them at all, even though they had signs up warning that the base was in a state of war and the soldiers had authorisation to open fire if they felt that they were in danger.

Kyle hated protesters on general principles – he'd never fired a shot in anger, yet some young bastards had called him a baby-killer or worse when he wore his uniform outside the base – and found himself hoping that the aliens shot them up when they attacked the base. Perhaps their sensors – no one knew how their sensors worked – would pick up the massive crowd on infrared and see it as a genuine threat.

He glanced up as another aircraft took to the skies, an F-16 that had been hastily refurbished and put back into service. The Boneyard had quite a number of aircraft that were still in operating condition and, with all of the reservists called back to the USAF, there were enough pilots for all the planes.

The newcomers were less obnoxious than the normal pilots assigned to Andrews, even through the base had been forced through a series of rapid changes. New fighters and their pilots had been moved in, while other aircraft had been moved out, hoping to preserve them in the face of inevitable alien attack.

Andrews normally handled tanker aircraft, but some had been moved out and based with the fighter squadrons that would protect them. The transports, including Air Force One, had been flown elsewhere. It was hoped that if the aliens saw them as no threat, they wouldn't bother to destroy them. Kyle privately suspected that the aliens would attack them anyway. Air Force One was a symbol to the American people and destroying it would send a powerful message.

Silently, he began to compose – again – the next discussion he would have with his reporter friend. He hadn't been able to tell her about the alerts – the CO had put the fear of God into everyone on the air base, even without sharing the exact truth of what was going on – and Kyle hadn't quite dared tell her what little he'd heard. Besides, the rumour mill had been completely wrong. They'd believed that the President was gearing up to go after Iran, or Russia, or China – or France, for God's sake – and only a few people had bet on aliens. The ones who had had collected hundreds of dollars from the others. His mind raged over possible points he could raise with her – his stock should rise if the aliens did attack the base – when everything changed.

Klaxons started to blare suddenly, warning of incoming attack. "Now hear this," a voice bellowed. "Incoming hostile aircraft. I say again, incoming hostile aircraft!"

For a moment, Kyle didn't believe his ears. No one could attack a military base on American soil. The worst they'd prepared for before the alien craft had been detected was a Chinese or Russian skipper sailing into cruise missile range and unloading his entire complement of missiles onto the air base. There were so many possible targets that the air base had an excellent chance of remaining untouched. It wasn't as if the Russians could launch their entire air force at America. He remembered seeing the Patriot missile batteries moved into position, along with the dedicated ground-to-air defence systems and soldiers carrying handheld MANPAD weapons…they intended to try and stand off the enemy!

His orders were simple. If the base was to come under attack, he and the remainder of the ground crew were to make their way to the shelters and hide there, so they could start repairing the damage after the aliens withdrew. Kyle hadn't been too sure it was a good plan – if the aliens used nukes, the entire base would be destroyed – yet it did have its advantages. Andrews was huge and even if it lost half of the runways, the remainder would still suffice to launch and recover aircraft. The aliens might even waste their firepower on the decoy aircraft he'd spent the last week placing into position. He started to run, but it was already too late.

A scream ripped across the sky as a delta-winged aircraft raced towards the Atlantic Ocean. Kyle recognised it as one of the F-16s – it was no alien craft – heading out under full military power. The sonic boom would upset a number of local residents, assuming that they survived the next few hours. The USAF had called it the Sound of Freedom ever since the fifties, but sonic booms were no laughing matter. Kyle smiled to himself at the thought of one of the fighter jocks having to explain himself to the CO before a flash of light in the sky marked the destruction of the F-16. The Fighting Falcon had been blown out of the sky!

His mouth fell open as three strangely shaped craft seemed to materialise out of nowhere, racing towards Andrews Air Force Base. He'd been expecting something like the scene from *Independence Day* when El Toro had been destroyed, but instead there were only three alien craft, firing brilliant bursts of light down towards the ground. A roar echoed over the air base as the missile batteries opened fire, launching missile after missile towards the alien craft, which separated and raced away from the base, before swinging around and coming back over the base at low level. None of the alien craft were shot down as they raced over the base, their weapons blazing.

The ground shook under Kyle's feet as the aliens pounded the dummy aircraft – the ground crews had thoughtfully included a small amount of jet fuel in the aircraft, ensuring a satisfactory explosion to deceive the alien pilots – before they turned back towards the hangars. A SAM struck one of the alien craft directly and it exploded, the shockwave knocking Kyle to the ground. It saved his life. One of the alien craft was firing into a nearby hangar and the shots were going right over his head. His hair stood on end as he *saw* the alien craft, looking so close it was as if he could reach up and touch it, before it was gone, chased by a handful of missiles. He imagined the alien craft being hit and destroyed like its comrade had been, but there was no second massive explosion. The craft had success-fully escaped.

A moment later, a second swarm of alien craft descended on the base. This time, they weren't unchallenged; a flight of fighters was chasing them, forcing them to keep dodging their fire. A MANPAD accounted for a second alien craft, sending it crashing down towards the ground where it crashed into a hangar and exploded, destroying the surrounding area. Fires raged through the base as the alien craft broke off a second time, leaving the base in ruins. Kyle might not have been one of the best and most dedicated servicemen, but even he knew that it was largely an illusion. The aliens had blown up a lot of shit and it probably looked good, yet with a little effort, the ground crews would have the base working again. The highly-trained crews were already springing into action.

He pulled himself to his feet as the fire engine raced by towards the nearest fire and followed them, running as fast as he could. The crew would need help and they'd have to deal with the most serious threats first. The air base held massive stockpiles of ammunition and a single alien hit in the wrong place would be disastrous. The fires might trigger the ammuni-tion, including the pallets pre-prepared for the returning aircraft, and put their lives at risk. He threw himself to the ground as dark shapes rocketed overhead, then relaxed as he realised that they were human aircraft. The aliens seemed to have broken off their offensive. It wouldn't last.

———

"Dark Shadows, Langley is under heavy attack," the dispatcher said. Will Jacob ground his teeth in anger. The Raptors had fired off their remaining missiles, apart from two pilots who were now taking the lead, and would be easy targets if the aliens decided to have another go at them. Their weapons, whatever they were, had definite advantages over the Raptor's weapons. They didn't seem to have to worry about shooting themselves dry. "Return to Andrews; I repeat, return to Andrews."

"Acknowledged," Will muttered. The Dark Shadows had landed at Andrews before, back during exercises and deployments to provide air security for the capital –why that involved shifting bases had been a mystery – yet they had never had to land on a base under attack. The HUD was pulling data from the AWACS and warning that Andrews Air Force Base, bare kilometres from Washington DC, had been attacked savagely. The aliens seemed to have retreated from the combat zone, yet he knew better than to take it for granted. They might have been waiting for the Raptors to land and allow them a shot at taking them out while they were on the ground.

And yet, there was no choice. Will had seen it himself; their cannons, which would have been lethal against any known human aircraft, were completely useless against the alien craft. He'd wondered at first if they'd simply missed when they'd fired – the alien craft did move with astonishing speed and dodging bullets was at least possible – yet he trusted his wingmates. They'd hit the alien craft and seen how useless the cannons had been. Without new missiles, the Raptors, the most advanced human aircraft in the air, would be sitting ducks when the aliens came back. They needed to rearm quickly. It didn't matter how tired the pilots were after their short nasty engagement. They had to get back in the air before the aliens returned.

The Raptors swooped down towards Andrews. The base had clearly been hit badly, yet it was still operative. Flames rose from a dozen fires and several hangars had been smashed by alien wreckage. It looked as if hundreds of jets had been caught on the ground and he silently cursed the base

CO, before realising that they'd been dummy aircraft intended to absorb alien firepower. It had been a waste of effort, he saw. The alien weapons seemed to have unlimited firepower. Their weapons might not be that accurate, or perhaps even destructive, but it didn't matter. A solid bombardment would hammer any human target into submission. He checked in with the emergency tower – the base's primary command station had been taken out in the first attack – and received permission to land on the one usable runaway. It was against any number of safety precautions, but as soon as he landed he taxied towards the ground crew, who were already rolling out the weapons pallets.

"Hurry up," he snapped at them, as he opened the canopy. He and instantly regretted it. They weren't ground crew in the old pre-alien world, where American bases were never attacked apart from a handful of terrorists, but ground crew whose base had been savagely attacked. He didn't want to fly back to Langley if their home base had come under a heavier attack. The base might have been completely disabled.

He looked at the HUD, barely watching the ground crew as they rearmed his aircraft. He felt tired and worn, as if he'd been flying and fighting for days, rather than the hours it had been. The reports weren't good. At least a dozen bases had come under attack and the aliens had inflicted heavy losses. They'd lost at least thirty craft of their own, but no one knew how big an impact it had had. How many craft did the aliens have to dispose of? What would they consider acceptable losses? There was no way to know.

"We're refuelling you now," one of the ground crew said. Will barely heard him. "Try not to blow up when we start pumping you up, sir."

Will snorted. Opening the canopy had been a mistake. He could smell the smoke in the air – smoke, and the unmistakable smell of burnt human flesh. The wind was blowing the smoke out towards the protesters at the fence – he was amused to discover that Andrews had its own mob of protesters as well – and he hoped that they were enjoying the smell. It would remind them of the human price of war. He continued to glance though the data and winced. A carrier had been sunk and two more were under heavy attack. The United States military had lost more in a few hours than it had in over forty years.

He relaxed slightly as the ground crew released the aircraft and allowed him to taxi back towards the runway. Whatever else happened, he'd meet the aliens in the air. Perhaps there would be a chance to even the score. He glanced over as the Raptor turned onto the runway and caught sight of a burned American flag, still flapping in the breeze. He hoped it wasn't an omen.

———

"Sir," Lieutenant Rogers said, "they're launching a second wave of attacks."

Colonel Thomas Mandell nodded, unsurprised. The aliens had scored significant hits on the defending forces and it stood to reason they'd want to capitalise on their success. The air defence forces were in disarray and the controllers were struggling to patch them back together into a unified force. The loss of the carriers had hurt them badly. It was, by all accounts, worse on the other coast.

"I see," he said, finally. "Where are they targeting?"

Rogers looked up at him. His face was very pale.

"They're going all the way, sir," he said. The display showed no room for error. The alien target was unmistakable. "They're headed directly for Washington, DC."

"Alert the President," Mandell ordered. The President had announced that he would be remaining in the White House. It had been intended to reassure the country that the President was sharing their peril, but it might have been a deadly mistake. "Tell him to get his ass out of there."

Chapter Thirty-Five

"Mr President, radar has detected enemy craft advancing on Washington," Pepper said, as she burst through the door. "You have to get to the bunker now!"

The President didn't argue. He'd chosen to stay in Washington – over the objections of the Secret Service, who'd wanted the President in one of the less well known bunkers – knowing that it might make him a target. The public had to know that the President was sharing the same risks, even though the President had a responsibility to remain alive and in control. The Vice President was well out of sight, buried in one of the secure locations, ready to take over if necessary, yet he knew that there would be some command confusion if he were killed.

He followed Pepper to the door in the rear of the office, a door that had only been opened on exercises. She opened it to reveal a shaft leading down into the bunker and the President jumped down it. The experience, he'd been told, had nearly defeated at least two prior serving Presidents, but it wasn't nearly as bad as Jump School. The shaft somehow cut his speed and allowed him to fall into the bunker safely – and very quickly. A Secret Service Agent at the bottom helped him out before Pepper followed him, bringing up the rear. The remainder of the White House would be evacuated by more conventional means.

The existence of bunkers under Washington was an open secret, but few outside the Federal Government really appreciated just how extensive the entire network actually was. The President had been taken on a tour after his election and had been astonished to discover just how far the tunnels actually stretched. It was a network of secret complexes, bomb shelters and storage compartments that could have housed most of Washington's population when it had been built, although now it might not have been able to protect much of the city. The President or his chosen representatives could have walked from the White House to Langley or Fort Meade without anyone on the surface being any the wiser. A handful of secret diplomatic meetings had taken place in the catacombs, yet no one in public knew that they had even been considered.

The President's bunker had a barren, almost Spartan look. It hadn't been designed as anything other than a short-term hole if Washington suffered a major terrorist attack – the possibility of direct invasion had been an illusion ever since 1815 – and was short of luxuries, although the President didn't care. There was a stockpile of MRE packs in the catacombs that would keep Official Washington fed if necessary – the President privately considered that most of the bureaucrats would probably prefer to starve than eat them – and a simple cot bed. He didn't need anything else.

"Mr President," the duty officer said. Ever since the alien craft had crashed, the bunker had been fully manned by its duty crew. It had links into the command network and could draw data from thousands of sources. It was a miniature NORAD in its own right. "Enemy craft are approaching Washington. Emergency signals are being transmitted now."

The President nodded. The Emergency Broadcast System was being utilised, along with Federal links into the main commercial broadcasting systems. The population of Washington would be warned to remain in their homes and seek shelter if possible, those who remained in the city. A large number of civilians had headed out into the countryside to escape the alien attack they feared, but countless others lacked the resources to do anything of the sort. They'd be hopelessly exposed if the aliens started bombing the cities.

"Show me," he ordered. He'd seen images from the battles over the East Coast in the White House – he never wanted to see any of those images ever again – yet he had no idea of the overall tactical situation. What were the aliens doing? Did NORAD have a handle on how they thought and acted yet? "Where are they?"

"Racing up the Potomac," the duty officer said. A swarm of red and green icons were moving steadily towards the centre of Washington. The red were alien craft, the green were American air defence aircraft...and many of them had been lost. Washington was defended by a formidable number of fighter jets, as well as ground-based systems, yet the aliens had inflicted heavy losses. "They're going to fly over the White House."

The President forced himself to sit down in his chair. There was no point in issuing orders, not any longer. The air defence controllers would have issued whatever orders were necessary, yet the battle was moving so swiftly that their orders might be outdated before the pilots even heard them. All he could do was watch, and wait. His city, his country, his *planet* was under attack...and he could do nothing.

———

Karen ignored the protests of her official bodyguard – a surprisingly hip young man from the Secret Service – and ran for the stairs, ignoring the warnings blaring out of the television. The population of Washington was being warned to remain calm and avoid panic, yet somehow Karen suspected that it wouldn't be enough. She and her family – along with SETI itself – had received death threats from various people who blamed them for discovering the alien ship, even though the alien signal had been powerful enough to be detected by conventional civilian equipment. It hadn't even been SETI's fault. It wasn't SETI that had found a crashed alien spacecraft and chosen to conceal it from all and sundry. Karen wouldn't have cared about her demotion from first person to make contact with alien life, except the death threats were still coming in. Someone had torched her home back in California and they had little choice but to stay in Washington. If the President hadn't been picking up the bill...

It still seemed incredible that the aliens were moving to attack the city, but the news broadcasts had made it far too clear. Fox, CNN and WNN had been warned not to broadcast anything the aliens could use against America, and so there had been a terrifying vagueness about the reports, but the overall theme was clear. American forces were taking a pounding every time they encountered the alien craft. America had a long history of taking a pounding in the opening rounds of any war – Pearl Harbour had smashed an entire American fleet – but this would be different. Karen had had time to think about the implications and knew that whatever happened, the world would be a very different place afterwards. The aliens wouldn't just go away, even if the mothership were to be blown up. There would always be new threats out there beyond the stars.

She passed Daisy on the stairs, heading down to the hotel's bunker, and barely waved. Daisy had been an interesting companion, but she'd been depressed after the aliens had turned out to be hostile, knowing that SETI would pick up the blame. California had provided heavy police protection to SETI's complexes and personnel, yet it hadn't been enough to save a pair of astronomers, one of whom had had nothing to do with SETI. She'd actually been on the record as opposing SETI and considering it a vast waste of time and effort that could be better spent on studying supernovas, nebulas and other objects in space. Her death had been bitterly ironic.

"Come on," she muttered. She was surprised that her bodyguard hadn't come after her, but perhaps there were limits to how far he was prepared to go to protect her from herself. The trickle of guests heading downstairs had become a torrent and she had to push her way through to reach the roof. No one seemed to want to join the crazy girl on her mad quest to see the alien attack in person. "Get out of my way!"

Daisy had taken Karen and her family out one night to a restaurant in Washington, one recommended by the President himself. She'd speculated aloud that the President might have been sending them a subtle message, for the restaurant had an odd role in American history. Donald Rumsfield, on the day that he left office, had taken his family there to eat, where one of the waitresses had refused to serve him on the grounds he was a war criminal. Daisy might have been a Democrat – she'd admitted as much when she met the President – but she'd been indignant at the waitress. If she hadn't wanted to serve people, whoever they were, she shouldn't have taken on the job. Her employer would have been quite within his rights to sack her on the spot.

She reached the landing and stepped out onto the roof. The hotel maintained a penthouse on the very top that cost more dollars for a single night than Karen earned in a month. It looked deserted now – the actor and his latest mistress who'd been using it had headed off to somewhere a little less likely to be a target – and she was able to look out over Washington without interference. She'd been impressed with the view before, when they'd first arrived at the hotel, but now it was different. Great pillars of smoke were rising up in the distance and the sound of aircraft engines echoed over the city, matched by the wail of countless alarms and panicking humans. The entire city seemed to be coming apart. Cars were crashing; people were fleeing – fleeing what? There didn't seem to be anything driving them onwards to an unknown destination. They might not even have a destination in mind!

A streak of light caught her eye and she saw a missile launched from somewhere near the Pentagon. She followed it with her eyes and saw an ominous black craft racing over Washington, twisting to avoid the missile. It didn't move fast enough and the missile struck home, sending the craft into a tailspin that ended when it came down smack in the middle of Washington. There was a flash of light and then a massive fireball, rising up into the sky. The explosion echoed over the city. Karen had been a baby when 9/11 had taken place and had only seen the videos, but this was nothing like a single terrorist attack. The aliens were tearing the city apart.

She ducked instinctively as a set of black shapes roared overhead, firing down at targets on the ground. For a moment, she thought that they were F-117s before realising that they were alien craft, firing odd bursts of light as they moved. She couldn't see precisely what they were targeting, but they didn't seem deterred by fire from the ground, or the handful of fighter jets chasing their tails. Karen wondered why the jets weren't trying to engage the alien craft before remembering that at least one alien craft had crashed in Washington and killed a lot of people. A second set of crashes might be worse than a precision strike against the centre of government.

Another sonic boom rocked the building as newer air defence aircraft raced into battle, firing missiles towards the alien craft. If they'd been worried about bringing craft down over a city, they'd lost their concern now. The cynical side of Karen's mind wondered if that was because the Pentagon and the White House were under attack, but whatever they were doing, it seemed to work. The alien craft twisted and broke off the attack, leaving flames and smoke rising up from their targets. One craft was unlucky and was struck by a missile, exploding in midair with staggering force. Karen flinched, covering her eyes against the glare, just before the sound of the explosion struck her. It had to have shattered windows all over the city.

The remaining alien craft seemed to have vanished, followed rapidly by the air defence aircraft. Karen hoped – prayed – that the fighters would catch up with their targets over the ocean and bring them down before they could reach orbit and escape, but she had admit that was unlikely. The alien craft seemed to be capable of reaching orbit at will and that implied staggering speed capabilities. She didn't know much about the USAF fighter jets, but she was fairly sure that none of them could reach orbit.

My fault, she thought, remembering the naive child she'd been only two weeks ago. She'd thought of the alien contact as being her ticket to fame and fortune, and humanity's ticket to a golden age. Even her suspicions and her meeting with the President hadn't been enough to deter her. The fires raging over Washington showed her how foolish she'd been. Daisy had encouraged her not to think of the aliens as anything other than a meal ticket and neglected to consider that they might have plans and ideas of their own. SETI had gone looking for alien life without ever really considering the consequences of success, yet what other choice had they had? The aliens had to have been travelling for centuries, long before the human race started broadcasting radio transmissions into space. No level of precaution, no ban on transmissions, not even a nuclear war reducing humanity to the Stone Age…nothing would have prevented the aliens from finding Earth. Karen had been the lucky one to discover their signal – and then decipher it – yet she had merely been in the right place at the right time. It would have happened without her. It would just have happened to someone else.

She looked down towards the burning buildings as Washington's fire department sprang into action, sending fire engines racing through the streets towards the fires. It wasn't an easy trip. Countless cars had been abandoned by their owners, forcing the firemen to knock them out of the way or find alternate routes. She flinched as she saw new aircraft high overhead, before realising that they were human aircraft. If there were alien craft as well, they weren't showing themselves. Her guests, the aliens she had discovered – and yet, hadn't discovered – seemed to have pulled back. What were they thinking?

She looked over towards the fence preventing a person from jumping off the roof and knew that it would be easy to climb over. She could jump…and what good would it do? It hadn't been her fault, no matter what various idiots thought, and it would all have happened without her. It was no consolation.

"Don't jump," a quiet voice said from behind her. Karen nearly jumped out of her skin. "It would be very irritating to have to clear you up afterwards."

She spun around to see her bodyguard sitting there. "How long have you been there?"

"Around twenty minutes," the bodyguard said. He winked at her. "You were rather distracted."

Karen flushed. She'd prided herself on being aware of her surroundings at all times – it had been drummed into her head at school, warning her to watch for men who might have bad intentions and who were merely waiting for a sign of weakness – and yet she'd allowed him to sneak up on her.

"Sorry," she said, finally. "I didn't want you watching me all the time."

"Consider yourself lucky," the bodyguard said. "If you were the President's daughter, I'd be watching you like a hawk."

Karen found herself giggling, even though it wasn't funny. The thought of a bodyguard following her everywhere was just insane. Her life at school would have been different, college, dating…would he have even followed her into the toilet? How could she have dated a nice guy if she'd had a bodyguard following her around everywhere? It might have been a good thing if she'd had a bad boyfriend, but really…

"Thank you," she said, finally. She looked back towards the pillars of smoke. "The President doesn't even have a daughter."

"The last one did," the bodyguard pointed out.

Karen nodded. "What now?"

"I have no idea," the bodyguard said. "Wait and see what happens, I guess."

———

There were more soldiers and marines on the streets of Washington than Abigail had seen in any number of unstable regimes, but with a combination of her press pass and some bluffing she was able to get closer to the

Pentagon than the security personnel might have preferred. It had been an impressive building when she had first seen it, yet now it was nothing but burning rubble. The heat from the flames could be felt even at her distance and she had a nasty feeling that the firemen pouring water and foam into the blaze were wasting their time. The building would have to be rebuilt from the ground up.

The White House, by contrast, hadn't been touched at all, although she suspected that was a deliberate choice on the part of the aliens. She'd seen enough of the battle from her vantage point to know that they could have taken out the building if they had wanted to. The handful of craft that had crashed in Washington had inflicted further wounds on the city and even though they seemed to have broken off for the moment, they could return at any time. The strikes not only served a tactical purpose, but a psychological one as well. The message was clear. Nowhere was safe.

She glanced upwards at a fighter jet racing overhead and wondered if it was hunting an alien craft, or merely providing what little protection it could. She had had no way of keeping track of the battle, yet the strikes in the heart of Washington suggested that it wasn't going well. The war was barely a few hours old and it was already being lost.

Abigail knew that she should file a story, something to back up or disprove the hysterical nonsense being put out on the Internet by the bloggers, but it all seemed futile. If the aliens could inflict such harm on the best-defended air space on the planet, what couldn't they do? Was she looking at the twilight of the human race?

Chapter Thirty-Six

The President ached all over as he stepped into the underground Situation Room. The cot bed in the bunker hadn't been very comfortable and the war news had been depressing, depressing to the point where he hadn't been able to get much sleep. He'd slept much better in Iraq, when he hadn't borne ultimate responsibility for every lost life, and he made a mental note to get a better bed installed in the bunker, even if he had to pay for it himself. The underground Situation Room was almost a duplicate of the normal situation room, apart from the absence of servants. The principals would have to organise their own coffee. He was sure that wouldn't tax their abilities too far. With alien attacks still underway, their servants had more important things to do.

"Please be seated," he said, as he took his place at the head of the table. The group had stood when he'd entered, a gesture of respect that was all the more meaningful when the country was at war. The atmosphere in the room was grim. The President doubted that there had ever been such an atmosphere of urgency and desperation since the Civil War. Even 9/11, as shocking as it had been, wouldn't have provoked such urgency. Only the Cuban Missile Crisis would have come close. "General, what is the current situation?"

"Grim," General Wachter said. He nodded towards the big plasma screen at one end of the room. The President's hatred of PowerPoint briefings was well known, yet there was no other choice. A map of the United States – marked with red icons representing enemy attacks – appeared in front of them. It only took one look to know that the situation was bad. "First, we have lost all of our orbiting satellites apart from the stealthed units deployed by the NSA. The vast majority of our command and control system, particularly for units deployed to Iraq, South Korea and Afghanistan, has been crippled. We have had to fall back on European satellites and communications systems, but we imagine that it won't be long before the aliens realise what we've done and either demand that the Europeans stop sharing their systems with us or simply take their satellites out as well. The NSA satellites were intended for covert reconnaissance and have only limited communications facilities.

"The attempts to prevent the aliens gaining a foothold in orbit failed completely," he continued. "Ground and air-based lasers appear to have been completely ineffective against the alien craft. Researchers at Area 52 have speculated that the reason they failed is because the lasers simply didn't have enough power to overwhelm their drive fields. The aliens, regardless of the actual truth, simply ignored them. The handful of KE-ASAT units that we activated was also completely ineffective. They were simply too slow to reach the alien craft before they were either avoided or taken out.

"THAAD missiles proved to be more effective against them, with at least two confirmed hard kills in orbit and nine more against targets that imprudently chose to enter the atmosphere over Montana. They seem to have difficulty manoeuvring in the atmosphere at very high speeds and the THAAD missiles were fired right into their path. We know we stung them because they never attempted to enter the atmosphere over land again. The vast majority of their craft chose to enter the atmosphere over the ocean."

His face darkened. "At least three hundred craft descended on the east and west coasts, engaging our air defence forces in a series of running battles. A full analysis is in your briefing notes for later examination, but the short version is that we inflicted losses, but were unable to prevent a series of attacks against targets on the ground. We downed around forty of their craft – we may have taken out more, but radar returns are sometimes inconclusive – at a cost of sixty jets of various types. We have no way of knowing just how badly we're hurting them. We may have taken out fifty percent of their forces, ten percent, or one percent. Missiles destroy the alien craft if they hit – analysis suggests that the impact overloads their drive fields – yet cannon fire is completely ineffective. The best guess is that the alien craft are capable of absorbing or deflecting cannon shells, but missiles are too powerful to prevent from at least inflicting some damage. Ground-based missile systems had similar results, although in at least two attacks the alien craft crashed onto the target and inflicted considerable damage.

"Their mindset may be alien, but their targets are understandable. They targeted air bases, radar stations, support systems and political targets. A handful of air bases have been damaged to the point where they can no longer support fighter operations and we've had to redistribute their units to other facilities. The Pentagon has been completely destroyed on the surface and the underground complexes have suffered significant damage. A handful of alien craft shot up power stations and transformers, causing blackouts in several cities before power could be rerouted. Outside Washington itself, civilian casualties have been minimal. The only significant civilian death was an idiot reporter who managed to convince a pilot friend to take him up to view the battle. The aliens blew him out of the sky."

There were some chuckles. "Do you think they knew who they were shooting at?"

"I doubt it," Wachter said. "They don't seem to discriminate between military and civilian aircraft, although all civilian air traffic has been grounded and will remain on the ground until…the, ah resolution of this crisis, one way or the other. We'd have stripped the idiot pilot of his licence if he'd survived. The majority of the destroyed aircraft went down with their pilots, although a handful of pilots did manage to eject in time to save their lives.

"The USN has lost three carriers so far, two in the Atlantic and one in the Pacific, along with almost all hands. A handful of crewmen were able to take to the boats and escape before the aliens finished them off. The escorts, being smaller and less well-protected, were generally sunk quickly. Their point defence proved unable to prevent the aliens from landing blows on their vessels and battering them to pieces. The carrier air wings were either destroyed or pulled back to the mainland."

He pressed on, as if he wanted to finish before he broke down completely. "So far, there have been no attacks on facilities outside the Continental United States, including carriers and air bases, but we don't expect that to continue. The *George Washington* is completely exposed in its current location and isn't yet in position to assist with Operation Wilson. In some ways, they're actually hampering their own operations – we're still drawing radar data from facilities in Canada, England and Japan – but my analysts believe that their forbearance has a political motivation. Officially, those bases belong to the host country and leaving them alone may convince the hosts that the alien quarrel is only with America. I suspect that the hosts will eventually get demands to take the bases over or the bases will come under direct attack.

"The bottom line, Mr President, is that we're taking a hellish beating," he concluded. "The fighter pilots and soldiers on the ground are doing the best they can, but the longer this war continues, the more pressure they'll be under. We'll have to start pulling aircraft out of their squadrons for maintenance and repair work, giving their pilots time to rest and relax and everything else. We may even run out of missiles and spare parts. We need to launch Operation Wilson now."

The President stared down at his hands. Operation Wilson – the attack on the alien base in Antarctica – would raise the ante quite some distance. He'd held off authorising the operation because it would have painted America as the bad guy, yet it no longer mattered. The country was under attack and Operation Wilson represented the best chance they had at hurting the aliens. The mothership was still bearing down on Earth, yet if they could take out the base, the aliens might be inclined to negotiate.

"The diplomatic field is not encouraging," the Secretary of State said. He looked, if anything, worse than the President felt. Hubert Dotson had spent the last day talking personally to world leaders and his opposite numbers, only to face a series of rebuffs. "Privately, we're getting messages of sympathy and covert help – as the General described – but publicly, the message the governments are getting from their own people is that we started this war and should therefore be left to face the aliens on our own. The economic fallout from the war is hitting the rest of the world badly, Mr President; Europe, Russia and China are all suffering serious economic disasters. Europe already has mobs on the street that will grow worse over the next week, while both Russia and China have clamped down hard. I doubt the Chinese will be able to maintain control for long. Their economy has effectively evaporated.

"And the normal suspects are acting up as well," he added. "Iran has been bullying the smaller Gulf States and acting as if it intends to challenge Saudi. North Korea has been making threatening noises towards its southern cousin and may be considering coming over the DMZ. The economic shockwaves may sweep over Africa and the Middle East – frankly, even if the aliens all dropped dead tomorrow, we'd be spending years rebuilding. The loss of the satellites alone has crippled our economy."

"And our media," Wachter said. "They're going to have problems broadcasting their lies without their satellites."

The President was too tired to see the funny side. "And the word on the streets?"

"Concerned, mainly," the FBI Director said. "The vast majority of the population is praying, although there have been a series of nasty incidents, mainly clashes between people protesting the war and people who are protesting the protests against the war. Several thousand people have been hospitalised after violent clashes; thousands more have been arrested. The fighting has caused people to rally round the flag rather than question the underlying nature of the war; it helps, to be fair, that the aliens chose the wrong forum to drop their bombshell. The UN is not well-regarded by the majority of the American population."

"The UN has been working to get a peace agreement going, despite opposition by various UN members," the Secretary of State said. "They've been beaming signals out from several facilities in Europe and Asia, but no response. The aliens don't seem interested in a truce."

"Of course not," the President said, sharply. "They're coming to settle our planet. The war won't end until we take out the mothership or force them to settle on our terms. We might as well admit now that the world is never going to be the same again."

"And the aliens are not UN members anyway," the Secretary of State added. "They might not be interested in *becoming* UN members. Why should they?"

The President shrugged. "Operation Wilson," he said. "Are you sure that we should move now?"

"The base is definitely supporting their attacks," Wachter confirmed. "We've tracked alien craft heading southwards at high speed after breaking off their attacks on our facilities. We're not sure what's waiting for the assault force under the ice, but taking out the base – even if we recover no alien tech – would definitely have an impact on their ability to conduct operations. We can no longer afford to care what the other involved nations think of us conducting military operations in the area. We have to take the base out now."

"Send the orders," the President said, coldly. The die was cast…but then, it had been cast when the aliens had forced them to fight or submit. "If the assault team is unable to occupy and loot the base, they are authorised to detonate the nuke and destroy the base."

No one objected. The President wondered vaguely if that was a sign of their increasingly desperate situation. Detonating a nuke for any reason before the aliens arrived would have caused a furious debate, even within his handpicked cabinet. Now, he'd authorised the deployment of a backpack nuke capable of taking out an entire city and might have to launch nuclear-tipped missiles at the alien mothership when it entered orbit, even though destroying the mothership might ruin Earth. Nukes were hardly as terrifying as public opinion would have people believe, yet there was nothing casual about their use. They'd been humanity's final resort for far too long.

"There is another issue," Jones said. He looked unshaven and tired as well. "We need permission to start dissecting one of the alien bodies."

The President considered it briefly. He'd given the order to hold off on any intrusive research procedures because it might have upset the aliens, but now they were at war, it hardly mattered any longer. Learning how the alien bodies actually worked might help prepare for the ground offensive he knew was coming – they might even work out how to construct a biological weapon that could be deployed against the aliens. If they could present the aliens with the threat of a biological holocaust, perhaps they'd talk terms. It was a possibility…and yet he had no illusions about how difficult it would be to identify possibilities and develop such a weapon. Alien biology had to be very different to human biology. Human-alien hybrids were the product of cheap science-fiction movies, not real life.

"Granted," he said, finally. "Keep me informed on the results."

"That does lead to another interesting datum," Wachter said. "Most of the craft we shot down exploded violently in the air or crashed into the ground and exploded, but a couple crashed fairly intact and were recovered. They both had two pilots who should have survived the crash, but both of them had liquefied brains. I think that the aliens are determined that none of their people are going to fall into our hands."

"Why?" The President asked, genuinely puzzled. "We wouldn't mistreat them."

"We might if we wanted information we knew they possessed," Wachter pointed out. "It might be a simple security precaution. Anyone who falls into enemy hands gets killed by an automated suicide implant. The CIA used to have a comparable idea…"

"No one liked the idea very much," the CIA Director said, quickly. "It became a system for volunteers only."

"The Special Forces do sometimes use similar implants," Wachter admitted. "The ones for soldiers are voluntary and can be triggered by the soldier if he felt that he was at risk of being tortured for information. The ones for captured terrorists are often inserted without their knowledge and have been used to lead us back to their bases, or their fellow terrorists. The aliens may just believe that anyone we capture will be tortured…"

"Or perhaps will talk quite willingly," the President mused. "The only information we have about them came from one of their leaders and we *know* that they lied to the UN. For all we know, they might be a repressive society with soldiers convinced that the human race is composed of monsters and assholes."

Wachter grinned. "You mean it's not?"

The President snorted. "Short of capturing a live one, we'll have to table it for the moment," he said. "When will Operation Wilson be launched?"

"Within the next two days, depending on conditions," Wachter said. "Lieutenant-Commander Nicolas Little will make the final call for when they'll jump off and hit the base. There's a Force Recon team watching the base now, but we're restricting communications in case the aliens locate them and realise they're being watched. Taking out the bases in Antarctica would be child's play for them and then they'd be safe – they'd certainly go after the *George Washington* as well."

The President nodded. The last thing a SEAL would want would be a politician – even an ex-military man – watching over his shoulder and micromanaging. He'd hated it back when he'd been in Iraq – it had been one of the reasons he'd resigned – and he trusted the SEALs to do the job. There was nothing else he could do. The only help the outside world could offer was a Tomahawk bombardment from the submarines waiting to pick up the surviving soldiers after they pulled back from the base.

"Good," he said, finally. "Keep me updated."

———

His quarters in the underground bunker were cold and harsh, almost like a monkish cell. It was a level of equality with the others in the bunker that a communist might have envied, although the communist would probably have argued that the President could have had the room upgraded at will and therefore there was no such thing as true equality. It wasn't the Lincoln Bedroom, but it would suffice. The President had slept in worse.

He'd spoken briefly to the country after the first wave of alien fighters had retreated back into orbit, but he knew that it hadn't been enough. The alien fighters had returned, broken off, and returned again, keeping on the pressure over the hours. The President had studied the Battle of Britain when he'd been younger and remembered how close the RAF had come to breaking. The British had been able to replenish their fighters over the weeks of war and train new pilots, but it took months to build a fighter jet – the Raptor production line had been dismantled after the project had been cancelled - and years to train a USAF pilot. The USAF might be worn down to nothing before the alien mothership entered orbit…

And what would happen then?

The President believed what Ethos had told him, because it fitted all the facts. One billion aliens were going to land on Earth and settle the planet, after sweeping aside humanity's resistance. The entire world would be theirs if America lost the war.

"Over my dead body," he muttered, and started to consider contingency plans. The war wouldn't be lost even if the aliens occupied all of America, or even the entire world. Biting off the entire planet might be beyond even their resources. There was still a chance for victory.

Chapter Thirty-Seven

Area 52, Nevada, USA

Day 40

"I thought I'd find you here."

Alex looked up from the comfortable, if ugly chair. "I'm doing what everyone else does when there's a national crisis," he said, dryly. "I'm watching television."

"Oh?" Jane asked. "Is it telling you anything you don't already know from intelligence reports?"

"Not really," Alex admitted. "It just keeps reminding me of how much the world has changed over the past month."

The loss of the satellites had sharply reduced the number of channels available to American viewers, although most of the foreign channels had replaced their scheduled programs with updates on the war raging over America and the EBS overrides kept cutting in, relaying warnings of new alien attacks. CNN, Fox and WNN had fallen back on their contingency plans and were broadcasting as they'd done in the days before satellites had become so common, while talk radio and other sources of information were enjoying a surprising boost in popularity. Local channels carried more specific information on battles between the American defence forces and the aliens, updates on dead or missing people and a vast amount of nonsensical speculation on the course of the war. The military was restricting information and few broadcasters were willing to risk federal charges for revealing classified military secrets, but most people could read between the lines. The war wasn't going well.

He flicked a channel to a British TV station, which was showing images of running street battles between French riot police and dark-skinned rioters.

The commentary was reporting that the French Interior Ministry was preparing to deploy paratroopers and Foreign Legion soldiers to the streets of a dozen French cities in the wake of the massive economic collapse. The aliens didn't need to invade Europe. It was coming apart quite nicely on its own. The news from China was even less encouraging. After some ritual fist-shaking at Taiwan, the Chinese Government had declared martial law and started putting troops on the streets. As those soldiers were unpaid, the results had not been pleasant.

"I keep thinking that…you know, I'm suddenly redundant because everyone knows now that aliens are real," he admitted. "I used to keep thinking that they weren't real, or that they were just classified military aircraft, and now…now, I feel useless. And then I remember that thousands of lives have been lost already and more will be lost unless we can figure out a way to stop them and…it all feels unreal."

He shook his head. "I felt the same about 9/11," he added. "It was impossible to believe that someone could do that to us, not until I saw the footage and realised that it had actually happened. I walked around numb to the changes in the world until it finally sank in. Does that make me sound selfish?"

"It makes you sound like a man," Jane said. She stuck out her tongue at his expression. "The human mind isn't capable of grasping big surprises all at once, even with the best of training. You're down in a base that gives you an increasing sense of unreality; of course you're going to question if this is really happening. I used to wonder if the whole alien crash scenario was just a test of how we'd react under the strain, until I saw the alien bodies. They couldn't have been faked."

She placed a hand on his shoulder and gave it a gentle squeeze. "I know what you need to cheer you up," she added. "Come watch while I dissect the alien."

"And then we can make a film of it and sell it for big dollars," Alex said, remembering several films that had claimed to feature aliens being dissected by military doctors. He'd had two of them analysed and they'd both proven to be fakes, with the alien bodies actually human children who'd been badly malnourished. It said more about the human willingness to be fooled than what alien anatomy might look like. "I'll split the money with you fifty-fifty."

"We'll have to put the data out on the web for free," Jane disagreed. "The entire world will need to know what makes them tick. Come and watch from the observation lounge in an hour. I'll have everyone ready by then."

Alex watched her leave and looked back at the television. An announcer he didn't recognise was reporting on an alien attack on an installation in Oregon and discussing the possible future implications for the state's military spending. It sounded like the least of America's concerns to Alex and it left him wondering if Jane was right, if the announcer was trying to hide from an unpleasant reality behind nonsense. He clicked the channel and saw a talking head going on and on about protesters who'd been killed in one of the alien attacks, calling them all martyrs to the cause of interstellar peace. Alex had no such feelings. Most people who were caught up in war zones didn't choose to be there. The protesters didn't have to be anywhere near the military bases under attack. It was hardly the military's fault that they'd been killed.

An hour later, he found himself in the observation lounge, flanked by Jones and an Army Medical Colonel from the US Army Medical Research and Materiel Command. The concerns about an accidental biological holocaust had faded somewhat with the apparent discovery that the aliens had no qualms about exposing themselves to humanity, but no one was interested in taking any chances. It was possible, although unlikely, that something the aliens rated as harmless would be lethal to humanity, or vice versa. The entire autopsy would take place in a sealed environment and the medical researchers would take the utmost care to avoid infection. It wasn't an easy task. If any of them were touched by alien biological material, their superiors might never be able to take them out of quarantine.

It grew worse. It wasn't hard to deduce that there would be a nuclear option – quite literally – for dealing with any biological contamination. The base was designed to allow the air to be pumped out, or flamethrowers used to sweep the entire complex clear, but as a final resort a nuclear weapon would be used to sterilize the base. Alex had never given much thought to working near jet fuel and aircraft weapons, yet the very thought of the nuke sent shivers down his spine, even though he knew that nukes were highly overrated. His one visit out of the complex only heightened the sense of returning to a death trap. Jane might have had a point about it being a test at the beginning. Missile crews in silos tended to suffer from similar cabin fever and other disorders.

"This is EBE1," Jane said, her voice echoing oddly through the speakers. Everything she said would be recorded by very sharp microphones, to the embarrassment of some medical technicians. The microphones picked up everything. "There has been no change in the alien since first examination, including no biological decay. The reason for that remains unknown, but may be connected with the sterile working environment. The bodies were not frozen or preserved by any human agency. It may be that Earth-based microbes or other lower life forms do not find the alien biology palatable, or it may have another cause."

Alex watched carefully as she started to dissect the alien, taking her time. The original faked videos had suggested a hasty procedure, but Jane moved slowly, carefully exploring the alien's internal organs. Alex was no expert on biology, human or alien, but it was evident to him that the alien had been designed for a specific set of tasks. He'd read several science-fiction novels in which aliens – or humans – had engineered castes that fitted various different roles, from warriors to breeders. They'd had societies rather like anthills, with the queens at the top and the lowly workers at the bottom. It was possible that the older aliens who'd spoken to the President and the UN were actually high castes, while the smaller aliens – or the big brutish aliens – were lower castes. The alien body actually looked less complex than a human body, yet there was a surprising amount of wasted space and seemingly useless organs.

Or I could be completely wrong, he thought, reminding himself that he wasn't a doctor and, even if he had been, it was only the first exploration of an alien body. Without a live specimen, it was difficult to know for sure what every organ did, even though Jane and her assistants were making educated guesses. The alien seemed to have a rather odd heart - by human standards - that seemed to be merged with the liver and lungs. If, of course, they *were* alien livers and lungs. They could have been something entirely different.

As the dissection proceeded, tiny sections of alien flesh and blood were cut away and passed to the sealed research spaces. There were hundreds of researchers who'd demanded a chance to look at an alien body – after the aliens had kindly told the world that the United States had a crashed ship and alien bodies – and Jane had been able to choose the best. They'd study the alien DNA – if they used DNA – and attempt to determine how the different alien subsets were related. Alex was inclined to believe that they were looking at different castes rather than different races, although he had no idea how such a system might have evolved. Humanity would have refused to try to engineer their bodies to fit a specific purpose.

Or maybe not. The Soviet Union had tried to convince itself that it had created the New Soviet Man. It had been nothing more than a delusion, yet there were hundreds of unanswered questions surrounding their genetic engineering project and biological warfare capabilities. Others, the modern-day Nazis and other extremist groups, would have been quite willing to domesticate large swathes of the human race, converting those they considered lesser into slaves and breeders. It might even be possible, in the future, to engineer human slaves who literally couldn't think of freedom as anything other than a word, worshipping the master race. It was the plot of thousands of science-fiction novels and movies – including a whole series of underground movies that were long on bondage and sadistic domination, but short on actual plot – yet with the alien technology, it might be possible to do just that. A human would be revolted, but aliens might not think like humans; they might think that it was a great idea.

"The alien fingers appear designed for extremely precise work," Jane said, her voice breaking into his thoughts. "They show a degree of precise control that is superior to the average human, although it is impossible to be sure without a live alien to examine. Despite their small size, they are apparently quite strong and would probably be capable of inflicting serious harm on a human in close-quarter battle. Combined with their other traits, including very sharp eyes and no apparent nose, I am inclined to wonder if I'm looking at a worker caste alien."

"Interesting," one of the other observers said. Alex hadn't even seen the USAF officer entering the room. "Is it actually intelligent?"

"It is in fact a he, as far as I can tell," Jane said, slightly nettled. "I have candidates for sexual organs on all five of the aliens and they're all male-type.

They may not be breeders, of course, but they are definitely male. They should be capable of the sexual act if given a partner."

Her voice tightened. "Without a live specimen, I cannot actually tell you if it is an intelligent creature," she admitted. "It is true that it has a brain that is actually larger than a human brain, but I cannot tell you what level of intelligence it possesses, or even if it is intelligent in any sense that we humans would understand. We may be dealing with creatures that are capable of making tools and developing technology by instinct. Man needs to think to challenge and reshape the world; the aliens may not need anything of the sort. My gut feeling, however, is that the aliens are definitely intelligent, perhaps not that different from us. They don't react to situations; they *create* situations."

Alex frowned, following her logic. A few years ago, a set of researchers had started to try to teach monkeys about the idea of money. It had sounded like a mad experiment when he'd first heard about it, but by trial and error, the researchers had finally managed to teach the monkeys that money had value, even though they couldn't eat it. The monkeys had developed to the point where they'd been able to adapt to their new situation, inventing bank robbery, shopping and prostitution. It had raised a number of disturbing questions about how intelligent monkeys actually were, yet they had clearly not invented money for themselves, or tried to communicate openly with humans. Was their behaviour, once they had grasped the concept of money, a sign of intelligence or merely a sign of *adaptation*? They had never invented money in the wild and there had been no need to invent it when they were in cages.

But if the mark of humanity – or intelligence - was the ability to *imagine*, and then *create*, wasn't it proof that monkeys were *not* intelligent… and the aliens were? Humanity had imagined thousands of alien contact scenarios before a UFO had finally crashed, scenarios that Alex – among others – had used to prepare for possible repercussions. Others had imagined uses for materials that simply hadn't been in existence when the writers had conceived them, yet once the technology was available, the dreams had flowered into reality. It seemed impossible to think of a race that couldn't *imagine*, or existed as anything greater than…well, monkeys. The aliens had to have some form of intelligence.

And had humanity gotten *smarter*? In the early days, brute strength and cunning would have been more important than brains, particularly in a weak body. Alex remembered the Special Forces soldiers he'd seen before they'd set out to Antarctica and knew that, in the past, they would have been far more important to society than any nerd, or a person like Alex. As humanity had developed, intelligence and imagination became more and more important...and when societies started suppressing innovation, they stagnated and eventually collapsed. The Dutch, the British, the Americans...all had prospered by rewarding imagination and innovation. The Germans, the Russians, the Japanese, the Chinese...all had rejected freedom of thought and speed, freedom of innovation, and had suffered for it. The Germans had thrown out the men and women who had created the atomic bomb! How innovative were the aliens?

He looked down at the half-dissected alien body, and then walked out of the observation room. There would be nothing he could contribute and he wanted to get his thoughts down on paper before they fell out of his mind. He barely realised where he was walking before he walked into the hangar holding the alien craft and stopped, looking up at its almond shape. There was no way that something so...elegant could be created by a race operating on instinct alone. The aliens had to be intelligent.

"We need results now," Jones was saying. Alex realised suddenly that he'd walked in on an argument between Jones and Frandsen, who looked tired and angry. "What the hell did they use against our carriers?"

"And I'm telling you that we only have theories," Frandsen replied, sharply. "We don't *know* what they did to those ships, only that the green fire seems to destroy electronic systems and ruin entire compartments! We thought it might be a focused EMP weapon, but if they had something like that, why aren't they knocking our aircraft out of the sky with ease? Our best guess is that it's some kind of electromagnetic field causing localised overloads and massive disruption.

"The other alien weapon is easy to understand. It's nothing more than bursts of superheated plasma, something we had under development ourselves in the labs. It moves very fast, but hardly at the speed of light and it can be dodged by our aircraft if they react in time. Its own nature makes it a very imprecise weapon, but they can spit out enough plasma pulses to make sharing the same airspace very unhealthy. We could even duplicate the weapon within a few months…"

"*We don't have a few months*," Jones snapped. He sounded on the very edge of collapse. Moving back and forth between Area 52 and Washington was wearing him down. "We have twenty-odd days before that mothership enters orbit and at this rate, the aliens will have smashed our entire air force well before they arrive! We need something we can use now!"

Frandsen took a step forward, and then managed to calm himself. "It takes months, at the very least, to develop an experimental piece of hardware," he said. "It takes years to put it into production once all of the bugs have been worked out. Even if we abolish safety rules put into place by people who don't have the slightest idea what they're talking about, even if we get an unlimited budget from a Congress that is notoriously unwilling to fund new technology, even if we have all the advantages in the world, we're still not going to be able to produce something completely new…"

He smiled before Jones could explode. "We do have one possibility," he admitted, slowly. "We've been studying the telemetry from the big battles and it seems that the reason the alien craft are being brought down is because their drive fields are being disrupted…"

"As you told me," Jones snarled.

"And that the impact from the cannon fire is apparently insufficient to bring down the craft," Frandsen continued, getting a small measure of revenge. "There are other ways to introduce vast amounts of energy into such a field. We might even be able to get one to implode with *really* dramatic results."

"Get me something, get me anything," Jones snapped. "Get us something we can use before the entire country comes apart!"

Chapter Thirty-Eight

Alien Base, Antarctica
Day 40

Sergeant Edward Tanaka had been a Marine on active duty for four years before he'd been transferred into the United States Marine Corps Force Reconnaissance unit, better known to the public as Force Recon. It had been an interesting career covering far too many countries that were too hot and dry for his taste, but one of the most interesting postings had been Antarctica. He'd spent two weeks at one of the research bases drilling for operations in the Antarctic after reports that terrorists intended to occupy one of the Antarctic Research Bases. The threat had never actually materialised and the Marines had been pulled out, yet it had clearly served as good experience. Edward would be among the first American soldiers to assault an alien base.

The Antarctic was a land of contradictions. The public thought of it as a massive icy continent, rather like the Arctic. There were places where that was all it was, but also places where there was little ice, places where later bases could be built. There were vast deposits of coal somewhere within Antarctica and Edward had been briefed that, one day, countries might start raping the Antarctic for resources they desperately needed. It would devastate the area and perhaps lead to the extermination of countless birds and sea mammals that inhabited the continent. The Antarctic wasn't to everyone's taste, yet it had a stunning natural beauty and Edward had already seriously considered trying to obtain a permanent posting to one of the research stations. A Force Recon Marine was a master of many skills and some of them would definitely be useful in the Antarctic.

It was also a very dangerous place. There were areas where snowstorms blew up out of nowhere, presenting a very grave hazard to life and limb. There were the famed Areas of Inaccessibility where aircraft ran into massive distortions and had to turn back, or crash. Dozens of aircraft had been lost over Antarctica and, it was becoming increasingly clear, some of those aircraft might have been helped to crash by the aliens. No one knew how long they'd been hidden away in the last great unexplored wilderness, yet Edward was becoming sure that it had been for a very long time. The Antarctic had the highest number of UFO sightings in the world, even though there were natural conditions that suggested that many of the sightings were caused by ball lightning or other more mundane causes. The presence of the alien base, however, was no joke.

He peered down from the hide towards what looked like a sheer cliff face. It would have been daunting to even an experienced climber, even men who'd been through the dreaded training exercises required for Special Forces. It also wasn't real. They'd seen hundreds of alien craft flying out of the sky right towards the cliff face and passing right through, somehow either moving out of phase with the rock or, more likely, passing through a hologram. It was a neat way to camouflage the base and the Marines had been impressed. Hell, they wished that *they* could do that. The Marine Corps had specialists in camouflage and blending in with enemy populations – Edward himself had once walked through a terrorist camp without being noticed or challenged, before calling in the air strike that had obliterated every last terrorist in the camp – but mobile holograms remained in the realm of science-fiction, until now. The aliens had somehow cracked another technological mystery.

As they watched, another flight of alien craft floated out of the sky, flashing down towards the cliff and stopping just before they crashed into it, then drifting slowly forward and passing through the hologram. Edward had wondered why the aliens had built the base like that until realising that it helped to conceal the base if the aliens flew right into a cliff face, rather than down into a dark pit. It suggested that the aliens didn't have a large hangar, but merely a small landing pad, although the only way to find out for sure was to pass through the hologram themselves. They'd been given strict orders to remain out of sight and merely observe, no more. The attack wouldn't begin until the entire force was in position.

"Send the signal," he muttered. They'd chosen not to bring their standard equipment to the base, knowing that the aliens would pick up the radio transmissions and deduce their presence. Instead, they'd brought a tiny laser communicator that could reach a British satellite high overhead, which would relay the transmission to their superiors. In theory, the laser beams were impossible to detect or intercept, but they'd been warned to keep their transmissions as brief as possible. No one knew for sure just how secure the entire system was. "How long do we have to wait now?"

A moment later, the reply flickered back down the laser. "Thirty minutes before the main body arrives here," his spotter said. They'd been a sniper team in the Middle East, but watching the alien base was far more fascinating. It was far too clear that the alien base was supporting the attacks on their homeland and both men had been tempted to open fire, even against orders. Their discipline had held, but both of them hoped and prayed that it wouldn't be long before the attack began. The Marine Corps had its own aircraft and they were engaged against the alien craft – and many had been lost. Both men wanted some payback. "And then we move."

"Thank Christ," Edward said. The alien craft were taking off again, returning to the fight. At their speeds, they would be over America within minutes. "Keep an eye on that hatch and see if you can find any other way into the base."

———

Nicolas cursed again under his breath as the Arctic Cat floundered, before catching itself and carrying on towards their destination. It was becoming increasingly clear that their estimates for how long it would take to get the entire force in position had been rather…optimistic. It wouldn't have taken so long in the Middle East, or even in the most sadistic training area in the United States, but Antarctica was something else again. The sudden sharp changes in the weather, combined with the need to spread the force out to make it look as if they weren't a single unit, were making their lives increasingly difficult. If the aliens hadn't seen them coming, they had to be blind. The only reassuring point was that a thousand angry UFOs hadn't already swarmed the convoy, or destroyed their base camp. Perhaps the aliens had other things to worry about.

He felt cold and it was nothing to do with the weather. They'd trained endlessly in the expectation of taking war to someone else's country, despite an increasing number of novels predicting political or ethnic strife within the United States itself. None of them had seriously expected to end up fighting a war in their own backyard, even though they had engaged terrorists on American soil, and many of them wanted to get back home and get stuck into an enemy who dared attack their families and country. Nicolas himself remembered his daughter and shivered at the thought of her being caught up in an alien attack, even though she lived well away from any logical target. The tactical experts all agreed that once the air defences had been softened up, a ground invasion would be the next alien move…and his daughter might be killed in the process. Her stepfather wasn't a military man. He might not be able to protect her as society came apart. Nicolas pushed the thought of his little girl out of his mind as they finally stopped at the planned location and stumbled out into the cold.

The United States GPS system had been destroyed along with its satellites, but the aliens had left both the European and Russian systems alone. Nicolas remembered complaining bitterly that both systems were used by enemies of the United States – along with plenty of countries that didn't want to be dependent on the United States for something of vital military importance – but now he was relieved that the capability existed. Whatever the aliens thought they were doing by sparing those satellites, it allowed the attack force to assemble without getting badly lost. It would have been much harder to navigate without the satellites.

"Check weapons," he ordered. Some of the early missions in sub-zero temperatures had ended badly when weapons had failed. The old hands had had plenty of horror stories to tell the new recruits, ending with dire warnings to test everything in conditions more extreme than they expected to face. It would have been embarrassing to have made to the alien base, only to discover that none of their weapons worked. "Move out."

The attack force had practiced marching in Antarctic conditions back at the research station, but now it was deadly serious. They spread out, wearing camouflage gear that would have made them hard to see against the snow and ice, while dampening their heat signature in case the aliens had scattered a few hundred tiny sensors around their base. If Nicolas had been running the base, he would have had patrols constantly checking and rechecking all of the approaches, but that would have risked exposing the base's existence. The Force Recon team had stated that they'd found no trace of alien patrols, yet that could change at any moment. Their orders were simple. Any alien patrols they encountered would not be given a chance to sound the alarm. They'd done it before, against terrorists and several Middle East countries, but this was different. No one knew what an alien ground combatant force might look like.

His gaze fell on the four men at the rear. The Wrecking Crew was just a legend to most of the military world, even the majority of the American Special Forces. They were so classified that their names were stricken completely from the records and former members tended to be treated as posers, simply for lacking a record. Nicolas himself had a record, even if most of it was highly classified, and he could have proven that he was a SEAL. The reason for the secrecy was terrifying. Two of the Wrecking Crewmen were carrying a single backpack nuke each. Just one of them would be enough to destroy the alien base.

"There," Sergeant Rawlings muttered. Nicolas followed his gaze towards a sheer cliff face, only a kilometre away from the team. Everyone froze as an alien fighter flew overhead and came down into the cliff face. Nicolas winced, expecting a massive explosion, but instead the craft passed through the cliff and vanished. The Force Recon Marines had reported that the base was concealed by a hologram, but being told about it and seeing it in person were two very different things.

The Marine position had been carefully hidden. Nicolas didn't see it until he was right on top of it. "No change, sir," Sergeant Tanaka said. "They're just landing hundreds of fighters and then launching them again. They seem to come in groups of five, at twenty minute intervals, and then vanish before the next group arrives."

"We attack just after the next group arrives," Nicolas muttered. There was no disagreement. Civilians found it odd, but if anyone who'd made it through the training and into the Special Forces disagreed with the CO, he would have said so. He might even have been right. "Pass it on to the men.

I want the Ravens in the rear scooping up everything they can, including prisoners if we can take them."

"It might be hard getting them back to the subs, sir," Sergeant Tanaka pointed out. "We don't have stuff for them with us."

"They can take their chances," Nicolas said harshly. He didn't want to take prisoners at all, if the truth were to be told, but a single enemy captive would be worth his weight in gold. It might allow them to finally figure out just what the aliens were really doing on Earth. "How long do we have until the next flight?"

"Seven minutes," Tanaka said. "They rarely seem to be early or late."

"Always a first time," Nicolas said. He looked over at Rawlings and the other Sergeants. The plan would include a large degree of improvising, but that was fine with him. SEALS were good at improvising, even against an enemy with unknown capabilities. "Get a Stinger fire team up ready to engage any other alien craft that arrive, while the rest of us go right through the hologram. Bring up a Javelin team just in case that hologram is solid half the time, but warn them not to fire unless I command it specifically."

The next five minutes passed in a whirlwind of activity as the force slipped closer to the alien base. Up close, there was no sign that the hologram was anything other than a cliff face, although Nicolas warned everyone not to touch it. The aliens might not have scattered any sensors around, odd as that was, but they'd definitely have rigged the base's entrance to sound the alarm. He pressed himself down to the ground as the first alien craft appeared and raced down towards the hologram, only stopping bare inches from the cliff face. The sheer power the aliens were showing, far beyond any human Vertical Take-off or Landing – VTOL - aircraft, was staggering. Was there any hope for victory against such a force?

Up close, the alien fighter looked rather like a larger version of an F-117. It was surrounded by a faint shimmer in the air – there was no sign of any of the thrusters so beloved by science-fiction artists – and seemed to be vibrating slightly. He stared at it and saw no trace of a cockpit, no alien faces peering back at him. The aliens, he deduced, probably flew their aircraft completely through their electronics…or maybe the interior allowed the pilot to look out. The craft that had picked up the President had allowed him to see the Earth from space before he reached the mothership.

The other four alien craft proceeded through the cliff face – he was pleased to see that one of them had a nasty dark scar along its fuselage – and he held up his hand, counting down the seconds. The Sergeant had refused to let him lead the assault in person, no matter how much he wanted to go first, and he'd reluctantly given the position to a group of hard-entry specialists from Delta Force. They'd pointed out that throwing grenades or explosive charges into the unknown might not have been a bright idea. If the alien craft were anything like human fighters, they might explode violently, blowing up the base and the assault team.

"Go," he mouthed.

The Delta Force men pushed up against the cliff face and went right through it. A moment later, shooting broke out and the illusion vanished, revealing a massive hangar that had been dug right into the mountain. He almost stopped dead as he saw the live aliens swinging around to stare at the humans invading their base, moving so…oddly that it was clear they weren't human. It was like looking at a spider or a crab. The sense of being in the presence of something totally alien almost rooted him to the ground. Only his training kept him moving into the base.

A flash of green light raced over his head, revealing that the aliens had recovered from their surprise. The smaller aliens were running for cover – a handful lay dead or dying on the ground – but the larger aliens were returning fire with short precise bursts. Nicolas levelled his rifle at one of them and fired three times, twice into the chest and once into the head. The alien staggered backwards and collapsed. Others fell back with blinding speed, leapfrogging from cover to cover, trying to stall the human force. One of their fighters started to rise up in the air and an antitank team put a missile into it, sending it crashing to the ground. Nicolas barely had a moment to realise that they'd had a very lucky escape before he was urging the team onwards, driving the aliens out of their hangar deck. If the craft had exploded, the entire team would have been killed.

"Secure the deck," he snapped. The aliens had been driven back to the lower levels, but they'd be regrouping and preparing a counterattack. He glanced from body to body and saw at least four different types of alien lying dead. The big ones – the warriors, he was coming to think of them – had fought and died hard. Three of the Delta Force soldiers had been killed, despite the advantage of surprise.

The elevator in the deck might have passed unnoticed, apart from a sharp-eyed Marine who realised that it was there. The demolition experts rapidly fitted it out with explosions and detonated them, sending the elevator plunging down towards the second level. There were a handful of smaller aliens hiding there who ran from the humans, although Nicolas couldn't tell if they were cowards or merely unarmed. Two were shot and the remainder managed to escape down a long passageway. The confusion would probably help the attackers.

"Group Two, remain on the deck and secure our line of retreat," he ordered. The alien base was larger than he had realised. It was quite possible that the aliens would be able to drive them back out and if that happened; they'd have to nuke the base and retreat on foot to the submarines. "Group One, down the passageway!"

There was no sign of any resistance as they inched their way down a dark corridor. NVGs revealed that there were odd heat patterns in the walls, suggesting that they'd knocked out a lighting system. The absence of resistance puzzled him. If he'd controlled the base, he'd have used his knowledge of the base against the intruders, although that might be exactly what the aliens were doing. They could be moving forces into position to flank him at any moment.

They broke into a massive chamber filled with transparent columns, filled with a murky liquid. A handful of alien warriors came at them from the shadows and killed one of the team before they were driven back to take cover. The columns seemed to be bullet proof, allowing the soldiers to bounce bullets off them and into the alien positions. The warriors wore armour that seemed to provide a considerable degree of protection, yet it wasn't enough. The soldiers broke through and kept moving.

"Sir," Rawlings said, suddenly. "Look at the columns!"

Nicolas followed his gaze. The murky liquid inside the columns was slowly thinning out, turning transparent. It revealed very familiar shapes.

"Humans," he said, in disbelief. Every column held a naked human. They looked alive, but frozen in suspended animation. "They brought humans here?"

Rawlings had another question. "Why?"

Chapter Thirty-Nine

Alien Base, Antarctica

Day 40

"Do you think that one of them is Elvis?"

Nicolas ignored the question, staring up at the body inside the column. The body was male, around thirty years old, with a faintly Arabic appearance. Nicolas had half-wondered if he might be a particularly infamous missing terrorist, but he didn't recognise him at all. He was naked, yet there were no signs of injuries or any suggestion that he'd been taken by force.

"Why?" Rawlings repeated. "Why do they have humans here?"

"Slaves, perhaps," Nicolas said, although something told him that wasn't the answer. Slavery was inherently inefficient in a technological society and the only modern-day roles for slaves were basic work or sexual services. He couldn't see the aliens being interested in either. There were places on Earth where there were real slaves, but they tended to be poor or undeveloped, neither of which fitted the aliens. "Take a look at each of them and make sure you get a good image. We'll compare them to the missing person records when we get home."

He moved to the next column and peered through the glass. This one held a black teenage girl, floating in the column's liquid. Again, there were no signs of violence or suffering. She looked surprisingly healthy in the liquid. Nicolas had been forced to learn how to breathe liquid during SEAL training and it occurred to him that the aliens might be doing the same to their captives, in which case it might be possible to free them. He placed one hand against the column and realised that it felt like glass. Breaking it might be possible - although bullets had been bouncing off it earlier - but what would that do to the girl? She might come out of it, or she might die from shock.

One of the more interesting innovations the Special Forces had adapted to their purposes was the tiny microscopic cameras; so tiny they barely could be picked out with the naked eye. The CIA had developed them for insertion in terrorist camps, which tended to have a shortage of advanced bug-detecting gear, but it hadn't taken long for the Special Forces to think of another use for them. Every man in the assault force had a similar camera system sprayed onto his forehead, allowing the post-mission analysis teams to see everything they'd seen in the base. The original idea had been to use it as evidence to knock down charges of abuse and unpleasant behaviour brought against American soldiers, but it had plenty of other uses as well. The entire SF community still chuckled when they remembered the captured soldier whose camera had led rescue teams right to his prison, along with two of the senior leaders of Al-Qaeda in Iraq. They'd been so confident they wouldn't be caught that they'd even come without a heavy escort!

The next column held a little boy, barely a year older than Nancy. Nicolas thought of all the milk cartons carrying images of missing children and shuddered. Thousands of people went missing every year in the United States, perhaps through a desire to drop out of sight or a genuine kidnapping - or perhaps they dropped dead in their homes and nobody noticed. Had the aliens been kidnapping a few of them and taking them to their base? The briefings had suggested that the aliens knew more about humanity than could be explained by remote study, yet if the aliens had filled every column in the room with a human being, they had over three hundred humans on the base.

"Spread out, seal this room," he ordered, moving to the next column. A Mexican kid looked back at him. Their faces were blurring into one. The All-American blonde teenager, the old man with little hair, a middle-aged woman who could have been someone's wife or mother, and a Chinese man whose body faintly suggested military service…he couldn't afford to think of them as *people*. They were trapped within the alien base and getting them out would be difficult. He considered the logistics quickly and shuddered again. They only had a handful of transports and moving three hundred naked people back to the station would be impossible. They'd freeze to death even without the aliens giving chase from the air. He keyed his radio thoughtfully. "Raven?"

"Raven here," a brisk voice said. "Yes, sir?"

"Tell me you can fly one of the alien craft," Nicolas said, knowing that it was futile. "Can you get one of them to fly?"

"I very much doubt it," the Raven said. The Air Force Ravens were trained to fly every kind of human aircraft in the world, yet that didn't mean that they'd be able to fly the alien craft. "They don't have controls that we can recognise. We push the wrong button and we're likely to start firing plasma bolts into our own people."

"Understood," Nicolas said, shortly. There was no point in avoiding radio now – the aliens knew they were there – but short broadcasts were the rule. He still cringed at the memory of an exercise where the enemy force had hacked into their radios and listened to his orders, then carefully deployed their own troops to counter the moves he'd kindly told them he was planning to make. "Get as much as you can, but be prepared to leave in a hurry."

He looked up into the next column and blinked. The girl – a brown-haired girl who could have come from America or Europe – was the first to show signs of violence. Dark bruises covered her arms and chest – a very well developed chest, part of him noted – and she looked to be in constant pain. The bruises looked fresh – Nicolas had seen the results of domestic violence on active duty – yet that might mean nothing. The alien liquid seemed to keep their human captives in suspended animation and the bruises might have been inflicted years ago.

"Two hundred and seventy captives, unless they have another chamber of horrors like this one," Rawlings said as they reached the end of the chamber. "None of them recognised by any of us; all of them stored in footage for later analysis."

Another doorway, large enough to take an Abrams tank, yawned open in front of them. Dark steps led further down into the base. Nicolas stared into the darkness and wondered just how far down the base actually went. If the aliens had established it before the human race started seriously exploring the area – after the Second World War – they could have built an entire city and slowly moved in an entire army.

"Get one of the techs working on trying to free them," Nicolas ordered, as the assault force reassembled at the top of the stairs. The enemy could have dug in down below and waited for them, or they could have killed all of the alien warriors defending the base. He doubted it. Someone who wiped out the guard post at Fort Hood would hardly have scratched the number of troops on the base at any one time. "Detail off a section to guard them and bring them back to the hangar deck if they're broken out of their columns."

"And then they all freeze to death from the cold," Rawlings pointed out, putting Nicolas's own early doubts into words. "Sir, we're not going to be able to get them out of here."

"We have to try," Nicolas said. "If we can't get them out of here, they'll be killed when the bomb goes off and the base is destroyed."

The assault force paused at the top of the dark steps, then hurled a pair of illumination grenades down the stairs, lighting up the entire area. There was no immediate response and the first group of soldiers dived down the steps, expecting heavy resistance. Bolts of green light flared up at them, splashing uselessly against the metal sheeting covering the stairs, as the soldiers took cover and unhooked their grenades. A large enemy force had been waiting for them. Nicolas watched as the grenades flew down into the enemy positions and detonated with stunning force. In the confined space, the grenades would be twice as dangerous and he heard voices screaming in pain. The sound sent a chill down his spine. He'd heard men begging for mercy or a quick death before, but those were alien voices, very far from human. The sound was both pitiful and enraging. How *dare* they come to his planet and make war on his people?

He winced as the ground shook as a second set of grenades detonated, allowing the second group of soldiers to punch their way through the enemy position and finish off the remaining aliens. Nicolas followed them, escorted by Rawlings and two Delta Force commandos whom the Sergeant had ordered to look after him, and saw a bloody mass where an alien position had once been. The stench was horrific, both familiar and unfamiliar. No armchair commando could grasp the smell of battle, the mixture of fear and sweat and blood, yet this was beyond Nicolas's experience. He saw a couple of hardened soldiers gagging and diplomatically turned away to allow them to be sick. The alien stench was tantalisingly familiar, yet far too alien.

They broke out into another level and stared into a giant empty room, so vast and dark that he couldn't pick out the far wall. It reminded Nicolas of a gym hall with all the equipment removed and converted into a place for exercises only, yet there was the spooky sense of *alienness* covering the entire room. It took him a moment to realise why. All humans, regardless of their ethnic roots, shared a general similarity. He could be comfortable in an Arab or Japanese dwelling, yet in the alien base, all of the proportions were subtly *wrong*.

"Killing ground," Rawlings muttered. Nicolas was inclined to agree. The aliens could have an entire force lurking ahead of them, ready to shoot them down when they attempted to cross the vast chamber. The semi-darkness meant that they could be hidden anywhere in the shadows, even if they didn't have a portable invisibility device. "We can't leave it unwatched."

Nicolas nodded. The other option was to go further down the stairs, but that ran the risk of being trapped between two enemy forces in a very confined space. What had happened to the aliens waiting for them could easily happen to his force if they got careless. They'd started with two hundred men, five were dead in the opening moments of the battle, and the remainder were starting to spread out. It wasn't a good thing. The separate forces risked being defeated in detail and wiped out.

In the movies, he would have been able to grasp the true dimensions of the alien base at once. In practice, it wasn't nearly so easy. He didn't know how the base went together, or what led to where; he merely knew about a handful of rooms and corridors. The aliens knew their territory perfectly and would have the time to deploy their own forces to wipe out the intruders. He keyed his radio, flicking briefly through the various channels, yet he was unable to build up a sense of tactical awareness. It might have been deceptive if he'd had. He'd grown used to Arab buildings from Iraq, and he'd grown up in America, but the aliens might have different ideas about how a building should go together. It would be easy to be lured into a false sense of security.

"We need to go further down," one of the Wrecking Crewmen muttered. "The device won't be as effective in the higher levels."

Nicolas nodded. "Take position, and then light the room up," he ordered. "Fire!"

Rawlings threw a pair of illumination grenades into the room and they flared into light, revealing heavy barricades at the other end and a handful of aliens lying in wait for them. He bit down a curse. The NVG goggles hadn't picked up a trace of the alien presence against the darkness, even though they should have been easy to detect against the cold walls. The aliens either had cold blood – although they should still have been able to pick up on them – or wore something that minimised their heat signature. Nicolas's own combat suit did exactly the same. The aliens didn't flinch from the light, or come running forward as the terrorists in Iraq had done; they merely opened fire from their position.

"Return fire," Nicolas snapped, as the commandos dragged him back. The position wasn't a good one at all. Both sides could make each other miserable, but the only way to win a decisive victory was to walk across the vast gym hall…where the soldiers would be a very easy target. They could have thrown grenades, yet even the best thrower in the force would have problems reaching the enemy position. On the other hand…there were options. "Get one of the Javelin teams up here."

The Javelin had originally been designed as an antitank missile, but it hadn't taken various soldiers long to realise that it could have other uses. Nicolas himself had used it for breaking through sealed doors, walls and even taking out entire terrorist hideouts, although that had probably been because the terrorists had stockpiled their supply of ammunition far too close to the door. The resulting explosion had ended the battle rather sharply. Using a Javelin against a handful of alien personnel might have seemed a little excessive, but Nicolas doubted that anyone would complain. The aliens only needed to stall the humans long enough to get a counter-attack organised. He glanced down at his watch and swore. They'd been assaulting the base for over thirty minutes and they were no closer to securing the installation. He was starting to suspect that the base was so large that an entire army division would have trouble securing it. For all they knew, the hangar deck they'd captured wasn't the only one. Parts of the base might still be supporting the alien war effort.

"Force them to duck," the Javelin operator said. He took up a position where the backfire wouldn't harm any of the soldiers and waited. The soldiers opened fire, casting away fire discipline to spray the alien position with bullets, forcing the aliens to duck and cover. Their weapons gave them an advantage, Nicolas realised. They didn't have to worry about reloading every time they shot a clip empty. "Ready?"

"Ready," Nicolas said. He braced himself for the noise. The Javelin lunged forward, right for the heart of the enemy position, and slammed into the barricade. The resulting explosion was deafeningly loud and left the alien position shattered. "Go!"

Four commandos ran forward, weapons raised and ready to take down any remaining enemies. One of them flew backwards as a green flash struck his chest and burned through the body armour; the others avenged his death and took down the remaining aliens. The warriors didn't surrender. Even the wounded kept fighting until they were put down. It was almost like battling fanatics again, except these fanatics were getting better organised all the time. They were making all the right moves, using smaller forces to weaken the attackers while preparing a counterattack of their own.

"My God," Rawlings said. He'd peered through the next set of doors. "What have they been doing here?"

Nicolas followed his gaze and felt his heart sinking in his chest. The room looked like a triage centre after a natural disaster, or a heavy round of fighting, with bodies lying on the ground waiting to be inspected by the docs. He knew the theory – patients were to be sorted into three categories; lightly injured, salvageable, certain to die – yet he also knew that he was looking upon a very alien interpretation of the concept. The bodies lying on the ground were unquestionably human. All of them were badly injured and some were near death.

He looked down at one body, wondering if the aliens had somehow teleported the missing USAF pilots out of their planes before they'd destroyed them, but the body was beyond identification. Terrorists and insurgents in Iraq and Afghanistan had mutilated their captured enemies, in hopes that it would break their enemies will to resist, but this was something more extreme. The aliens had been dissecting humans with a very inhuman lack of concern for their survival, or feelings. He saw a girl with staring eyes that didn't see him, a boy who'd lost his entire lower body and had it replaced by a giant mechanical spider, a man old enough to be his father taken apart piece by piece. The whole scene was beyond imagination.

"I think we know what happened to some of the aircraft they lost over here," one of the soldier said, holding up a bloodstained uniform. It took Nicolas a moment to recognise it as an Argentinean uniform. They had claims to territory in Antarctica and had established several bases on the continent. Their loss rates were comparable to those of the other bases, yet they'd never imagined the truth. Who would have conceived of an alien base under the South Pole abducting entire aircraft – apart, of course, from a science-fiction writer? Even if someone *had* come up with the idea, Alex had made it clear that it wouldn't be taken seriously, not until it was too late.

His radio earpiece buzzed. "Sir, we have company," Sergeant Tanaka said. "We have four alien craft making an approach now. I think they know something is up."

"Take them down when they enter range," Nicolas said. Their time had just run out. "We'll be pulling out in ten minutes."

He looked over at the Wrecking Crew. "Are you ready to emplace that device and get out of Dodge?"

"Yes," their leader said flatly. Nicolas didn't even know his name, but his face was as pale as the rest of the soldiers. The mutilated humans were shocking to them all, feeding a desire for justice – and revenge. "We're ready."

Chapter Forty

Alien Base, Antarctica
Day 40

"My God," Edward breathed. "Just look at them."

There were four alien craft hovering in the air, watching the base. They weren't making any attempt to hide, convinced – apparently – that nothing the assault force had could reach them. They weren't the little fighters, or the egg-shaped transports, but almond-shaped craft. It took him a moment to place them as being of the same class as the ship that had crash-landed over a month ago, warning humanity of the new danger. He wondered; were they troop transports, or reconnaissance craft, or what? The aliens seemed to just be waiting.

"I have a lock," Corporal Singh said, pointing the MANPAD towards the lead alien craft. "I can definitely hit him. He's just a sitting duck like that."

Edward smiled. "Fire," he ordered. "Take the bastard out."

The missile launched from the tube, joined a second later by three other missiles from the SAM teams scattered around the base's entrance. The alien craft looked totally surprised. One vanished – flew off so fast that the human eye couldn't follow it – but the other three had barely started to react before the missiles struck home and sent them crashing towards the ground. They impacted hard enough to send shockwaves all the way back to McMurdo Station – assuming that the base was still intact and the aliens hadn't attacked it as punishment for its role in the assault – and exploded violently. There was no point in attempting to pick up any of the remaining wreckage. After such explosions, the craft would have been completely atomised.

He keyed his radio. "Sir, we took down three of four hostiles," he said. "The fourth hostile may have decided to bolt, or may be back."

"Understood," the CO said. "Hold your positions and wait."

Edward looked back down towards the tantalising gateway into the alien base. Now that the hologram had vanished completely, he could see the interior of the alien base and the damaged alien fighters. He was tempted to go down and stare into the unknown, but training and discipline held him in place. The CO was depending on the Force Recon Marines to keep their exit open and allow them to escape. The bug-out order meant that there was no hope of taking and keeping the base. The aliens were probably mobilising already to counter the unexpected threat. How long would it take them to bring reinforcements in from the mothership?

He was throwing himself to the ground before he even realised that they were under attack. A pair of alien fighters had raced by at low-level, strafing the ground and shooting up every human they could see. A MANPAD team on the other side of the base was wiped out before it could fire back at the fighters, or dive for cover. The alien craft lanced around and vanished as another crew fired a Stinger at them, forcing the Stinger to burn itself out and come crashing back to the ground. Edward guessed that they would circle around and come in again, before launching another series of attacks. If they went after the transports instead of the assault force itself, they might prevent the assault force from escaping, leaving them to freeze to death in the cold.

"They're coming back," someone shouted over the radio. "There are three of them now!"

Edward recognised the larger almond-shaped craft in the middle of their formation and braced himself. The alien fighters didn't seem to be capable of tracking individual human soldiers – or maybe the uniforms they wore were working perfectly and they had hardly any infrared signature – but it hardly mattered. They were strafing almost at random, yet with the sheer level of firepower they were putting out, they were bound to hit someone eventually. They were keeping the assault force pinned inside the base and trapped, buying time for reinforcements to arrive.

A MANPAD team took a risk and fired a missile right into their teeth. This time, the results were rather more spectacular. One of the fighters exploded with terrific force and shoved the other fighter into a spin that came within millimetres of crashing into the ground. The larger craft apparently decided to call it a day and vanished, although Edward suspected that it hadn't gone very far. The alien reinforcements would be on their way.

"The Ravens are coming through now," his radio said. "Cover them."

"Understood," Edward said. The Ravens were running out of the base, carrying with them an astonishing amount of alien gear. The Ravens had the same training as the remainder of the American Special Forces – as well as specialist USAF training – and he hoped that they knew what they were bringing. It would be the height of irony to discover, later, that they'd carted away junk or alien toilets. "Recommend we move fast. This area is becoming hazardous."

"So is the base," the CO said. "We're on our way."

———

"You have to leave us here," the Wrecking Crewman said. Nicolas glared at him, unwilling to comply. It was a code as strict as anything else from the military. No one – but no one – was to be left behind. He would have risked the entire team to bring back dead bodies if necessary. "We'll be out of here before the bomb goes off."

"I'm not leaving you behind," Nicolas said, sharply. "Set the bomb and then we can all get out of here."

"The bomb needs to be guarded until we can trigger the anti-tampering system," the Wrecking Crewman said. "If we set the bomb now, one of the aliens could disable or destroy it before it goes off. The anti-tampering system will trigger the bomb the moment someone actually touches it. We have to stay and guard it until the rest of the team is out of the base. Go!"

Nicolas stared at him, seriously considering dragging them along, before snapping a salute. "Come on," he ordered, and urged the remainder of the assault force back up the stairs and out of the alien chamber of horrors. Behind them, the Wrecking Crew would be selecting their positions and waiting for the signal that would warn them to set the bomb and make their own escape. They should be able to hold out long enough, yet the odds of them making it to safety were low. He wanted to run back and drag them out, but they were right. Cold logic ordained that their lives were placed at risk. "Move!"

They double-timed it up the stairs and back into the chamber of suspended people. "No luck, sir," the tech said. The handful of soldiers guarding him shook their heads in agreement. "Whatever these tubes are made of, I can't break it without killing the person inside. I've tried to drill through only to lose good drill bits and small amounts of explosive are just as useless. They're trapped until we can figure out a way to break them free."

Nicolas swept his gaze from column to column. Humans – perhaps kidnapped from Earth, perhaps cloned by the aliens. Humans – like him and the rest of the team. Humans – who he'd condemned to certain death. The United States military existed to prevent civilians being killed by enemy action, not to condemn them to death. Nicolas served the finest military force in the world, a force that never took part in political repression or gunned down protesters in the streets…and yet, the cold equations demanded that he sacrifice the alien captives, the mystery of their presence still unsolved. Perhaps, if the base survived, they could negotiate with the aliens to retrieve the captives…

He shook his head. "Leave them," he said, finally. He keyed his radio to the general channel. "Saigon. I say again, the heat is on in Saigon."

It would make no sense to the aliens, he hoped, but it was one of a set of codewords they'd arranged back at Fort Benning. It warned that the nuke was being prepared for detonation and that it was time for all of the team to fall back to the hangar deck and prepare to leave the alien base. He took one last look at the columns and then pushed them out of his mind, saying a silent prayer for the souls of the innocent men and women who were about to die at his hands. He hadn't brought them to the base, he hadn't organised their use as experimental subjects – he was sure that was what the aliens had had in mind – but they would die at his hands. He pushed the thought out of his mind as he concentrated on returning to the hangar deck. The teams had strung rope ladders down to allow them to escape.

"We really could do with taking one of the craft," a remaining Raven said. "Sir, four of us could carry it and…"

"If you think you're Will Smith and you can fly it out of here, do it," Nicolas snapped. Carrying an entire alien craft back to the transports would be difficult, even if the aliens hadn't thought to include a transponder on their craft. They would certainly have learned that lesson after losing one of their craft, either to an engine fault or a base's defence systems. "We can't carry it out of here and that's final."

Green flashes burst out in the distance as a group of enemy warriors mounted a counterattack. They seemed to have realised that the humans were retreating and were trying to drive them out of the base, or wipe them out before they could get home. The real question was how badly they'd been hurt and if they'd try to get to the Wrecking Crew and disarm the nuke before it could be detonated. The remaining soldiers returned fire, but there was no point in making a stand.

"Hit them with two more Javelins," he snapped at Rawlings. "We'll get out of here in the confusion."

"Yes, sir," Rawlings said. The Javelin teams had been held back for emergencies. Two antitank weapons flashed past the team and into the enemy position, detonating in a massive explosion. Nicolas felt the heat even at their distance and realised that they had to have hit something explosive. "Sir?"

Nicolas took one last look into the alien base. They'd fought through it, but they still didn't know how big it really was or what it had really been for, apart from sadistic medical experiments. The aliens might have been using it to study Earth a long time before they marked the planet down for conquest, or perhaps they had another reason behind all the sadism. He doubted that they were an entire race of sadistic monsters. That would have been beyond reason. There had to be a point for all the horror. He just wished he knew what it was.

"I'm sorry," he whispered. "Move out!"

———

Jeremy Damiani braced himself as the four Wrecking Crewmen gathered around the nuclear weapon. It was really nothing more than a metal box, wrapped in a rucksack that would have passed unnoticed in any American city, a thought that never ceased to give him chills. It had been the Russians who had pioneered the backpack nuke, but it hadn't been long before the Americans had built one that was "bigger" and "better." If the bomb had detonated somewhere in New York, the entire city would have been trashed. Jeremy wasn't blind to the level of trust the President had placed in him – the Wrecking Crew reported directly to the President through the Chairman of the Joint Chiefs of Staff – yet he knew something he hadn't told Commander Little. The Wrecking Crew would have to remain with the weapon until it was detonated.

A nuke wasn't a weapon that could be triggered by another weapon, not like high explosives or Fuel Air Explosives. The enemy could simply destroy the nuke with their plasma weapons, or do something beyond human imagination to reduce the weapon to useless dust; they couldn't take the risk of leaving the weapon unprotected. Jeremy had accepted the risk of a suicide mission ever since he had been recruited – his files had been wiped to the point that no one even knew that he had existed as anything other than a Wrecking Crewman – yet now he was faced with the possibility, part of him quailed. It wasn't for himself – he had no family and few friends – but for the other three. They'd shared so much together, yet they'd have to share their deaths as well. What other choice did they have?

He pushed the weapon into a corner and opened the access hatch in the top. The specialists back at the base had removed the standard system – intended to prevent a terrorist triggering the weapon, even if they somehow stole it from the most secure complex in the United States – and replaced it with a system that could be triggered very quickly, by anyone. Commander Little would probably have been rather upset to know that someone could have wiped out the entire force by accident, yet there was no other choice. The weapon might have to be triggered too quickly for a standard protocol. He pressed his fingers against the fingerprint reader and typed in the activation code. The weapon was armed and ready to fire.

They exchanged a look of shared understanding as they listened to the brief exchanges between the other commandos, retreating from the alien base. By Jeremy's estimates, it shouldn't take them longer than twenty minutes to get out of range, although he knew that it was an estimate based on other estimates. The base might absorb most of the blast and channel it up and down to destroy everything the aliens had built, or the blast might melt through the rock and come raging after the assault team. Nukes could be unpredictable at times, particularly when almost nothing was known about their target.

"They're coming," one of the team members said, using sign language. Speaking aloud or using the radio might betray their presence. Jeremy hoped that the aliens wouldn't search the base as soon as they drove out the remaining members of the assault team, but in their place, that would be the first thing he'd do. Any Special Forces soldier had plenty of training in leaving IEDs behind to confuse and irritate any pursuers and they would all have to be disarmed, carefully. "Stay down."

Jeremy grasped his rifle, leaving one hand on the bomb's detonation switch, as the lights suddenly came up to full intensity. The sheer horror of the room had been hidden from them by the semi-darkness, but now he saw it clearly. The aliens who'd done this – who could do this – deserved to die, even at the cost of all of their lives. Was that, he wondered as his hand tightened on the trigger, what the aliens had in mind for all of humanity? Had they been studying the human race to determine the most effective means to gain control?

The first group of aliens were from the little caste, followed by two taller aliens. They seemed to miss the Wrecking Crew at first, and then they saw the soldiers and started gibbering away in an alien language. Jeremy wasn't unused to such reactions – they'd happened in various countries as well – and he levelled his weapon at the aliens and started firing. The alien bodies blew apart very satisfactorily, but a group of warriors came charging into the room and returned fire, blazing away at the Wrecking Crew. They didn't seem to be inclined to press the issue, but they had to know that there was no way out. They could sit back, keep the pressure on and wait for the team to starve.

"Now," Jeremy said. The longer they delayed, the greater the chance that something would happen they couldn't predict or handle. He pushed down on the trigger. "It's been an honour…"

The world went white.

———

Nicolas and the rest of the survivors hadn't bothered with trying to be stealthy. They'd just run as fast as they could from the alien base, praying that the alien fighters high overhead wouldn't consider them reasonable targets and start attacking them from the air. They hadn't bothered to engage troops on the ground in America, but they might have a different opinion of the humans who had invaded their base. They'd moved as quickly as they could, but the earthquake when the nuke detonated sent them all to their knees. The ground had shaken violently.

He turned to look back towards the base and saw a glowing mushroom cloud forming in the air. It reminded him of a volcano erupting as secondary explosions shook the ground, sending towering flames high into the sky. The Wrecking Crew had clearly been lost in the explosion – it might have been what they'd had in mind all along – but they'd hurt the enemy. They'd *definitely* hurt the enemy. The alien base had been completely destroyed.

The alien craft overhead seemed to agree. One moment they were hanging in the air, flying bearers of bad news, the next they were gone, leaving the humans alone. Nicolas was too tired to be relieved, but there was no time to sleep. They had to get back to the transports, and then to the subs, and then back to the United States. The raid's objectives wouldn't be completed until they'd gotten themselves back home. He had a nasty feeling that they'd have problems leaving the continent. The aliens would have to know where the attackers had come from, and they could easily take out a defenceless base. If the station were gone, they'd have to make contact with the submarines on their own to get home. It wouldn't be easy.

He smiled inwardly as the team started to walk again. If the job had been easy, they wouldn't have needed the combined force to take the base out. No matter how powerful the aliens were, that had to have hurt. He just hoped that it had hurt them enough.

Chapter Forty-One

Washington DC, USA
Day 41

"They took them *all* out?"

"Yes, Mr President," Wachter said. "They took out every research station and tourist site in Antarctica. Just after the nuke went off, they swooped around the continent and blasted all of the stations from the air. There might have been a few survivors, but without any shelter or help they'll freeze to death within a few days."

The President rubbed his eyes. Part of him knew that the loss of so many lives was a tragedy. Part of him wondered if there was a way to use the deaths of so many foreign nationals to encourage the rest of the world to resist the aliens as well. Even if they chose to fight, it wouldn't help the United States. Their fighters would be bounced and destroyed by the aliens when they tried to cross the Atlantic to come to America's aid.

"And then they took out the *George Washington*," Wachter added. "The last signal we picked up from the carrier reported that the ship had taken heavy damage and the Captain had given the order to abandon ship. Since then, nothing. We've spoken to several governments in the area and convinced them to launch SAR missions, but the odds of rescuing more than a handful of crew are very low. I think they're probably going to start taking out the remaining carriers as well."

"Probably," the President agreed, bitterly. He wasn't used to being so helpless. An American carrier was normally an untouchable weapon the United States could bring to bear against anyone who offended it. Now they were just...targets, targets that could be overwhelmed and sunk by alien fighters. Their fighter wings needed to be redeployed to ground bases in order to keep flying against the aliens. The bases on the ground could soak up much more damage and keep going. "Anything on the diplomatic front?"

"The news is still sinking in," the Secretary of State admitted. "Most of our allies have their own problems at the moment, even without direct alien attacks. They've got millions of people who are suddenly unemployed and rioting in their streets. The British and French have been sending their armies into their cities in hopes of stemming the tide of rioting before it does more damage. The bottom line is that I doubt we'll get more help than we already have – all of which is covert and very deniable."

"Which might not matter to the aliens anyway," Wachter said. "Mr President, I feel that we should look at a few important details."

He nodded towards the big display, showing the current situation. The aliens were still pressing their offensive against the United States and losses were mounting rapidly. A handful of USAF and Air National Guard bases had been rendered completely inoperative and their aircraft – those that had survived – had been redeployed to other military or civilian air bases. The national airports had been rapidly converted into fighter bases – there had been contingency plans for that ever since World War Two – but the aliens had responded by widening the scope of their attacks to take out civilian airports as well. Civilian airports were simply less capable of taking and absorbing damage than their military counterparts. Air travel over the entire United States had become much more hazardous and could no longer be risked for anything but the greatest emergency.

"Our assets are being worn down day by day," Wachter said. "Our pilots are growing tired and making mistakes. Our ammunition is starting to run low, even with emergency orders placed at all of the factories and health and safety regulations completely disregarded. We're losing pilots to errors they would normally never have made, because they're not getting nearly enough sleep. We're trying to rush forward the next crop of trainee pilots, but they'll just be easy targets for the aliens. And, of course, we're running out of planes. The war is not going well."

"I know," the President said. He looked over at a timer, showing the days left before the alien mothership entered orbit. Once that happened…

no one was sure what the aliens would do, but the President suspected that it involved a ground invasion, once the United States had been softened up by the air raids. He liked to think that America wouldn't be broken so easily – neither Britain nor Germany had been broken by bombing raids in the Second World War – and yet, they were in completely uncharted territory. No one had invaded the United States since 1812.

The reports made it clear that the fabric of American society was starting to break down. There were reports of food hoarding, looting and panic on the streets. People were buying guns and stockpiling ammunition. States that had enacted harsh gun control legislation were discovering that their citizens suddenly wanted guns to defend themselves and the laws had simply been ignored. The President had never been a gun control advocate – although he conceded that there were some people in the world who should never be trusted with a gun – and while part of him found the whole display to be amusing, he knew that it heralded the breakdown of American society. The trust that formed the underlying basis of that society was being torn apart. People were already starting to look for scapegoats. One nasty riot in San Francisco had seen a left-wing march set upon by a counter-march and over a thousand people hospitalised. There had been a spate of attacks against peace groups, Jews, Muslims and others. It was a nightmarish mess.

"Then we need to start facing up to the possibility that we might lose the war," Wachter said. He sounded bitter. The man the President had met as a young officer would never have conceded that the United States could be defeated. He would have been right – then. "We have to start making preparations to carry on the war once the aliens land and occupy the country."

"You mean an underground war," the President said. He had nasty memories of fighting to suppress one in Iraq, yet the Iraqi insurgents had been beaten, long after he'd resigned from the army. Very few insurgencies had ever been successful without massive help from outside and that wasn't likely to happen. Those states that had an interest in helping America would need to keep their resources back to defend themselves. "Has it really come to that?"

"Yes, Mr President," Wachter said. They both knew that he was right. "We need to start preparing now. We have thousands of soldiers we can spread out around the country as the first line of resistance. We can set up weapons stockpiles and make preparations to produce more weapons in isolated locations. We can distribute our command network so it won't go down when the aliens land and destroy the remainder of the official command network. We can…"

"Tear the country apart," the President said, slowly. Decades ago, General Lee had been faced with the choice between surrendering to General Grant – and ending the Civil War – or scattering his army and engaging in an underground campaign against the North. General Lee had been wise enough to know that the war was over and had surrendered his men, but he'd been surrendering to a fellow American. The South hadn't done badly in the years following the Civil War – some said that it had done too well – but the aliens would have no interest in rebuilding the United States, unless it was in their image. He didn't want to admit it, but Wachter was right. They had to start making preparations for defeat.

A vision seemed to shimmer in front of his eyes. He saw America, not the land of freedom and liberty, but an occupied land under enemy rule. There were alien soldiers marching through the streets, bullying humans as they moved from building to building, perhaps assisted by collaborators, willing or forced into serving the enemy. There were bombs detonating on the streets and shootings every day. There were alien forces advancing through the corn fields of Kansas and climbing the mountains of Virginia, hunting for human resistance fighters. It would be nothing like Iraq. The Americans who had occupied Iraq had no intention of staying for longer than they had to stay. The aliens were coming to a new home. They literally *could not* go elsewhere.

He held up a hand. "Make the preparations," he ordered, simply. "Keep it as secret as you can, just to avert panic." He looked down at his hands for a long moment. "How long until the survivors of the assault force reach home?"

"They're currently in submarines on their way back to the United States," Wachter said. "Unless the aliens have some way of tracking them underwater and sinking them, we're looking at around eleven days before they get back home, then perhaps another day or two before we can get them into Washington."

"Good," the President said. "We're going to need heroes before all of this is done. I intend to tell the world this afternoon about the successful strike on their base, although perhaps I won't go into specifics. Jones and his people weren't able to deduce what the aliens were doing with human captives and mentioning that will only cause panic."

"It might also convince others to rally around the flag," Wachter pointed out. "There's still a hard core of idiots who think *we* started this war and the aliens are here to bring them the New Age of Leo or some crap like that."

"True," the President agreed. "We'll get that out into the public domain as well."

Wachter nodded. "Yes, Mr President," he said. "Did they identify any of the captive humans?"

"No, but Jones was at pains to point out that means nothing," the President said. "They could have been kidnapped from anywhere and no one might even have noticed that they were gone, or they could have been reported dead or…"

He shrugged. "We'll run the question past our allies, but I doubt we'll identify any of them," he added. "It doesn't really matter anyway. They're all dead."

"And it might have been for the best," Wachter agreed. "I'll get started on the preparations at once."

———

Washington was a ghost town these days, Abigail decided. The city's richer and more successful inhabitants had decided to evacuate before the aliens even started their attacks, leaving their homes close to the centre of power for the less dubious safety of their mansions and estates well away from the city, or other cities. The middle-class residents had booked themselves holidays away from the city, taking advantage of their money while it was still worth something, although they might not have jobs waiting for them when they returned. The poorest of the city had rioted when the alien craft had crashed on their heads and FEMA had moved most of the remaining population out of the city. They'd promised that it could be done in hours, but it had taken nearly a week before the city was almost empty. The remainder had chosen to stay and see what happened, either because they didn't believe in the threat or because they expected Washington to be invaded and intended to fight when the aliens came for the city.

The other major populations on the ground were soldiers and reporters. The soldiers patrolled the city – Washington was under martial law – and had shot a handful of looters when they'd caught them in the act. Abigail had heard that some of the more liberal reporters intended to brand those soldiers as merciless killers, but somehow she doubted that would get very far. A few hundred other criminals had been lucky and had merely been arrested, transported to one of the stadiums and left there to rot. They'd probably face a civilian judge at the end of the emergency period – if it ever ended – and would probably get away with it. The hundreds of reporters in the city merely reported, although some of the more famous names had decided that their services were required in safer locations. Washington was attacked at least once a day and several reporters had been killed in the crossfire.

She glanced up sharply as the roar of jet engines echoed over the city and saw a pair of fighter jets making lazy contrails in the sky. It didn't look as if an attack was inbound, although she'd seen enough to know that the situation could move from peaceful to all-out war within seconds. The news on the alien attacks was largely classified, yet she'd picked up quite a bit, even if she wasn't allowed to broadcast it to the population at large. It wasn't a decision she approved of – there were so many rumours flying around that panic was starting to set in across parts of the country – but it wasn't one she could argue. Fort Leavenworth was currently playing host to several reporters who'd broken censorship and reported on the results of two alien attacks. No one doubted that there was room for plenty more.

The White House remained miraculously intact, although the same couldn't be said for much of the rest of Official Washington. Dozens of buildings had been damaged or reduced to outright rubble, from the Pentagon to the Senate. She'd heard several reporters say that it was a shame that the Senators hadn't been in the building when the aliens had hit it, on the grounds that the country would run a lot smoother and have more money, but she couldn't agree. Hitting the Senate was a direct blow at the very heart of American democracy. The aliens had probably intended to make a statement, with or without taking out the Senators. Abigail had no difficulty in understanding the statement. They were coming to take over. The White House probably remained intact because the aliens intended to use it for themselves.

She stepped past a pair of armed Marines after showing them her ID card and pressing her fingers to a fingerprint reader. There was no longer any informality, not when the aliens might be watching and waiting for their own shot at the President, decapitating America's leadership in one blow. A handful of reporters who'd tried to crash the last press conference had very nearly been shot by the Marines and had been unceremoniously evicted from Washington. There could no longer be a free-for-all. A handful of reporters were invited to each press conference and all footage was shared among the networks, such as they were. The loss of the satellites had sent most of the networks to their knees.

The old Press Room had had room for hundreds of reporters. The new one barely had room for more than a handful of people, without even a stage for the President to stand on. She wasn't sure why they'd chosen it, although she suspected that the President had to be somewhere near an emergency escape route at all times. The media knew more about the security surrounding the President than the Secret Service was comfortable with, even if it had never been broadcast. The President might have been the most powerful man in the world, yet he could hardly call his life his own.

"Ladies and Gentlemen, the President of the United States."

Abigail straightened up, fighting down an absurd desire to salute. The President looked tired and worn, with hardly any make-up or preparation for the press conference. It suggested that he was worse than he looked. As much as politicians sought to deny it, looks were important in politics and appearing haggard and worn sent entirely the wrong message. The war wasn't going well…but then, everyone knew that. The reporters knew the truth.

"My Fellow Americans," the President said. It wasn't a live broadcast, of course. That would have revealed the President's location and the aliens might have tried to attack the White House and take him out. The reporters had cooperated when that had been pointed out to them, although cynics had wondered if that had anything to do with the fact that the reporters would be in the same location. "We have struck a blow against the aliens and hurt them badly."

Abigail found herself straightening up sharply. "Days before they landed in New York, we discovered the existence of an alien base at the South Pole," the President continued. "An attack force composed of Special Forces soldiers was sent to attack it, a mission they successfully completed with the destruction of the entire alien base, along with a number of their fighter craft. The attack force successfully departed the South Pole and is on its way to a base in Africa.

"The assault force discovered that the aliens have been kidnapping humans from Earth and conducting medical experiments on them. They may have been abducting American citizens for years. Their claims to come in peace are at variance with the facts. We do not know why they carried out such experiments, or what they had in mind, but they showed a frightening lack of concern for human rights. The footage, exposing the true horror of the alien threat, will be released for study by the entire world."

He leaned forward. "I ask all American citizens to give thanks to God for the victory and pray for the souls of our fighting men who lost their lives in the battle," he said. "Their sacrifice may mean that we continue to hold our freedoms, our right to be who we are. They may have struck a decisive blow against the aliens."

There was a long pause. "I wish to discuss another matter as well," the President said. "Over the last few days, there have been hundreds of...incidents involving guns, the gun control lobby, and American citizens desperate to obtain what they believe to be necessary to protect their families against a possible alien invasion. Many citizens have been arrested for violating or trying to violate gun control legislation. A pair of BATF agents has been shot for attempting to arrest others in violation of that legislation – people who were guilty of no other crime.

"By executive order, I am removing all legislation involving the private possession of firearms, with a single exception," the President said. "The private possession of nuclear, chemical and biological weapons is still forbidden, but all other bans and laws are hereby overturned. Those arrested for possession of illegal weapons will be released from prison and pardoned. I am also removing restraints on private research into firearms development and production. Thank you for your time."

The President departed, leaving the reporters behind. Abigail found her mind racing, knowing that WNN would need its own spin on the President's words. The President had never been a friend to the Gun Control Lobby, yet why would he turn them all into sworn enemies? Why take such a desperate step? The only reason that made sense to her was that it was a tacit admittance that the guns might be needed, and the only reason for that was a possible alien invasion. That, in turn, suggested that the war wasn't going well at all, despite the successful strike on the alien base.

And *that*, she knew, was something that could never be broadcast.

Chapter Forty-Two

Over Virginia, USA

Day 47

It was a gamble, one that could cost them their lives, but desperate times required desperate measures. The farm in Virginia had been taken over by the military, who had deployed a dozen AN/TWQ-1 Avenger and MIM-104 Patriot mobile missile launchers to the farm and the surrounding area. Normally, the systems would have their own organic radars sweeping the horizon, but the analysts had concluded that those systems would have given the game away too soon. Using passive sensors only, emplaced near silos or hidden under camouflage, there should be nothing to tip off the aliens that a large section of farmland had suddenly become a great deal more dangerous.

Lieutenant Andrew Summerlin glanced down at the live feed from the AWACS a few kilometres away and winced. The United States Army Air Defence Artillery had played the Army's lead role in the fighting against the aliens, although everyone expected that would change when the aliens actually started landing ground troops. Andrew had been deployed to four airbases that had been under attack – along with soldiers and USAF personnel armed with MANPAD systems – and fired missiles against attacking alien craft, scoring two hits and a near miss. It hadn't stopped the final airbase from being battered to uselessness by the aliens, who hadn't even bothered to engage the air defence systems before vanishing back into space. He'd expected redeployment to another possible target, but instead…

He looked around at the handful of vehicles scattered around, pretending to be haystacks or civilian vehicles. Everything looked different from the air – or space – and even though he could see through the camouflage, he was fairly sure that the aliens would have problems doing so at high speed. They'd get in at least one good shot before the aliens reacted, if they came overhead in the first place. The plan worried him because it was too dependent upon the aliens playing the role allocated to them, yet there was no other choice. The aliens knew to expect surface-to-air missiles near airbases and the handful of civilian airports that had been pressed into service. They wouldn't be expecting a missile battery in position miles from anywhere important, or at least that was what the plan said. The United States was vast. It would be difficult to cover all of the United States even if every vehicle in the army were replaced by a mobile missile launcher and the aliens flew freely over much of American territory. They'd been doing it for years, according to the President. It was very definitely payback time.

His earpiece buzzed. "Make it so," a voice said, in a passable imitation of Captain Picard. Andrew rolled his eyes as he looked back down at the console. They'd agreed on a set of code phrases for certain situations, yet he knew that the unexpected might occur at any moment. 'Make it so' meant that the Dark Shadows were engaging the enemy fighters, before preparing to bug out.

"Check the systems," he ordered, quietly. There was no need to whisper, but somehow he couldn't help it. "Get ready to bring them all up as soon as we get the alert."

The problem with radar, as all operators were warned on their first day of training, was that it had a limited range. The signal would be fired from the antenna, hit the target and bounce back, yet if the target was too far away, the signal would fade away before it reached the sender. Worse, any passive receptor could pick up a radar signal, ensuring that the target would *know* that it had been targeted. If a given radar range was written as X, the distance in which a radar system could be detected was 2X, allowing an enemy a chance to skirt his way around the radar or, alternatively, target it before the defenders knew that they were under attack. The USAF deployed HARM missiles to track down and destroy any enemy radar system and the aliens seemed to have their own version, a strange weapon that somehow suppressed radar systems across the United States. They'd also brought down several AWACS aircraft, forcing the USAF to add additional aircraft to their escorts, or pull them completely out of the targeted area. The USAF was slowly being worn down to a nub.

"Ready, sir," the operator said.

Andrew nodded. Now, all they could do was wait.

————

"Incoming enemy fighters," the AWACS said. "Stand by to repel attack."

Captain Will Jacob braced himself as the alien fighters materialised on his HUB, shedding speed as they prepared to engage the Dark Shadows, such as they were. The squadron had absorbed survivors from other squadrons and lost several experienced officers to command other units. The smoothly-functioning machine he'd built up over the years was being ground away by the aliens, although he'd been lucky enough to keep the squadron as Raptors only. He'd seen other squadrons that were a crazed mixture of Raptors, Super Hornets, Falcons and Tomcats; the latter pulled out of the junkyard and refurbished. The pilot shortage was affecting everyone. He'd heard that every reservist had been called back into service, along with people who'd last flown an aircraft during Vietnam. It sounded insane to him, but the entire world had gone insane. In the last ten days, he'd flown more than he'd ever flown in his life, seen friends – almost family – get blown out of the air and he'd come closer to dying than he'd ever thought possible.

Langley Air Force Base no longer existed. The aliens had systematically overflown the base and hammered it into the ground. Their weapons had breached the massive fuel bunkers under the airbase and sent most of the base up in a massive fireball. The remainder had been wrecked beyond repair. They'd even destroyed the B-52G Stratofortress that had been on display, an aircraft well beyond refurbishment, just because they could. The melted wreckage of the plane had been strewn across the entire airbase. A handful of MANPAD teams waited in case the aliens intended to have another go at the base, even though it would be pointless, but the remaining survivors had been redeployed to other bases. Their services were required elsewhere.

The aliens had learned and adapted their tactics as well. The USAF had learned not to fire missiles at them from long range – the aliens had time to accelerate and simply outrun the missiles – but the aliens had been pressing them hard. Will still remembered the four Raptors that had fired off all their missiles and had tried to return to their base…and had been hunted down and destroyed by the aliens, who had known that the Raptors were defenceless. Now, every aircraft had to retain at least one missile for personal defence and any aircraft returning to base had to be escorted, which put yet another strain on the defences. Will hadn't had enough sleep since the war began and knew that others had been far less lucky. The CO had seriously considered booking them hotel rooms so they could sleep safely well away from the base.

"Fire at will," he ordered, as seventeen alien craft swooped into view. "Fox-three."

There were no jokes now, no suggestions that surely he didn't mean they were to fire at him, just grim determination. The battles were wearing away at the squadron's morale as much as their aircraft – the number of aircraft going unserviceable was rising sharply – and their humour was gone. The Raptor jerked as he launched a missile right towards the lead alien craft and had the satisfaction of seeing the bastard twisting, trying to run, before a hail of flickering colour flashed past his cockpit. The alien shooting hadn't improved, thank God, but they hardly *needed* to improve. Their weapons filled the air with lethal bolts of plasma. Back in Iraq, soldiers had joked that the safest man in the platoon was the man the enemy were shooting at, but the joke wasn't so funny now. He'd seen several pilots die because they'd flown right *into* an alien plasma bolt, their aircraft blown apart before they could eject. Only a handful of pilots had survived losing their aircraft in this war. The remainder had gone down with their planes.

Another alien craft appeared in front of him and he launched a Sidewinder at it, hitting the alien craft before it could escape. The explosion shook the Raptor badly, saving his life as another alien craft poured fire towards his tail. He yanked the Raptor back, trying to evade before his luck finally ran out, and breathed a sigh of relief as one of his wingmates put a missile into his tormentor. It didn't seem fair, somehow. Even when the alien craft were destroyed they were still hazardous. He launched another missile at an alien craft and saw it twist away, the missile going wide and harmlessly flying off without reacquiring the target. He bit off a curse. That had been happening more and more lately and the best theory anyone had been able to come up with was that the aliens had been improving their countermeasures to evade the missiles.

He broke through into clear space and took a moment to survey the battle. Like so many encounters with the aliens, it had devolved into a high-tech dogfight, with both sides taking roughly equal losses. It was a game of attrition that the aliens played to win. Their weapons simply gave them more staying power than the Americans, who had to fall back when they ran low on ammunition, often pressured by the aliens, who were intent on cutting down American numbers as much as possible. Their attacks just kept coming and coming. For the first time in his life, Will felt a certain measure of sympathy for the Iraqis and everyone else who had faced the USAF. The experience of facing a vastly superior foe was humbling.

"Ah, Shadow-Lead," the AWACS said. "We assess that you have another twenty contacts bearing down on you."

Will smiled. The alien tactical manual seemed to allow them to lure the USAF into a dogfight and then swamp the American aircraft with their reserves. It had cost hundreds of lives in the opening days of the war, but now perhaps it could be turned against them. The aliens wouldn't hesitate to give chase if they felt there was a chance to take down the remainder of the Dark Shadows.

He launched a missile at an imprudent alien craft that had swooped up to challenge him, had the satisfaction of seeing it explode, then keyed his radio. "All Shadows, run," he ordered. He'd tried to put a hint of panic into his voice, but he'd failed. Hopefully the aliens wouldn't know the difference between a panicking human and a human pretending to panic. "Run for your lives!

The Raptors twisted, triggered their afterburners, and fled. Will scowled at the thought of being the first USAF Squadron Leader to lead a headlong flight, even though he knew it was only meant to *look* like cowardliness in the face of the enemy; he'd never live it down. The USAF would never let him forget it, ruse of war or no.

"Flee, flee," another pilot called. Will thought that he was hamming it up too much, but the aliens probably wouldn't notice. "They're coming!"

The aliens didn't hesitate. They wheeled around and gave chase at supersonic speed.

———

"They're coming," Andrew said. The timing had to be just right. The alien craft were catching up with the fleeing Raptors, yet if they had even a moment's warning they could put hundreds of kilometres between them and the trap. "Get ready to deploy on my command."

The live feed from the AWACS gave them all the targeting data they needed. The aliens probably intended to go after the AWACS next, even though it was protected by thirty jet fighters and orbiting an area covered with surface-to-air missile launchers. They might have been alien, but their tactics were understandable. Their craft were battering down the United States and its ability to coordinate its defences. If all of the radars were taken down, the aliens would be able to roam at will and land wherever they pleased. And, when the mothership arrived, they would be able to begin colonisation.

He watched as two of the alien craft broke off, leaving over thirty in hot pursuit. There was no reason why the alien craft seemed to have departed, but it hardly mattered. If they'd scented the trap, they would have all scattered, or fled at high speed. Instead, they were coming right into the trap, fat and happy. He wondered, vaguely, if the aliens had the concept of aces and if the pilots flying those craft intended to win their spurs. They were taking a hellish risk to take down the Raptors, even though it did make sense. They thought that the Raptors were no longer armed and therefore could be wiped out without risk.

"They will enter engagement range in thirty seconds," the operator said. "All systems are ready to go."

Andrew smiled. "Trigger the engagement sequence," he ordered. "Fire at will."

He glanced out towards one of the haystacks, in time to see it rotate and reveal four heavy missile boxes mounted on a truck. A moment later, there was a flash of fire and the first missile was launched upward, right into the teeth of the alien craft. There was no longer any point in hiding and every launcher was spitting missiles upwards, striking the alien craft before they had a chance to either respond or escape. A thunderous explosion echoed out over the noise of the missiles being launched, revealing that at least one of the missiles had struck its target. He looked back down at the display from the AWACS and saw that at least a dozen alien craft had vanished.

Two more were clearly falling out of the sky, heading for a crash-landing; the remainder seemed confused, almost hesitant. The missile launchers kept firing, emptying themselves even as the aliens started to return fire.

"Sir, run," the operator snapped. Andrew dived out of the command post and ran, seconds before a hail of alien plasma bolts blew it to pieces. It had either been a lucky shot or the aliens had some kind of advanced detection system, for the command post hadn't been emitting anything to mark its nature. The ground shook violently as one of the alien craft came down hard, exploding on the ground and sending a massive fireball rising up into the sky. The remaining alien craft were pounding the ground, tracking down all the puny humans who had dared to challenge them…

"Stay down," he snapped, as the operator made to sneak away. Their only hope now was to stay down and hope that the aliens continued to ignore them, even though they acted *pissed*. They had already destroyed all the launchers and their crews, unless they'd managed to get to safety as well. "Stay…"

An instant later, a green-blue bolt of light blew them both to atoms.

———

"Turn around," Will ordered. The Raptor seemed to quail under the strain, but the aircraft managed to come around in the tightest turn it could, aiming right at the remaining alien craft. They'd shed their speed completely as they destroyed the ground-based missile launchers, their fury marking the ground perfectly. They'd taken heavy losses as well. The ground-based launchers had shot down over twenty-four craft after they flew right into the trap. No matter how inhuman they were, that had to *sting*. "Fire at will."

He launched a Sidewinder towards the nearest alien craft, which vanished. A moment later, the skies were clear of anything but human aircraft. His HUD, showing the feed from the AWACS, revealed that the aliens had taken off at speeds of over Mach Nine, despite the risks of flying so fast over human territory. For the first time in the war, they'd suffered a very definite defeat. Their humiliation might even convince them that humanity was too dangerous to fight. They might even come to terms. Will and the remainder of the USAF would quite happily have traded the Middle East and Africa for alien technology. Let the aliens worry about the population. There was very little sympathy left in America for the inhabitants of the Middle East.

"I think we got them," one of the pilots observed.

"No shit," another agreed. "How mad do you think they'll be after that?"

"Mad enough to nuke us," another said, sourly. Will winced at the mixture of bitterness and tiredness in his tone. They all needed hours of sleep and they weren't going to get it. There just weren't enough pilots, or planes, or airbases. "There's no reason why those damn flying saucers can't carry nukes. What happens if they blow up a city or two?"

"They wouldn't do that," a fourth pilot said. Will was vaguely amused to note that no one had protested on the grounds that nukes were evil. The USAF fighter pilots knew better. Besides, the aliens might not share the human taboo on using nukes. "We'd nuke them back, surely."

"Nuke where?" the third asked. "We can't hit their homeworld from here, can we?"

There was a long pause, broken finally by the first pilot. "How many did we lose?"

Will nodded, silently. Seven more Raptors had been lost, with three more unarmed and needing escort back to Andrews Air Force Base. If the aliens jumped them again, the results would not be pleasant. The President's tacit admittance that the United States might face a ground invasion was worrying. He knew what it meant. No matter how many alien craft they brought down, the USAF was coming to the end of its tether. The USN and Marine Air had been pressed into service, along with the Air National Guard, but it might not be enough. The meaning was all too clear.

The United States was losing the war.

Chapter Forty-Three

Schriever Air Force Base, USA
Day 50

Master Sergeant George Grosskopf braced himself as the klaxons sounded, warning of yet another incoming alien raid. Schriever Air Force Base had come under attack repeatedly since the war had begun, with alien craft blasting through the defending jets and strafing the ground, reducing several buildings to rubble. A handful of dummy aircraft had drawn fire and blown up with satisfactory explosions, but the aliens had returned time and time again, steadily wearing down the defenders. Nearby Peterson Air Force Base had come under attack as well – it had been rapidly opened for defence duties and played host to several squadrons of fighters – but Schriever seemed to have been targeted for particular malice. The daily briefing claimed that it was because of Schriever's vital role in monitoring near-space and tracking alien attacks, but George suspected – and knew that others shared the same suspicion – that the real reason was because the alien craft had crash-landed near the base. If the aliens believed that it had been shot down, they might be out for revenge.

He watched, his face expressionless, as a line of soldiers carrying MANPAD weapons took up positions around the base, followed by a pair of mobile missile launchers. Schriever might have had an important role to play, but it wasn't as important as the fighter bases and units that had been rapidly reassigned to cover those bases. The USAF had managed to hurt the aliens – the daily briefings were constantly updated with known alien losses – yet the aliens just kept coming. Nothing seemed to deter them for long. The more damage they did to the USAF and its ability to defend

America, the more they widened their targeting list. George had heard from his sister and her husband in Alabama and she'd told him that they'd had repeated power outages as alien attacks took out transformers and power stations. They didn't go after nuclear plants – thank God – but everything else seemed to be fair game. That had occurred to others as well and there'd been a mass exodus from anywhere under a dam. An alien attack that took out a dam could cause thousands of civilian deaths.

The alien craft made no noise as they swooped down, but he heard the sonic booms from fighter jets fighting a running battle over Colorado. Their presence increased the risk of a friendly fire incident, with the ground-based missiles locking onto American fighters instead of alien craft, but the senior officers believed that allowing the aliens a chance to attack unmolested increased the chances of them learning to shoot straight. It was humiliating to admit that the only reason hundreds of bases hadn't suffered worse damage was that the aliens had lousy targeting, yet George had to admit that it didn't seem to matter. The aliens could spray and pray all they liked. They had practically unlimited firepower to expend on their targets. The American fighters were limited to as many missiles as they could pack on their wings.

He winced as the missile launchers starting firing, throwing a hail of guided and unguided rockets into the air. One of the brighter sparks in the USAF had come up with the idea of using unguided rockets for both ground and air-based defences, fitting out the older fighters with missile pods that were normally designed for hitting targets on the ground. It had given the aliens some unpleasant surprises until they'd figured out that the rockets weren't actually guided and could be evaded easily, yet they still risked losing craft to the aerial version of Close Quarter Battle. George hoped that the idea of falling to such a primitive weapon annoyed them. They were pounding the USAF into the ground.

The base shook as explosions billowed up at the other side of the complex. The aliens were bombarding almost at random, yet there was a method to their madness. Even a hole in the ground in the wrong place could disrupt repair work and make putting the base back online difficult. Worse, Schriever wasn't a fighter base with massive runways that could easily be filled in, but a base equipped with billions of dollars worth of advanced radars and sensor systems. A single hit in the wrong place could cripple the base. It was ironic, but the aliens had actually reduced Schriever's workload when they'd taken out the satellites, although after they'd devastated Antarctica the USAF had gained access to foreign satellites. George didn't expect that to last for long – when the aliens caught on, they'd take down all human satellites – but for the moment it was a lifesaver. The USAF could use the satellites to coordinate its defences.

He lifted his M16 as a dark shape flashed overhead and into the distance, but held his fire. It would have been nice to have something to fire back at the aliens, yet it had become increasingly clear that cannon and rifle fire did nothing to them. They just shrugged it off and kept going. Two bases had attempted to coordinate their machine guns in hopes of overloading the alien craft and bringing it down, but it had failed, although no one was quite sure why. Post-battle analysis had suggested that they just hadn't been able to hit the aliens hard enough to make them take notice. It wasn't as if there were any protesters outside the base any longer. The aliens had slaughtered enough of them – probably by accident – to convince the remainder that perhaps they'd be safer protesting elsewhere. It would be hard to continue to believe that ET was coming back to Earth – bringing peace, love and Elvis – when alien plasma bolts were blasting their fellows apart.

"Incoming," someone shouted.

George ducked on instinct as an alien fighter flew overhead, weapons sending pulses of light towards the ground. He saw a hangar explode violently as a series of plasma bursts found their target, sending flaming debris flying everywhere, and then noted a missile reaching up towards the alien craft. He had a moment to curse the idiot who'd fired it – the craft would explode over the base and actually cause more damage – before throwing himself to the ground. A moment later, the alien craft flipped over and plummeted towards the ground, crashing right into the hard surface. By some miracle, it didn't explode.

He pulled himself to his feet, wincing slightly. He'd hit the ground hard enough to hurt, yet there was no time to delay. The briefings had been clear on what to do with a crashed alien ship – it had taken them weeks to come up with a procedure, far too late for George and the men who'd found the *first* crashed alien ship – and it had to be secured at once. A crowd of airmen had already assembled, staring at the downed alien craft. It had clearly been badly damaged in the crash – George doubted that anyone was going to be flying it up to the alien mothership and blowing it into a pile of debris anytime soon – but it was still largely intact. He remembered seeing the first craft and the awe and fear he'd felt when he'd realised just what it actually was. Now, looking at a crashed alien craft, it was merely another problem to solve.

"Get the area cordoned off," he barked. In every other crash site, the aliens had been dead – killed, apparently, by their own people to prevent them falling into human hands. George figured that there wouldn't be any aliens coming boiling out of the craft, intent on shooting their way to freedom, but taking chances had never been his thing. The reluctant crowd dispersed back to their work, as if they'd never seen a crashed UFO before. George and the remainder of the security team had found themselves very unpopular once the rumours had been confirmed and the base's personnel had realised that they'd prevented them seeing a genuine alien craft. "Move it!"

The heat from the alien craft was fading rapidly, although George wasn't sure if that was a good or bad thing. It had scorched the surrounding area when it crashed, but luckily it hadn't set fire to the surrounding area. Rumour had it that at least one alien craft had come down in a National Park and set fire to the forest, forcing the evacuation of the entire area. Fire-fighters had fought valiantly, but the aliens had kept attacking their aircraft, apparently unaware that they weren't military craft. The net was full of conspiracy theories suggesting that the aliens had intended to burn the forest down on purpose, although no one was quite sure why. The most popular theory had something to do with Global Warming.

Up close, he could feel a tingle in the air surrounding the craft, as if he was tasting iron and feeling sparks in his mouth. Several people had collapsed up close to an alien craft, although there seemed to be no rhyme or reason as to who collapsed, or why. The general theory was that it was the result of coming so close to a craft from another world, but George didn't believe it. Repeated exposures didn't seem to render someone immune. Carefully, he touched the hull, ready to snatch his hand away at the slightest hint of burning, and was relieved to discover that it was cool. The alien fighter was safe to touch.

"Here," he said. There had been twelve other craft recovered – not counting the first craft he'd seen personally – and the daily briefing had included information on how to open the hatch and get inside. The aliens seemed to favour the KISS principle – Keep It Simple, Stupid – for their craft, something that seemed oddly akin to humanity. He found the latch and pushed at it, expecting resistance, but it opened as easily as a car's front door. He stepped backwards sharply as the spicy scent assailed his nostrils and peered into the gloom. There was nothing to see apart from a handful of lighted consoles, so he drew his flashlight and shined it into the compartment…

And found himself staring into a pair of very dark eyes.

"Shit," he breathed, staggering back and grabbing for his pistol. The idea of meeting a live alien had seemed remote, impossible. No one had met a live alien apart from on their terms. "You…stop!"

The last was addressed to two of his men, who'd stepped up with their M16's pointing at the alien. It recognised the weapons for what they were, for it quailed backwards, trying to avoid their notice. Now his eyes were more accustomed to the gloom, George could see two more aliens in the craft, both clearly dead. Liquid was leaking out of their mouths and their faces were contorted with agony. It was a very alien expression, yet it seemed to transcend the cultural and social barriers between races.

"Sir, that's…"

"Get an ambulance up here," George snapped. The alien was affecting them all, just by its sheer presence. Anyone looking at it could tell that it was a creature from another world. It didn't seem to be injured, but they knew nothing about its internal anatomy or what kind of inhuman injuries it might have suffered. It was wearing a simple one-piece tunic that covered up any traces of sexual identity – it was impossible to determine if it were male or female, or either. For all he knew, he was looking at an asexual drone.

If the alien had been a human intruder or terrorist, George would have treated it harshly. As it was, a single alien prisoner might be worth its weight in…well, anything. He leaned toward the alien, carefully returning his pistol to his holster, hoping that the alien would understand that they didn't mean it any real harm. Human history tended to suggest a wide range of possible treatments for prisoners - an American captured by the Russians would be treated fairly well, while a prisoner of the Taliban would be better off blowing out his own brains before he was captured – and the alien might have been expecting everything from medical experiments to immediate death. It might even have a reason to expect to be dissected. The news about what the aliens had been doing at their polar base had caused widespread outrage across the globe. The aliens couldn't expect any more mercy from humanity…

Except, of course, they have the entire world as hostages and we have just one, he thought, looking at the alien. It wasn't the same as the two types of alien in the first crashed ship. It was taller, thinner, and seemingly more cerebral, although he wasn't sure how he knew that. Just for an experiment, he pictured an unimaginably violent scene of torture in his head, but the alien showed no reaction. It wasn't telepathic then, or maybe he just couldn't recognise an alien reaction. Its face wouldn't lend itself well to expressions. Its tiny mouth looked as if it was permanently on the verge of kissing someone. He wondered if the alien had a mate, or kids, and felt a sudden burst of sympathy for it. It had to know that unless its comrades organised a rescue mission, it was trapped among the human race for the rest of its life.

The ambulance pulled up beside the crashed ship and, for the first time, the alien showed a reaction, quailing away from the vehicle. George stood up as the drivers opened the door and allowed the doctors to disembark. Someone had to have warned them because they showed no surprise at seeing the alien, but carefully recovered the other two bodies before turning their attention to the live alien. George beckoned it forward and it slowly uncurled itself from where it had been crouching, coming forward into the light. He'd wondered, from the darkened interior of the craft, if bright light scared them or hurt their eyes, but it showed no reaction. Just looking at its walk made him shiver with the urge to stamp hard, like looking at a spider or something else completely inhuman. It made his skin crawl.

"Should fucking crack its fucking skull," one of the soldiers muttered, just loudly enough for the alien to hear. George had wondered if it spoke English, but again it showed no reaction to the words. "Or cap it, right now…"

"Quiet," George snapped. There was no time for a lecture on the proper treatment of prisoners – including not hurting them unless they tried to escape – not when the aliens could return at any moment. The alien seemed to be staring upwards, looking for signs of a rescue mission, but the skies were clear. He waved the alien into the ambulance and it climbed inside with weary dignity. It was easy, somehow, to feel sorry for it.

"You're being detailed to serve as his escort," the CO said. "I've just been on the secure line to NORAD and they've issued orders for the captive to be moved to a secure location and the complete decontamination of this site. Take four men and whatever weapons you need, then ride up with the captive and get him to safety."

George winced. Complete decontamination was expensive, painful and humiliating for everyone involved, and it was probably unnecessary, even though he couldn't blame the senior officers for wanting to ensure that there was no possibility of a biological contamination from the alien craft. Schriever had been through the same process when the last craft had crashed and no one had enjoyed it. It was too sadistic to be enjoyed even by a bondage-submissive.

"Yes, sir," he said. He glanced over at his men. "You, you, you and you, draw your weapons and equipment, then go get us a pair of hummers and some MANPAD weapons. You" – he addressed the soldier who had threatened the alien – "go report yourself to Sergeant O'Flynn and tell him that I am *extremely* displeased with your conduct and he's to take corrective measures."

"Yes, Sergeant," the soldier said. He looked unhappy and George didn't blame him. A few weeks of cleaning out toilets with a toothbrush – assuming the base lasted that long – would teach him a lesson. There were some things that should not be said even in jest. "I'll go now."

George watched him go and then looked up at the ambulance, feeling a chill running down the back of his neck. The alien's big dark eyes were looking at him. It was a terrible absence of expression, no fear, no hatred, no love…just nothing. Its tiny hands, somehow inhuman in their very structure, seemed to twitch constantly. George wished that he'd read more science-fiction as a kid. It might have helped him learn more about the alien. For all he knew, the aliens communicated by sign language and they literally couldn't talk…no, that was untrue. The aliens had spoken to the President and then to the UN. They knew how to speak English…

But not *all* of them would know how to speak English. George's brother-in-law had seen service in Baghdad and he'd had hundreds of horror stories about American soldiers who hadn't known a word of Arabic. The confusion that had resulted had been terrifying, with soldiers accidentally insulting civilians or giving them inaccurate information. There had even been cases of signs being switched around to cause more confusion and irritation. It was easy to understand why the President had quit in disgust. He watched as the doors were closed and the ambulance drove off to a holding area and smiled to himself.

If their captive could learn to speak English, if it could talk to them, it might turn the war around. The things they could learn…they'd have to keep the prisoner safe, of course, and make sure that the aliens had no way to track him. They'd get a secure truck first, transfer the prisoner into it, and then move him by road to his final location. Air travel was unsafe these days and it would have been the height of irony to lose their alien captive to another alien attack.

An hour later, they departed Schriever on the first leg of their journey.

Chapter Forty-Four

Area 53, Nevada, USA
Day 54

"We got a live one!"

Alex smiled as he followed Jane into yet another highly-classified base in Nevada. Like Area 52, its official designation had been stricken from the records and it had been re-designated – somewhat inevitably – as Area 53. According to Jones, before he set out on a road trip back to Washington, it had been designated as a place to take and examine alien captives even before the war had begun. Someone in Washington, for once, had been thinking ahead, even though not all of the ideas had been good. A former biological warfare laboratory would make an excellent prison, particularly as it had been designed to be comfortable. The base designers had assumed that terrorists would infect Typhoid Mary-like people – a civilian innocently spreading disease without even knowing what he or she was doing – and they would need secure, but comfortable accommodation, even if they were prisoners in all but name.

The entire American Medical Association had demanded access to the alien bodies once they'd realised that the bodies existed, and Washington had been happy to parcel out the bodies from the other crashed alien craft, knowing that the more minds focused on a specific problem, the better. No one outside Area 53 and a handful of people at Schriever Air Force Base knew that there was a live captive, and Jones intended for it to stay that way. The aliens had made no attempt to recover any of the fourteen craft they'd lost in the war – the wrecked craft had been scattered around the country, with one being prepared for transport to Britain – but they might be desperate to recover a live alien. The real question was impossible to answer. Did they know that the suicide implant on one of their pilots had failed and left the pilot alive?

There was no way to know. Jones and Santini had nearly gone ballistic when they'd realised that the aliens might have seen the soldiers escorting the alien into an ambulance, but no rescue mission had materialised. The secure truck might have passed unnoticed in all the confusion and the sudden increase in road traffic – all flights were permanently grounded now, apart from military fighters and support craft – or perhaps they'd been worried about accidentally killing their own people in any rescue attempt. The soldiers who'd escorted the truck all the way from Colorado to Nevada had been on edge, expecting an attack at any moment, but they'd made it safely. They'd been detailed to Area 53's defences until they could be released, simply because they knew too much. They'd have to remain on the base until the President could decide what – if anything – to tell the nation.

"Welcome to Area 53," a man wearing a Colonel's uniform said. Area 53 had never been shut down completely, unlike Area 52, and the entire base looked a great deal more professional. "I'm Colonel Brent Roeder, Base Commander. I understand that you've both been briefed on the base and the security requirements?"

"Yes, sir," Alex said. It was questionable which one of them outranked the other – the President's authorisation had given them considerable powers over even officers of vastly superior rank – but there was no point in being hostile. "We've both been decontaminated repeatedly."

"My sympathies," Roeder said. They shared a rueful grin. "The preliminary teams checked the alien, the soldiers and the truck they rode in and found no trace of a biohazard, but we are currently keeping the alien under Biohazard Level Four and decontaminating everyone who goes in and out. There are some doctors who have volunteered to remain within the biohazard lab wearing normal clothing, rather than lab clothes and biological suits, but most of the staff have gone in and out suited up. Do you wish to meet the alien in person first, or study him through the surveillance system?"

Alex looked at Jane, who shrugged. "The surveillance system first," she said, firmly. "Has he said anything or tried to communicate in any way?"

"Nothing that we can detect," Roeder explained, as he led them down the corridor into a small office. "We've tried talking to him in English, but it's hard to be sure if he really understands, or if he's just picking up on our body language. We're not even sure if he *can* speak, as we understand the term. His mouth is too small to form all of our words." He snorted. "He's very clever though. One of the researchers gave him a Sudoku book and he started solving his way through it, faster than I could – and I'm pretty good at it.

"We gave him some basic foodstuffs that analysis of the alien bodies suggested that he should be able to eat without problems, but he only took a few sips of water," he added. "We're not sure if he's unwell, or doesn't like the food, or if we're accidentally poisoning him. The doctors think that he can eat pretty much everything on Earth without problems – they wouldn't want our planet if they couldn't live here – but he might be missing out on vital trace minerals or nutrients specific to their homeworld. We had all of the crashed ships searched and found a handful of what we think are alien foodstuffs, so we're having them shipped here. We'll see if our friend can eat them."

"Good thinking," Alex said. He'd heard soldiers joking about preferring to starve rather than eat MREs, but he rather suspected that the alien would be glad of the food when it arrived. "If we have one of them analysed, we might be able to determine what they actually eat and produce it for ourselves."

"Indeed," Roeder agreed. "As you can see."

He clicked a button on the desk and the plasma screen sprang into life, revealing a surprisingly luxurious apartment. Alex had once had an old girlfriend who had enjoyed watching reality television about a group of fame-seekers who'd locked themselves inside a house and been given a series of embarrassing and stupid tasks to complete, struggling not to be voted off for another week. It had been incredibly stupid, in his rather less than humble opinion, and had led to the break-up of the relationship. Looking down at the alien, poised on a chair, he felt faintly dirty. He'd spent days in secure environments before, where there were cameras everywhere, but he'd volunteered to be monitored. The alien – and the humans who would have stayed in that room if the base had ever been used for its intended purpose – hadn't volunteered for anything.

On the other hand, he reminded himself, it – he – was a representative of an enemy power that was attacking the United States. How could it reasonably expect to be treated?

"Interesting," Jane observed calmly. "That's the same kind of alien as met the President first, but not the same as their apparent leader, or their spokesman in front of the UN. Have you tried to take blood and stool samples?"

"The alien does not apparently need to go to the toilet," Roeder said, looking faintly embarrassed. "The doctors say that it's just a matter of time, but it was taken prisoner six days ago and hasn't been to the toilet since, nor has it simply wet itself through lack of understanding. We haven't done anything more than a handful of scans since he arrived here. We don't want to accidentally harm the captive."

He frowned. "I'll tell you one thing," he added. "We x-rayed that massive head and found a set of implants embedded in the creature's skull. We don't think that it has a way of phoning home, but just to be sure we have the entire base firmly secure and heavily guarded. I have orders from Washington to ensure that the alien doesn't return home alive unless a peace deal is worked out. He's simply seen too much."

"Indeed," Jane said, coldly. Only someone who knew her well could have picked out the disapproval in her voice. "He's a helpless captive."

"He was flying a craft that was engaged in a hostile action," Roeder corrected her, bluntly. "He was attacking Schriever Air Force Base when he was shot down and captured. He is a prisoner of war, *Doctor*, not someone to be treated as an innocent victim. I have no intention of torturing him, or killing him, but he represents a priceless source of information that we *must* have access to, whatever the cost."

"Schriever Air Force Base," Alex repeated. "The aliens crashed there again?"

"They've been getting a greater number of attacks than anywhere else that isn't actually a fighter base," Roeder pointed out. "I supposed statistically their chance of getting a live captive was as good as anywhere else."

He stood up. "Would you like to meet the alien?"

"I think we need to get freshened up first," Jane said, sharply. "We'll call you when we're ready to meet ET down there."

She marched out of the office and Alex followed her. "What an asshole," she said, once the door was shut and she was raging down the corridor. "That alien is a helpless captive, not someone we can perform Nazi experiments on or cut up for the tabloids. We can't..."

Alex caught her shoulder. "Monitored environment, remember?"

"Oh," Jane said, and flushed. "I don't suppose they'll have kept the cameras out of the shower room, will they?"

"Just go shower in the dark," Alex advised, as they found their rooms. They were tiny compared to the alien's quarters, although they did have the advantage of not being inside a Level Four Biohazard Zone. Alex was fairly sure that there was no biohazard any longer – if there had ever been one – but there was no point in taking risks. He put his bag down on one of the beds and chuckled to himself. "That's what we used to do at those wretched exercises when we were playing at being Russians or Chinese and gaming out what we'd do if we controlled enemy forces.

"And then someone decided to have a fit about it, so some of us accidentally on purpose blocked the cameras, or acted really badly in front of them...one of the men got a reprimand for masturbating on camera and one of the girls got a rocket from the CO for pretending that she was making out with another girl..."

"You're making it up," Jane said, doubtfully. "Wouldn't you all have been tossed out of the Air Force?"

"I would have hated to have been the CO who had to give any of us a Bad Conduct Discharge for the offences," Alex said. "It was just a way to blow off steam. Apart from that, we aced the exercise and several of us got promoted. The system works!"

He lay back on the bed. "Go have your shower if you want," he added. "We'll go see ET in half an hour."

The entrance to the Level Four Biohazard Zone was comparable to the entrance back at Area 52, except that it was clearly more modern. The briefing papers had warned that secret stockpiles of Smallpox, Ebola, Lassa fever, Crimean-Congo hemorrhagic fever, and other various hemorrhagic diseases had been stored in the base after talks with the Russians broke down – again – on the issue of trust and verification. The ink on the treaties had barely been dry when the Russians had started cheating, forcing the United

States and several other countries to follow suit. Alex had seen papers that suggested that the United States population had been secretly immunised against hundreds of different diseases, preventing a virgin field pandemic, although he privately doubted that the government could have been that effective.

They stripped, went through the showers, and were allowed to dress on the other side, before passing through three airlocks and a host of automated sensors. Ominous signs warned that all cuts, bruises and other injuries might become infected and had to be reported instantly, regardless of how small and harmless they appeared. A smaller sign warned that the inhabitants of the secure zone were innocent victims and were to be treated as such, regardless of their visitor's inclination. The final airlock allowed them access to the inner chamber and he caught himself taking a breath, as if it would be his last. He had to remind himself that the aliens themselves believed that there was no biohazard.

"Unreal," Jane muttered, as they stepped into what looked like a standard apartment. Alex silently agreed. It was a bizarre mishmash of the mundane and the strange. It would have been an ordinary apartment in any apartment block, save for the single occupant sitting on a chair, watching them with massive dark eyes. He – Alex resolved to think of the alien as a male until he knew better – seemed very alien. Alex had had over a month to mentally prepare himself for meeting a live alien and yet…it was hard to look the alien in the eye. The massive lidless eyes didn't even blink.

Up close, there was a faintly spicy scent surrounding the alien, as there had been in their crashed ships. It wasn't unpleasant at first, but as he breathed it in, it seemed to grow thicker, until he wanted to physically push it away. Maybe the aliens communicated using scent, he wondered, or perhaps it was merely part of their physiology and perhaps humans smelt worse to them. The alien had made use of the shower and a handful of other facilities in the room and so perhaps it was how they smelled normally. He realised his mind was wandering and forced himself to concentrate. Jane was staring at the alien as if he were suddenly the most attractive man in the room.

"Hello," she said, very softly, as if she were speaking to a child. "My name is Jane. What's yours?"

The great head turned to face her, but the alien didn't speak. Alex couldn't hear anything, except a very faint whispery exhalation as he breathed. He was suddenly aware of just how close he was to the alien, except that he looked too puny to inflict much damage. The alien warriors had fought viciously against the assault team at the South Pole, but what role did *this* alien play in their society? The different types of aliens, all coming from a single source, suggested that the aliens had a number of different castes – was he looking at a creature that had been *bred* to be a pilot? The entire concept was revolting and yet he knew that there were training officers who'd love the thought of pilots who were all natural talents.

"I think you can understand me," Jane continued, calmly. "I think that your people wouldn't have let you down to Earth without some way to talk to the natives. We don't know anything about you and we might kill you by accident. You'd have to be able to tell us to stop."

Alex suspected that it might have made perfect sense, to the alien leaders, to let their people fly without a translator of some kind. They gave their crews suicide implants and killed them when they crashed, even though they would have survived the crash and would have been well-treated. It didn't suggest a mindset that cared about losses, even their own losses. It suggested a frightening lack of concern for the death toll. Every contact with the aliens had been on their own terms...until now. The mothership was approaching Earth, with invasion and settlement as its goal, and they'd *have* to deal with human governments, if only to negotiate a human surrender.

Jane picked up a notepad and examined it. The alien had drawn strange diagrams on the paper, but little else. Alex peered over her shoulder at them, yet they made no sense to him, even though he had an inkling that he'd seen something like them before. Jane flipped over the paper and started to draw a mathematical diagram of her own, showing it to the alien. The long grey-green fingers took the pad and pencil, and then drew another image on the pad. The alien had matched her diagram and added his own. Jane wrote down a mathematical sequence and allowed the alien to complete it. Alex realised that the doctors had been right. The alien was at least as smart as a human, perhaps smarter.

"We'll be back soon," Jane promised, at the end of a long hour. It had been fascinating, yet it was astonishing how quickly the unique became mundane. Humanity had rapidly grown used to the concept of alien life, even alien war. Somehow, there was nothing enchanting about it anymore. First Contact was over and any further contact with other alien races would be...common. Who knew how many other races there were out there, waiting for the human race to meet them? "I promise."

The alien nodded, bowing his great head. Alex realised that Jane was right. The alien might or might not speak English, but he sure as hell *understood* it. It might not be an insolvable problem either. They could ask yes-no questions, or teach him how to speak or write English. The alien made a funny chattering noise – like a host of insects - that Alex chose to interpret as *goodbye*, although it didn't wave when they stepped back into the first airlock. It was already drawing new diagrams on the pad.

"He understood me," Jane said, firmly. "All we need to do is teach him to speak."

Alex nodded. The thought of all that information locked up inside the hairless alien skull was unbearable. They needed to know what the alien knew, before the mothership entered orbit. It was only fifteen days away and then, everyone agreed, the situation would get *really* bad. If the aliens could inflict so much damage with only tiny fighter craft, what could they do with an entire mothership and a billion aliens?

Chapter Forty-Five

Washington DC, USA
Day 57

Nicolas could smell smoke as they gathered inside a large warehouse that formally belonged to a trucking company, judging from the markers on the wall. It was easily large enough to hold the hundred and twenty survivors from the assault force, as well as a small gathering of other personalities in the Special Forces world. He recognised some of them from prior operations and took the opportunity to bullshit a little with them about the successful assault, as well as outlining how the aliens had reacted to the human intrusion. Their warriors – no other term seemed to fit, although one of the soldiers had suggested Orcs – had been taken by surprise, but even so had fought savagely. Nicolas had spent most of his career trying to prevent nuclear explosions, not trigger them, but the sacrifice of the Wrecking Crew had probably saved their lives. If the aliens had come boiling out after them, across the ice and snow, it could have only had one ending.

The journey back to the United States had been nightmarish. He'd felt a twinge of guilt as they viewed the remains of McMurdo Station, smashed by vengeful alien fighters, and remembered the expressions on the base's scientific staff as they'd been bundled onboard the USN aircraft to return home. Their ability to carry out scientific studies in peace were what the military existed to defend and it hurt to know that they'd ensured the destruction of their station. The assault force had probably saved their lives by transporting them back home before hitting the alien base, yet they wouldn't see it that way. Academics rarely understood the realities of combat missions.

They'd made it to the submarines and had a few nerve-wracking moments before managing to board the boats for a fast journey home. The eleven days onboard the ballistic missile submarine had been claustrophobic, but Nicolas was used to that. Some of the other SpecOps personnel hadn't coped nearly as well, despite the success of their mission, and had had to be sedated by the submarine's doctor. The SEAL teams had been inserted into hostile territory by submarines before and had lived in far worse conditions. Nicolas had been glad of the rest and used it to write letters to the families of each of the men he'd lost. It was the duty of a CO, yet he couldn't tell them the truth. Very few SpecOps missions were ever publicly acknowledged these days until long after they'd taken place. They certainly weren't going to get a trip around the White House and a chance to shake hands with the President.

The discovery that their mission had been headline news around the world might have changed that, but instead they'd been given a day's leave, strict orders not to mention a word to anybody, and told to meet up at the mystery warehouse the following morning. Nicolas had written his daughter a letter – keeping it bland and very casual – and spent the evening in one of the more upscale brothels. They'd been happy to see a man with money. These days, with an ongoing economic crash and alien fighters flying at will over the United States, even the whores were doing badly. It wouldn't be long before they started attaching themselves to men who might be able to keep them safe. The news had been vague and probably censored, but it had suggested that vast parts of the United States had broken down.

He looked around the room and scowled, once again, at the oddness of the concept. It wasn't the first time he'd met up with the rest of a team in a strange location, but downtown Washington would not have been his first choice for a covert meeting or debriefing. There were so many soldiers in the building that he would be very surprised if the media didn't already know that they were there, perhaps even preparing to swarm the soldiers with cameras and shout inane questions. SpecOps personnel tried hard to stay out of the public eye and avoided cameras like the plague, yet for some reason hurting a reporter was considered bad practice. Nicolas had met some particularly unpleasant reporters in his time and only training and discipline had kept him from punching some of them out.

"Ladies and Gentlemen," a commanding voice said. "The President of the United States of America."

Nicolas came to attention automatically as the President entered the room. There was no mistaking him, even though he looked older and gaunter than the last time Nicolas had seen him on the television. The President might have been a regular soldier rather than a Special Forces soldier – and he'd been an officer, to boot – but he was all right in Nicolas's book. On command, they snapped a salute, which the President returned. Unlike some other Presidents, he'd never appeared scared of the human wolves, perhaps because he'd been a soldier himself and knew that there was nothing particularly superhuman about a SEAL. Anyone could become a SEAL with the proper training and dedication to the role. It did require a great deal of physical and psychological toughness, as well as high intelligence, but they could be learned.

"I am not here," the President said, flatly. There was an icy note in his voice that discouraged questions. "Officially, I am currently hosting a meeting of the Boy Scouts of America. I am here merely to confirm your orders. You are about to receive a set of orders that you will find…unusual. You will feel inclined to follow your training and question them, or refuse to carry them out without further information. You must not do so. Once you listen to the briefing, you will understand why. If we had time, we would have asked for volunteers or taken other steps, but time is no longer on our side."

He looked over at General Wachter. Nicolas had a sudden flash of Déjà vu, remembering the meeting at Fort Benning, when he'd been told that he would be commanding the first strike against the aliens who had attacked Earth. There, a senior officer had confirmed the orders…and now the Commander-in-Chief himself was confirming the new set of orders. He sensed the realisation settling in around the room. This was some serious shit, all right, perhaps something decisive.

"General Wachter will brief you on your mission and give you specific instructions," the President continued. "You may not see me again, now or ever, but I expect that you will each carry out your orders to the best of your ability. The future of America – the *survival* of America – may depend upon it."

For a moment, his expression softened. "If we had time, I would reward those who attacked the alien base and ensure that you had the thanks of a grateful nation," he concluded. "There is no time, but please know that you have my gratitude and that of the remainder of the Government. Thank you."

He stepped off the podium and vanished through a door, followed by a pair of Secret Service Agents. Nicolas had heard rumours of vast networks of bunkers and tunnels under Washington and guessed that the warehouse was owned by the CIA or one of the other intelligence agencies. It probably had a hidden access point to an underground railroad linking Official Washington and allowing politicians to move around secretly, without anyone being aware of their movements. He knew that he shouldn't even speculate on the possibilities, even in light of the war. God alone knew what the enemies of the United States – or the entire human race – would do with the information.

"At ease," Wachter ordered, shortly. "What you are about to hear is not common knowledge. We've invested a great deal of effort in keeping it that way. Some of it will already be familiar to you; some of it will be new and startling to the newcomers. You've all been tapped for Operation Allen and, I'm afraid, there is no release from this mission. If there was another way…"

He leaned forward. "The blunt truth is that we are losing the war," he said. Nicolas heard the reactions only vaguely, through his own shock. A handful of men swore aloud, another thumped the ground savagely, but the majority just stared at Wachter. He could have pulled out a gun and started shooting at them and they would have been less surprised. "We've kept the loss rates and suchlike out of the media – no point in giving the aliens a useful source of intelligence – but they're bad. We're losing irreplaceable aircraft every day. We've adapted our tactics and scored some significant successes, yet we are being steadily ground down to nothing. We're losing bases and support units and that is hampering our ability to keep our fighters flying.

"We've effectively ceded the airspace over parts of the United States because we can no longer plug holes in the defences. The aliens have not been slow to take advantage of our weaknesses and there have been an increasing number of strikes against military bases and other vital targets.

There are parts of the country without power or other essential supplies because the aliens took out power plants, transformers, bridges and other targets. They don't seem to target civilians directly – at least as far as we can tell, although there have been some incidents where civilians were killed for being too close to a targeted base – but the civilian population is suffering. We believe that it is only a matter of time before they move on to the next logical step, a ground invasion."

"Like we did to Saddam fucking Hussein," someone said, from the rear.

"Exactly," Wachter said. "The mothership enters orbit in twelve days. We don't know why they're following the exact targeting pattern they are, but we suspect that once they have the mothership in orbit, they'll land vast numbers of ground troops. We may have problems stopping them from establishing a foothold and occupying the entire United States. But we cannot let the war end there."

Nicolas met his eyes for a moment and saw the desperation written there. "We think that they targeted us first because they believed that we posed the greatest threat," he said. "They will probably seek to complete the job once they have the troops on hand and…I'm telling you now, we may be unable to prevent them from landing and taking the country. If – when – that happens, you men will be the core of an underground resistance movement to take back the country.

"The President, as some of you have heard, recently nullified all laws concerning firearms ownership and suchlike in an attempt to ensure that the civilian population will be armed and ready to fight the aliens. This has not gone down well with some elements of the country" – Nicolas smiled at the thought of the multiple heart attacks that would have struck the gun control nuts – "but on the whole it has proved a popular policy. The problem is that most of the armed civilians out there won't have the slightest idea of what to do and will probably end up being easy meat for the aliens. Your task is to change that and to prepare them for an underground war."

Nicolas scowled. He'd seen some of the militia movements during one of his leaves – they frequented gun shows and shooting competitions – and he hadn't been impressed. Some of them would have made good soldiers, with the right training and leadership, but most of them were nothing more than wannabes, without even the right mindset to be a trained soldier. Their massive collections of guns wouldn't be much use without training and discipline and they lacked it. They also tended to be frighteningly intense, sometimes fanatical, but almost all talk. A handful were dangerous and had caused the FBI some sleepless nights, some were ex-military trying to keep their skills sharp, but the majority were harmless nuts, more dangerous to themselves than others.

He remembered a man with a beer gut who had claimed to be a SEAL. Nicolas had quizzed him without his knowledge – if he'd been close to any SEAL, it was a seal in a sea life centre – and then out-shot him in the shooting competition later that day. It had been easy to outshoot the poser, but some of the odder people had been more surprising challenges. There had been a cheerleader with a skirt that was shamefully short who had been a sharpshooter, even though she was only a few years older than Nancy. She would have made an ideal recruit for a resistance movement. Her father would have been proud.

"You will operate with authority from the President and leave no paper trail," Wachter said. "You will emplace weapons stockpiles around the country, including explosives and other nasty surprises, and recruit other soldiers as necessary. You will be responsible for establishing your own communications networks and linking in to the underground communications systems, although you will have to bear in mind that it might become compromised at any moment. In the event of Washington being destroyed and the National Command Authority being lost, you are authorised to continue the war until the enemy is removed from our land."

Or we die, Nicolas thought. He had no illusions about the task. He'd studied insurgencies during training and then fought them in his career. Insurgents could be deadly enemies, yet very few insurgencies had come close to success without massive support from outside, or an incompetent opposition. The Warriors they'd fought…how well would they handle an insurgency? Would they go in soft or hard? Would they torment the civilian population until they broke and handed over the insurgents, or turned on the aliens…? There was no way to know.

"Your group is not the only group involved," Wachter concluded. "You will have no contact with those other groups, however, until the aliens land. OPSEC will be maintained until we know the full extent of the threat. You will not talk to civilians or anyone outside your group about your duties – if some asshole in a procurement office refuses to hand out weapons and materials without a requisition form in triplicate, you will put them in touch with my office and we'll send that bastard to a posting in Alaska. I suspect that there will be rumours about your activities, but your lives and success may depend on how well you maintain your secrecy.

"If we are lucky, there will be no need for your operation and you will be able to disband and return to normal duties. I do not expect that to happen, and nor does the President. You are to assume the worst and prepare for the long haul. The country may well be occupied, but as long as one of us remains fighting, we will never be defeated. Good luck."

Nicolas watched him go, still unable to grasp what had happened. No one had ever seriously expected that the United States would be invaded. It just didn't happen. NATO had created stay-behind units in Europe to prepare for a Soviet invasion, but the Soviet threat had collapsed and the stay-behind units had been disbanded, although not before getting their names into the media in the worst possible way. Stay-behind units in Italy and Germany had been implicated in political assassination, media manipulation and other criminal acts, poisoning the political scene. It hadn't been NATO's finest moment. The only reason it hadn't blown up into a full-scale Atlantic crisis was because the stay-behind units had been a mixture of American and European personnel.

And even if the aliens were defeated, the insurgents would cast a long shadow over American politics for the foreseeable future. The vast majority of American citizens had been content with their lot, but there had been plenty who'd wanted a change, even if they had to wade through oceans of blood to force change. The tactics they'd learn in the course of the insurgency would also serve well – perhaps better – against an American government. He wasn't blind to the level of trust being placed on their shoulders, and the desperation. Nullifying all firearms legislation was one thing. Teaching thousands of American citizens how to be terrifyingly good insurgent fighters was quite another. The government knew that it was on the verge of losing the war. Once the mothership arrived, all bets were off.

The soldiers spilt off into smaller groups and began good-naturedly arguing through the possible options, discussing the value of different tactics and operations. Nicolas looked up at the map and realised that most of the soldiers came from the same general area, Virginia and the surrounding states. Many of them had grown up with military families, or knew other veterans in the area who could be recruited into an underground army, men and women who would be motivated to fight for the United States. The official military bases would probably be destroyed or occupied, but there was plenty of room for covert military bases…and all the chaos caused by the alien attacks would only cover their movements. The mountains would provide a great deal of cover for insurgent operations.

He ran his hand through his hair as he remembered Nancy. She could never know the truth…or perhaps he should tell her and her stepfather, warn them to run and hide. The aliens could have a list of every soldier in America and have them all marked down for immediate arrest and execution when they finally invaded, or perhaps they didn't know or care about individual humans. Human history showed a wide range of possible precedents. They might be nice and concentrate on winning hearts and minds, or they might be cruel and devastate hundreds of miles to wipe out insurgent groups. There was no way to know.

"We'll find a base of operations over the next few days," he said, finally. They'd discovered that he was the senior officer in the group, although he'd only have nominal overall command. Leaderless resistance would work far better than an attempt to coordinate against vastly superior firepower. He attempted to sound confident, yet he knew that it was going to be nasty. Insurgent wars were never clean and tidy. "Once we know where we're operating, we can start gathering supplies and making contacts. The bastards won't know what's going to hit them."

Chapter Forty-Six

RAF Fairford, United Kingdom
Day 60

I wonder if I'm making a mistake, Prime Minister Arthur Hamilton thought, as he watched the alien craft settling down to the tarmac. RAF Fairford was something of a pointed choice for a secret meeting, one that implied that the aliens were going to make more than a few demands of the British Government. The base might have officially been a RAF station, but until comparatively recently it had actually been run by the United States Air Force and still played host to a handful of stealth fighters, although all of them had been placed in reserve. The base was currently operated by a RAF maintenance crew who'd started the task of bringing it up to full operational status after the alien mothership had been detected. The RAF might need to operate from Fairford if, as seemed likely, the other bases were hammered by alien fighters.

The alien craft was a spectacular sight as it glided out of the air, but the Prime Minister's thoughts were elsewhere. Britain had been in a weak economic position for the past decade and the shockwaves from the alien war against the United States had pressed huge financial damage on Britain, and the rest of the world. The country had been making slow progress towards full employment when the shockwave hit and instantly put millions out of work.

The government had done its best to prevent a crisis, but nothing had worked for longer than a day, if that. There had been rioting on the streets, ethnic warfare in a dozen cities and a massive loss of confidence in the government. Martial Law had been declared across half the country and tens of thousands of even vaguely suspect characters had been put behind the wire, something that might do even more damage in the long run. The prisoners had to be fed and watered and, after the crisis was over, would probably try to sue the government. The hell of it was that most of them *were* innocent, but there was no way to tell the difference and some of the truly guilty were really dangerous.

The former USAF base wasn't *that* far from London and the heart of the British Government, but the Prime Minister felt uneasy at being even that far from Parliament. The Leader of the Opposition had been giving the Government his full support, which had prevented outright challenges to the Prime Minister's authority, but the backbench MPs were muttering rebelliously. Some of them thought that the government had gone too far. Some of them thought that the government hadn't gone far enough. Between them, they could bring down the Government.

His gaze slipped to the SAS soldiers patrolling the perimeter with loaded weapons, including a handful carrying Stinger missiles and other weapons. There shouldn't be any problems – protests had been banned since three of them had turned into riots and left hundreds dead in their wake – but if the aliens came with hostile intent, the Prime Minister suspected that they wouldn't be enough. The news from America was growing darker by the day. The Prime Minister's military advisors had been following the USAF's battle very closely and had advised the Prime Minister that while the RAF could learn from the American experience, they would still lose aircraft and eventually run out of planes and pilots.

Britain had one of the most advanced military forces in the world, yet it was tiny, a legacy of successive defence cuts by various governments. The Government had been trying desperately to repair the damage, but rebuilding a capability took years, and anyone who might have been willing to sell the needed equipment to the British required it for their own defence.

"They're coming, Prime Minister," his aide muttered. A hatch was forming out of the alien craft – despite himself, the Prime Minister was impressed by how...*organic* the craft seemed to be – and allowed a single alien to step out of the ship. "There's only one of them?"

"Hush," the Prime Minister said. The American President had been taken to the mothership, the UN had had three alien ambassadors...he suspected that it was a calculated slight, best handled by ignoring it. Britain probably didn't rate as important compared to the United States, and if the aliens could grind down the invincible USAF, they were probably confident that they could do the same to the RAF. "Ambassador. Welcome to Britain."

The alien looked at him and, despite himself, the Prime Minister shivered. He'd seen the recordings the Americans had made of their President's visit to the mothership – he had no idea how they'd managed to smuggle a camera onboard – yet it didn't compare to meeting an alien in person. It was a warm summer day, but he still felt cold. It was almost like meeting a diplomat from one of the more unstable world states, yet somehow different. The aliens could threaten Britain's very existence.

"Thank you for meeting us," the alien said. He spoke in a voice that sounded like a loud whisper. "I am Ethos. I speak for my people. You speak for yours?"

"Yes," the Prime Minister said. The aliens had clearly done their research – *probably by kidnapping a few hundred people from the UK*, the Prime Minister thought sourly – and knew how the Prime Minister was elected. Britain might still be a monarchy, in theory, but as long as the Prime Minister had a majority in the House of Commons, the Government could run the country to suit itself. "I have authority to speak for my people."

The alien said nothing for a long moment. He had an excellent poker face, without any of the facial tells that a human would have shown. The Prime Minister was an excellent chess player – he had always regarded poker as rather uncivilised – and recognised the pause. The alien was silently running through his possible options in his mind. The Prime Minister had negotiated with countless diplomats before and had faith in his ability to bring two parties together, yet this was very different. The aliens had the power to dictate to the entire world – what was happening to America proved that – and would presumably insist on a large degree of political control. Ethos – an odd choice of name, the Prime Minister considered – might have come to demand that Britain surrender.

"We are currently on final approach to this planet," Ethos said, finally. The alien voice sounded slightly more human, all of a sudden. "Once we enter orbit, we will begin landing our people on the surface and establishing living spaces for ourselves."

The Prime Minister's eyes narrowed. "How will you establish living space for yourself?"

"We will remove the local human governments and take over," Ethos said, flatly. There was no hint of compromise in the alien tone. "It is our observation that many of the humans in the targeted area would be happy if their governments were smashed and replaced by benevolent authority. We would certainly not slaughter thousands of humans merely for being the *wrong* sex, or the *wrong* skin colour, or the *wrong* religion."

The Prime Minister said nothing, thinking hard. If the description was taken at face value, that meant Africa or the Middle East, perhaps both. It made a certain kind of sense. The aliens claimed to have a billion settlers on their ship and Africa and the Middle East were under-populated by humans who might get in the way. Ethos might even be right about their reception. Only a week ago, there had been yet another bloody coup in Africa and thousands of supporters of the defeated government had been put in front of a wall and shot, while the rebels looted, raped and burned their way through the capital city. War – and famine and drought – were the curses of Africa, curses blamed on the Europeans who had colonised the continent over a century ago. The truth was more mundane, and tragic. The African Governments, as a general rule, were corrupt and their leaders looted as much as they could before rebels overthrew them and took control for themselves. The rebels promptly repeated the same process until they too were overthrown. There were seeds of hope, but most of the continent was a hopeless disaster area.

"We are prepared to make you an offer," Ethos continued. "We do not intend to settle on your territory. We wish merely that you do not become involved in the inevitable and futile struggles between humans and our people. If you agree to remain uninvolved, we will provide you with fusion power systems, batteries of a vastly superior design to your own tech, and synthetic oil that will meet your requirements until you switch over completely to electric systems. We will even consider purchasing supplies we need from you in exchange for further technology and other supplies."

The Prime Minister knew he was gaping, all reserve gone, but he couldn't help it. The chaos in the Middle East had stopped the oil tankers from moving, ensuring that Europe was on the verge of freezing in winter.

The price of petrol had already skyrocketed despite heavy rationing and shortages were setting in everywhere. The Government had established a vast underground storage network for oil in calmer times, yet even that would run out eventually. The European Union had been giving serious thought to putting together a multinational force and seizing the oil wells in Saudi Arabia, perhaps with the help of the remaining American forces in Bahrain. The EU normally moved very slowly, yet they were desperate. The worst that could happen was that the oil wells would be destroyed. They weren't getting any oil from them anyway. Rumour had it that the Russians were even considering invading *Iran* and taking their oil by force.

"I see," he managed finally. "And the catch?"

"We do not wish you to become involved with our operations," Ethos informed him. "We wish you to remain uninvolved. We will be extending comparable offers to other governments and forging ties with them. You can join us or not, as you please. Your refusal will not change anything for us, merely for you."

The Prime Minister could read between the lines. Which other governments had been approached? The French? The Germans? The Russians? The Japanese? The Chinese were in the middle of a civil war, so they probably hadn't been contacted, yet perhaps the aliens were backing one side, or both. The alien approach was sneaky, in a way. The nations that had access to alien tech in one form or another would face immense pressure from the other nations to share, or else. The aliens might be hoping that Europe would go to war over their technology, weakening them for a later invasion. It would make sense from a cold-blooded point of view.

"I understand," he said, finally. "How long do we have to decide?"

Ethos reached into a pocket and produced a small black device, barely larger than a walkie-talkie. "You can contact us on this at any time," he said. "If you do not contact us within a week, we will assume that you do not intend to accept our offer and will consider other steps. Thank you for your time."

The Prime Minister watched as the alien wheeled around and marched back to the alien craft. A moment later, the hatch had flowed closed and the craft floated slowly off the ground. It seemed to pause at about five meters, then simply vanished, rocketing out of the area so fast that the Prime

Minister didn't see it go. He shook his head in awe and nodded to his aide. The young man was flushed and very pale.

"Say nothing for now," he said. The black box in his hand might transmit everything he said back to the mothership. He turned it over and over in his hands and discovered a button marked PUSH THIS. The aliens, he realised suddenly, had a sense of humour. "Once we get back to London, we'll discuss it with the Cabinet."

He passed the black box to one of the RAF staffers, who'd take it to a research lab and study it as much as they could before it was used, and headed towards his car. Their next destination was half an hour away and he intended to use the time to think, carefully. The alien offer came with strings attached. Just because they were invisible, as any good diplomat knew, didn't mean that they didn't exist.

————

Normally, in the mid-afternoon, Britain's motorways would be utterly jammed up with cars, lorries and other vehicles. The Prime Minister had attempted to promote public transport in the hopes of cutting down on pollution and congestion, but even he had to admit that the efforts had failed. One of the more ironic side effects of the alien invasion and the resulting economic chaos was that thousands of cars had been forced off the roads and the air was cleaner than it had been in years. The Prime Minister's car and its police escort rocketed along until they reached a mansion belonging to one of Britain's noble families, although one with dire financial issues. The British Government had stepped in with an offer the family couldn't refuse and, in exchange for having their home designated as an emergency government facility; their home had been saved from being sold. It had never been used for its intended purpose, until now.

The Prime Minister passed through the security check impatiently, but knew better than to push matters. He still remembered going to the Russian Embassy for a diplomatic gathering and coming back to his office with no less than five bugs attached to his person. It was all part of the game, he'd been assured, but he'd taken security very seriously since. The aliens might have taken the opportunity to put him under surveillance as well. No one knew the extent of their capabilities.

The Home Secretary and the secondary Chief of Joint Operations were waiting for him. The British Government had been dispersed around the countryside to avoid a single strike decapitating the entire government, although a handful had had to remain at PINDAR, the command and control bunker under Whitehall. The primary Chief of Joint Operations was at the Permanent Joint Headquarters, watching and waiting for the first sign of an alien attack on the United Kingdom. The Prime Minister didn't envy him. Northwood had to be high on the list of alien targets if they chose to invade.

"Listen carefully," he said, and ran through a brief outline of the meeting. His aide had transcribed everything despite his shock and they read it quickly. Now that the shock had faded, the Prime Minister found himself getting angry. Who did the aliens think they were? "So, what do we do about it?"

"From a national point of view, accepting the offer works in our favour," the Home Secretary said. He had been Deputy Prime Minister until the mothership had been detected, whereupon a coalition government had been formed and the Leader of the Opposition had accepted that position. Collective responsibility, the Prime Minister considered, otherwise known as sharing the blame. "We need what they're offering desperately. The country is on a knife-edge."

"There's also the other aspect to consider," the CJO said. "I think they're not warning us about the Middle East at all. I think they're warning us about not interfering with *America*."

The Prime Minister frowned. "Explain," he ordered. "Why would they care?"

"They may be aliens, but their tactics are understandable," the CJO said. "They went after the most powerful nation on Earth to scare the shit out of the rest of us..."

"Succeeded too," the Home Secretary injected.

"And they probably intend to invade America directly once they've finished tearing the USAF apart," CJO continued, ignoring the interruption. "We and Canada could provide material support to any resistance movement in American territory, play host to American refugees and their military equipment, even accept and promote an American government-in-exile. That has to concern them unless they intend the wholesale extermination of America's population."

"It wouldn't bother them that much," the CJO said. "Look, I'm a soldier. The politics of the situation are beyond me and they're hardly my responsibility anyway, but I have to tell you that if the aliens can eat the Americans for lunch, they're not going to have problems eating us for dinner. The entire combined force of Europe couldn't match what the Americans are throwing at the aliens – and losing. We'd get in a few solid hits – we're outfitting our own aircraft to benefit from the Yanks' experiences – but we'd lose. There is no question of that. We just don't have the numbers to stand up to the aliens."

The Prime Minister stared down at his hands. "So…we're already making preparations to give the Americans what covert help we can," he said, thoughtfully. "Do we continue with that, or do we accept the alien offer and refuse to help the Americans any further?"

"It may not matter," the CJO pointed out. "The level of material support we can offer to the Americans is actually quite low. We couldn't fly the RAF over there to help without the aliens taking countermeasures. We could accept the alien offer and continue to help the Americans at the same time."

"You're talking about a double-cross," the Home Secretary said. "If they catch us at it…"

"They'll be…rather annoyed," the CJO agreed. "The problem is simple. I think that the aliens have come to invade, and they're not going to be satisfied with just America, the Middle East and Africa. Just by what they've done so far, they've hurt the entire world badly. I think that we might get Britain moved to the final place on their list of targets, but eventually we *would* be targeted, or kept in permanent subordination. They won't risk us developing to the point where we could threaten them and drive them off the planet."

"It does make a change from waiting for the Yanks to put together a plan and lead us all against the aliens," the Prime Minister agreed, ruefully. "Very well. We slip them as much help as we can. Something totally covert – and deniable. If they find out…"

"I understand," the CJO said. "It's all my fault."

"A rogue operation," the Prime Minister said. "Don't get caught."

Chapter Forty-Seven

International Space Station, Earth Orbit
Day 69

The mothership was showing up clearly now, even through the small telescope that had been mounted on the ISS. It was a massive structure, so vast as to be beyond human comprehension, yet somehow it was now hard to get a clear image of its actual shape. It seemed to be surrounded by a vague field that obscured the telescope's view, concealing vital hull details. There were countless theories on how it was somehow slowing down and preparing to inject itself into Earth's orbit, but none of them mattered a damn. It could be matter-antimatter propulsion or a drive field out of a science-fiction nightmare – NASA had had a research program into advanced propulsion concepts for over twenty years – yet all that mattered was that it was finally entering orbit. The alien colonists had arrived at their new home.

Captain Philip Carlson watched from the International Space Station as the mothership seemed to grow larger on the screen. No one knew why the aliens had spared the ISS – the current theory was that it would have spoiled their claim to come in peace, although Philip thought that was ridiculous – and the five-man crew had had a perfect view as the aliens had systematically dismantled America's defences. He'd expected the call to action to come at any moment, when he and Felicity would have cut loose from the ISS and steer *Atlantis* right into the path of the alien mothership, but it had never come. Intellectually, he supposed that he should have been relieved, but emotionally he would have sooner tried and failed than been kept out of the fight. He'd lost friends and family down on Earth, some from the massive air battles raging over America, others from being too close to the alien targets and killed in the attacks. He wanted to strike back at the aliens, yet cold logic told him that it would be futile. *Atlantis* carried exactly eight nuclear-tipped missiles and two laser cannons that might as well be popguns, for all the harm their bigger brothers on Earth had accomplished against the alien craft. They might take out a handful of alien craft – the shuttle was primitive compared to their ships and it might make them overconfident – but the outcome was inevitable. The shuttle would be smashed and their lives would be lost, for nothing.

"I wonder what they're using as a power source," Colonel Irving Harrows said. There were only three men left on the ISS as permanent crew, the remainder having been evacuated after the alien mothership had been detected. Philip suspected, reading between the lines, that the Russians and Europeans had been quite happy for the Americans to have the ISS as an observation platform. The two shuttle crewmen had fitted in quite nicely. "They can't be using anything we'd recognise as a power source without leaving a massive drive trail behind."

Philip nodded sourly. The alien craft seemed to have problems manoeuvring in the atmosphere at high speeds, yet such constraints didn't seem to bother them in space. He'd seen alien craft racing past the ISS at speeds well over Mach Twenty, taunting the humans before flying down to continue the war. They flew their craft like starfighters out of a bad movie, daring the humans on the station to open fire and see their missiles hopelessly outmatched by the alien craft. Whatever tech the aliens used, it was fantastically advanced over anything the human race had deployed, or was it? He'd followed the Advanced Propulsion Program as closely as he could – his security clearance was high enough to at least get the gist of what was going on – and he'd heard rumours of breakthroughs that would change the face of space travel forever. Nothing had ever materialised, however, and NASA's attempts to develop a replacement for the shuttle had kept floundering. The agency couldn't have found its rear end with terrain-following radar and a map for dummies.

The Director of NASA had been forced to resign – more accurately, he had been unceremoniously sacked – after the alien attack had begun. Congress had been looking for a scapegoat and NASA had been an easy target, with reports of trillions of dollars being funnelled into the agency and yet producing little usable hardware. Philip knew that the problems ran much deeper than the Director and the horde of yes-men he had surrounding him and was doubtful as to what had been achieved, apart from covering Congress's collective butt. The aliens hadn't hit NASA's centres – cruel rumours had suggested that they didn't need to bother – but everyone agreed that it was only a matter of time. The United States was not going to be saved by something coming out of NASA's endless paper-generation programs.

"It doesn't matter," he said. He would almost have preferred to face the Death Star, or perhaps an alien mothership from a more primitive group of aliens. The Death Star had had a massive design flaw that had allowed the rebels to destroy it – the Second Death Star hadn't even been completed when *it* had been destroyed – yet the heroes had also had the help of the scriptwriters. He doubted that even the most insane Hollywood scriptwriter could write the United States a way out of its current predicament. "It's going to enter orbit any time now."

He hoped – prayed – that plans had been made for a massive nuclear strike by all of Earth's nuclear powers, yet he knew that it would be lethal. The mothership might be powered by antimatter, resulting in an explosion that would have catastrophic effects on Earth, or it might be shattered and the debris would crash down onto the planet. The entire human race now knew what the aliens had been doing to human victims at the South Pole – even if none of the humans had been identified by various police and intelligence services – and Philip hoped that there would be an alliance against the aliens, yet nuking them wasn't the answer. It would have ensured the destruction of both races. No, the *humans* would be exterminated. The aliens would still have their homeworld and however many other worlds they'd colonised.

The thought had taunted him over the past couple of weeks, while the alien attacks had been underway. There was no reason to assume that the aliens had *only* headed for Earth. Their technology was so advanced that even the mothership might only have required a tiny fraction of their resources, allowing them to build hundreds of the ships and launch them in all directions. The astronomers were still unsure which of the many stars near Earth had birthed the alien mothership – there were a handful of possible candidates – yet there were plenty of possible other destinations. The human race might fight off one invasion to discover that the stars belonged to the aliens.

Philip winced. Back when he'd been a kid, his father – a space buff himself – had told him that he might be on the first starship leaving the solar system. He'd kept it to himself in the USAF and NASA, but he'd always been fascinated with the idea of travelling from star to star. He had studied it obsessively and concluded that the human race could have populated all of the nearby stars within a hundred years. It had never happened. NASA had become a bureaucratic monster, the Russians and Chinese had cut back on their space programs…and humans had never returned to the Moon.

And now it was too late. The human race had told the universe that it wasn't interested. The universe hadn't taken the hint.

Philip no longer expected to have children, but if he had had kids, they would have grown up in a universe where humanity played second fiddle to a mysterious alien race that had laid claim to all the real estate. The human race might continue to exist as slave labour, or pets, or…human history showed a wide range of possible precedents for natives when the colonists arrived. The human race might be enslaved, or exterminated, or pushed into reservations, or…perhaps treated as equals. It was a possibility Philip found hard to believe. He'd seen debates on internet discussion forums over the ethical implications of committing genocide against the aliens and while he liked to believe that humanity would never commit such an act, there was no reason to believe that the aliens shared humanity's conception of morality. They might regard extermination or enslavement as perfectly moral solutions to the human problem. They might regard humanity as too primitive to control its own destiny…

"I'm picking up an unusual energy signal from the mothership," Doctor Melvyn Heights said. He'd been on the ISS to conduct a series of experiments – he'd once tried to explain them to Philip, but he hadn't understood a word of them – and had insisted on remaining on the station to observe the mothership when it arrived. Philip would have sent him down to the planet with the remainder of the crew, but apparently Heights had friends or enemies in high places, who'd authorised his remaining on the station. "It's fluctuating…"

The mothership exploded.

For a long moment, Philip wondered if someone had fired on the mothership after all, or if another alien faction had joined the battle on humanity's side, or if one of NASA's secret programs had led to workable hardware after all. He'd read a set of novels centred around the idea of a top-secret fleet of interstellar-capable warp ships being based on the Moon and had found the idea rather insulting – he wanted to fly such ships, if they existed – but perhaps they did exist and they'd destroyed the mothership. He braced himself for the expected shower of debris and recoiled as he realised the radars were picking up hundreds of chunks...no, they were moving spacecraft. The mothership had launched hundreds of spacecraft as it entered Earth's orbit, rather than exploding. Many of them were bigger than anything humanity had yet seen other than the mothership itself.

"I'm...I'm reading over four *hundred* spacecraft," Harrows said. He couldn't keep the stammer out of his voice. NASA hadn't selected a coward to command the ISS, but the worst he'd had to deal with was a possible collision with a manmade object. No one had seriously expected an alien invasion...and even after the alien mothership had been detected, they'd expected the ISS to be destroyed in the opening moves of the war. "They're coming this way."

Philip watched over his shoulder. There were so many spacecraft that the radar was having problems keeping track of them all, making it hard to tell just how many there were, although it probably didn't matter. The alien spacecraft were *massive*, each one large enough to land thousands of aliens on Earth...and they were all heading towards their new home. The mothership itself was hidden behind the radar distortion caused by the presence of so many smaller spacecraft, yet somehow he knew that it was entering orbit and preparing to send down the next set of alien craft.

"Update Washington," he said, slowly. The ISS wouldn't last a second against the alien armada. It was overkill. So many ships could probably take out hundreds of worlds like Earth. "Tell them that we'll do our best."

"They've taken notice of us," Heights said. Somehow, the scientist remained calm. "One of the really big ships is heading our way."

Isabel Paterson peered over from her console. The brunette woman had been one of the engineers before the crew had been recalled to Earth, but her

USAF commission had kept her on the station. Philip barely knew her, yet his superior officers had been impressed with her and predicted that she'd probably serve a term as ISS commander, provided she passed the political handicaps. Every country that had an investment in the ISS got a say in how the station operated. Personally, he would have operated it by the rules of the Republic of Gondor.

"Big bastard, too," she said. The alien craft was showing up clearly on the radar screen now as it separated itself from the stream of craft heading towards Earth. "It's over five kilometres long."

For a moment, Philip quailed. What could they do against such a force, but die bravely? "Felicity," he said, slowly. "Prepare *Atlantis* for launch."

Felicity didn't argue as she left the control module. Harrows did. "Captain," he said. "What do you hope to achieve?"

"If we hit that...*thing* with one nuke, we'll take it out and make life easier for those down on Earth," Philip said. He wasn't inclined to argue, not when time was rapidly running out. "I have instructions to launch a strike on my own authority if..."

The entire station shook violently. Alarms sounded as oxygen began to leak out of the station. "What happened?" He demanded. "Felicity! Are you all right?"

There was no answer. "Felicity!"

"I'm alive," Felicity's voice said. "I've got a mask on, but there are at least two breaches in this compartment and we're probably spinning in space."

"*Atlantis* got hit badly," Heights said. He swung one of the cameras mounted on the station's exterior hull around to show where the shuttle had been. Fire didn't burn in space, their only saving grace, yet the shuttle had been completely wrecked. The cockpit had been destroyed and the cargo bay had been ripped open. There was no hope of launching any of the nukes now. "Sir, the station is no longer viable."

Harrows gritted his teeth. "We'll have to get to the escape pod," he said, pulling masks out of the walls. The emergency systems had failed, Philip realised dully. They hadn't been designed to deal with an alien attack. "We don't have a choice but to abandon the station now and hope that we make it back down to Earth. I'll set the station's sensors on automatic and they can keep feeding information to Washington..."

"I don't think it will matter," Janet said, as the station jerked again. "They've come to get us."

Philip stared in frank disbelief as the looming bulk of the alien spacecraft settled over the station. The station was shuddering under its presence, as if it were generating turbulence in space, as impossible as that was. He saw a hatch the size of an aircraft carrier opening up, revealing an eerie green light that seemed to somehow reach out towards the station and pull. He felt himself drifting *downwards* towards the deck as a gravity field pulled them towards the spacecraft, taking the entire ISS onboard. It was completely insane, it was unbelievable…yet it was happening. He saw a look of shock on Harrows' face, disbelief on Isabel's face, before the station was pulled completely onboard the alien craft and crashed to the deck. The ISS had never been designed to operate under gravity and rapidly crumpled under its own weight.

They've abducted the entire station, he thought, realising that they had to get out before it crushed them. He silently cursed the decision not to arm the ISS with anything more lethal that ASAT missiles, wishing that he'd strapped on his sidearm before leaving the shuttle. It hadn't seemed like something he'd need onboard the ISS, but who would have imagined that the aliens would bring the entire station – and the wreckage of *Atlantis* – onboard?

"We have to get out of here," he snapped, helping Isabel to her feet. The sudden return of gravity was affecting them all, making him feel dizzy and weak. It would be worse for the three who'd spent months onboard the space station. Too long in orbit made the muscles atrophy. It occurred to him that the aliens might breathe poison and they'd die, except they knew what humans breathed…they'd have provided a breathable atmosphere. If they hadn't, the humans were dead anyway. "Come on."

They stumbled through connecting tubes – all warped and twisted now – until they found Felicity in one of the storage compartments. Her leg had been broken by the fall. Philip helped her to her feet and supported her as they staggered out of the station, exiting through a gash in the hull that would have been lethal in orbit. The alien air smelt faintly spicy, with an odd hint of something he couldn't place, but it was breathable. They could live on the alien ship. He looked over at *Atlantis* and winced. The shuttle might have been a creaky ship that was older than her pilots, yet she'd deserved better than to die on an alien hangar deck. There was only one shuttle left now, if the aliens hadn't taken out the Cape and destroyed that as well.

He turned around a piece of debris and came face to face with a group of alien warriors. He'd seen pictures of the dead warriors from the crash – and, later, from the attack on the alien base – yet seeing them in the flesh was terrifying. The aliens lunged forward, grabbed the humans and sliced away their clothes. He heard Felicity scream as her broken leg was bumped and tried to struggle, but the aliens held him too tightly.

"You are our prisoners," one of the aliens said. His voice was rough and very hard. It was oddly accented, spoken as if the alien had memorised the phases for the occasion. "You will not attempt to resist and you will be treated well."

"I understand," Philip said. Harrows should have spoken to the alien, but he was in shock. "My friend needs medical care."

"It will be provided," the alien said. The tone hadn't changed at all. "You will accompany us."

The alien holding him half-pushed, half-carried him towards an exit on the far side of a room large enough to play several games of basketball in. It was massive, yet mundane, and hardly special to the aliens. He saw a group of smaller aliens moving past them towards the remains of the ISS and wished for a nuke. A single nuke would have destroyed the entire alien ship. They could have hurt the aliens badly…

Instead, they were just prisoners, while the aliens descended on Earth.

Chapter Forty-Eight

Robin was a past mistress at reading and understanding the input from radar stations and the other sensor systems deployed around the United States and in orbit, but even she hesitated when she saw the mothership seemingly disintegrate. The overall radar picture had been badly degraded ever since the war had started – the aliens had targeted every American radar station and AWACS aircraft – yet she could still study the mothership through optical sensors and foreign satellites. It didn't take long to realise, from the live feed coming from the ISS, just what had happened. The mothership had finally reached orbit and the aliens were starting to land on their new home.

"I'm reading at least six hundred alien craft," she said. She barely had hard locks on a handful of them. The alien craft were spreading out, but even so it was impossible to track them all behind the haze of distortion they caused. The mothership might not have disintegrated into nothingness, as she'd feared before realising what had happened, yet she'd lost track of it entirely. It was somewhere behind the massive cloud of alien ships.

"My God," General Sandra Dyson said. She looked appalling and Robin knew that *she* didn't look much better. She'd never cared about her personal appearance very much – apart from one interview where she'd been assured she'd get a position if she looked pretty – and it didn't bother her, but the General was clearly at the end of her tether. Colorado Springs had never been attacked – the aliens had clearly decided that it wasn't worth the effort of hacking their way through the reinforced rock protecting the base – yet they'd had to watch as the aliens had hammered the USAF all over America. They'd struggled desperately to coordinate the defences against a threat of unprecedented power – and lost. The sheer weight of craft slipping into orbit and preparing to descend to Earth spelt certain doom. "How big are they?"

Robin studied the readings, trying to make sense of them. "Most of them are around the size of a destroyer," she said, finally. So many alien craft would be able to ride out any human attack with nukes or THAAD missiles and just carry on. "There are four that are truly massive, at least five kilometres long. One of them is closing in on the ISS now."

As she watched, the two icons merged together. "They've taken out the ISS, or taken it onboard," she said, slowly. There were some pieces of debris floating away from where the ISS had been – the station had been attacked by one of the alien fighters, but most of it had remained intact – but there should have been much more debris, or a larger explosion if the station had been completely destroyed. "One of the other large ships is heading for America; a second is heading for the Atlantic Ocean. The third seems to be hanging back, waiting to see what we'll do."

"Target them with the remaining THAAD missiles and ground-based lasers," Sandra ordered, tartly. The aliens had never attempted to take out the lasers, a backhanded insult. Clearly, they had never considered them worth the effort of destroying, even after they'd chipped away the air defence aircraft and left the lasers undefended. "Prepare a firing solution for the ballistic missiles if we can get launch authority."

Robin had been running that subroutine ever since the alien craft had been detected. "They're going to be operating at extreme range," she warned. The alien fighters hadn't been bothered by the THAAD missiles, except when they'd tried to enter the atmosphere over America and lost a handful of craft. They'd learned from the experience and never tried it again. "I don't think they're going to cause the aliens many problems…"

"Target them anyway," Sandra ordered, sharply. She picked up a phone and tapped a switch rapidly. "Get me the President, now!"

The massive alien craft seemed far less manoeuvrable than their smaller brethren, even in space. Robin amused herself by attempting to visualise the limits on their capabilities, such as they were, and decided that it was probably a result of how much mass the aliens were moving around. The smaller alien craft could travel FTL, but the larger ones had never shown any such ability. The general theory was that they were simply too large to be pushed past sublight speeds, even with alien technology. The analysts had concluded that the power requirements would be colossal and that implied limits to the alien tech base, yet even she had to admit that it wouldn't matter. The aliens weren't hundreds of light years away, but sitting in Earth's orbit, preparing the invasion.

She tracked their fighters swooping away from their running engagements with the USAF and heading out over the Atlantic, actually evading the remaining American air defence fighters. It made no sense until she realised that there were hundreds more fighters streaming down into the atmosphere, rendezvousing with their comrades and preparing a likely final sweep through American airspace. Other alien craft seemed to be clumping up over North Africa, watching and waiting. Robin tracked them carefully, knowing that the other NATO countries would have access to the data, even though there was little they could do about it. The aliens were probing steadily eastwards, over the Middle East, India and war-torn China...

"You are cleared to fire when ready, Gridley," Sandra said. Robin keyed the command sequence into her console, authorising the thirty laser weapons to open fire. They had all been targeted on the massive alien ship coming over the United States, yet there was no trace of any damage. The craft seemed to be growing warmer, as if the lasers were transferring heat to the alien protective field, but there seemed to be no other damage at all. The missiles roared off their launch platforms and screamed up into the sky and for a moment Robin allowed herself to hope, before they started to vanish off the radar screens. "Result?"

"No detectable results," Robin informed her. The massive alien craft was an easy target, yet it was simply too large and powerful to be affected by lasers that took minutes to burn through ballistic missile coatings and incoming enemy warheads. They could burn away at it for hours without any results; indeed, she suspected that they were actually *feeding* the craft energy it could use. The drive fields propelling the alien craft certainly seemed to absorb energy from the surrounding area. "It's just hanging there."

A moment later, the display updated again. "General," she added, "the second alien craft is descending into the atmosphere, along with hundreds of escorts. It's on a direct course for Washington!"

"The President has authorised the use of nuclear missiles," Sandra said. There was a desperate hope in her voice. "They're going to take the bastard out."

Robin might have argued about the virtues of taking a ship that size out, when the debris would come crashing down on America, but there was a more practical concern.

"General," she said. "There is no reason to believe that the nuclear missiles would be any more successful than the THAAD missiles. The aliens shot *all* of the THAAD missiles down before they struck their target. They could do the same to ballistic missiles. They're easier targets, in fact."

Sandra stared at her. She might have been a General, having struggled her way through the ranks, but she respected Robin's abilities even as she despised her inability to follow proper procedure and protocol. Robin – and hundreds of nerds like her – were tolerated because they were necessary - and because they'd never be on the front line. They'd never imagined that they'd face serious danger or life-or-death decisions.

"Do you have a better idea?" Sandra asked, finally. "That craft is dominating the sky and…"

She broke off as a new contact appeared on the display. "What is that?"

Robin felt her blood run cold. The contact was an object falling from the alien craft, directly towards Colorado Springs. It didn't seem to be powered, but it hardly needed to have a power source to reach its target. It didn't take more than a second to perform the calculations required to know what would happen when it finally crashed into the base. The entire complex would be cracked open like an eggshell. There was no time to evacuate.

"I'm sorry, General," she said. The object was coming closer and closer, unstoppable by the Patriot missile batteries emplaced nearby. It was simply too large to be destroyed or deflected. "I'm very sorry."

She heard Sandra shouting orders, transferring tactical control to other secure bases around the United States, yet Robin knew that it was too late. The aliens could stamp on any other base with as much ease as they could stamp on NORAD. The war was on the verge of being lost along with the bases.

Slowly, she closed her eyes and waited for the end.

———

The massive kinetic energy weapon impacted directly with the base. Soldiers and airmen at nearby Peterson Air Force Base saw it as a streak of light and wondered if it was a laser weapon, before the massive explosion and earth-quake marked the end of the complex. Those looking directly at the blast might have thought that it had been a nuclear attack, before the flash burned out their eyes, leaving them blind and stumbling around for help. The KEW punched right through the base and down into the underlying rock, melting the works of humanity and erasing them from existence.

There were no survivors.

———

"They want us to fight that thing?"

"Quiet," Captain Will Jacob snapped. Somehow, he'd survived two weeks of heavy fighting, only to face the aliens in one final battle. The alien craft was so massive that he could see it with the naked eye, even at such a distance. It was moving forward slowly, as if it had problems moving faster than a crawl in the atmosphere, yet there was a ponderous inevitability about its steady course. It was heading right for Washington DC. "Stow that chatter and concentrate on your duties."

The Dark Shadows were no more. Only three of his squadron mates had survived. The squadron hadn't been officially disbanded, but pilots now flew with whatever wingmates they could scrape up, flying a disparate mismatch of aircraft. Will was leading seventy aircraft into the fight, yet it was hardly a unified force. There were only four Raptors, backed up by Fighting Falcons, Super Hornets, refurbished Tomcats, Marine Harriers, F-117s and even a pair of Warthogs. They couldn't even fly at the same speeds, forcing the faster aircraft to either speed forward or remain with their slower brethren. The desperate struggle for survival had brought USAF, Air National Guard, United States Navy and Marine Corps pilots together, fusing them into a single fighting unit, yet it hadn't been enough. The aliens had ground them down over two weeks of heavy fighting and now they were moving in for the kill.

He looked at his HUD and winced, unable to believe his eyes. He'd flown enough different types of aircraft to have an idea of how much power was required to hold something like that in the air, far more than any human technology could produce. He'd watched a television show which had featured a giant flying aircraft carrier – the USAF had actually considered the concept before deciding that it would be far too vulnerable to attack – and the aliens had actually made it real. It was no mere fighter craft, or even a landing craft. He couldn't help but draw a comparison between the alien craft and the City Destroyers from *Independence Day*, which boded ill for Washington if they couldn't stop the alien craft. The only consolation was that the aliens could probably have taken out the city at any moment if mass slaughter was part of their plan. They'd certainly stripped the city of defences more than once.

The alien craft wasn't a massive flying saucer, yet it was more than surreal enough. It reminded him of a B2 bomber, a massive flying wing, yet this flying wing was large enough to pass for a flying city. It seemed to be launching and recovering escorting fighters all the time, challenging the humans to close in and attack it, yet Will wasn't sure if they dared. The smaller alien craft had gone up in massive explosions when they'd been shot down. The massive alien craft might go up like a nuclear bomb, or come crashing down in the sea. They were so close to the coast that the results of either would be disastrous.

"They're coming down everywhere," the AWACS operator said. The radio seemed to be more disrupted than standard. Will heard a wave of static and winced as his ears suddenly hurt. "There are thousands of alien craft, landing all over the States!"

Will stared into the distance. The alien fighters seemed to be bunching up, preparing to come right at the humans fighters and sweep them out of the air before they could threaten the mothership – no, not the mothership, only a smaller ship. The aliens worked on a scale that dwarfed anything humans had ever attempted. His mouth was suddenly dry and he had to swallow twice before he could speak. The sheer presence of the alien craft scared the crap out of him. It was just hanging there, supremely confident in its ability to withstand everything the human race could throw at it…and he had a nasty suspicion it might be right. A single Sidewinder wasn't going to do much more than annoy it.

"All right," he said, clearing his throat. There was no point in delaying any longer. He was tempted to pinch himself, to see if he could wake up, but he knew it was real. "On my command, execute Watchman and follow me in."

There was no dissent, even though they knew – they all knew – just what he was asking. Watchman had been designed as an emergency option, not something that anyone sane would try without desperate need. It would almost certainly cost the lives of at least half of his force, and even so, there was no guarantee of success. The alien fighters were wheeling around, their tactics so familiar to him now that he knew when they would come at them before they finally straightened out and accelerated towards the human aircraft. Brilliant sparks of light raced ahead of them as they opened fire, forcing the human aircraft to evade. Will braced himself as the alien craft swooped closer...

"Now," he ordered.

The Raptor lunged forward as he triggered the afterburners, driving right towards the alien fighters. The other supersonic aircraft followed, closing with the aliens at well over Mach Two. The aliens reacted quickly and scattered in surprise, and then found themselves under attack by the subsonic Warthogs and Harriers. The Harriers had proven themselves as fighters during the Falklands War, yet the Marines had never flown them in air-to-air combat until the aliens had arrived. They'd made up for it since then. A massive explosion marked a collision between an alien fighter and one of the human aircraft, the alien having failed to get out of the way in time to escape.

"Lock missiles on target," he ordered. The alien craft was so large that it was impossible to deduce where a vital system might be installed. He designated a target quickly and flashed the information to the other aircraft. The aliens had recovered from their surprise and were rapidly counter-attacking. "Fox-three!"

The Raptor jerked as he launched four missiles right towards the massive alien ship. A moment later, the remaining fighters added their own fire, launching a swarm of missiles right into the teeth of the enemy defences. If a single missile could bring down an alien fighter, Will had reasoned, a handful of missiles might bring down one of the big alien ships. He was only vaguely aware of the AWACS vanishing off the air and the loss of radar data as the missiles bored in, before the alien craft opened fire. It filled the air with countless multicoloured sparks of light, shooting down a handful of the human missiles before they could strike home. The remainder slammed into the alien craft's drive field and exploded, but the ship seemed undamaged. The drive field didn't collapse. The craft didn't fall out of the sky.

Shit, he thought. *We're going to need a nuke.*

He yanked the Raptor aside microseconds before an alien craft could blow him apart. The aliens were counter-attacking savagely, vectoring hundreds of their fighter craft in on the impudent human aircraft, wiping them out of the sky. The formation, such as it had been, was coming apart as the aliens pressed in and picked the human craft off, one by one. He twisted desperately to avoid a second craft, realised that it was useless and expended a Sidewinder on the enemy, wasting it to preserve his life for a few more seconds. The alien craft exploded, shaking the Raptor violently. There was no hope of a clear sky. He saw a Warthog explode as an alien craft wiped it out of the sky, fired another missile to save a Tomcat from an attacker who killed it a moment before it followed its target into oblivion. If there were more than a handful of human aircraft left in the air, he'd lost track of them. His entire force had been wiped out and it would be his turn in seconds. He didn't even have any missiles left. Once the aliens realised that he was unarmed, they'd simply pick him off with ease and put an end to the affair.

Quite calmly, he pointed the Raptor at the massive alien craft and rammed it. There was a brilliant wave of fiery pain, a sudden awareness of his entire aircraft disintegrating against the drive field, and then nothing.

Untroubled, unharmed, the alien craft rumbled onwards, towards Washington.

Chapter Forty-Nine

"Mr President, NORAD is gone!"

"Gone?" The President repeated. "What happened?"

"Unknown," the operator said. "The report from Peterson AFB suggested that the base was nuked. All communication links with Cheyenne Mountain and NORAD are down. The base is no longer broadcasting on any frequency. General Dyson began the command transfer procedure just before the base…ah, went off the air, but most of the command links are down."

"They're heading directly for Washington," Wachter said. The display showed thousands of alien craft slipping out of orbit and heading down towards the United States. They'd be coming down all over the nation, the President realised. "Mr President, we have to get you out of here!"

The President stared at the display. The remaining AWACS had been shot down, and the radar stations surrounding Washington had been hammered over the past two weeks, but the alien craft were putting out so much energy that they were easy to track. Their mammoth…invasion transport, or command ship, or whatever the hell it was seemed to be gliding slowly, but surely towards Washington, while the smaller ships were fanning out over the country. The last of the American fighters had been shot down or driven away by superior alien firepower. A direct attack would be suicide.

"I'm not leaving," he said, flatly. He'd refused to leave the White House when the alien attacks had begun – leaving the White House would have caused panic across the nation – and he had no intention of leaving now.

The bunkers would provide more than enough protection. If the aliens could detect and destroy the bunkers directly, the war was within shouting distance of being lost anyway. "What about the SAM missiles?"

"The batteries on the coast tried to engage the massive ship, but they didn't cause any damage," Wachter said. "Mr President, you cannot stay here! They're either going to invade the city or destroy it and either way, you must survive."

"Mr President, we just had a FLASH message from Andrews AFB," the operator said. "Alien craft are landing around the base and engaging the defenders. Other bases have dropped completely off the air. We're losing command and control networks everywhere."

"That big bastard will be overhead in ten minutes," another operator added. "The Marine Barracks and Air Defence Artillery are on alert, for whatever good they'll do."

"It we shoot that thing down, it'll come crashing down on the city," Wachter said. "There won't be much of a city left afterwards."

The President stared at him. It was hard, almost impossible, to comprehend the sheer magnitude of the disaster. It would have been easy to fall into delusion, or to move imaginary units around the map. The situation was so...*surreal*. He'd had over two months to get used to the concept of aliens, he'd met the aliens personally and knew what they had in mind, yet...no one invaded Washington, no one. The British had burned down the White House in 1814, during a war neither side had really wanted, and no one had ever repeated the feat. Lee and the Confederates had never attacked Washington; the Germans and Japanese had never had a prayer of reaching the city. Even terrorists had only managed to cause some damage and panic. The aliens...the aliens were going to take the entire city. The population had fled, apart from those who wouldn't or couldn't go...

It was going to be a nightmare. Cold logic told him Wachter was right and he had to flee, to raise his standard somewhere else and organise the underground resistance to the aliens. The oath he'd sworn to protect the United States against all enemies demanded that he stayed and fought alongside the Marines now deploying to defend the White House. No other President had ever faced such a nightmare, but no other President had ever failed so badly. Richard Nixon, Bill Clinton, Jimmy Carter...they'd all called America into disrepute, but they'd never done any permanent harm. President Chalk had lost the entire country.

"I can't," he said, finally. He'd taken the precaution of carrying his old Desert Eagle, something the Secret Service praised and condemned in equal measure. "I won't..."

Wachter nodded to someone behind him. Before he could protest, he felt cold hands grasping his body and holding a cloth to his mouth. He breathed in a tiny amount of the fumes, enough to send him falling into darkness. His last thought was absurd. They weren't even going to let him die bravely.

———

Pepper held the President's body as he lost consciousness and the darkness claimed him. The drug on the handkerchief was military-issue only, causing anyone who breathed in even a tiny amount to collapse for at least an hour. There were concerns about releasing it to the public, even though it would have been very useful in riot control work, because a tiny percentage of the population suffered from allergic reactions to the drug. For someone whom the Secret Service had a full medical profile of, like the President, it was possible to calculate the precise dose required to cause a longer period of unconsciousness. Pepper just hoped that the President wouldn't sack her on the spot when he woke up and realised what she'd done.

"You three," Wachter said, waving to a set of uneasy-looking soldiers. They wore nothing beyond basic combat uniforms, but Pepper knew that they were all Green Berets. "Escort the President and his protective agent to the secret bunker and then place yourself under his command. Tell him that it was all my idea and he shouldn't blame anyone else."

"Yes, sir," the lead soldier said. Pepper had never caught the man's name, but she'd read his record. He'd protected Ambassadors and Special Representatives in several of the world's more hostile countries and never lost one yet. "Shouldn't we get a stretcher?"

Pepper was already well ahead of him. The President was always escorted by a medical team, just in case of a heart attack, poisoning or another medical emergency. Two of the medics had already come into the room when the President's monitor had revealed that he'd collapsed. At her orders, they took the President and placed him gently on the stretcher. They'd carry him through the maze of tunnels to the secret bunker. If the aliens knew where that was, the war was over anyway.

"Send out a general signal," Wachter was ordering, as they left. "Tell them that EGGPLANT is now underway."

Pepper shivered as she checked her sidearm. EGGPLANT was a contingency plan no one had ever expected to have to use. All over Washington and the rest of America, government buildings would be destroying paper files and wiping computer databases, before destroying them with shaped charges. The records of everything that America had left; from underground forces waiting to strike back at the enemy to the command codes to contact the SSBN submarines would be destroyed. The aliens wouldn't be able to use Washington's fondness for paperwork against it. It was a tacit admission that the war was lost.

"Sir," she said, "shouldn't you come with us?"

"My place is here," Wachter said. "Get him out of here."

———

Abigail couldn't remember if Washington had even tiny earthquakes, yet the entire city was shaking now as the alien craft advanced. It was incredibly massive; so vast as to be beyond her comprehension, mocking anything that humanity might have put in the air. She heard the sound of cars crashing and people fleeing – the groups that had planned to oppose the aliens having suddenly realised just how powerful the aliens were – above the sound of windows shattering into shards of broken glass.

The alien craft just took her breath away. She'd never imagined anything like it outside of a Hollywood flick where lots of shit was blown up. She didn't have the slightest idea how something that large could even fly, or if it intended to land in the middle of Washington and crush all the skyscrapers below its bulk. It seemed close enough to touch even though she knew that it was an illusion. It seemed large enough to be the mothership itself. As it advanced, it cast an unholy shadow over the land. She heard shooting not too far away and risked glancing away from the alien ship. A cop was standing in the middle of the road, firing madly up towards the alien craft. If the alien craft even noticed, if the bullets even hit the target, there was no sign of any reaction. It just lumbered on towards the White House.

Its shadow seemed to leap forward and envelop her, plunging her into darkness. She felt a warm trickle running down her leg as the air seemed to shimmer all around her, casting her into sheer terror. She found herself on her knees, staring up into the darkness – Washington's power grid had gone completely down and all of the streetlights were dark – and shaking uncontrollably. Staring up at the alien craft was like looking up into absolute darkness. A human would have outfitted the craft with running lights, surely, but the aliens hadn't bothered. She knew she should be recording the entire scene, yet there was no point. The aliens had won the war.

Others seemed to disagree. She heard a roar behind her and turned to see SAM missiles lancing up towards the alien craft. She wanted to scream at the defenders – if they shot down the craft, it would come down right on her head – yet how could she blame them? She wanted to flee, back to her apartment and hide under the bed and pretend that it wasn't happening, but she was rooted to the spot, unable to move at all. The missiles splashed against the alien craft's drive field, sending waves of oddly beautiful light shimmering out over the city, but accomplished nothing. The alien craft hung in the air, as enigmatic and threatening as ever. The soldiers fired again and again, but nothing short of a nuke would touch the craft.

The panic down below was only getting worse. She saw a mixture of government workers, wealthy citizens and poor gangbangers from the suburbs fleeing together, suddenly rendered equal by the aliens. The shadow was nightmarish, casting the human race into gloom and setting off the worst of humanity. She caught sight of a pair of gangbangers dragging a teenage girl off the streets and into a building, then of a cop shooting the pair down without even trying to arrest them. Humans were scurrying around like ants that had had their nest smashed wide open, trying desperately to find an elusive safety. There was no hope for any safety any longer, Abigail realised. The aliens had shattered every one of humanity's illusions about its role in the universe. The men who'd wandered the streets proclaiming that the end was nigh had had the last laugh after all. The end *was* nigh.

Another spread of missiles reached up towards the craft…and this time, the aliens reacted. A beam of light, bright enough to break Abigail's paralysis and send her hand racing to shield her eyes, lanced down towards the remains of the Pentagon. There was a brilliant flash of light followed by a massive fireball; a moment later, the ground shook violently. The entire building shook and for a terrifying moment, she wondered if it was going to come crashing down, killing her in the process. As a child, she'd had nightmares about living in skyscrapers because they seemed too fragile, yet when she'd grown up she'd dated a guy who designed them and he'd convinced her they were safe. Rick had never imagined an alien craft shaking the entire city, even though he'd assured her that tornados and earthquakes could be handled. He'd been a nice boyfriend, but their careers had clashed and they'd eventually broken up. The last she'd heard, he'd married someone who specialised in building mansions and they had been trying to set up a business together. She hadn't thought of him in years.

The aliens kept shooting, picking off targets she couldn't even see. The defenders were no longer firing, trying to keep down the casualties. The alien craft had settled in over the White House, daring the human race to keep firing and wreck their city. It was so large that she hadn't even realised that it had escorting fighters and smaller transports until one flew right over her head, breaking line of sight with the alien craft. She found herself lying on her back, able to move again. Her ears hurt badly. The alien craft was making hardly any noise, but it was clearly producing something she could almost hear. She rubbed at her ears in hopes of making the pain go away, yet somehow it refused to fade.

A green light flared out from the alien craft, casting the darkened area of Washington into stark relief. It looked oddly like an alien landscape under their glare. The aliens had opened a massive hatch in the underside of their vessel and hundreds of aliens were spilling out of it, falling towards the ground faster than a HALO parachutist. She wondered absurdly if they intended to die like lemmings, but the green glow seemed to be some kind of tractor beam. They were invading the very heart of Washington.

Slowly, she pulled herself back to her feet, and staggered over to the door. She wanted to get downstairs now, change her clothes, and then escape. Washington was no longer a suitable place for human habitation. It was alien territory now. The interior of the skyscraper had taken a terrible beating. Windows had smashed, pictures and vases had come off the walls and crashed on the ground, while the power was almost completely off. Emergency power provided a faint dim light as she made her way down the stairs, choosing to leave the elevators strictly alone. The shortage of power might leave her trapped inside, unable to escape. There was no one else around at all.

Her apartment was a mess as well, but she was relieved to see that everything she had was still intact. She wanted a shower desperately – now she was calming down, she had realised that her clothes were filthy – but when she checked the shower she discovered that there was no water, so she used wipes before changing into a more practical outfit. She'd packed a getaway bag weeks ago – it was standard practice when she might have had to leave at any moment – and took a moment to check the pistol she'd bought after the President had nullified all gun control legislation. It had been far too long since she'd fired a gun, but the principle remained the same. Point and shoot.

She took one final look around her apartment, picked up a necklace that had been a gift from her mother, and closed the door behind her. She never expected to see it again.

———

General Wachter watched in absolute disbelief as the alien warriors duelled it out with the Marines defending the centre of Washington. It might have been an even fight without the presence of their craft high overhead, calling down fire on any Marine target that showed itself. There was little wrong with how the warriors comported themselves; they moved in unison, with one group covering the next, as they advanced towards the White House. It seemed to be the only target safe from alien fire. The aliens would have to dig the Marines out by force.

He checked his M16 as he rallied the inner defenders. The vast majority of the staff had been sent through the tunnel system to places where – he hoped – they'd be safe, or at least would be able to get out of the city. The reports that had come in before the aliens had somehow disabled communications suggested that the aliens were landing everywhere, yet they couldn't overrun the entire country within hours. They didn't have the tech or the numbers to do anything like that. America had one of the highest ratios of guns to people in the world...and most of them, unlike the Iraqi insurgents and terrorists Wachter had fought, knew how to use them. The aliens might still win, but by God they'd know that they'd been in a fight.

"Ready, sir," the operator said. "I've primed the charges as you ordered."

Wachter nodded. "Good," he said. The aliens had overrun most of Washington, but they hadn't discovered the tunnel network, not yet. The charges had been placed to collapse sections of the network, making it harder for the aliens to locate an entrance once they deduced its existence. The second set of charges had been placed in the White House itself. Wachter didn't know what the aliens wanted with the President's official residence, but he was damn sure that they weren't going to get a chance to use it. The charges would blow the White House to rubble and kill all of the aliens inside the building. By then, there would no longer be any defenders.

He flicked from camera to camera, but the view was always the same. The aliens were crashing into the building, fighting it out with the Marines, who'd turned the White House into a complicated network of IEDs and other unpleasant surprises. The warriors seemed to have a sixth sense for some surprises and almost nothing for others, although they were learning quickly. They also showed little in the way of restraint. They threw grenades into a room before entering and seemed unconcerned about the possibility of civilian deaths. It was a far cry from the restrictive rules of engagement the United States had used in Iraq. The aliens took no chances.

"Set the timer now," Wachter ordered. He hefted his M16 and headed up the steps towards the final redoubt. The aliens would take the remains of the White House over his dead body. "Good luck."

Chapter Fifty

Washington DC, USA
Day 69

Pepper hadn't known the full extent of the tunnel network until she had been briefed about the emergency escape plans from Washington. At the time, the Secret Service had considered them a burst of official paranoia rather than a serious plan, even though it was primarily focused on preserving the President's life. The plan existed only for when air or ground escape was impossible – a major nuclear or chemical strike on the heart of Washington – and consisted of a set of bunkers and tunnels that were only linked to the main tunnel complex at two locations. Pepper and her escorts had triggered charges as they'd passed and now there were no clues that the Presidential Bunker existed – unless EGGPLANT had failed and there was a reference to the bunker in files captured by the aliens. It wasn't impossible. A few years ago, the Secret Service had investigated a science-fiction author for revealing details of the bunker, a task made harder by the fact that the author possessed a security clearance and might have heard something in his military career. It had taken some very expensive investigation to prove that the author had made it all up.

She watched as the President slowly recovered from the drug. The medics had injected him with a counter-agent, at her instructions, but she was dreading the coming discussion. No Secret Service Agent had ever drugged the President before. The most controversial act in the history of the Secret Service had been Presidents being knocked down to keep them out of the line of fire, something that was generally applauded. The President would be angry with her, maybe even sack her on the spot. She wasn't sure she'd blame him either. *She* would have been furious if someone had drugged her, even if it had been for the best of motives.

The President pulled himself to his feet, rubbing the side of his head. Unlike some residents of the Oval Office, he had maintained a regular exercise routine and worked out every day, so he should be strong enough to shake off the drug quickly. It had few side effects when the dose was properly calculated, but that wasn't very reassuring. Drugging the President was regarded as an absolute last resort and not something to be entertained lightly.

"I assume," he said, finally, "that you have a very good explanation for this?"

At least there's nothing wrong with his mind, Pepper thought, although it was cold comfort. "You had to remain alive and out of enemy hands," she said, as practically as she could. She wouldn't have appreciated such an explanation and she doubted the President would disagree. "The country needs the legitimate President alive and free."

"And so you drugged me," the President said, angrily. "Why?"

Pepper took a breath. If she was going to be fired, she might as well go out with a bang. "The President isn't just the Head of Government, but the Head of State as well," she said. "The person holding that title becomes a symbol of American government, the core of the country. He has more responsibilities than dying bravely beside his defenders. All of us swore to keep you alive because as long as you are the President, you're the heart and soul of the country. We could not allow a disputed succession or a President in enemy hands. The country needs you alive and free."

"And in hiding," the President said. He looked over towards one of the operators. "How long have I been out and what's happened since I...left the White House?"

Pepper had been surprised by the sheer size of the bunker when she'd first seen it, expecting a small installation buried deep under the outskirts of Washington. It was small, but there was room for a permanent staff, a set of sleeping quarters and a shower, as well as links into every civil and military command network. It drew power from a nearby nuclear power plant – apparently, the staff at the power plant didn't know where the power was going – and had enough stored power to maintain operations for years, if necessary. Five men operated the bunker, four of them wearing earphones and muttering away into microphones. The fifth – a Colonel who'd been on reserve until the alien mothership had been detected - came over to brief the President personally.

"Mr President, welcome to the Tomb," he said. Pepper could have quite happily killed him for that joke alone. "I'm Colonel Mikkel Ellertson. We have been attempting to monitor the military situation from here, but the command and control networks have been hammered very badly and we've lost contact with a number of bases. The direct links to overseas installations and forces have been cut. We're currently working on linking though landlines. All foreign satellites have been downed."

"Shit," the President said. He rubbed the back of his head. "Very well. Give me a full rundown. Start with Washington."

"The aliens have been landing troops in Washington for the last hour, even after the White House was blown up, and have been encircling Washington. As you know, most of the civilians had fled the city before the aliens invaded and civilian casualties have been mercifully low. There has been some resistance to the aliens – mainly cops, soldiers and armed civilians – but the aliens have been strong enough to overcome all such resistance. They're establishing a ring of steel around the city and have been turning back the remaining civilians. Any attempt to push through the cordon is met by lethal force.

"I was able to speak, very briefly, to the base CO at Quantico, the Marine Base. He reported that several alien craft had landed on the base and there was a major firefight going on, before the line went dead. The Marines have not been heard from since. Andrews AFB reported that the base was on the verge of being overrun before contact was lost; several other installations reported alien invasion and landings before they too broke contact. Fort Hood reported that soldiers had dispersed into the training grounds to carry on insurgencies against the aliens.

"Reports from several major cities suggest that the aliens have been landing around the cities rather than crashing into their hearts, like they did to Washington," he added. "There's only one massive…City Destroyer or whatever the hell it is, so they don't seem inclined to force their way into the cities yet. The reports basically add that the aliens are turning back refugees and are responding to attacks with lethal force. Without NORAD or the foreign satellites, I am unable to give you a complete picture of the alien landings, but we did pick up a vague report from the BBC that alien craft were descending over Africa and the Middle East. There's so much confusion on the internet that I can't rely on anything until the spotters get back in touch with us. They're reporting everything from cities destroyed to hordes of alien women raping human men."

Pepper rolled her eyes, and then concentrated on the important issue. "Are we safe here?"

"I honestly don't know," Colonel Ellertson admitted. "The Webcam images we have from Washington show the aliens swarming over the centre of the city, but we don't know if they have access to any part of the tunnel network. The security system is badly damaged and may collapse completely at any moment. I would advise against trying to escape the city entirely until nightfall. The situation is unstable."

"Show me," the President said, standing up.

Ellertson led them over to a big screen and started to flip through images from the various cameras. "That's where the White House was," he said, as the screen displayed a pile of flaming debris. Alien shapes moved over the debris, rounding up human survivors and pushing them towards the nearest open space, where they were guarded by other aliens, who were searching and tying the prisoners. Many were injured, some badly, but the aliens weren't providing any medical support. Civilians and cops seemed to have been mixed up with the soldiers, all lumped together into one mass. Dead bodies – human and alien – were being gathered together in a pile. "That's the Mall, that's the view from a skyscraper towards the north, that's…"

"Enough," the President said, sharply. He sounded shaken and Pepper didn't blame him. Scenes like that just didn't happen in America. "If they keep the population penned up in the cities…"

"Easier to control," Ellertson finished. "The last reports we had included several alien landings in the countryside. They may intend to settle the country, or they may have other plans. What do we do now?"

"What do we do?" The President repeated. Pepper heard the note of icy determination in his voice and cheered inwardly. "They've taken our country. We'll fight to take it back."

Pepper nodded and started to plan their escape from the bunker. They couldn't stay in Washington for much longer. It wouldn't be long before the aliens stumbled across the tunnel system and started to search it, looking for insurgents and fugitives from their authority. Even if no one betrayed the complex – and Pepper had no way of knowing what the aliens could do to induce someone to talk – they'd eventually run out of food and supplies. Their only hope for escape was to leave before the cordon around Washington became an iron noose, strangling the life from the city.

She looked over at two of the soldiers. Three Special Forces soldiers, five men who hadn't seen front-line service in years and one PPA wouldn't be able to provide much protection if the complex was attacked. An idea was already taking shape in her mind, but it would require careful planning – and intelligence.

"Tell me something," she said, to the senior Green Beret. "How good are you at sneaking around?"

———

Abigail had barely any warning before a pair of strong hands grabbed her and yanked her into the alleyway. There was no public transport, or working cars any longer, which forced her to walk. It was a decision she bitterly regretted as the mugger – or worse – slammed her against a wall. Cold hands reached for her jeans, sending shivers running down her spine. His intent was all too clear.

"Let me go," she demanded, and kicked out at him. He laughed and thrust her against the wall again. She tried to bring her foot down on his, but he slapped her back hard enough to stun her, just long enough for him to start pulling down her jeans and panties. His cold hands roamed over her bottom and between her legs, making her cry out in pain. "You don't have to do this!"

There was no answer, just deep excited breathing. She felt a wave of anger, and determination. No one raped her. No one! "I'll let you fuck me," she said, desperately. It was easy to pretend to be scared. "I'll let you do what you like, but not like this. Turn me round and I'll suck you off before you fuck me…"

The breathing seemed to grow harsher. She guessed that her would-be rapist had never had a willing girl before. He finished pulling off her jeans and stroked her buttocks again, before twisting her around. She saw his face and his engorged cock for the first time and fought to keep the revulsion off her own expression. He was actually excited by her submission, pulling her towards his cock. She took a breath and pursed her lips, before bringing her knee up as hard as she could. He screamed in pain and tried to lash out at her, but it was too late. She kicked him again and saw him topple over, before bringing her foot down hard on his throat. He wriggled and tried to escape, yet somehow she kept pushing down on him until he died. She vomited over his body as she stumbled back from him. She had been in dangerous places before, but this...this was *America*. Law and order had broken down over the entire city.

Never a cop around when you need one, she thought, trying to avoid thinking about the man she'd just killed. She pulled her jeans back on, feeling dirty and ashamed even though he hadn't done worse than grope her before she'd killed him. She wanted a shower desperately and perhaps a stiff drink or two, but there was no time. She removed her pistol from her bag and put it in her coat. Perhaps she should have carried it openly, or perhaps she would have been disarmed as easily as she had been dragged into the alley. Leaving the dead would-be rapist behind, she started to walk towards the edge of the city. Surely, out there somewhere, she could meet up with someone else from WNN and the world would be understandable again.

She encountered crowds of other people streaming towards the outskirts of the city and gave them a wide berth, apart from a group of soldiers heading into the city. The crowds grew larger as they approached the way out and discovered that it was blocked. A group of aliens were parked right across the road, their weapons clearly ready for use, blocking the human escape route. Several of them were firing from time to time, aiming over the crowd and forcing them to turn back. They'd encircled Washington already.

"RETURN TO YOUR HOMES," the alien voice thundered. It was harsh and terrifying. "DO NOT ATTEMPT TO LEAVE THE CITY. ANY ATTEMPT TO CROSS THE BARRIER WILL BE MET BY LETHAL FORCE!"

Abigail stared at the alien warriors. It was her first sighting of them and she had to admit they were terrifying, like a monster from a low-budget science-fiction movie. Behind the aliens, there were armoured vehicles shaped like tanks, providing support to the alien infantry. If the humans tried to force their way out, the aliens would clearly be able to stop them…and, judging from the pile of bodies nearby, had already proven their ability to do so. Abigail caught back a sob as she caught sight of one of the bodies and realised that it was just a little girl, barely older than seven. Her body had been burned through by an alien weapon and dumped in the pile.

She thought about drawing her pistol and joining the group of armed citizens who were preparing to try and break through the alien cordon, but there was no point. The aliens had enough firepower to stop a handful of humans in their tracks and they probably had more out there beyond the city. Their massive craft was still looming overhead, casting the city into unnatural darkness. There didn't seem to be any other choice. Slowly, she walked away, back to her apartment. There was nowhere else to go.

Behind her, shots broke out, followed by the sound of alien weapons firing.

It didn't last long.

———

Sergeant Arun Prabhu cursed under his breath as he saw the aliens wiping out the civilian group. He'd come up through the sewers and scouted around, knowing the dangers if the aliens or criminals caught him, but it hadn't taken long to realise that the aliens were rapidly tightening up the noose. Their forces had clearly been deployed with considerable forethought and they'd trapped almost all of the remaining population of Washington within the city. It wasn't as if they had any use for them either. They just had to be prevented from swarming out over the countryside.

He checked a possible escape route and frowned. The massive alien craft was the real joker in the deck and he had to admit that it made one hell of a convincing argument against any resistance. The tactic seemed simple enough. The alien fighters cleared the way; the massive landing ship moved in and took control. How much trouble would the United States have had in Baghdad, he wondered, if they'd parked a flying aircraft carrier over the city and plunged it into shadow? Probably far less than they'd actually had. The aliens were still swarming over the centre of town, but now they were flooding into the suburbs, concentrating on rooting out any resistance. He had strict orders to avoid contact if possible, but part of him wanted desperately to forget his orders and go after the aliens. Years ago, he'd lurked in a Middle Eastern town and watched as a captive was brutally raped and then murdered, unauthorised to intervene. This was worse. Far worse. Washington itself was being raped in front of him.

But he knew his duty. Slowly, remaining out of sight, he backed away from the aliens and headed towards the warehouse that concealed one of the entrances into the tunnel system. They'd have to slip out under cover of darkness – real darkness. The sight of sunlight at the edge of the city was tantalising and inaccessible. If they were lucky, the plan would work perfectly. If they weren't lucky, the aliens would be snapping at their tail for the entire escape. He was halfway to the warehouse when he stopped dead and saw something that almost made him forget his orders again. The aliens had prisoners.

He'd seen them through the cameras, of course, but it wasn't the same as coming face to face with soldiers, people he *knew*, being taken prisoner. Very few Americans had been taken prisoner in the Iraq War, although there were still question marks over the fate of prisoners from the Gulf War, or Vietnam. He stopped dead as he saw a line of prisoners, some badly injured, being marched out of the city by the aliens. There was no way of knowing where they were going, or what the aliens had in mind to do to them, and he wanted desperately to rescue them. But he couldn't do anything. He'd left most of his weapons behind in the bunker and he was just one man. The resistance would have to liberate the prisoners, if they could, before they were dissected for medical experiments. The entire planet knew, now, what the aliens had been doing at the South Pole.

Slowly, he backed away and found another route to the warehouse. There was no longer any time to delay.

Chapter Fifty-One

Washington DC, USA (Occupied)
Day 69/70

The night sky was dark, unbroken by even a single glimmer of manmade light. The alien craft hovering high over the centre of Washington was a dark shadow in the air, casting a darker one over the land below. Washington was normally brightly lit, but with the power failures and the presence of the aliens, there were few lights piercing the darkness tonight. The city was dying.

"Come on up, sir," Pepper said. "There's no one around."

The President climbed up out of the hatch and into the warehouse. It was easy to recognise it as the warehouse where he'd briefed the Special Operations soldiers, back before the aliens had invaded and the world turned upside down. The only illumination came from a set of glow-in-the-dark strips intended to assist workers if the power cut out, leaving him barely able to recognise Pepper's shape in the darkness. It had been a long time since he'd used night vision gear in Iraq, but he hadn't forgotten how to use it. The outside streets took on an eerie deserted look through the goggles. The crowds of civilians and the criminals that preyed on them had either fled the city or were lying very low. They wouldn't want to attract attention from the aliens.

They'd had an emotional farewell with Colonel Ellertson and his staff. The Colonel had volunteered to remain behind in the Tomb and continue to monitor the situation in Washington for the Resistance, now that contact had been re-established through the Internet. It wasn't something the President would have been happy about, not with the massed might of the aliens bearing down on them, but someone had to remain in the city. The five operators and a handful of spotters might be all that the Resistance had left in Washington. Intellectually, he was sure that others had survived the landings, but none had made contact yet. They might be completely alone.

A shadow detached itself from the wall and revealed itself to be one of the Green Berets. Even with the goggles, he'd been hard to see, the result of wearing an urban combat uniform designed to conceal the infrared signature of his body. The President hoped that it would be just as effective against alien scanners, although no one knew what the aliens would use to hunt for human fighters on the ground. The reports had suggested that their ground-combat technology wasn't significantly advanced over humanity's tech, but few trained observers had survived the landings all over America. The President had read the reports after he'd rested and knew what they meant. There would be no safety anywhere until the aliens were driven out of America and back into space.

The original evacuation plans were all so much junk now. Air Force One was no longer at Andrews Air Force Base - it had been moved to a civilian airport to keep it safe – and it was inaccessible, even if it hadn't been captured or destroyed by the aliens. The other plans, involving Marine helicopters and even stealth craft, were even worse, and most of their possible destinations would have been compromised. Camp David would have been occupied – he couldn't imagine the aliens missing it – along with several of the better-known bunkers. There were a dozen command and control bunkers that had never made it into the media and might still be safe, yet the aliens had landed in Washington and might have seized the human archives. If they hadn't been destroyed in time, they might be able to use them to track down the remaining bunkers and destroy them. The Vice President was in one of those bunkers, the President knew, sparing a thought for his old friend. His security staff should be able to take care of him if all hell broke loose.

"There's no sign of enemy activity," the Green Beret hissed. "We can make our move now."

The President hefted his M16 and nodded. Despite himself, the thought of seeing action again was seductive. He'd traded in his suit and tie for a more practical outfit, although he still wore body armour under his shirt.

The soldiers had proposed putting the President in a uniform like theirs, but a quick search of the Tomb had revealed no spare uniforms, nor could he have fitted into one of theirs. If they were lucky, they'd be mistaken for a group of refugee soldiers trying to make it back to their units, or perhaps cowards fleeing the battle. The President might be a known public figure, Pepper had reasoned, but the aliens might not recognise him after a little effort at altering his features. She'd cut off his hair and played around with a make-up set, changing his appearance subtly. The President no longer recognised himself.

"Come on," Pepper hissed. "Let's move."

The air was thick with the smell of burning, although all of the fires seemed to have been put out by the aliens or the Washington Fire Department. The cameras had showed images of the alien craft picking up vast amounts of water from the Potomac and dropping them over the fires, extinguishing them one by one. The President had been silently relieved that they didn't seem to intend to burn Washington to the ground, yet it was somehow ominous. The aliens had come as colonists, he knew. Did they intend to move into humanity's very homes? It dawned on him that no one had seriously considered what the aliens might do with humanity's population. Did they intend to enslave the humans or simply ignore them?

Pepper herself had changed her outfit again, looking more like a cheerleader than a Secret Service Agent. Her original plan had been to escort the President out herself, claiming to be a couple out on the town if anyone asked, but some covert scouting had revealed that they would need the help of the soldiers to get out of the city. It was more proof that the aliens were in firm control. The alien forces had ringed the city and were still turning back anyone trying to leave. At least they weren't shooting humans at random. The President took a certain amount of consolation from that, even though it suggested that the aliens might have other fates in mind for humanity. Keeping them penned up in the cities might have been intended as a first step towards enslaving the human race.

He followed Pepper carefully, keeping to the shadows, barely able to pick out the sounds of the remaining soldiers bringing up the rear. Washington was deathly quiet, with barely any noise echoing through the darkened air. He looked out at the alien craft's giant shadow and shivered. There was no doubt that the country – his country – was in the grip of a massive invasion. His position as President was meaningless in all but name. He thought about some of the more drastic plans to ruin the planet and prevent the aliens from using Earth and wondered if his successor would be forced to use them, or if the aliens would somehow prevent them destroying the planet. Would they compromise if the alternative meant both races dying?

They passed a body lying on the ground, a half-naked man who had been kicked to death. The President wondered what his life story had been and who had killed him, as if it mattered. It was the civilians who mattered. They were the ones that the military existed to defend. They didn't deserve, no matter how little they understood the realities of the world, to die like that. They deserved better. Three months ago, everyone had *known* that the United States was the world's sole superpower and had a bright future ahead of it. Now, the United States President was crawling through his own capital city, trying to escape, while aliens occupied the countryside and prepared to colonise the world. The remainder of the world would be intimidated into submission, or perhaps, now that the aliens had occupied America, they'd occupy the rest of the world as well. He imagined alien fighters cutting through the British, French, German and Russian air forces and shivered. They'd wreaked enough havoc to completely destroy the world as mankind had known it. It was the end of an era.

Pepper held up a hand and the President stopped dead. A troop of five alien warriors was marching right down the centre of the road, their heads swinging from side to side as they watched for signs of trouble. The scene was so unbelievable that it was almost surreal, something right out of a low-budget movie, yet it was happening. He felt his hand clasping the M16 and fought down a desperate desire to leap out and start shooting. The aliens passed them by, missing them…or perhaps simply ignoring them as long as they didn't pose a threat. They hadn't made any announcement of a curfew to the population. The only announcement they'd made had been the order to remain within the city and wait.

It seemed like hours before Pepper motioned for him to move again, yet it couldn't have been more than a few minutes. He felt stiff, as if he'd been standing still for days, yet as he followed her, he rapidly regained ease of movement. The outskirts of Washington loomed up in front of him, revealing a network of old warehouses and utilities that had been abandoned in the wake of the economic collapse and the alien invasion. Businesses had been going out of business all over the world. If the aliens had promised a new order of peace and prosperity, the President knew, much of the world's population would have followed them. So many citizens had been in debt that the sudden banking collapse must have been something of a relief.

The thought was a bitter one. He'd been elected on a promise of reform, after convincing the Republican Party that he could win – mainly by defeating the Party's preferred candidate – and he'd had great plans to reform and rebuild sections of America. All of his great plans had come to nothing. The aliens had occupied the country and there was nothing left, but endless underground warfare until they either defeated the aliens or were wiped out entirely. The government he'd sought to reform – that he *had* reformed – was gone. The proud military he'd lavished care and attention on had been wiped out, or reduced to an insurgency force fighting a vastly superior foe. The thought kept echoing in his head. No other American President had lost the entire country.

"In here," Pepper hissed. The President followed her into a darkened building, completely abandoned. His nostrils twitched at the stink, although he'd smelled worse when he'd gone to war. She'd played her cards close to her chest about where they were going, but it didn't take much effort to deduce that they were about to enter the sewers. The underground tunnel network had once been linked to the sewers, despite the risk of discovery, but a careful check had revealed that part of the network had collapsed. "Take off your goggles."

The President did so, and then covered his eyes as a light shone out in her hand, revealing a set of steps leading down to the sewers. He'd seen the sewers in his hometown years ago and remembered that they pumped the sewage out to a reclamation plant well outside the city, where it would be recycled as best as possible. He'd been a kid at the time and he'd thought that it was funny, even though he hadn't wanted to think about it too much. Pepper glanced around, looking for signs that the aliens were ahead of them, before leading the way down towards the tunnels.

"This place has been completely shut down," one of the soldiers muttered. "There's going to be a backlog of shit all the way back to homes and toilets."

The President winced. A modern city was constantly under threat of being drowned in its own refuse. The aliens had blocked the ways in and out of the city, which meant that the population would rapidly run out of food, water and other vital supplies, while they wouldn't be able to wash or even go to the toilet. Disease and deprivation would spread rapidly. He'd served in several Third World cities where the balance had been lost, never to be regained, leaving the population at the mercy of fate. The lucky ones – the powerful ones – had had all the luxuries they could wish for. The unlucky ones had had no hope of anything but death. They had had no schools, no health care, nothing…not even hope. They'd been born waiting to die.

"Then we'd better get moving," Pepper said, tartly. "They'll probably try to round up technicians and get everything moving again before long."

She led the way down the stairs into a long tunnel. The stench was even stronger down in the tunnels, but there was no sign of sewage. "These are the inspection tunnels," Pepper explained, when he asked. "We can walk through them without having to swim, I hope."

"Run through them," one of the soldiers said. "I can hear something."

The President tensed. There was a faint scraping coming from high above them, back where they'd entered the building. The aliens…or a refugee trying to escape? There was no way to know. Pepper nodded and pulled at his arm, leading him along the tunnel, followed rapidly by two of the soldiers. The third paused long enough to rig up a grenade as an unpleasant surprise for anyone following before coming after them. Great clouds of dust rose up from their footsteps, nearly causing the President to cough. They passed hundreds of inspection hatches, each one marked with warning signs in several different languages, and even a disused trolley that would have carried them to the far end in comfort, had it been working. Hours seemed to pass in the tunnel, hours marred by the flickering flashlight, raising nightmarish thoughts of being trapped down in the dark. What would they do if they ran out of light? There was no illumination in the tunnel, not even emergency lighting.

"Nearly there," Pepper said, encouragingly. Behind them, the President heard the sound of an explosion. Someone had tripped over the grenade. "Come on!"

His heart was pounding inside his chest as he pushed himself to the limit. Only the thought of letting Pepper and the soldiers down kept him going, that and the knowledge that Pepper wouldn't hesitate to encourage him with a kick to the ass if necessary. The end of the tunnel came as a surprise and he almost ran past the stairs before Pepper caught him and motioned for him to follow her up to the surface. They'd run over five miles. The President had thought that he'd kept himself in shape, but when he'd been younger, he would have laughed at such a distance.

"We're clear," Pepper said. "All we need to do now is meet up with the Resistance and get out of here."

"Oh," the President said. He felt better than he had in months. "Is that all, then?"

———

From a distance, the looming shape of the alien craft covered the horizon, somehow visible as an area where no stars shone. Jones watched, barely aware of the ship's engines coming to life and the freighter sailing away from the Potomac, joining hundreds of other boats fleeing the country, trying to find an elusive safety. This ship was headed for Britain, along with many others, mainly the rich trying to find a new home in a hurry. They had no intention of being caught up in the middle of an occupation, or an insurgency. He considered them nothing better than traitors – they'd never sent their children to war, or understood the real world – yet he too was fleeing, even if it was under orders. Perhaps MacArthur had felt the same when President Roosevelt had ordered him to abandon the Philippines. MacArthur had been leaving his men behind in serious danger…and many of them would die in Japanese POW camps.

The President's orders had been beyond dispute. "You will take the two crashed ships to Britain for them to study," he had said. The original crashed ship was still at Area 52, but others had been recovered during the war. Now that America had been crushed, the study might not be continued, even if the aliens didn't hit Area 52 and recover their missing craft. "Once there, you will assist them to the best of your ability and report to the Ambassador. There will be work for you there."

Jones caught sight of a sailboat that looked tiny, too tiny to make the trip across the Atlantic, and felt a moment's pity for the sailor. He'd have to fight Mother Nature as well as the aliens, if they came out to sink the refugee human fleet. An ironclad guarding the waters would be very helpful now, but if there were any American naval vessels left in the area, they weren't advertising themselves. The submarines had been ordered to escape to Britain and make contact with the British, as well as American forces stationed overseas. The reports that the aliens had been landing in North Africa and the Middle East had suggested that American forces in Iraq might be in trouble...but there were so many reports and no way to know which were accurate and which ones were not.

Bright lights shone overhead when he looked up at the stars. The night sky had been enhanced by hundreds of new lights, alien craft in orbit around Earth. There looked to be hundreds, if not thousands, of them; the ship's Captain had told him that all of the world's satellites had been taken out. Jones hoped that the stealthed satellites had survived untouched, yet there was no way to know for sure. Outer space belonged to the aliens.

He watched an alien craft flying overhead, scaring the people below, but making no hostile moves. The hundreds of ships couldn't have been of much interest to them – hell, perhaps the refugees were making their lives easier by fleeing. They'd missed the crashed ships in the freighter...

"Enjoy it while you can, you bastards," he muttered, staring towards the alien craft. "We'll be back."

Chapter Fifty-Two

Area 52, Nevada, USA
Day 75

There was no longer any television, apart from a handful of local channels. Alex had never believed that he would miss television, or the sheer volume of shit pumped out by Hollywood producers and newsreaders, yet it would have been a link to something outside the base. The aliens had shut the television channels down, however, even without intending to do so. Their place had been taken by talk radio and the Internet, yet neither of them were reliable. The Internet had been badly damaged by the alien attacks, but somehow it had kept going. It had been originally designed to resist a nuclear strike and the aliens hadn't inflicted quite *that* much damage.

The reliable spotters and observers for the Resistance – as well as a few of the more reputable bloggers – had been providing useful data, yet most of it was depressing. How could it not be? Every military base had been attacked and occupied by the aliens, forcing the defenders to stand and fight or vanish into the shadows to carry on an insurgency against the invaders. Fort Hood's terrain was making it a nightmarish battleground for both sides, yet the aliens had time on their side. Every major city had been ringed by alien ground forces, all aircraft were grounded, and all of the regular military forces had been scattered. The Resistance was working desperately to pull them all into the underground, but it was taking time, time the aliens were using to solidify their grip on the country. The reports from Washington and several other cities suggested that the aliens had started to feed and water the population, giving them a vested interest in seeing that the aliens remained undisturbed. Other reports had large alien landings in areas with small human populations, and humans being evicted from their homes without warning. The alien colonists were landing and taking over their new home.

He wished, desperately, that Jane was here, but she was at Area 53, trying to talk to their alien captive. Jones was also gone, ordered to leave the country by the President for knowing too much, leaving Alex in charge of the Tiger Team. He had never expected command in his life – the FTD Directorship was about the most he could hope for – and now he was the senior officer in the base. Colonel Fields still ran the day-to-day operations, but he'd made it clear that Jones had had supreme authority and as his successor, Alex shared that authority as well. Alex privately suspected that Fields simply didn't want to do anything that might draw alien attention to the base – so far, they hadn't attempted to occupy it – and Alex couldn't blame him. The problem was that they needed to hit back hard…

And they had no weapon capable of scratching the massive alien craft over Washington. A nuke might have done it, except that the command and control links had been crippled in the last hours of the war. With the President hidden away somewhere in Virginia, there was no way to order the submarines to strike – and, if they had, the ballistic missiles would have been shot down by the aliens a long time before they reached their target. The Resistance had a handful of tactical nukes, and others had been hidden around the country, but how could they get them to the alien craft? He'd wondered about slipping one into Washington and detonating it, but the others had nixed that idea, pointing out that there was no guarantee that the nuke would take out the alien craft. Frustrated, he walked into the hangar to see Neil Frandsen. The advanced propulsion specialist might have some idea how to scratch the alien ship's paint.

He looked up at the alien craft as he entered the hangar. It never failed to take his breath away, even if it had been half-dissembled by the researchers trying to understand how it worked. Parts of the ship's computer core had been moved to one of the lower levels where a team of researchers were trying to hack into it, although all they'd recovered so far had been gibberish. Alex had pointed out that they might be reading alien signals sent in the clear and they wouldn't know about it – after all, the aliens would hardly speak English amongst themselves. The hackers had agreed, but pointed out in turn that certain basic principles of computer language would be recognisable and they would be able to use that to unlock the rest of the database. Alex hoped that they knew what they were talking about, but he knew that it had taken over five years to create the F-22 computer system and the alien craft were considerably more complicated. Some of the alien tech seemed to be barely two or three years ahead of humanity. Some of it was so advanced that Alex doubted they'd figure it out in less than a decade.

It might not matter anyway, he reminded himself. The alien FTL drive, whatever its limitations, wouldn't give them any tactical advantage in the long term. They'd be better off figuring out how the alien weapons and sublight drives worked, which would even the odds between the human air forces and the alien fighters. The plasma weapon alone would be useful, unless the alien craft could absorb power from plasma shots as well. It would explain why the aliens never seemed to worry about the prospect of friendly fire. Superheating plasma seemed to be possible provided there was enough power on hand to generate a magnetic field, but no one had managed to do it in a research lab, let alone in the field. Besides, accuracy seemed to be almost a matter of luck rather than skill.

"Hey, boss," Frandsen said. "I finally found something cool!"

Frandsen been quick to discover that Alex hated being reminded that he was the boss and took ruthless advantage of it. The only one who understood was Santini, who'd had to send men and women to their deaths before. He'd been talking about leaving Area 52 to join the Resistance and Alex had had to promise him that when they finally developed something that could be used to hit back at the aliens, he'd be in the lead.

"Wonderful," Alex said, dryly. Frandsen might have been overjoyed at each new discovery from the craft, but Alex found it hard to think about such wonders when the aliens were sucking the life out of his entire country. The longer the aliens had to establish themselves, the harder it would be to drive them into the sea, or space, or anywhere that wasn't America. "What do you have to show me?"

"This," Frandsen said. He pointed to a bizarre combination of devices that had been worked together on the table. "What do you think of her?"

"It looks as if a toaster has been unfaithful with a radar set," Alex said, dryly. Toaster jokes had been floating around Area 52 ever since the craft had been moved in and studied. Some wise-ass had even posted a picture of an Asian movie star on the toaster in one of the common rooms. "What is it?"

"This, my friend, is the prototype of a weapon for bringing down one of the really big alien craft," Frandsen said. "What do you think of her now?"

Alex's eyes narrowed. "What is it?"

Frandsen dropped into lecture mode. "The alien craft generate drive fields that absorb energy being shot at them up to a certain level," he said. Alex, who knew this already, nodded impatiently. "This explains why bullets were completely ineffective against the alien craft and missiles worked perfectly, sometimes too well. They exploded against the drive field, overloaded it, and either caused a second explosion or forced the craft to fall out of the sky. Unlike our craft, they don't have much in the way of aerodynamics, but I imagine that they wouldn't need them in space."

"Maybe," Alex said. The aliens had claimed not to know about humanity until their craft had drawn close to Earth, but they had still come loaded for bear. It suggested either that they were as fundamentally warlike as humanity, or perhaps that they'd been lying all along and that they'd always had invasion in mind. There was just no way to know for sure, unless Jane managed to get their captive to talk. "How does this apply to one of the really large craft?"

Frandsen grinned. "I haven't been able to duplicate their drive fields yet, but I *have* been able to produce computer models of how they must behave," he explained. "The bigger ships have to lift much more mass and – obviously – have greater tolerance for additional energy than the smaller craft. The massed missile attack just before the Fall of Washington was simply insufficient to bring the craft down, which might have been a blessing in disguise. If the craft had exploded, Washington would certainly have been badly damaged and every aircraft in the sky would have been swatted out of it."

"They got swatted out of it anyway," Alex reminded him, tightly. He'd lost friends in the war, men and women who'd given it their all and lost their lives. He knew better than to blame them, no matter what some morons were saying on the internet; there had hardly been a secret government plan to sell America to the aliens. "Can you get to the point?"

"It's impossible to be sure, but a nuke might not be enough to overload the drive field and bring the craft down," Frandsen said, tightly. "The drive field would be able to spread the energy over the entire hull. The results might not be pleasant for the aliens, but I doubt it would bring the craft down. This, on the other hand, might just be enough to give the aliens a serious jolt."

He tapped the device fondly. "A year or so ago, DARPA produced a design for a plasma warhead, something that would produce an awesome amount of energy over a relatively small area. The idea was to hunt down terrorist caves in godforsaken parts of the world…and probably melt Russian and Chinese ships as well. A standard cruise missile wouldn't suffice to take out a major carrier with a single shot, but a plasma warhead would certainly render the carrier useless even if it didn't sink it. The design was tested a few months ago and it worked, once they worked all the bugs out. Half the time, the warhead simply refused to detonate."

"How reassuring," Alex muttered. "And are you sure that this one will detonate?"

"Like I said, they worked all the bugs out," Frandsen assured him. "I had them ship one over here for comparison to the alien system, but that was useless…never mind. The point is that with a little finagling, we can hit the alien craft with one of these warheads, properly configured to create a *local* overload in the alien system. The results should be…interesting."

"We're talking *Independence Day* here," Santini said. Alex jumped. He hadn't heard the soldier coming into the room. "Your device might bring the alien craft crashing down on Washington."

"*Might* being the operative word," Frandsen agreed. "Alex, I don't know exactly what it will do to the alien craft. They might manage to compensate – my computer models say that is unlikely, but they can't account for every-thing – or the craft might simply shrug off what does happen and carry on anyway. All I can say for sure is that they'll know that they've been kissed."

"Very well," Alex said, ruefully certain that he'd face a mutiny if he disagreed. "How do you intend to get it to Washington and then to the alien ship?"

Santini grinned. "I'll take the device and four of the soldiers in one of the trucks," he said. "We've got links to the truckers anyway, so we'll pass for truckers until we reach Virginia. The aliens aren't interfering much with traffic outside the major cities yet – more reason to move now while we still can – and we'll make contact with the Resistance – and the Army of Northern Virginia. They've got a deserted airbase that hasn't been touched by the aliens, and one of the aircraft there will carry the warhead to the alien ship."

"Suicide," Alex said, flatly. "Who's going to fly the mission?"

"The ANV flies Predators – in this case, a modified stealth Predator Remotely Piloted Vehicle, an RPV" Santini explained. "They intended to arm several of them with nukes and fly them right into the path of incoming alien vessels, but the war situation overran them before they managed to get them all prepared and launched into the air. We know that the aliens ignored a handful of RPV craft during the air battles, apart from two that engaged the alien craft with missiles and got shot down. Our RPV won't be shooting at them, but will be flying up to the alien craft and detonating the warhead as it impacts with the drive field."

"They'd have to be mad to let it get so close," Alex objected. "They certainly had no trouble tracking the Raptors…"

"Which were shooting at them, and operating in broad daylight besides," Santini said. "The RPV I intend to use is stealthy enough to give even the aliens pause…"

"Their detection systems aren't much better than our own," Frandsen added. "The stealth coatings should work as long as they don't do something stupid like emitting a signal or opening fire. We can operate the RPV through the stealthed satellites and laser communications – the aliens won't be able to detect that unless they accidentally fly through the laser beam and pick it up. Alex, we can make it happen."

"We don't know how long we have either," Santini added. "The aliens are running right down a damned checklist. They took Langley and Fort Meade pretty quickly. What's to stop them overrunning the airfield and destroying the Predators? We can't stand up to them in open combat…"

"One point, then," Alex said. "Consult with the President first. This is well above our pay grades."

"Yes, sir," Santini said. "I'll see to it at once."

———

The American military communications system had been built to withstand terrorist attacks, nuclear strikes and massive EMP pulses that could have blacked out the entire continent. An alien attack was nothing compared to an EMP, or even a massive nuclear strike, and elements of the command network remained intact. Hundreds of nodes – those representing military bases and a number of vital installations – had gone offline, marking the areas the aliens now controlled. Complex verification protocols had been implemented to make it harder for the aliens – or anyone else, for that matter – to hack into the system and gain control, but Alex had his doubts about how useful they actually were. The more complex a system, in his experience, the easier it was for some unhelpful soul to gain entry and cause some real damage.

There was no way of knowing where the President actually was, a security measure Alex thoroughly approved of. Given enough time, the aliens would probably find a way to hack into the network and try to download data from it, either by themselves or with human quislings assisting them. Alex and the rest of the Resistance had studied – frantically – tactics used by resistance and counter-resistance operatives in other countries, but few Americans had ever seriously considered fighting an underground war in their own country. The few that had tended to be militia groups that believed that the government had sold out to ZOG – a Zionist group that somehow ruled the world – or the UN. Alex had a private suspicion that most of them would wet their pants the moment they came face-to-face with an alien warrior.

"It's the President," Dolly confirmed. She was part of the base's security staff, a small woman with a very sharp mind. "Voice print analysis confirmed. Stress analysis indicates a mild level of stress, consistent with his current situation. He's not under duress."

"Thank God," Alex said. They'd only heard the basic story of the President's escape from Washington, but the Internet had spun it up into a story involving stealth helicopters and a daring midnight flight in Air Force One, leaving hundreds of dead aliens in the President's wake. "Mr President, we have something of a possible option here."

He ran through the entire proposal in basic terms, passing over the specifics. "If it works, we risk bringing the craft down onto Washington and destroying the city," he concluded. "We need authorisation to hit the craft that hard."

The response was immediate. "Granted," the President said. Alex was surprised, and not a little horrified. The decision had been made so quickly! "I'll issue the supporting orders from here; the Resistance can secure the airbase and prep the Predator for flight."

"Ah...yes, Mr President," Alex said. "I'll..."

"Good luck," the President said. His voice hardened. "I'll contact you when it's time to discuss further measures."

The connection broke.

Santini dismissed Dolly with a wave. "Surprised?"

"Yes," Alex admitted. It was hard to speak. "Why...?"

"Because the President knows that there are no rules any longer," Santini said. "The old Rules of Engagement went out the window when the aliens landed and occupied our cities. Everything we used to justify binding our hands, to keep them clean of blood by not killing people who deserved death no longer matters. This is our country under occupation."

"And Washington?" Alex asked. "Everyone in the city?"

"Expendable," Santini said, flatly. "All that matters now is hurting the aliens as much as possible. We have to get rid of them quickly, whatever it takes, or our descendents will spend the rest of their lives in slavery. Washington is expendable against the rest of the country and anyone who stayed there when the aliens were breathing down their necks deserves everything they get."

Chapter Fifty-Three

Washington DC, USA (Occupied)
Day 82

The small airfield seemed completely deserted, but Nicolas and his team checked around the surrounding area before they finally cut their way through the fence – carefully avoiding triggering the alarms – and made their way inside. From the outside, there was little more to the airfield than a pair of buildings – one hangar, one control shack – but inside, they discovered a high-tech operations centre. Nicolas had to smile inwardly as they checked out the various rooms in the building, taking nothing for granted. Someone might have thought that the airfield represented a way out of America, or at least away from Occupied Washington, and hidden in the buildings when they discovered they couldn't fly the RPV. The team found no one, much to Nicolas's relief. They might have had to shoot them to maintain security.

He glanced into the hangar and stared at the RPV. He'd seen Global Hawks and Predators on deployment while he'd been in Afghanistan, but the stealthed Predator was a very different design. It reminded him of seeing an F-117 for the first time, yet it was smaller and somehow lighter than any of the manned stealth fighters. It was completely black, as if it absorbed all the light in the room, without even a flag or any other American markings. It was the ultimate deniable asset – or it would have been, if any other country in the world had the ability to produce such a craft. Perhaps, he reflected, now that aliens were present on Earth, maybe they'd get the blame in future. The F-117 had been mistaken for an alien craft before…

The USAF had *hated* the very idea of RPVs and for a long time, any pilot who seriously considered going into RPVs found it career suicide. The

USAF had been so fixated on the next generation of manned fighters – which had eventually led to the Raptor and the JSF – that it had largely ignored RPVs until it had become impossible to resist their introduction. The CIA, on the other hand, had loved the concept and had expended a great deal of its own funding in building a private air force of Predators, often arming them and sending them against targets of opportunity. They'd come hellishly close to disaster more than once – Nicolas had heard, in Afghanistan, how a Predator had come far too close to ramming a British Harrier – yet they'd persisted. The RPV program had provided SpecOps teams like his own with support they needed desperately, even though they did have their limits. Enemy forces had managed to hack into the Predator control links on more than one occasion.

His earpiece buzzed. "Truck coming," one of his men said. "The cargo?"

"Take positions," Nicolas ordered, quickly. In theory, the tiny microburst transmissions were undetectable except at very close range. In practice…he intended to keep their use down to a bare minimum. The aliens might be able to track the team down by their radio signals. "Stand by…"

The truck turned off the road and came to a halt near the hole in the fence. Nicolas braced himself, just in case a swarming alien army came out of the truck, before a man climbed down with his hands conspicuously empty. Nicolas peered through the night scope and relaxed slightly as he recognised Santini from the briefing before they'd gone to hit the alien base. The three other men with him didn't look familiar at all, although they were clearly soldiers, even out of uniform. They'd probably been regulars rather than Special Forces, he decided. They didn't have the same attitude and ability to blend in with the mundane world surrounding him.

"Cover me," he subvocalised, and stood up, walking right towards the truck. Santini turned to face him, holding up his hands. Nicolas raised his voice. "Code?"

"Fat Lady Singing," Santini replied. Nicolas relaxed slightly. "Rather obvious if you ask me, but no one did."

"Me neither," Nicolas agreed. Someone at the Presidential bunker – wherever that was – had obviously watched too much *Independence Day*. "Do you have the device?"

"Yep, and a guy to install it," Santini confirmed. "Can you open the gate? We'll have to get the truck right up to the hangar."

Nicolas watched as Santini backed up the truck and his ground crewman started to work. One advantage of the whole RPV program – or so he'd been told – was that a person who had spent most of their lives playing video games could pick up flying the Predator easily. He'd been assured that some Predator pilots had believed that they had been playing video games up until the moment the Predator had returned to base, although he didn't believe a word of it. CIA was over-funded and under-worked, even after President Chalk had started to reform the intelligence sector, yet even they would have balked at risking a Predator on such a folly. What if the pilot smashed it into the ground, unaware that it was more than just a game? Nicolas himself had been taught how to fly one from the ground – he'd had to operate a smaller Dragon Eye drone back in Afghanistan – yet he wasn't a master pilot. He hoped that the ground crewman knew how to fly the RPV. It wouldn't be the first time someone had to scrub a mission because of a minor oversight like that.

"We're ready," the crewman said, finally. "She's all armed up and ready to fly."

"Good work, Joe," Santini said. They walked into the small control room. Someone with a sense of humour had rigged it out to look like a cockpit from a plane, complete with stick and video monitors in place of a canopy. He wasn't sure if it was meant to encourage the pilots to remember they were flying a real plane or merely for the amusement of their superiors – either explanation fitted the CIA – but as long as they worked, he didn't care. "Are you sure you can fly this thing?"

"If I can't, we're all dead," Joe replied, tightly. Nicolas liked his attitude. "Get the hangar doors open. I'll do the rest."

The briefing had said that the Predator wouldn't be guided by standard radio transmissions, but by a laser link to one of the stealthed satellites floating around the Earth. The aliens, so far, had either missed them or chosen to ignore them – Nicolas hoped that it was the former. It didn't seem likely that, after they'd blasted the remaining satellites – regardless of who they belonged to – out of orbit that they would have ignored the stealthed communications satellites. That might change after his group mounted their attack. He wasn't sure if it was worth the price.

He shook his head, angrily. The country had been invaded – no, the country had been *occupied.* The Resistance was already fighting, yet most of the population had been badly shocked by how quickly they'd been defeated and they needed hope. They needed a sign that the aliens weren't invincible after all. The mission, if it succeeded, might convince them that there was still a chance for victory. Otherwise, the Resistance might die out quickly and the alien conquest would be complete.

"No emissions, apart from the laser beam," Joe said. "There'll be nothing to guide them to the Predator. They won't get any warning at all. Their craft, at least, is putting out enough energy that a blind man flying an Avenger could track it easily."

Nicolas heard the faint sound of the RPV powering up and advancing towards the runway. The CIA hadn't stinted on the sound-dampening system. A regular jet would have produced a deafening noise, yet all he could hear was a dull hum. In the air, the briefing had assured him, the Predator was completely silent, a legacy of the time when a sound-detection system had brought down an F-117 in 1999. The aliens shouldn't even know that it was in their airspace.

"Here goes nothing," Joe said, and pushed the stick forward. Nicolas saw the dark shape racing down the runway and vanishing into the gloom. "We're off…"

Nicolas found his lips shaping a silent prayer. The Predator wasn't moving at supersonic speed and it would take time for it to reach its destination, time in which anything could go wrong. They'd considered trying to warn the people still within Washington and the surrounding area, but that might have got back to the aliens. Nicolas had spent time in places where the local population might have preferred the Americans, but didn't trust their ability to protect them, and knew that the occupying power had probably already found some friends in Washington. Hell, for all he knew, the thousands of government bureaucrats had already sworn allegiance to their new master.

And, if the mission succeeded, a lot of people were going to die.

He didn't consider himself a monster, despite the vitriol frequently aimed at the SEALs and other Special Operations Teams by their detractors, yet now they might have a point. Thousands of Americans were at risk because of him. They'd die under the craft or perhaps be killed when the aliens retaliated for the strike. Who knew the rights and wrongs of it? Their deaths might serve a greater purpose – the salvation of the entire planet – or they might just be petty acts of violence carried out by terrorists. Whoever wrote the history books would determine how the future looked upon him and his men. He shook his head in frustration. He'd sworn an oath to protect and defend the United States and as for the rest…

God would judge him.

———

The majority of the population of Washington – those who had remained, cursing themselves for not having fled with the remainder of the population – had moved, almost as a group, to the edge of the city, away from the looming alien craft. The aliens hadn't objected, even though they'd been registering and monitoring the humans in-between feeding them and putting them to work. Abigail had never felt so sore in her life. The alien leader – she was already thinking of him as the Commandant – had put her to work clearing rubble from the streets, along with thousands of others whom the aliens had deemed otherwise useless. Doctors and other medical professionals had been allowed to carry on their work, soldiers and policemen had been rounded up and taken away somewhere – no one knew where – and utility workers had been pushed into getting the power and water supplies back on. Resistance was useless. The aliens simply shot anyone who dared to resist. A group of gang members had been cut down right in front of her, screaming about their rights to the last. The aliens hadn't cared.

There were, she knew, a handful of humans who hadn't registered, yet the aliens didn't seem to care all that much. They wouldn't have to care. They handed out food to those who worked for them and insisted that it be eaten onsite, apart from men and women who wanted to take it home to their families. The hidden ones would have to eat their own food or eventually sign up with the alien program, or starve. She hoped that they were soldiers, watching, waiting and plotting the liberation of Washington, but there was no way to know for sure. She kept her distance from them. Every day, dozens of new human bodies were discovered and taken away by the aliens. No one knew who was killing them, or why. The aliens didn't seem to care.

She clutched the ID card around her neck as she stumbled into the apartment she'd claimed. It had once belonged to a rich young lobbyist, she'd deduced from a brief check of his belongings, who'd worked for one of the more exclusive lobbying firms. He and his wife had gone missing somewhere during the invasion and she'd felt only a brief twinge of guilt when she'd moved in. She tried to keep it in good condition, in hopes that the real owners would one day return, but she knew better. They'd never come back to reclaim what was theirs.

"Damn it," she muttered, looking over at the laptop she'd salvaged from one of the other apartments. It had taken several hours to dissemble the security precautions someone had built into the unit's hard drive, yet all she'd found had been a vast collection of porn, much to her private amusement. She'd managed to hook it into the Internet – now that the power was back on, so was the Internet – but WNN seemed to have completely vanished. Some of the more reliable bloggers were still going strong, but the sheer volume of rumours and lies on the net dwarfed the truth. She'd checked a vast registry of missing people that someone had compiled and her name hadn't been on it. It made her wonder if anyone cared, or if the aliens had wiped all of WNN out of existence. She might be the only WNN employee left in a world gone insane.

There hadn't been any shortage of men willing to 'protect' her in exchange for sexual favours – however expressed – but she'd declined all such offers. It helped that the aliens kept a tight leash on their human slaves; rapists, thieves and murderers got the death penalty, often at once. The handful that had tried to continue, keeping themselves well away from the aliens, had been driven away by the other humans, just to protect the rest of the group. Civilisation was breaking down and all that was left was to protect themselves. The aliens just…watched. They just didn't seem to care.

She'd studied them while she laboured for them and had reached her own conclusions. There was only *one* alien race, but it came in many forms. The Warriors fought and guarded the human prisoners. The Workers seemed to do all of the menial work, although they'd been pressing humans into service to assist them with that. The Leaders issued orders and seemed always to be obeyed. The Leaders were also the only ones who spoke English. The Workers just ignored any questions put to them and the Warriors motioned for the humans to go away and stop pestering them. They all wore the same uniforms and it was impossible to tell them apart, yet she was sure that there were layers to the alien society she wasn't seeing. They couldn't just be ants in an anthill, could they?

This isn't an informal setting, she reminded herself. *They're not at their best.*

She would have liked to see an alien city, to see how they interacted without humans around, but that seemed impossible. Her horizons had shrunk to Washington DC – or what was left of it. There seemed to be no way out. The most optimistic postings on the net only confirmed it. She was trapped.

———

"Getting closer," Joe muttered. The live feed from the Predator was showing up clearly now. A massive dark object hung in the air, visible only because it was darker than the surrounding night sky. Nicolas couldn't pick out any of the details, apart from a vague sense of its shape. It could have been anything from a giant flying saucer to a hovering aircraft carrier, yet it was alone in the night sky. The hundreds of fighter craft that had escorted it to Washington were not in evidence. They could be anywhere – either on the mothership in orbit or overseas fighting it out with other human powers – but Nicolas didn't care. As long as they weren't watching for threats to their massive ship…

"This is pretty much our last chance to back off and forget this," Joe said. "Are you sure you want to proceed…?"

"Get on with it," Santini snapped. "Now!"

Joe nodded. Nicolas saw tears glistening on his cheeks. "Yes, sir," he said. "Impact in ten…nine…eight…"

Nicolas swung over to the window and ripped away the curtain, staring towards Washington and the massive dark shape over the city. He was just in time to see a brilliant flare of white light in the darkness, casting the entire city into stark relief. The protectors on his goggles darkened automatically, saving him from going blind, although he knew that others wouldn't have been so lucky. The entire ship was glowing…

———

The light burned through the curtains, shocking Abigail as she showered, trying to wash the grime off her body. The noise hit a second later, shaking the entire building, convincing her that someone had nuked Washington. Naked as the day she was born, she staggered towards her armchair and scooped up a dressing gown, pulling it on as she ran to the stairs and down to the streets. If someone had nuked the city, she had to get out, whatever the risk. The warm air struck her as she ran onto the streets and she looked up. The massive alien craft was blazing with light.

Shielding her eyes with one hand, she peered up towards it, just in time to see explosions rippling through the craft. Chunks of material, each one the size of a small house, were falling towards Washington, bombarding the stricken city. The craft was somehow trying to manoeuvre away from the city, trying to get out over the ocean, but it was too late. In terrifying slow motion, disintegrating as it moved, it fell towards the ground and crashed. The force of the impact took her to her knees, but she couldn't look away. A pearly-white flash of light, followed by a massive fireball, rose over the city. The entire alien craft had been knocked out of the sky.

Abigail couldn't help herself. She burst out laughing. Even as smaller alien craft raced overhead, searching for the humans who had been so impudent as to hurt their carrier ship, she laughed. The explosions and fires that might devastate the city no longer mattered. All that mattered was that the aliens had taken one hell of a bloody nose.

———

"Take that, you bastards," Santini was shouting. The light of the alien craft's death was still visible, even at their distance. "We fucked you up good!"

Nicolas laughed. "Get everyone out of here," he said, keying his radio one final time. The aliens would take a careful look at their sensor records and probably deduce what had happened…and where the RPV had come from. Even if they didn't, there was no point in remaining at the airfield any longer. "Prime the destruct charges and get out of here."

He took one last look towards Washington, where flames were towering into the sky and smaller alien craft buzzed around, confused and uncertain what to do, unable even to see an enemy to hit back at…

And then he started to run.

The War Will Continue In
Under Foot
Available NOW!

Afterword

I don't believe in a UFO Conspiracy.

Let me step backwards a moment and explain myself. I started reading UFO books when I was around seven and one image, in particular, stuck in my young mind. A massive flying saucer stuck in a canyon, recovered by American soldiers and taken away to Hangar 18 (or wherever). It wasn't until I was a bit older that I heard about Roswell for the first time, yet it fascinated me – until I started to think about it. If Roswell had been a genuine UFO crash (genuine in the sense that it was an alien spacecraft, as opposed to a top secret weather balloon) it would have changed the world, yet the world was not changed. UFO Researchers believe that the world wasn't changed because the US Military covered up the crash – but, if that were the case, it was a remarkably incompetent job. Roswell's very notoriety comes from the fact that no one knows for sure what happened, or do they?

But then, the military's position on UFOs has always been a little odd. The USAF made several attempts to bury the whole issue (the name Project Grudge is quite indicative) and tended to treat UFO reports as hoaxes. The British Ministry of Defence classed all UFO reports as being 'of no defence significance,' an odd choice of words when UFO reports include UFOs flying over British military bases and buzzing British military aircraft. How could such incidents *not* be of defence significance? The KGB and various other intelligence agencies looked into the whole issue and several concluded that the US knew more than it was telling, yet they found nothing significant – or so they said. Just what is going on in our skies?

One of the problems with doing a detailed study of UFOs is that the field is vast. It starts with the Great Airship Scare of 1896-97, touches upon Nazi secret weapons and 'Foo Fighters' in World War Two, 'ghost rockets' over Sweden, sightings of alien occupants after 1945, reports of benevolent alien contact merging into the far more sinister and hostile abduction phenomenon…if any of them could be proven to have some real explanation, it would change the face of the world, yet there is so much nonsense written in the field that sorting out 'truth' from 'fiction' would be the work of a lifetime. Which events are real? Which are not?

I believe that the vast majority of UFO reports are not alien spacecraft.

The odd reluctance of the military to investigate what seems like a clear and present danger to their respective nations, I believe, supports my view. Why this reluctance? There are only a handful of possible answers. We can probably dismiss most of the conspiracy theories out of hand. I believe that the most likely explanation is that the 'unexplained' UFOs are really classified military craft and that the military's reluctance to expose them is why they rarely comment on such reports. (Although it is common in the UFO Community to disregard any governmental denials.) The F-117 would have looked very odd to anyone who caught a glimpse of it before it was officially acknowledged. They might even have filed a UFO report! Bear in mind that the vast majority of any air force would not be involved with the development and testing of new aircraft. It is quite likely that a military pilot would file a UFO report and his superiors realise, without telling him, that he actually saw a new experimental aircraft.

Does this explain why the military prefers not to investigate UFO reports?

There are other explanations, of course. One is that the UFOs are actually Russian or Chinese aircraft. Another says that they actually are alien spacecraft and the military is unable to stop them, or has made an agreement with them to allow them to operate in our airspace without interference, perhaps in exchange for technology. I find some of those explanations unbelievable. The aliens, assuming that they exist, possess command of technology well beyond ours. They must. Even if they come from Mars, they have a technology capable of crossing the interplanetary gulfs that separate us from our nearest neighbours. Their technology becomes all the more formidable if we assume they come from the nearest star, or further away…why would they *need* to make a deal with the military? All they'd have to do is drop a few rocks and the human problem goes away.

Independence Day, although a bad movie as far as plot and character goes, actually illustrates my point quite nicely. The UFO crashed at Roswell in 1947. If we assume that ID4 took place in 2000, the US Military wasted 53 years it could have been using to prepare for the aliens. Sure, we couldn't make head or tail of their technology – even though we had Data to help – yet it doesn't matter. The mere presence of the alien craft should have alerted the entire world that there was a potential threat out there. Think about how the movie would have turned out if the aliens had launched their first strike against Area 51 and destroyed or recaptured their missing craft. Could even Will Smith have saved us then? Given a priceless opportunity to prepare for war against the most implacable foe humanity would ever face, the opportunity was squandered so badly that they brought humanity to the brink of destruction instead.

What would we do if we faced an alien threat?

I like to think we'd do better.

Let us suppose, as put forward in this novel, that a UFO does crash – in America, Britain, France, China, darkest Africa…or anywhere. What next? Most UFO crashes seem to take place in isolation, yet that doesn't stand up to scrutiny. The F-22 Raptor didn't appear out of nowhere. It came from a production line, which produced hundreds of other Raptors, in America. The presence of an F-22 implies the existence of a country capable of creating them. Why, then, do UFO researchers so often dismiss the fact that a crashed alien ship automatically *confirms* the existence of an alien society? If alien ships *have* crashed on Earth, why haven't the aliens demanded them back, or recovered them by force? And, for that matter, why are we not going on planetary alert?

I think that the answer is obvious.

In this book, I have blended 'fact' and 'fiction' from UFO lore. Roswell, as most people know, was a reported crash in 1947. It was debunked by Karl T. Pflock in his *Roswell: Inconvenient Facts and the Will to Believe*. He also provides an excellent debunking of Philip Corso's *The Day After Roswell*. (A copy of *The Day After Roswell* is online.) The Manhattan Abduction, in which Linda (Cortile) Napolitano was allegedly abducted by little grey aliens, was supposedly witnessed by Javier Perez de Cuellar, then Secretary-General of the United Nations. I find the report largely unbelievable. There were simply too many witnesses. People interested in UFO Abductions may wish to consult *The Uninvited* (Nick Pope) and *Alien Encounters* (David Jacobs). It's hard to say how seriously one should take them. The introduction of the Greys to popular culture through mediums such as *The X-Files* and *Dark Skies* means that many people could 'construct' an alien abduction report under hypnosis without intending to mislead the researcher.

I guess the best advice I can give is keep watching the skies.

Or, as HG Wells put it…

"At any rate, whether we expect another invasion or not, our views of the human future must be greatly modified by [The Martian Invasion.] We have learned now that we cannot regard this planet as being fenced in and a secure abiding place for Man; we can never anticipate the unseen good or evil that may come upon us suddenly out of space. It may be that in the larger design of the universe this invasion from Mars is not without its ultimate benefit for men; it has robbed us of that serene confidence in the future which is the most fruitful source of decadence…"

Christopher G. Nuttall
New Years Day, 2010

Cast of Characters

The US Government
President Andrew Chalk, President of the United States
Vice President Jacob Thornton, Vice President
General Gary Wachter, Chairman of the Joint Chiefs of Staff
Janine Reynolds, NSA Director
Hubert Dotson, Secretary of State
Tom Cook, Secretary of Defence
Dahlia King, Secretary of the Treasury
Tom Pearson, CIA Director
Richard Darby, Director of Homeland Security
Pepper Reid, Secret Service Protective Agent

The Tiger Team, Area 52
Tony Jones, Chair, Special Advisor to the Presiden
Ben Santini, Military Adviser, Former SF
Alex Midgard, Foreign Technology Division
Jane Hatchery, MD. Medical researcher
Neil Frandsen, advanced propulsion specialist
Gayle Madison, communications and cultural specialist
Steve Taylor, Intelligence Analyst
Colonel William Fields, Base Commander, Area 52

The Military
Colonel Mikkel Ellertson, CO The Tomb, Washington
Colonel Brent Roeder, Base Commander, Area 53
Sergeant Arun Prabhu, Green Beret, Washington
Lieutenant-Commander Nicolas Little, SEAL, CO Operation Wilson

Airman First Class Robin Lance, Radar Specialist, Schriever Air Force Base
Technical Sergeant Dave Heidecker, Radar Specialist, Schriever Air Force Base
Master Sergeant George Grosskopf, Base Security Team, Schriever Air Force Base
Captain Will Jacob, USAF F-22 pilot, Dark Shadow Squadron
General Sandra Dyson, CO United States Strategic Command, NORAD

NASA
Director Jack Buckmaster, NASA
Colonel Irving Harrows, ISS Commander
Isabel Paterson, ISS Officer
Doctor Melvyn Heights, ISS scientist
Captain Philip Carlson, *Atlantis* Captain
Felicity Hogan, *Atlantis* co-pilot

SETI
Karen Lawton, Radio Specialist
Daisy Fairchild, Director

The UN
Secretary-General Abdul Al-Hasid
Ambassador George Hutchmeyer, US Ambassador

The Media
Abigail Walker

The Other Governments
Evgeny Vikenti, President of the Russian Federation
Mu Chun, President of China
Prime Minister Arthur Hamilton, Prime Minister of Britain
President Vincent Pelletier, President of France

The Aliens
Ethos (Leader)

18554878R00251

Printed in Great Britain
by Amazon